PROOF
POSITIVE

FORGE® A TOM DOHERTY ASSOCIATES BOOK NEW YORK

PROOF
POSITIVE

Philip Singerman

This is a work of fiction. All the characters and events portrayed in
this novel are either fictitious or are used fictitiously.

PROOF POSITIVE

Design by Heidi B. G. Eriksen

A Forge Book
Published by Tom Doherty Associates, LLC
175 Fifth Avenue
New York, NY 10010

www.tor.com

Forge® is a registered trademark of Tom Doherty Associates, LLC.

Library of Congress Cataloging-in-Publication Data

Singerman, Philip.
    Proof positive / Philip Singerman.—1st ed.
        p. cm.
    "A Tom Doherty Associates book."
    ISBN 0-312-87686-6
    1. Undercover operations—Fiction.   2. Alps, Austrian (Austria)—
Fiction.   3. Conspiracies—Fiction.   4. Florida—Fiction.   I. Title.

PS3569.I5743 P76 2001
813'.54—dc21

                                                            00-048452

First Edition: January 2001

Printed in the United States of America

0   9   8   7   6   5   4   3   2   1

FOR ALAN AND CAROLYN LUCE

PROOF
POSITIVE

I

Solomon Kessler heard the sharp crack of a high-powered rifle and saw a bundled figure come off the ridgeline as though it were trying to fly. He knelt quickly behind a tree and watched the figure tumble partway down the slope toward the river before coming to rest against a fallen log. As the figure tumbled Kessler heard two more shots, less powerful than the first and fired in rapid succession, probably from a pistol, followed by what sounded like a far-off cry, though it could have been the wind. He waited for several minutes behind the tree, his eyes on the ridgeline, straining to see at a distance through the snow. Halfway between the ridgeline and the log he saw something—a scarf perhaps, or a hat—that had come off the tumbling figure and lay on the white slope, rising and falling forlornly in the wind. The echo of the shots was long gone; the wind was now the only sound he heard. As far as he could tell no one from up above was coming after the bundled figure.

According to the blazes slashed on the trunks of two trees angling southwest from where he knelt, it was time for Kessler to leave the trail he had been following along the river and begin climbing toward the old hunting lodge where he was to spend the night. His path would take him within yards of the tumbling figure that now lay in a motionless heap. He would have preferred to continue waiting and then follow a different route to the lodge, or better yet, circumvent the lodge altogether, but he had no choice. The light was fading, the snowfall was increasing, and since he could carry nothing that might indicate the direction of his journey, Kessler had no map. If he didn't reach the lodge by nightfall he would surely freeze to death in the mountains. There was nothing for him to do but begin climbing directly toward the place from which the shots had come.

9

Kessler had been walking since he jumped from the back of a truck early that morning just north of Brenner Pass in the rugged mountains between Austria and Italy. The truck was loaded with crates of chickens, and as he moved south, following the river, the acrid odor of chicken droppings moved with him. The smell didn't bother him. Neither did the snow that began falling shortly after he paused at noon to eat the sandwich and drink from the flask of tepid coffee the truck driver had given him. After what he had been through in the death camp, after what he had seen, the smell of chicken manure and some bad weather were as insignificant as the occasional feather that worked loose from his clothing and drifted to the ground with the snow.

The hunting lodge had been built more than a hundred years earlier in the dense, precipitous woods outside the town of Merano, along a route laid out for him by the underground transport network—the *Bricha*—that took its name from the Hebrew word meaning escape. He was to spend one night at the lodge. The following morning he would be escorted into Merano where another truck would take him to Genoa. There he would board a freighter bound first for Lisbon and then for Baltimore. In the United States he would begin a new life, assuming something didn't happen to him before he reached the ship.

Solomon Kessler had been captured once, two years earlier on his seventeenth birthday, by an SS squad on patrol outside the small Hungarian town where he was born. The SS officers put him on a train to Auschwitz. In the five months since the Allied soldiers liberated the camp he had gained thirty pounds but he still looked gaunt, his haunted eyes smoldering from dark hollows in his face like a pair of flickering lanterns at the bottom of a well. Though he continued to suffer sporadic pains in his chest and fits of dizziness, the results of malnutrition and numerous beatings, Kessler had made the decision to flee through the underground rather than run the risk of being transported east to Russia. In the pocket of his coat was a 9 mm Luger taken from the body of a German soldier he found in the forest shortly after the liberation. Before beginning his climb, he reached into his pocket and touched the cold metal, wrapping his fingers around the stock and carefully releasing the safety. He was determined not to be captured again.

The bundled figure lay face up in the snow. Though the dark hair framing a pale, round face was quite short, he could tell at once by the smooth skin and the delicate hand that rested palm up on the fallen log that it was a woman. She had been shot in the back and was still conscious, but just barely, her life seeping darkly into the snow. Her large eyes were open. As they fixed on him with the crazed, desperate gaze of a wild animal caught in a trap he felt as though he were looking into a mirror.

"What happened," he said, speaking to her in Yiddish. "Who did this?" She opened her mouth to answer but could manage only a hoarse, croaking sound, a weak groan. A small, pinkish bubble appeared between her lips. She groaned again, and died.

The face of death was nothing new to him. For more than a year he had been forced to pull gold from the teeth of dead bodies, reaching into the twisted, gaping mouths of the gassed with a pair of pliers specially designed for his job. The work had numbed him, leaving him bereft of almost any emotion, yet as he looked at the young woman in the snow, he shuddered. She had survived as he had only to end up like this, another dead Jew, soon to be a forgotten pile of bones as anonymous as the rest. For what? The few American dollars or British pounds she was carrying? A piece of jewelry she had somehow managed to bring with her? A passport that like his had been forged?

He reached down, closed the woman's eyes, quickly mumbled the Kaddish—the prayer for the dead—and was about to move on when he saw something under her coat she seemed to be clutching with her other hand. He knelt in the snow, hesitated for a few seconds, then opened the coat. A book, spattered with the woman's blood, lay across her frail chest. He leaned closer and saw that it was an album filled with photographs and that its leather cover was embossed with a circle surrounding two vertical lightning bolts—the seal of the SS. Again he hesitated for several seconds, glancing up at the ridge, listening for something other than the sound of the wind. Hearing nothing, he moved the woman's tiny cold hand, lifted the album from her chest, and opened it.

The cruel, bloated face of SS Blockfuhrer Konrad Stuebbe, frozen in a half-smile, looked back at him. He knew that face well. Stuebbe had walked the platform next to the railroad siding at Birkenau, meeting incoming trains, deciding with a wave of his riding crop who would be sent to a labor detail and who would die at once in the gas chamber.

11

The photograph had caught Stuebbe in mid-stride, the riding crop held aloft, a shaft of light glancing off a raised, polished boot. In the confusion during the liberation of the camp Stuebbe had managed to escape.

Solomon Kessler watched snowflakes fall on the photograph of Konrad Stuebbe and on the face of the woman whose name he did not know. She had not been shot for money or jewels or a forged document, but because of this album. Of that he was certain. That was why she had been running when the bullet struck her in the back. Someone had tried to take it from her and she had refused to give it up. But why hadn't this person come down the slope to retrieve the album? Maybe the two pistol shots were the answer to that question. Maybe the woman had a friend, but if so, where was this friend? It was pointless, Kessler realized, to stand there wondering, for no matter what the answers, he was going to the lodge. He brushed the snow from the snapshot, closed the album, placed it in the inner pocket of his coat, and took one last look at the woman's face, fixing it in his memory. Then he resumed climbing, ignoring the woolen scarf lying on the slope, now almost covered by newly fallen snow.

"My son killed a stag a short while ago," the man said. "It's being dressed at this very moment in the shed outside the kitchen. You may, in fact, have heard the shots."

The man was beetle-browed, short and squat, with long arms and a heavy beard. He looked, Solomon Kessler thought, like an ape. A dangerous ape. He was one of the professional smugglers who ran the lodge. He spoke to Kessler in German.

"I heard nothing," Kessler said, studying the man's face. "Nothing but the wind."

The two of them were sitting in a tiny room on the second floor of the lodge, Kessler on the narrow bed, the other man on an old wooden chair. The room was thankfully quite cold, allowing Kessler to remain huddled in the coat that he did not want to remove.

"Maybe you would like a broiled chop before we leave in the morning," the man said. "Or do you eat stag?"

"I eat whatever is placed in front of me," Kessler said. "I am not a fussy eater."

"No," the man said. "I don't imagine you would be. Not now."

He rose, walked to the door, and turned, his hand on the knob.

"They fought a fierce battle less than two kilometers from here," he said. "The forest is filled with . . . reminders. Reminders of what took place."

"I saw nothing," Solomon Kessler said. "The reminders must all be covered by the snow."

The man smiled and nodded. "There is a bathroom at the end of the hallway," he said. "To the right. Feel free to use it. But do not, under any circumstances, go down to the first floor. Is that understood?"

"Yes," Kessler said.

The man nodded again and left the room. Kessler continued sitting on the bed, listening to his footsteps on the rickety wooden stairs across from the tiny bedroom. He knew why he had been warned not to go down to the first floor. The smugglers, owing allegiance to no one, were willing to run anyone or anything across the border if the price were right. They kept Jews on the second floor, Nazis on the first, and contraband in the long shed where supposedly the freshly killed stag was being dressed. For all Kessler knew, Konrad Stuebbe himself could be sleeping in a room below him, or lying dead in the forest with the young woman. It had been made very clear to Kessler that the smugglers would do whatever they deemed necessary to keep their business running smoothly.

Late that night, by the light of a tiny kerosene lamp placed on the nightstand next to the bed, Solomon Kessler carefully examined the rest of the album. It was filled with pictures of prisoners in the death camp where he had spent two years, some of whom were from his hometown and had been his friends: Otto Rothberg, the champion table tennis player; Michael Epstein, the mathematics genius who wanted to become an astronomer; Esther Kolodny, who used to sit out in the fields and paint landscapes; Rabbi Likovski, who had been his teacher; his older sister Freda; all of them as dead as the young woman in the forest. Intermingled with these faces were the photographs of the brutal

13

men who had run the camp, among them Helmut Weber, the very young but vicious SS officer in the section where the prisoners' belongings were stockpiled, an area known as Canada because of that country's wealth of natural resources. Weber prided himself on his ability to kill a man with a bullwhip. He saw the face of Stefan Butowski, who threw babies into the air and caught them on the end of his bayonet, and Wolfgang Reiger, who had sex with teenage boys and then shot them. He looked again at Konrad Stuebbe, the selector, the man who had separated him forever from his family. There were others, young men not much older than he, every bit as good at dealing out death and torture as their elders.

Only two people had been allowed to have cameras in the camp, an SS officer named Walter Kroner, the man in charge of identification, and Rolf Gormann, his assistant. The two of them ran a photo lab next to one of the killing facilities. Undoubtedly they had taken the photographs, but how had the woman in the forest gained possession of the album? Where had she found it? Solomon Kessler studied the faces of the prisoners carefully, but could not find the young woman among them.

Finally, when he could no longer keep his eyes open, Kessler closed the album and put it back in the inner pocket of his coat. He extinguished the lamp and lay down on the narrow bed. Still wearing the coat, he pulled the single blanket he had been given up to his chin and listened to the wind howling through the forest, the wind that was covering the dead woman's body with snow. He felt the Luger, heavy along his right side, and the album, resting against his chest, as it had rested against hers. Silently, in the darkness, he began to cry.

Standing in the doorway of the kitchen on the first floor of the same hunting lodge that was a way station—an *anlaufstelle*—along his escape route, SS officer Helmut Weber heard the sharp crack of the rifle and knew the woman was dead. Stuebbe was a superb marksman, and in her boots and heavy coat she would have been moving far too slowly through the snow for him to miss. Now it was a simple matter of taking the album from her and destroying it, and the two of them would be safe. Equipped with their new identities they would travel

14

first to Syria and then, when things calmed down a little, to the United States where a legitimate business was already in place, well financed by plunder funneled out of Germany during the past year and a half.

Once secure in America, they would wait some more, many years perhaps, but one day he and Stuebbe would return to Austria and retrieve the millions in gold they had buried there. It didn't matter how long it took. Though only twenty-one, Helmut Weber was a very patient man, and gold lasted forever.

It was fortunate that the woman disobeyed the smuggler who ran the lodge and came downstairs looking for something to eat, and that he and Stuebbe had just then stepped into the kitchen. Had she not seen them, had she not screamed out their names and dropped the album in her panic, she would have escaped with it, carrying irrefutable evidence of their complicity in the activities at the camp. It was fortunate too that in her panic the woman scooped up the album and ran from the lodge into the woods rather than back upstairs where it would have been much more difficult to kill her without attracting attention. Stuebbe, skilled at gunning down moving targets from his time in the camp, had instantly grabbed the rifle hanging on the wall above the table and pursued her into the snow.

Weber stood in the doorway of the kitchen, listened to the echo of the rifle shot and smiled. Then he heard two more shots, fired in rapid succession, from a smaller weapon, probably a pistol, and his smile vanished. Stuebbe had no pistol. He was carrying only the smuggler's rifle. Quickly, Weber walked through the kitchen and down the hallway to the bedroom he and Stuebbe were sharing. He closed the bedroom door behind him, sat down in the easy chair next to the window and waited.

An hour went by and Stuebbe still had not returned. Weber watched the snow that was falling heavily now on the wooded hillside behind the lodge. He was thinking about going out to look for his companion, weighing that against the danger of walking through a strange forest in the fading light, when the door opened and the smuggler, the man who looked like a partially shaved gorilla, came into the room.

"Almost always the guests at this lodge abide by the rules," he said. "Your friend, however, was one of the few who either didn't understand them, or chose to ignore them. That was most unfortunate for him. If I were you, I would spend the remainder of the night right here in this room. In the morning someone will come for you. You'll be making the remainder of your trip alone. Be very careful, Herr Weber. The war is over. You aren't in charge anymore."

So, Weber thought, after the smuggler left his room, Stuebbe killed the woman, and those who are in charge up here in the mountains, now that the war is over, in turn killed him. So much the better. Stuebbe was a pompous, hot-headed ass who would have caused them both plenty of trouble sooner or later. And anyway, he had had enough of the subservient role the older officer demanded, even now, after the war was over, after they were no longer in charge and their respective rank meant nothing. He was smarter than Stuebbe and considerably more ruthless. He would prosper infinitely more without him, especially since he, Weber, had the map showing the location of the gold and now would not have to share it with anyone. Weber smiled at his sudden good fortune. The young Jewish woman and the smuggler unwittingly conspired to do him a great favor since sooner or later he would have ended up killing Stuebbe himself. As for the album, it was probably lost forever in the forest along with the woman and was not something he planned to worry about.

Weber opened the pack that held his belongings and took out the small leather folder containing the papers with his new identity. He opened his passport and studied the photograph of his face. The features were hard, the mouth cruel, the eyes unflinching and devoid of emotion. Unlike the soft, pudgy face of his late companion Stuebbe, there wasn't an ounce of extra flesh, reflecting the self-discipline of which Weber was very proud.

Weber's gaze focused on the right ear in the photograph, the ear with the top third missing. He was proud of that as well. At the age of twelve he had organized a group of boys his age into a band of thieves. He did this not for the money—Weber's father was a wealthy Bavarian businessman—but for the thrill, for the excitement he derived from sneaking into homes at night when the occupants were asleep and stealing their belongings. When the gang was caught the local magistrate went easy on Weber because of his father's position in the community. His father, however, was furious, accusing Weber of disgracing his name. In a moment of rage he grabbed Weber by the hair and cut off part of his ear with a pair of garden shears. He told his son that now he would forever bear the mark of his family's shame. With blood running down his neck, Weber stood in front of his father, refusing to cry. "I am only ashamed that I was caught," he said. Then he bent down, picked up the severed piece of ear, put it in his mouth and ate it. A month later Weber left home and traveled by himself to Berlin where he enrolled in a special training center for Nazi youth.

Weber looked at the name stamped below the picture in his new passport. Indeed, he thought, Helmut Weber was no longer in charge. From this moment on Helmut Weber no longer existed. He was as dead as his former comrade Konrad Stuebbe. He was now a man named Novac DuCharme with a whole new life ahead of him.

II

Special Agent Stan Erland was sound asleep in his desk chair when the phone rang. He opened his eyes and waited for someone else to pick it up, then, after the sixth ring, remembered it was Sunday and he was the only person in the office. He cleared his throat and answered.

"CID," he said.

"Is this where you call if you got information about an old crime?" a woman asked.

She had a catfish drawl straight out of the Big Scrub, or farther north even, maybe from somewhere up in the panhandle. It was the kind you didn't hear that much anymore now that the city had grown and was filled with people from the North and Midwest.

Erland had majored in psychology in college. He had written a thesis for his master's degree on personality disorders of the criminal mind and considered himself an astute judge of human nature, far better at sizing people up than anyone he had worked with in his six years as a federal agent. Even half awake he believed he already had this woman pegged. She'd gotten married at seventeen, had two quick kids before her husband left. Now there's a boyfriend with a four-by-four, they're living in a double-wide with an air conditioner that works part-time, and she leaves the kids with her mamma while she puts in a shift at the Winn-Dixie deli counter. Probably wants to blow the whistle on the ex-husband who won't give her a dime's worth of child support. Or else it's the boyfriend she's turning in if she caught him with another woman or he's taken to smacking her around.

"Yes ma'am," Erland said. "This is where you call."

"Then why'd you say 'CID'?" she asked. There was a hint of petulance in her voice, but it could be she was just nervous. Odds were

19

good she was at a public phone outside a convenience store and was afraid someone would see her.

Erland rubbed the bridge of his nose and took a deep breath. He tried to concentrate. Something about the woman's voice seemed familiar but he was still not fully awake and was unsure whether he'd actually talked to her before or whether she reminded him of one of the waitresses he'd questioned in Cocoa Beach or Indialantic. He'd talked to at least two dozen over there along the coast in the past few days. Or maybe it was one of the psychics up in Velvet. It was a fine line, he thought, between the waitresses and the psychics. All their voices ran together in his head with the plaintive sameness of a country-western refrain.

"CID is the Criminal Investigation Division," he said. Erland was a man who more than anything cherished order and logic. He believed in solving cases unemotionally through a careful, systematic process. It seemed to him that of late, however, he'd given in to a demon that filled his life with a disconnected, chaotic hodgepodge of random information he wished would disappear. He extended his left arm, raised his thumb and pointed his index finger at the stack of files on his desk.

"Bang," he whispered.

"What did you say?" the woman asked.

"Ma'am, the Joint Federal and State Anticrime Task Force—the unit dealing with old crimes, hate crimes, crimes that violate someone's civil rights, that sort of thing—is electronically linked, for the time being, to the criminal investigation division of the sheriff's department. We live in a quaint little two-story building nearby. We're upstairs. The tractors and lawn-mowing equipment are downstairs. It's a temporary thing. Until we get our permanent quarters. Like staying at grandma's house while they're remodeling yours, if you see what I mean."

"Right," the woman said. "I see what you mean."

"So," Erland said, "if you have information pertaining to a crime— in particular a murder—that took place awhile back, you dialed the right number."

"Who are you?" she asked.

"I'm Special Agent Erland," Erland said. "Who are you?"

"I know who killed Freddy Hatton," the woman said. "You remember him?"

Freddy Hatton had been a Caterpillar Tractor distributor who made a fortune leasing heavy-duty construction equipment to various government agencies. Early in his career, before he cleaned up his act and became a model of civic responsibility and a member of the governor's economic development commission, Hatton had been a grand dragon of the Florida Knights of the Ku Klux Klan. When a federal racketeering indictment was handed down accusing him of bribery, extortion, and fraud, Hatton volunteered to provide the FBI with all manner of information about his former associates.

In November of 1989, a week before Freddy Hatton was to testify, he slipped from under the watchful eye of the agent who was guarding him and drove to a nearby motel where, telephone records later revealed, a topless dancer named Michelle Cornel was waiting for him. Two days later Freddy Hatton's body was discovered floating in the marsh grass on the shore of a lake less than a mile from his house. He had been shot twice in the back of the head at close range with a .22 magnum. The topless dancer vanished and the murder weapon was never found. Robbery was ruled out as a motive since Hatton was still wearing a $15,000 Rolex and had $2,000 in sodden cash stuffed in his wallet. No witnesses surfaced and no one was ever arrested.

Stan Erland was the agent assigned to guard Freddy Hatton. At the time, he had been with the central Florida office of the FBI for less than a month. Shrewd student of human nature though he may have been, Erland never imagined that Freddy, fifty-four years old and considerably overweight, would crawl out an upstairs bathroom window and shinny down a sycamore tree to meet a bimbo. At least not in the pouring rain with his wife watching TV in the entertainment room less than six feet from the tree.

"Yeah, I remember him," Erland said. "What's your name?"

"Teresa," the woman said. "I'm not gonna tell you what I know over the phone."

"You got a last name?" Erland asked.

"Strowbridge," the woman said. "There's money for this, right? I mean if you catch somebody."

"Yeah, there's money."

"Well, meet me in an hour. At Hobot's Riverside. You know where that is? Down where they rent canoes off Watchula Springs Road."

"I have some things to finish here, Ms. Strowbridge. How about you call me back in twenty minutes? Would that be all right? Then we can work out when and where we're going to talk to one another."

"It's me that's gonna be talkin'," the woman said. "All you'll have to do is listen."

"Twenty minutes," Erland said. "That'd be ten after six."

"I can tell time," the woman said, and hung up.

Having been judged blameless in the Freddy Hatton matter, Erland was not disciplined. Still, in spite of a subsequently spotless record, Freddy's murder continued to gnaw at him, privately sullying his lofty self-image. He kept copious notes on the case and was secretly obsessed with the missing dancer, the woman he came to believe was the cause of his embarrassment.

To his credit, Erland kept his obsession reasonably under control, but when word got out about the formation of the Joint Task Force, he immediately volunteered. Erland had nothing but disdain for the sheriff's department, but politically it was a smart move, demonstrating his willingness to work with local law enforcement. His real reason for wanting to join the special unit, however, was that it would give him an excuse to search methodically for Freddy Hatton's killer. The idea for the Joint Task Force came from a commission that included a federal judge, a U.S. senator, and a couple of powerful congressmen. They obviously wanted some tangible results they could point to at election time, but since their real motivation for forming the unit was political appeasement and many of the cases were old, there was no frantic rush to solve anything. Once Erland had been chosen and the Joint Task Force became operational, he was free to devote time to his obsession.

For six months Erland ran down leads and got nowhere. Then, two weeks earlier, while working on another case—the murder of a psychic in the tiny hamlet of Velvet, Florida—he discovered what appeared to be a connection to Freddy Hatton. He was going through the stack of composition books containing the psychic's handwritten records when he came across the name Michelle, followed by the words "former dancer or model, now works with food, blond hair, tall, watched over by animal spirits, lives near water." Another notation a couple of pages later indicated that this Michelle had returned to visit the psychic with a friend named Tito, who, the psychic wrote, "smelled like the sea."

Convinced there was a link between the psychic's death and these entries in the notebooks, Erland spent four days driving up and down the coast from Titusville to Vero Beach stopping at restaurants and bars and talking to every commercial fisherman he could find, but no one knew anything about a waitress or barmaid called Michelle or someone known as Tito. One fisherman did remember a woman with long blond hair he'd seen at a party on another man's boat several months earlier but he had no idea what her name was.

"This woman," Erland said. "Did she have a scar along the bottom of her chin? One of her front teeth chipped?"

"That's her," the fisherman replied. "Kind of tall. Nice body. Sexy, but mean looking. Not a woman you'd want to bring home to mama."

"No," Erland said. "But you might slide down a tree in a rainstorm to meet her."

"You might," the fisherman said. "But I wouldn't."

Erland had fallen asleep rereading the psychic's notebooks on this Sunday evening in March. Now, reasonably awake, he ran a computer check on Teresa Strowbridge and drew a blank. The Florida Department of Law Enforcement had no record of a woman with that name. The motor vehicle bureau did, but their Teresa Strowbridge lived in Naples and was seventy-nine years old.

What Erland should have done next was call McKenzie Rockett, the captain from the sheriff's department who had been assigned to run the Joint Task Force. Either that or call Detective Angela Becker, the local law enforcement member of the unit who was, in effect, Erland's partner. Calling one or the other was certainly not mandatory. Erland and Becker did fieldwork and met with sources on their own all the time. But given the results of the computer check, it would have been the prudent thing to do, and Stan Erland was generally a very prudent man.

Erland, however, was uncomfortable with both of his co-workers in the unit. It wasn't because Rockett was black and Becker was a woman, he told himself. That wasn't it at all. Erland bent over backward not to be in any way discriminatory. It was that Rockett, though always soft-spoken and polite, seemed, at some level, to be judging him, weighing his performance against a standard Erland couldn't quite define. It's like I'm his kid, Erland thought, every time he was in the presence of the captain, a powerfully built ex–football player who looked as though he might at any moment burst the seams of his suit. I'm his kid and he's waiting for me to screw up so he can sit me down and lecture me.

Angela Becker, meanwhile, was as alien to Stan Erland as a Watusi warrior and nearly as tall, standing just a shade under six feet. In high heels she towered over Erland, who considered her to be bizarre and basically unstable. She lived out in the woods, in the swamp somewhere with the alligators and snakes, in an Airstream trailer, so Erland had been told, along with several pet goats and a couple of vicious dogs. She smoked a corncob pipe, had a diamond stud in her nose, and drove an old 1973 Trans-Am that had belonged to a drug dealer she busted when she was with the narcotics squad. Erland heard she'd gotten into some trouble drag-racing the car on the street late one night but had been cleared when she claimed the race was part of her undercover work.

Erland heard that before she was assigned to the Task Force under McKenzie Rockett's command, she had been taken off the street to work as a counselor for convicted felons who were youth gang members or skinheads. Erland was sure that had something to do with the drag-racing incident, although she sure as hell didn't act repentant. One day she'd show up for work in a silk designer suit, a remnant, no doubt, of her days as a fashion model in New York, made up as though she were being photographed for *Vogue*. The next day she'd be wearing torn jeans and a flannel shirt, or a scruffy old leather flight jacket and a pair of jungle fatigue pants with her hair done up in pigtails. She packed a .44 magnum with a 4-inch barrel, definitely not standard issue, though Captain Rockett didn't seem to care. As far as Stan Erland was concerned, people like Angela Becker had no business carrying any sort of firearm at all.

In any event, Erland regarded the Freddy Hatton case as his and his alone and had no intention of sharing the news about his recent phone conversation with anyone, at least for the time being. Since his conversation with the fisherman, he had been convinced a rendezvous with Michelle Cornel, the missing dancer, was imminent. That the computer had turned up nothing on a woman named Teresa Strowbridge only confirmed this in Erland's mind. Somehow Michelle had gotten wind of his recent search along the coast. For one reason or another—most likely for protection or revenge—she had decided to seek him out, to trade information for money and immunity. In addition to Hatton's death, she knew about the psychic, a man who had been murdered in a similar fashion—a couple of .22 magnum rounds to the back of the head. He revised his earlier assessment of the woman whose phone call woke him up. The petulant drawl now belonged to a hardened fugitive looking to make a deal.

When the phone rang again at precisely ten minutes after six and the woman on the line identified herself as Teresa Strowbridge, Erland firmly believed he was talking to Michelle Cornel. Feeling better than he had in months, he grabbed his jacket off the coat rack and hurried from the office. He had plenty of time for a nice dinner before their meeting, plenty of time to consider which of the two murders he wanted to hear about first.

"Well, sugar, how'd I do?" the woman said, putting down the phone. "Do I get the part?" She was sitting in an easy chair in a hotel room just off the interstate in Orlando, ten miles from the place where she and agent Erland were to meet.

Reclining on the bed across the room, the Argentinean assassin known as El Papagayo, the Parrot, watched her light a cigarette and blow a stream of smoke at the ceiling. He ran a finger up and down the sharply hooked nose that gave him his name and smiled.

"You were splendid," he said.

"Easiest two grand I've made in a long time," she said. "For another hundred I'll show you what I can do besides talk. You won't even have to move."

"Sure," El Papagayo said. "Why not?"

She was a small, thin brunette who had once been very pretty, back when she was an understudy on one of the soaps waiting for her big break, before the drugs. She lay the cigarette in an ashtray, stood up and took off her clothes.

"I left my shoes on," she said as she walked toward him. "And my pantyhose. I figured you'd like that."

"Yes," he said. "That's nice."

"I never wear panties," she said. "I like the feel of the pantyhose against my skin. I like to leave them on when I have sex. Any kind of sex. It's a fetish I have. I'm glad you like it."

She had freckles on her shoulders and across the top of her chest above her small breasts. He found that appealing and ran his fingers gently over them as she bent down and took him in her mouth, first running her tongue slowly around the head of his penis, then circling him with her lips, watching him all the while with her cold blue eyes.

"Stand up and touch yourself," he said after he had come. "Make a hole in your pantyhose with your fingernail and touch yourself through it."

He leaned over, turned on the radio and spun the dial until he found a station playing soft Latin jazz.

"Sure, baby," she said. She stuck a long red fingernail through the nylon material and looked at him, licking her lips. She was four feet from the head of the bed, swaying slightly to the music. He studied her with his dark restive eyes as she reached the finger through the hole and began to stroke herself. Her lips were parted, her hair disheveled, and the skin on her neck was flushed.

"Touch your nipple with your other hand," he said. "Make yourself come."

She began moving her finger faster, breathing audibly and closing her eyes, getting into it, maybe acting, but maybe not. She never saw him reach under the bed for the gun with the silencer, never saw him pull the trigger and put three bullets into her chest.

At eight o'clock Sunday night, Stan Erland drove into the parking lot of Hobot's Riverside. Hobot's closed at six on Sunday and the darkened lot was empty except for a white Ford Taurus, parked, as the woman on the phone had said it would be, in the far corner, next to the dock where the canoes were moored. The woman was sitting on the dock, her back to the lot, huddled against the chilly March evening in a sweater-coat. Her long hair spilled over the shawl collar, and as he climbed from his car, Erland could see that the hair was blond.

"Michelle," he said.

"No, I am not Michelle," El Papagayo said from beneath his wig, swiveling on the dock as he spoke. He had his silenced automatic aimed straight at Erland's chest. "Get into that canoe. The first one. You do exactly as I tell you, perhaps you will live."

III

Cortez the rug man listened while Angela Becker talked and the cool night wind, laden with the scent of orange blossoms, blew through the pine trees outside her trailer. The trailer was an old one, a '64 Airstream, thirty-one feet long, the inside finished all in wood. It was set up on blocks in the middle of twenty acres Angela owned north of Orlando in the swampy forest bordering the Coacootchie River. She'd purchased the land two years earlier at the estate auction of a drug-dealing banker who had been murdered. She owned a condo as well, a two-bedroom duplex with a hot tub and wood-burning fireplace in a gated community closer to town. She kept many of her things there—clothes, books, pottery and small carvings she collected from places she visited—but since she bought the land she rarely stayed at the condo for more than one night at a time. She used to tell herself she needed more room and was going to sell the condo and build a post-and-beam house in a clearing fifty yards from the trailer, but so far she hadn't gotten past looking at plans. Then Cortez told her the Airstream felt exactly like the cabin of a ship, even the way it rocked a little in a storm. As a birthday present for Angela he put down navy blue carpeting in the trailer that was left over from a theater job and would last forever. It made the trailer very quiet and even more peaceful and cozy, a perfectly self-contained sanctuary, Angela thought.

"You sit in here you could be anywhere in the world, sailing the seven seas," Cortez had said. After that she decided she could wait a while before building the house.

Angela was lying on her back on the bunk set against one side of the trailer three quarters of the way toward the rear. Her head was propped up on a pair of embroidered pillows, her dirty-blond hair cascading down over her shoulders, picking up light from the ship's lantern hanging on the wall. She wore old jeans, a gray sweatshirt with a hole in one elbow, and was barefoot. With her long legs stretched out straight, you could see the tiny tattoo on her right ankle of an angel done in cobalt blue and red with gold-tipped wings. A Mozart piano concerto played softly on the stereo. A holster with her 4-inch .44 hung on a wooden peg set in the wall above her feet.

"There's two of 'em left," she said. "Three more weeks talking to those creeps and then I file my report and I'm done with it . . . done cajoling and shouting and psyching. . . . Isaac, it's like trying to gnaw through a brick wall with your teeth. A year I've been doing this. Two nights a week. The rehabilitation of skinheads. What a noble concept. Help them to see the error of their ways. A futile attempt at the conversion of the swine would be more like it. And to think I volunteered. I told Rockett, I finish with these two and then I'm all yours, forever and ever. Two leftovers, you know, like a couple of moldy sandwiches you find stuck in the back of the fridge after you think you got it all cleaned out. One of 'em's a lost cause. No hope for that piece of crap, got his trousers pressed and his shoes shined, not a hair out of place, mellow as a Buddhist monk. All full of that yes ma'am, no ma'am bullshit, but he's got eyes like cement. I show him a church full of babies on fire he doesn't flinch. That boy's heart pumps liquid nitrogen, know what I mean?"

Isaac Cortez nodded. Once, years before he was Cortez the rug man, he had been Cortez the undercover agent, working for the Florida Game and Fresh Water Fish Commission, posing as an airboat desperado, reeling in poachers who got fifty dollars a foot for alligator hides and a hundred and fifty for the carcass of a deer. A poacher who knew what he was doing could make fifteen hundred a week year round, considerably more if he were willing to work for the drug runners who made fly-over drops into the swamp. Wading in that pool was dangerous business but Isaac Cortez seemed to have the touch, until one night at a redneck honky-tonk in the middle of the woods a man he'd busted two years earlier walked in and recognized him.

Angela Becker was twenty-three years old, working narcotics, parked on a backwoods dirt road on her first drug stakeout when Isaac Cortez, bleeding from multiple stab wounds to his body and a severed right hand, managed to crawl to his Ford Bronco and call for help.

Angela, by pure chance, was less than two miles away and reached him before he bled to death. Cortez lost his spleen and a kidney in addition to the hand. When he recovered, he decided to give up his career in law enforcement and went to work in his brother-in-law's rug business.

He sat facing her on a canvas deck chair, his feet propped up on a plastic crate. He was a small man, nearly fatless and a good four inches shorter than Angela, who was five-eleven, but despite his size and his missing parts he had surprising strength. Angela had seen him pull a 250-pound roll of carpet from his truck with his good left hand and the titanium claw that protruded from his right sleeve, swing the carpet onto his shoulder, and walk with it up a flight of stairs. He raised the claw now, ran it through his thick black hair, and tilted the chair back against the cupboard next to the trailer's stove. The lantern's light shone on the angry scar that ran from the tip of his chin down his neck and upper chest, disappearing beneath his worn flannel shirt.

"My last two skinheads," she said. "Sounds like the title of a poem. But the one—not the neat and polite one, the other one, who's always jumping up and down, just about foaming at the mouth—there might be hope for him. He makes all kinds of nasty faces and squints his eyes and folds his arms across his chest like a bad guy, but at least I know his blood pressure goes up and down. The other one runs the temperature of a shark. I'm thinking I can get to the one with emotions. Either that or get something out of him. Finish up the gig with a check mark in the win column. Make the trip worthwhile."

Just then, Angela's female Rottweiler, curled up on the couch at the front of the trailer, growled deeply and raised her head. The male, who'd been lying outside the door, stood up, chuffed a couple of times and lay back down. Something was moving through the underbrush down near the river.

"It's just an animal come to take a drink," Angela said. "He won't go after a wild animal. Not unless it's standing upright on two legs."

"So you've told me," Cortez said.

"You don't look like you believe me."

"Sure, I believe you. I just wouldn't want to wind up wearing his teeth. Hers either. There's enough of me gone already."

"Your my friend, Isaac. He can tell that. Both of them can. They feel it, same as I do."

"They're dogs," Cortez said. "Dogs make mistakes. Just like people."

Inasmuch as it indirectly resulted in the arrest and conviction of a major central Florida cocaine distributor, Angela Becker received no disciplinary action for her involvement in a drag-racing episode late one night on the street. Soon afterward, however, she was transferred from the narcotics and vice division of the sheriff's department, and before McKenzie Rockett tapped her for the Joint Task Force, she spent six months working with skinheads and various other fringe fanatics as a liaison between the courts and the police. This assignment was not a punishment, but rather a compliment to Angela's intelligence and persuasive talents, both of which were considerable.

"I wouldn't really call her a loose cannon," her commanding officer told one of the criminal court judges. "She's more of . . . how can I put it? An unusual person. She does things in an unconventional manner and therefore needs to be watched, but she gets results. Personally, I like having that woman on my team, though I may live to regret I ever told you that."

Her job was to work with young perpetrators of hate crimes in a program designed to make them see the hideousness of their ways and hopefully turn over a new leaf. She showed them movies, took them to lectures, involved them in discussion groups with Holocaust survivors and Black and Asian victims of racial violence. She spent hours with them in her office at the Holocaust Memorial Center, one-on-one, or sometimes talked with two or three of them at once in the conference room where the walls were lined with photographs of Hitler's victims. The work drained her, frustrated her, and nearly drove her crazy, but even after she began working with Rockett she continued devoting two nights a week to it. Her success rate was less than 20 percent, but even so she had trouble letting go. "Maybe this one," she would tell herself, as another young felon with a cocky walk and a face filled with disdain came through the door of her tiny office. "Maybe I can turn this one around."

"So now let me get this straight," Cortez said. "This kid, the one you think you got a chance to straighten out, the one who jumps up and down and makes tough guy faces, he's the younger brother of the dude you're gonna run against tonight?"

"Half-brother," Angela said. "His name is Jason Badger. They have the same mother."

A gust of wind came through the small screened window next to Angela's head blowing her hair over her face. Cortez watched her pull it back with an unconsciously graceful sweep of her hand. She turned her head slightly and the light from the lantern shone on the sprinkling of freckles across the bridge of her nose and along her upper cheeks. For an instant she looked like a complete innocent, like a naive, beatific child. Cortez shook his head. That look had fooled a lot of people who had underestimated her and paid the price. He had known her for nine years and it still could have fooled him.

She caught him watching her and smiled. "What?" she asked.

"Nothing," he said. "Tell me about Badger's half-brother, the one with the car. What's his deal?"

"Mr. Tough-Guy. Mr. Slick. At least he thinks he is. His name is Ernie Viens, a coon-ass from Louisiana. They call him Peacock. He was a gopher for his cousin, a right-wing fanatic oilman in Morgan City named Joseph Didier, who got shot by his mistress about three years ago. After Didier was killed, Ernie came here. Spends his free time in topless joints. The expensive ones, like Rachel's. Leaves hundred-dollar tips. Runs an outfit that produces radio commercials for car dealers. You've probably heard 'em. They're the ones with the screaming voices. He runs a bunch of these skinheads too. Sort of a Klan version of a scoutmaster. They idolize him. He takes 'em to clubs in his stretch limo, takes 'em out to eat, pays their rent if they're out of money, buys 'em clothes. That sort of thing. The half-brother, the younger one, thinks he's God. Peacock did two years in Angola for extortion. He was arrested for hijacking another time but he skated. Been clean as a whistle since he moved here. Personally, I think he's indirectly responsible for all sorts of badness up to and including a murder or two, to say nothing of a synagogue bombing and three or four cases of arson involving the homes of African Americans. Could be even directly responsible, only I can't prove it and neither can anybody else. Can't prove shit. But I can take his car."

"Take his car? You mean beat him in a race or take it away from him?"

"I mean win his car from him by beating him in a race."

"Then the younger brother won't think he's God anymore. Is that the plan?"

"That's a possibility."

"And you'll get yourself a conviction of sorts," Cortez said. "An out-of-court settlement, so to speak."

"Peacock loves that car," Angela said. "His brother told me so at least a dozen times. Imagine how pissed off he's gonna be. Maybe he'll do something stupid."

"This Peacock who's doin' things that nobody can prove, this tough guy who loves his car, he's gonna go out at night to the middle of nowhere and race it against a woman who's a cop? Is that what you're tellin' me?" Cortez said. "Sounds to me like he's already done something stupid."

"The kid doesn't know I'm a cop," Angela said. "The kid believes I'm a social worker. A bleeding heart liberal cooze social worker who thinks she can drive. We got to talking cars in one of our enlightenment sessions. The kid told me all about his brother. I thought, Hmm, what have we here? So I checked ole' Ernie out."

"He's never seen your tattoo, the kid."

"Or my diamond stud. I kept it au naturel with the youthful felons in my charge."

"The woman of many faces."

She smiled at him and stretched her long arms over her head, pressing her hands against the low ceiling above the bunk. "Men are funny," she said. "Tellin' 'em you can out-drive 'em is like tellin' 'em you can out-fuck 'em. They'll walk on their hands to the North Pole to prove you're wrong. Even tough guys like Ernie Viens. Especially tough guys like Ernie Viens. No offense, Isaac, but he's short. And he isn't all that bright. What I'm wondering is who's running him. I'm wondering where he gets all the cash he throws around. The radio commercial business isn't that good."

"I think you're nuts, Angela," Cortez said. "You're thorough, and smart, but you're nuts. And self-destructive too. You're gonna piss your career into the swamp."

"My career? You mean the one with the cases that have been buried so long they got trees growing up out of them, the one with an obsessive-compulsive G-man for a colleague who's so fucking secretive he won't tell me what he's working on and just about jumps out of his skin if I so much as go near his files? That career? Or do you mean this other one where I get to play Doctor Freud to a bunch of young Nazis? Which one is it, Isaac, that I'm gonna piss into the swamp?"

Cortez was about to tell Angela she needed a vacation when the phone rang twice and stopped.

"Well now," Angela said. "I believe we have received the signal to go racing. And if I play my cards right, I'm gonna need someone to drive my extra car home. I was hoping that would be you, Isaac."

"Yeah, I know," Cortez said. "And if you lose, then what? We walk twenty miles? Or maybe you were thinking I'd carry you over my shoulder. Like a rug."

"Trust me, Isaac," Angela said. "We won't be walking. Not tonight. You got a gun in your truck or you want one of mine?"

IV

"She ain't comin'," Peacock said. "She ain't gonna show. I dragged my machine all the way out here for nothin'."

Peacock's machine, a dark blue '92 Mustang, sat low to the ground on its extra-wide tires in a little clearing at the side of the road. It had been modified by a company out in Oklahoma City for $25,000. The wheels alone cost six hundred apiece. Oliver Reavis had glanced inside the car for a moment when Peacock climbed out and saw it had a six-point roll cage, special racing seats, and all kinds of gauges. He was unimpressed. Oliver Reavis's talent was assembling incredibly fast cars that looked like piles of junk.

"She'll be here," Oliver Reavis said. He shuffled his feet and bobbed his head, doing a little dance, putting on a show for this Peacock and the two guys he brought with him—the skinny kid with ears like dinner plates who was trying to look mean, and the other one, the big one in fatigue pants with the red bandanna on his head and the wad of chewing tobacco in his mouth who *was* mean.

"She's reliable," Reavis said, jabbing an index finger a couple of times at the night sky as though he were invoking a deity. "As reliable as her car, and I know that's reliable 'cause I'm the one done the extra work on it. Relax. Have yourself a smoke or somethin'. Here, you want a piece of gum?"

Peacock snorted and spit into the weeds. He smoothed back the sides of his dark, oiled hair with his palms, drew himself up to his full height, which even in his cowboy boots was about five foot six, and strode off down the road, away from the clearing, away from his chain-smoking half-brother Jason who was leaning against his car, and Tito Pettibone who was sitting on one of the front fenders.

"I should have my head examined," Peacock mumbled. "Listenin'

37

to this dumb-ass kid. Gets me into a race with a woman. With a social worker bitch got a nigger for a mechanic. Shit. At least if she does show up I ain't got nothin' to worry about. Ain't a nigger been born knows how to build a car."

Oliver Reavis sat down on the tailgate of his pickup and watched Peacock move, wondering whether that was his real name or a nickname given to him because of the way he puffed up his chest, jutted out his ass and kept his head tilted back when he walked.

Reavis listened to the click, click, click of the man's boots on the concrete. The sound faded into the darkness, blending into the chorus of frogs and insects, then grew louder as the Peacock turned and headed back.

Wouldn't take no gum from a black man, Reavis thought. 'Fraid the color rub off from my hand. 'Fraid he catch him some incurable disease. Struttin' fool. Struttin' fool just might be about to part company with his money.

The road they were on, shrouded in mist, lay straight and flat through stands of pine, scrub oak, and palmetto, halfway between the city and Cape Canaveral—the space coast, as it was known. Other streets, slightly narrower and equally straight, leading off into nothing but woods and swamp, intersected this road at regular intervals. Once, many years ago, a developer had planned to build a community there, a thriving, futuristic enclave called Satellite City, but shortly after laying in miles of pavement he had gone broke. Someone else had followed in the first developer's wake, erecting a smattering of dwellings, but he too ran out of money. All that remained of his endeavor were the shells of the few houses he built, ravaged now by wind and rain and inhabited, from time to time, by vagrants, outlaws, people on the run.

Occasionally, dope smugglers landed aircraft there, unloaded onto waiting trucks and took off, but even though the pavement was as level as a commercial runway it was risky business since ground fog was constant and the truckers' lights were unreliable. The swamp was littered with the twisted remains of planes that missed the road. From time to time, alligator hunters and fishing guides who traveled the swamp in air boats or canoes reported there were people living in several of these hulks but as long as they didn't bother anyone the law left them alone.

PROOF POSITIVE

One of the men who hung around Oliver Reavis's garage said the woman they were waiting for lived in one of the wrecked planes, but then another one said no, she lived in a deserted barn way on up the Coacoochee. A third man swore she lived in one of the old trapper's shacks along the river and kept snakes as pets. Every time Angela came by to have something done to her car they got into it, the debate sometimes raging for an hour after she left. Oliver Reavis, who knew precisely where Angela lived, never said a word.

"Angela, huh?" Reavis's wife had said. "She better have her a guardian *angela* looking over her shoulder she come around your place late at night like she do."

"*Angela* means messenger, not angel," Reavis said.

"Is that right?" his wife said. "Well then she better have her a guardian messenger who can run for help when someone goes to carve up that pretty face of hers. What's a white woman doin' with her car in your garage?"

"She's a most unusual white woman," Reavis said. "She's tall and skinny and walks like a day-old horse but don't be fooled. I was the only black man around that night out in Barnes when she happened along. Come slidin' out of nowhere and saved my ass."

"I done heard the story," Reavis's wife said.

"You done heard it, but you didn't see it," Reavis said. "That Angela be somethin' to watch when things get tense. Any carvin' go down it be her doin' it. She can keep comin' 'round my place long as she like."

That night in Barnes, Reavis had gone out with his wrecker to tow a car and had blundered into the lair of an outlaw motorcycle gang. A half dozen of them surrounded him, brandishing chains and baseball bats. One of them had some sort of Japanese sword. They told Reavis they were going to cut his balls off and stuff them down his throat. Reavis was convinced he was a dead man when suddenly he heard a car door slam and saw a very tall woman step out of the shadows and walk right into the middle of it, like a movie director stepping from behind the camera into the center of a scene. She was wearing combat boots and a tiger-striped jumpsuit with a gold detective's shield hanging from the chest pocket. She got everyone's attention in a hurry. When she cocked the hammer of the .44 she was carrying the click sounded

39

like the crack of a tree limb. That's how quiet it was. Legs shaking, Reavis waited for one of the bikers to do something—there were six of them, after all, even if she was a cop—but not one of them moved. It was the strangest thing he had ever seen, almost as though she had them hypnotized.

"Party's over, fellas," she said.

She had been sitting in an unmarked car, staking out the bikers, waiting for a drug dealer she'd been chasing for months to show up, when Reavis stopped to ask for directions and got pulled from his wrecker.

When the bikers were gone, Reavis dug one of his business cards out of his wallet. "You ever need your car fixed, anything along that line, you come see me," he said. "I'll take care of you. I do real good work. I build race motors too, you ever want something that'll really book."

"Yeah," the woman said. "I might take you up on that. Might be I could use something that'll really book."

"Hey, detective," Reavis said as the woman began to move off. "You mind if I ask you your name?"

The woman studied Reavis for a bit. "Angela," she finally said.

"You *my* lucky angel tonight," he told her.

"It's Greek for messenger," she said. "It doesn't mean angel."

"Either way," Reavis said. "You delivered the message when I needed it."

"I'll see you in a while," she told him.

Two weeks later she showed up at his garage driving her old red '73 Trans-Am with its big-block 455 motor that burned a quart of oil every three hundred miles, an automatic transmission that had begun to slip, and the huge gold and black firebird decal, now chipped and cracked, that covered the hood.

"It's still quick," she told him. "A lot quicker than people think, even with the automatic. But it's getting tired. To tell you the truth, I was thinking of getting rid of it."

"You got anything else to drive?" Reavis asked.

"Yeah," she said. "I have a Jeep."

"Leave the Trans-Am with me," he told her. "Let me look it over, think about it some, see what can be done. Give me a number where I can reach you. I'll call you before I spend any money."

Oliver Reavis kept Angela's car for three months. When he was through with it, the exterior didn't look any better than the day Angela drove it into the old cinder block orange grove packing house that Reavis had converted into a shop. If anything it looked a little worse, since the faded red paint was now speckled with primer where Reavis had removed patches of rust. But as she examined the car it seemed to Angela that it sat differently, that instead of sagging slightly on its worn-out suspension, it was now poised, like an animal ready to spring. When she fired it up she knew instantly, without even bothering to look under the hood much less drive it around the block, that it wasn't the same car.

"I got no idea how many horsepower that engine's puttin' out now," Reavis told her, "but it's plenty enough to get the job done. Horsepower don't necessarily mean a damn thing anyway. What's important is the way everything works together—the motor, the tranny, the gears in the rear end, the way the suspension transfers the power to the wheels—understand what I'm sayin'? It's like a symphony orchestra. You have one little horn out of tune the whole concert's gonna sound like a barnyard at dinner time. Same with a race car. And then of course with a street machine where there ain't no rules and regulations to contend with, you got the element of trickery, and I'm a sneaky ole' son of a bitch, don't you think I ain't. There's things I've done, deep down where no one can see, little extra things that can make the difference. To the untrained eye what you got here is a car that looks like it's been stuck together with Scotch tape and dried goose shit, but in a quarter mile drag race it'll run with anything on the road."

Reavis wiped some grease off his hands with a rag he'd been holding, cocked his head and grinned at her. "Assuming, that is, you can keep it in a straight line."

Oliver Reavis saw Peacock come back into view through the mist. He was walking down the center of the road, his chest puffed up, his short arms swinging stiffly at his sides, in perfect rhythm with the click, click, click of his boots that sounded now to Reavis like the metronome his daughter used when she practiced the piano. An image of his daughter's head bent over the keys as she played her scales again and again had just appeared in Reavis's head when he saw both of Peacock's boots leave the ground together, saw his legs fly into the air, and heard the rifle. Maybe it was two shots he heard, maybe it was three, he would never be certain, but Reavis had been to war, and one thing he was sure of was the sound. He was off the tailgate and under his truck almost as fast as Peacock's body hit the pavement.

Lying on his stomach beneath his truck, Reavis saw Peacock twitch a couple of times, then lie motionless, belly to the sky, legs splayed, one arm stretched above his head, the other bent across his face as though he were shielding his eyes from a bright light. He saw the skinny kid sprint toward the body, howling out a curse as he ran. The other one, the one with the bandanna, jumped into the Mustang, fired it up, and pulled onto the road spewing dirt and gravel behind him. He hesitated for just a second or two, thirty feet from where the kid knelt, then gunned the engine and was gone.

"He's dead," the kid screamed after him. "My brother's fuckin' dead and you took his car. You cocksucker. You fuck." Then the kid began to cry.

Oliver Reavis waited another minute until it was clear to him that the shooter had only been after one man. Dude's probably halfway to Titusville by now, he thought as he crawled from under his pickup and climbed into the cab. The kid heard him and glanced his way, desperate now, looking for help. He rose and took a couple of steps in Reavis's direction.

"Son, you're on your own," Reavis said under his breath as he started the engine. "I'm outa here. Ain't gonna be no nigger around to blame this one on. Uh uh. Not tonight." As he turned from the clearing he could see the kid running after him up the road and heard him holler something, but when he glanced in the outside rearview mirror mounted on the driver's door all he saw was darkness.

Angela Becker was telling Cortez about the transmission in her car, how Reavis had it set up with a dual-stage stall converter so the engine would idle down around eight hundred rpm all day long, no problem, for around-town driving, but then when she threw a switch under the dash the second stage would kick in and the motor would idle on up to four grand without the car so much as moving an inch off the line. She was telling him how, if she wanted to hold it with the brake, she could bring the revs up close to six grand for a launch and have half a car length on a guy like this Peacock before he ever got his clutch off the floor. She was about to tell Cortez why this would happen, how in addition to dealing with her car, Peacock would be all knotted up inside because in the first place she was a woman, and in the second place he'd had to wait for her to show up, and then on top of that Oliver Reavis was black, when both she and Cortez saw the body in the road.

"Judging from the snakeskin boots and the gold bracelet I'd say this here's your boy," Cortez said. "If it is, his racing days are over."

"It's him," said Angela. "He looked considerably better the one other time we met, but that's him."

The two of them were standing over Peacock's body illuminated by the headlights of Angela's car. There was no sign of anyone else, and besides the frogs and the insects, the only sound was the rumble of the Trans-Am's engine.

"What do you think happened?" Cortez asked.

Angela shook her head slowly. "Damned if I know, Isaac," she said. "Oliver Reavis didn't shoot him. He wouldn't hurt a fly. Even if the guy called him a dumb-ass nigger he'd just laugh and walk away. The brother sure as hell wouldn't have done it, and if it was someone else Peacock brought with him then the brother would probably be lying there dead too. At least that's my guess. By the looks of that churned-up dirt and the tire marks on the road it appears everyone who was left alive cleared out in a big hurry. Can you tell anything by the wounds?"

Cortez squatted down and peered at Peacock's chest. "For sure he wasn't shot close up," he said. "Could even be long range. Not a heavy caliber, I don't think. Maybe a two-twenty-three. Dark as it is out here, even with a night-vision scope it had to have been one mother-fucker of a shooter. There ain't two inches between these holes." He looked over at the Trans-Am. There was a two-way radio and a phone in the car.

"You gonna call it in?" he asked.

"Oh yeah," she said. "I'll call it in, but not until I get you the hell out of here. No point getting you mixed up in anything."

"You sure you want to do it that way?"

"Hell yes, Isaac. He isn't going anywhere. And they aren't going to find anything other than his body until morning anyway. With this fog rolling in, they aren't even going to look. They'll just seal off the road and wait until it gets light, so what's another hour or two gonna mean?"

"Animals," Cortez said. "He's nothin' but road kill now."

"Well that sure as hell doesn't bother me," Angela said. "Probably be the first time he served a useful purpose."

It was quarter to one, Monday morning, when Angela Becker finally turned out the lights in her trailer and went to sleep. Just over five hours later, at ten minutes to six, she was awakened by her phone. It was McKenzie Rockett, her boss.

"Meet me in an hour at Jimbo's and don't be late," he said, and hung up.

Jimbo's Cafe was a cavernous restaurant in west Orlando stuck in between a barber shop and a store that sold tropical fish. Once, many years ago, it had been a pool hall. The long, metal-shaded lights still hung above the rows of round tables covered with red-and-white-checked tablecloths and above the horseshoe-shaped Formica counter with high-backed, vinyl-covered stools. Jimbo, a six-eight black man who weighed well over three hundred pounds, stood behind the counter, all day, every day, doing the cooking along with his wife, Bernice, and his mother-in-law, Thelma, while assorted nieces and cousins waited on the customers, and Clarence, his father-in-law, ran the dishwashing machine in the back. There was an air conditioner that was always running, and several paddle fans as well, interspersed among the lights, but in spite of this a layer of smoke from the grill always hung just below the ceiling like a perpetual blanket of clouds.

Smoky though the place might be, the food in Jimbo's was beyond compare. When Jimbo moved to Orlando from Houston and turned the old pool hall into a restaurant thirty years earlier he brought with him the recipe for the secret sauce that dripped from the beef and pork ribs that were his specialty. The ribs, along with Bernice's fried chicken and Thelma's grilled catfish sandwiches, kept Jimbo's packed with people from every ethnic background and all walks of life every night at dinnertime.

No matter how crowded it got in the restaurant, however, there was one spot far in the back—a long, rectangular, wooden-plank table surrounded by a dozen chairs—that day and night was always reserved. This table, known as the wheelhouse, was where leaders of Orlando's black community gathered every morning for breakfast. It was at this table that city councilmen, school board members, lawyers and businessmen, ministers from the major black churches, and various other influential figures came to debate the issues of the day. It was there, over grits, fried eggs and bacon or sausage, and steaming mugs of coffee, that major problems confronting the community were discussed and often resolved, and where any white politician interested in garnering the support of the black community came at election time to pay homage.

McKenzie Rockett was sitting at the wheelhouse with two men Angela Becker didn't recognize when she walked through the door of Jimbo's at precisely three minutes to seven on Monday morning and took a seat at one of the round tables in front. Her hair was done up in a French braid, and she was wearing a burgundy double-breasted silk suit jacket with a matching short skirt, a stretch lace T-shirt and heels the same color as the suit. The heels put her more than an inch over six feet tall, and not a man in the place, whether he looked or pretended not to, was unaware of her presence. Rockett said something to the two men he was with, stood up, and walked the length of the room carrying his coffee, some of which sloshed out of the mug as he reached her table and sat down. Angela put down her menu and smiled at him. She put her long slender hand over his enormous one that was wrapped around the coffee mug and stared into his eyes with mock innocence.

"I didn't do it, Rock," she said.

Rockett didn't smile back at her and she let go of his hand. The top button of his starched, pinstripe shirt was undone and his tie was loosened but his thick, corded neck still looked like it didn't have enough room. He was an inch shorter than she was but one of the most powerfully built men she had ever known. She had heard that when he was a running back for Kansas City he preferred going through defenders than around them. When he rested both arms on the table and leaned toward her she felt consumed.

"Which one didn't you do?" he asked. "The guy lying in the road out there in Satellite City, the one you called in, or your former partner, the late Stan Erland who was found with his head full of holes sitting in a canoe?"

"Somebody killed Erland?" she asked. "Jesus Christ. When did that happen? What the hell was that asshole doing?"

"It happened last night out at Hobot's Riverside," Rockett said, "where he apparently went to meet a woman who claimed on the phone she had some information for him. She's dead too. At least I think it's her. Her body was found in the motel room where she made one of the calls, but that's another story. First tell me about Ernie Viens."

A young waitress came over, turned Angela's coffee mug right side up, filled it, and stood with her pencil poised. Angela shook her head and told the woman she wasn't hungry.

"Erland's dead?" she said after the woman walked away. "Shot?"

"You think I dragged you down here at this hour of the morning to tell bad jokes?" Rockett said. "Yeah, Erland is dead. Now what about Ernie? Tell me about you and the Peacock."

"They ID'd him already?"

"No thanks to you. He still had his wallet tucked in his boot. Don't mess with me Angela, I'm not in the mood. A deputy picked his brother up wandering down one of the side roads out there. He told us you and Ernie were supposed to be having a race. He says this other guy out there, someone named Tito who was supposedly his brother's friend, took off with Ernie's car after he was shot. He thinks you had him set his brother up. The little weasel thinks you pulled the trigger.

I know better. I know you're not that good a shot. What I don't know
is what the fuck's going on, but I plan to find out, and I'm starting
with you."

The two black men McKenzie Rockett had been sitting with passed
by on their way out of the restaurant. They nodded, but didn't stop
walking.

"One of those guys is the state trooper who found Erland," Rockett
said. "He called the other one who's a fed. The fed called me. Thanks
to that trooper you ain't gonna be reading about this in the *Journal-
Express,* nor will you see it all over the TV on the evening news. At
least not right away. It's good to have friends, Angela. But you gotta
be straight with 'em. You understand what I'm sayin'?"

"Ernie Viens had his hooks in these kids I've been working with,"
Angela said. "Somebody has . . . had his hooks in Ernie Viens. I was
trying to shake his tree a little, see if maybe something would fall to
the ground."

"So you decided to go racing. Again?"

"That was make-believe. Haul his ass all the way out there for
nothing. Get him real pissed off. This thing with these kids, Rock . . .
It's been very frustrating. I told you all that before. It was probably a
dumb idea, but I didn't shoot him."

"I know you didn't shoot him, Angela," Rockett said. "But what I
want you to do now is look me straight in the eye and tell me you
weren't going to engage that son of a bitch in an illegal drag race. I
want you to . . ."

Rockett sighed deeply and sat back in his chair. He brushed some
crumbs off the sleeve of his dark blue blazer and took another deep
breath.

"Fuck it," he said. "Don't tell me. I don't want to know. Let me
tell you. You listen, and listen carefully. Stan Erland, your partner,
your ex-partner, who wouldn't tell you, or me, for that matter, exactly
what the fuck he was up to, was obviously eyeball deep in something
that got his ass blown away. Supposedly he was working on the case
of that psychic that got murdered two years ago up in Velvet, the old
guy whose name wasn't really his name and who took pictures that
weren't really pictures, and no doubt he was working on it, sort of. I
mean he spent the last two weeks up there nosing around, talking to

the old man's fellow psychics, doing whatever it was he did as an investigator. But of course you and I both know he was preoccupied with Freddy Hatton."

"Stan Erland was fucking crazy, Rock. He saw Freddy Hatton clues in the night sky, in his tea leaves, in his soup. For all I know he saw them in the urinal when he took a piss. The man was delusional."

"Yes he was," Rockett said. "He was delusional. But I think he was onto something anyhow. See, the woman who called him in the office yesterday evening, the one I think got her ticket punched in the motel, told him she knew who killed Freddy Hatton. That's what got him runnin' out to Hobot's, which is where he got plugged. So maybe he saw Freddy Hatton clues in his soup, and in the urinal, and maybe he saw them up there in Velvet too, in the land of the crystal ball and the dearly departed who are still with us."

"You think there's a connection between Freddy Hatton and the murdered psychic?"

Rockett took two quick sips of his coffee and leaned toward her again.

"I can do even better than that," he said. "In the most recent chapter of his search for the killer of Freddy Hatton, Stan Erland was looking for a man named Tito, who he heard about up there in Velvet."

"Tito," Angela said. "Ernie Viens's Tito? The guy who took his car?"

"I don't know," said Rockett. "Wouldn't it be interesting if he was? Wouldn't it be ironic, you and Erland actually stirring around in the same pot? But now listen to this. There's nothing in Stan Erland's written files about anyone named Tito. In fact, there *are* none of Stan Erland's written files at all for the last two weeks. I looked for them at two this morning because I wanted to beat the feds to 'em. They were piled on top of his desk. I saw 'em when I stopped by the office earlier in the day. Somebody else went and took 'em out of the office. Only thing is, Stan Erland was not only delusional, he was, as I'm sure you observed, anal retentive. He made copies of everything. Every single note he took on the road, every phone conversation he had, every description of every person he interviewed, all carefully cataloged in his computer and backed up on floppy disks. Whoever took his files knew Stan Erland's habits very well. Hardly anyone knew Erland put the stuff in his computer, but this person did, because not only were Erland's notes gone, his computer was cleaned out. God knows what they did to the poor bastard to get him to give up his password. But what they didn't know was that he took the floppy disks home with him every weekend. I did. I even knew where he hid 'em."

Angela drank some of her coffee and studied McKenzie Rockett's dark, impassive face. As usual, he was conveying far more than the simple facts he had just related to her. Obviously he thought someone on the inside—someone in the department or closely connected to it—either took Erland's files or was involved.

"You don't think—" she began, but Rockett cut her off.

"C'mon, Angela," he said. "Don't even ask that question. I don't think you had anything to do with it. I learned all I needed to know about you when you worked for me in narcotics. That's why you're working for me now. Because I trust you completely. But you better be careful. You and I both better be very careful. Somebody whacks a sleazeball like Ernie Viens, big fuckin' deal, right? Somebody whacks a federal agent, even one who's delusional, that's a whole different ball game. Someone out there is serious."

"So what's our plan?"

The tables in Jimbo's were filling up and the noise level had increased considerably. Rockett leaned closer to Angela so that he wouldn't have to raise his voice. "I'm going up to Virginia where they're burying Erland to pay my last respects," he said. "His body'll be shipped as soon as the autopsy's completed later today. The whole thing will be done very quietly."

"You want me to come with you?"

"No. That's not necessary. I need you here. Find out what you can about this guy Tito. Find out what the homicide guys turn up. If they bring him in, listen in when they question him. You won't have a problem. I already cleared it. Unless I can get an old friend to exert some influence the feds'll be all over Erland's murder. Be nice to 'em. I made you copies of Erland's disks. Go through them. See if anything looks promising. And watch my back, you understand what I'm saying? I'm not coming straight home from Virginia. I'm gonna take a little trip up to Vermont."

"Vermont? Kind of an odd time for a vacation, Rock, if you don't mind my saying so."

"It isn't a vacation. I'm gonna see if I can talk someone into signing on with us. Be your new partner."

"That's a long way to go for help. He must be pretty damn good. Assuming it's a man, that is."

Rockett smiled at her for the first time that morning. "I'll bring you back some maple syrup," he said. "C'mon, let me get you those disks out of my car. I have a plane to catch."

V

Although it was cold, Roland Troy awoke drenched in sweat. He had been having the dream again, the dream he couldn't put to rest, the dream about the river of blood. In the dream he was back in Austria, in the mountains just south of Innsbruck, driving a small car on a narrow, winding road. Just after a sharp curve in this road, he turned onto a dirt lane that ended in front of an old farmhouse on the shore of a tiny alpine lake. He got out of his car, walked up the path to the farmhouse and climbed the steps onto the front porch. He approached the front door but forced himself not to open it. He knew what he would find if he went inside. He knew his wife Clara and Bruno Schleifer, the French filmmaker, and two of Schleifer's helpers were all lying dead inside, murdered while they ate lunch at a table in front of a large window overlooking the lake. He knew that if he hadn't been sick that morning with a stomach virus that kept him in bed at the inn where they all were staying he probably would have been dead too. He knew that now, a year and a half later, though when it happened and he actually climbed the steps and opened the door he had known nothing until he went inside and found the four of them gunned down where they sat.

In the dream he stood there on the porch trying to keep his hand from twisting the doorknob. He looked down and saw that blood had begun to ooze between the threshold and the door. He turned and tried to run but his feet wouldn't move, and then the door burst open and a torrent of blood rushed toward him. It swept over him, tumbling him off the porch and back onto the path. He tried to cry out for help but couldn't make a sound. The blood was a river now, carrying him away from the farmhouse into the countryside, through a wooded landscape he had never seen before. The river bore him faster and faster through a canyon cut between strangely shaped outcroppings of rock from which trees protruded at weird angles, and hurled him toward a sheer wall of rock. Closer and closer to the wall he came until he could see dark fissures bisecting its face and patches of moss and bramble growing randomly on its surface. There was no avoiding this wall. He was going to be pulverized against it by the raging river of blood, but just as he was about to smash into the rock he woke up.

In the distance, Roland Troy heard a siren and at first thought he was still asleep, listening to the sounds of the police and the ambulances racing up the mountain road to the farmhouse in the Austrian Alps. Then he saw the half-finished mug of herbal tea sitting on the low wooden table next to him alongside the book he had been reading, a biography of Crazy Horse, the Oglala Sioux Indian chief, and realized he was awake and that it wasn't a siren at all he heard but the screaming tires of a car stuck in the mud somewhere down the rutted dirt road that ran through the woods to his cabin in the northeast corner of Vermont.

He was wrapped in an old tattered sleeping bag, lying on the couch in front of the potbellied stove in the living room. He stared at the dark red tea mug with the gold insignia of the University of Alabama imprinted on it. Long ago, before he went off to Okinawa to study karate in the school of the famed master Myazato; before he was recruited as a scout to crawl through the jungles of Vietnam and Laos and was then nearly killed in an ambush in the Mekong Delta by a man whom he thought was his friend; before he was a husband and a father and the best homicide detective in the southeastern United States, maybe even the best in the entire country; before his first wife ran off and left him with their baby daughter and then, many years later, he finally married his second wife, his long-lost love, Clara, whom he found dead on that farmhouse floor, on their first trip together, on their honeymoon; before all of that, when Roland Troy was young and filled with hope, he had left his home in Florida to play football at the University of Alabama.

He came home to central Florida from Europe with the body of his wife and buried her on the land along the Coacoochee River that had been in his family for five generations. Then he boarded up his house, the house built by his great-great-grandfather, where he and

Clara had planned to live out their lives, and moved north to the cabin in Vermont he bought sight unseen from a friend who had worked as an undercover operative with him for the government. He found the mug stuck away in an old trunk in the attic while packing for the move. At first he was going to trash it but remembered it had been given to him when he left Alabama by his coach, Bear Bryant, and decided to take it with him. Staring at the mug now, just after waking from the dream, the irony of holding onto it occurred to Troy for the first time, and he let out a short, sardonic laugh. Alabama, he thought. The Crimson Tide. What do you know? Crimson Tide. River of blood. He was a long way from everything up here where the thick forests and undulating fields ran uninterrupted to the Canadian border; far from everything but the river of blood that one way or the other seemed to have followed him all his life.

He extracted himself from the sleeping bag, stood up, stretched, and walked slowly to the kitchen, taking care not to drag his bare feet on the rough wood planks of the kitchen floor and pick up a splinter. He stripped off the sweat-soaked long-sleeve undershirt and gym shorts he was wearing and stood naked in front of the sink. He was a month shy of his forty-ninth birthday but his six-foot-one-inch body was still lean, his stomach flat, the muscles of his arms and torso still clearly defined. Jagged scars, reminders of the ambush in the Mekong Delta, were visible on the left side of his face beneath his beard, across his upper back and left shoulder, and along his left hip. On his right biceps a tattoo of a tiger on its hind legs pawed the air above the Chinese characters representing danger and opportunity. The tattoo was the mark of an ancient and secretive martial arts society known as Prancing Tiger that traced its roots back to the fourteenth century, back to a small, ferocious band of sailors who patrolled the East China Sea, protecting peaceful merchants from marauding pirates. In more than six hundred years, Roland Troy was the only Caucasian ever to become a Prancing Tiger.

Troy turned on the tap and splashed cold water on his face. He took a couple of small towels from under the sink, washed himself off with one of them and dried himself with the other. Then, shivering slightly, he went into the bedroom and got dressed in old jeans, a T-shirt, a frayed flannel shirt and a pair of wool hiking socks. He returned to the living room, opened one of the windows and listened. The high-pitched whine of tires spinning fruitlessly in the mud had stopped and except for the sound of a crow wheeling high above the stand of maples below the cabin the cold March air was noiseless.

Still in his stocking feet but carrying a pair of rubber-bottomed Maine hunting boots Troy walked out onto the front porch and lit a cigar. He hadn't worn a watch or checked a clock in months, having no real concern for the time of day, but now he looked up at the sky and judged it to be somewhere between four and five in the afternoon, not a good hour to be stuck in the mud in the woods. He was about to pull on the boots, get his tractor out of the barn, and go pull the stricken vehicle to dry ground when he saw someone trudging up the road through the maples. From a distance Troy could see it was a black man, which in itself was unusual in that part of the country, but his eyesight wasn't what it used to be, and though there was something vaguely familiar in the way the man carried himself, Troy wasn't certain of his visitor's identity.

Troy sat down on the porch railing and watched the person approach. Shortly, the man came out of the trees onto the last stretch of road, which was actually a rock-strewn, muddy path just wide enough to accommodate a four-wheel drive truck. This path passed thirty yards in front of the cabin, made a sharp left turn, and came to an end at the door of Troy's small barn.

"I'll be a son of a bitch," Troy said, as the figure came clearly into view. The man was wearing a suit, the pants of which were caked with mud. His tie and shirt were spattered with mud as well, and there were dried flecks of it all over his face. Still, Troy had no trouble recognizing who it was.

"McKenzie Rockett?" he shouted. "That was you stuck in the mud? What in hell are you doin' up here?"

"Why you askin'?" Rockett yelled back. "You don't allow black folks on your property?"

"Well shit, I never had to deal with that issue, Rock, inasmuch as you're the first black person who's ever come by. At least since I've been here."

"So what's it gonna be then. Are you going to invite me in, or tell me to move on?"

"Do I have a choice?" Troy asked. "I mean you're stronger than me, you're faster than me, and it's just the two of us here."

Troy came down off the porch and made his way down toward Rockett, who had left the path and was slowly climbing the slope to the cabin. Halfway up the slope Rockett stopped and watched Troy walk. It had been two years since he'd seen his old friend and colleague and considering what Troy had been through Rockett thought he looked pretty good. His limp was a bit more pronounced, there was a little more gray in his beard, and as Troy got closer Rockett could see a touch of sadness in his eyes, but he still stood without the slightest hint of a stoop, and when Troy reached him and the two of them embraced his body felt as hard to Rockett as a solid oak post.

"When I rented the car at the airport in Burlington they told me the snow had melted," Rockett said. "They didn't say anything about the mud."

"They don't like to divulge too much in these parts," said Troy. "Solzhenitsyn lived up here for twenty years and when outsiders came looking for him none of the locals would tell them where he was at. They respected his desire for privacy and would just say they had no idea there was a famous Russian writer living nearby."

Rockett took a step back and raised his eyebrows. "Meaning?" he said.

"Meaning I'm not surprised about the mud," Troy told him. "You ain't an outsider, Rock. I'm glad to see you. Come on inside and I'll get you some dry clothes and bowl of my homemade soup."

"How *did* you find me anyway?" Troy asked. They sat facing each other at the kitchen table in front of large bowls of Troy's lentil-and-tomato soup. A platter piled high with chunks of his freshly baked whole wheat bread lay between them alongside a gallon jug of apple cider. McKenzie Rockett, dressed in a pair of Troy's sweat pants and an old wool sweater stretched tight across his shoulders dunked another piece of bread in his soup, crammed it into his mouth and chewed noisily.

"Katherine told me where you were," he finally said. "She made me swear I wouldn't say it was her, but what the hell, Tooth, she's your daughter. She's worried about you. She thinks if you stay up here all by yourself much longer you'll go off the deep end."

Rockett was one of the few people left from the old days who still called him Tooth. The name referred to a case Troy solved a long time ago when he was a young homicide detective. On and off for three years he tracked a vehicle he was convinced had been involved in a hit-and-run murder, questioning dozens of people and searching through four states until he finally unearthed the car in a barn in north Georgia. He linked it to the crime by finding one of the victim's teeth wedged under a rubber grommet on the hood latch. Troy's discovery resulted in a widely acclaimed conviction and earned him the nickname Tooth. Among those who worked with him in law enforcement and criminal prosecution it was an appellation signifying the utmost respect.

Troy leaned back in his chair, relit his cigar, and watched McKenzie Rockett eat. "You think I've gone off the deep end?" he asked.

Rockett mopped up the last of his soup with another piece of bread, chewed it slowly and swallowed. "No," he said at last. "No, you seem to be in pretty good shape, to tell you the truth. At least on the outside. But I don't know what it's like for you on the inside, Roland. I don't even know what to say. There are times I look at my wife and think about what happened to Clara. I wonder what the hell I'd do if something like that happened to Carolyn. I just don't know." Rocket sighed. "You got another one of those cigars?" he said.

"Sure," Troy replied. He got up from the table, walked into the living room, and returned holding a wrapped cigar. He handed it to Rockett and sat back down on the kitchen chair.

"It's a real live Cuban," he said. "Guy I know does business over in Russia. He gets 'em there and sends 'em to me. All the way up here, in the middle of nowhere. Got my *New York Times,* got my books, got my jazz CDs and a real good radio, and I got my Cuban cigars. Only one thing I never got . . ." he leaned across the table and held a match to Rockett's cigar.

"What's that?" Rockett asked.

"I never got the people who killed my wife," Troy said. He looked straight at McKenzie Rockett and Rockett looked away.

"It's all right, Rock," Troy said. "I don't mind talking about it."

"I never really knew what happened," Rockett said. "I mean I heard stories, but I never heard nothin' about it from you. I wanted . . . I would have . . . next thing I knew you up and left . . ."

"We were in Paris," Troy said. "Clara and I. She'd never been to Europe before. She was loving every minute of it. She wanted to look up this guy she'd met in Orlando, this French filmmaker named Bruno Schleifer she met when he gave a lecture at the Holocaust Memorial Center. She called him and he invited us to dinner. Good guy. Very interesting. He was making a movie about how the Nazis escaped capture after the war. He was leaving in a couple of days for Austria to shoot some scenes along one of the escape routes. Next thing you know he asks us if we want to go with him to see firsthand what he was doing. I wasn't so hot about the idea but Clara was real excited and wanted to go. She even volunteered to help Schleifer out, you know, lugging stuff, setting up lights. She wanted to be involved. She felt it was important that she make even a small contribution to preserving the memory of what happened. She had never been a religious person at all, but she felt the need to connect somehow with the Jewish people. I understood that. I respected it. Matter of fact, after a while her excitement kind of rubbed off on me.

"I have to admit the place we went, where Schleifer was filming, was beautiful, way up in the mountains in an area filled with all these little alpine lakes. Schleifer didn't really need more than one of us—he already had a couple of technicians on his payroll—so while Clara was off helping him I went hiking in the mountains. The weather was perfect, and actually I was really enjoying myself because we'd been spending most of our time in cities and I was glad to get away from the crowds for a while.

"Anyway, this one night, just after we'd eaten dinner at the hotel where we were staying, I got me a wicked case of stomach virus. I was up with it all night. The next morning I stayed in bed while the rest of them went back to this old farmhouse where some of the escaping Nazis had hidden out.

"I'm lying there in bed, in the hotel, and sometime around about noon I get this funny feeling something wasn't right. A premonition. Don't ask me how or why, but I had this overpowering sense that

Clara and Schleifer were in trouble. I actually thought I heard Clara cry for help. So I got up and got dressed and drove out to the farmhouse . . . and I found them."

He blinked a couple of times, ran the back of his hand across his forehead, and stroked his beard. Then he cleared his throat and continued.

"I went back, after I buried her," he said. "Before I moved up here. I spent nine months there, Rock. I worked with the local cops, with Interpol, with U.S. military intelligence, German antiterrorist guys, some company ops over in Europe. I mean I left no stone unturned, but I didn't find shit. Nothing. Someone, some neo-Nazis or old Nazis, or someone else that no one knows about didn't want Schleifer making that movie. They didn't want it in a major way. I'm not sure why but my guess is that Schleifer knew considerably more than he let on. He wasn't murdered just for making that movie. And there had to be big money involved, of that I'm certain, 'cause whoever did the killing cost plenty. They left no tracks. No footprints, no fingerprints, not even a shell casing. He'd been warned, though, Schleifer. His wife told us he got a couple of threatening phone calls back in Paris. If I'd known . . ."

Troy stopped in midsentence, as abruptly as he'd begun, took out a handkerchief and blew his nose. Rockett sat in silence puffing on his cigar, waiting for him to continue. He could hear the gurgle of the stream running ten yards from the kitchen door and the hiss of burning wood from the stove in the next room, but somehow these sounds seemed unrelated to where he was and the events of his day. Stan Erland's funeral early that morning, his flight from Washington to Vermont, the drive across the state over roads of decreasing navigability culminating in an impassable quagmire all appeared in his mind as unrelated vignettes told to him by someone else. He suddenly felt terribly ashamed of having come all this way just to ask Troy for a favor when it was apparent his old friend was suffering badly and needed help himself. He looked across the table and saw that Troy was smiling at him. He had read Rockett's mind.

"So Rock," he said. "You didn't come all the way up here in a suit just to hear me spill my guts. It's all right, man. Ain't no reason for you to feel bad. What can I do for you?"

Rockett lay his cigar in the ashtray on the table and took a deep breath.

"They made me a captain," he said. "Pulled me out of narcotics and gave me a position running the community relations division. You know, promote the black guy then give him a job making sure there ain't an uprising in the jungle. Then some politicians got the idea of forming a joint federal and local task force. An excavation crew for unsolved murders, especially ones with hate crime tags on 'em or a civil rights violation. Great for public relations, right? You could ride the back of that one to the polls. They put me in charge of it and I thought I was reborn, but guess what? They only assign two people to my unit, one fed, one local. Said I'd get more help as soon as our productivity required it."

"Gonna buy you some dynamite just as soon as you dig that tunnel with a spoon," Troy said. "Or better yet, with your fingernails."

"Politicians," Rockett said. "The good part is I got to pick the local person. The bad part is the fed they sent me was deranged . . . well, maybe deranged is a little strong. Just say the dude was fucked up."

"Was?" Troy asked.

"Right," said Rockett. "Was. He's dead. Got himself drilled. I was at his funeral this morning in Virginia, which is why I was wearing a suit when I got stuck in your bog down there. Six months into this gig, man, and I got me a dead agent and we haven't closed a case."

Rockett picked up his unlit cigar and studied it, then set it back in the ashtray and scratched his head. "So here I am," he said. "Me and that car, both up to our asses in mud. I'm in trouble, Tooth. I was hoping to talk you into pulling me out. The car I wasn't planning on."

Troy got up from the table, carried the soup bowls over to the sink and rinsed them out. "You want anything else?" he said. "I got some real fine homemade apple pie I bought from this lady over in Barton who bakes 'em. Let me cut you a piece."

"I'm full, man," Rockett said. "The soup and bread did the trick. I couldn't put another thing in my mouth. Maybe later."

"Come on then, let's go sit in the living room where it's comfortable," Troy said. Rockett followed him and, at Troy's invitation, stretched out on the couch. Troy sat in the easy chair next to the couch and put his stocking feet up on the coffee table.

"I work outdoors all the time," he said, "hauling wood, tapping the maple trees, digging rocks out of the hillside for a garden. This winter I learned to cross-country ski. Went out every day there was snow. So yeah, I know I look pretty healthy for an old fucker. But I ain't got it in me anymore, Rock. Whatever it was that sent me down the trail day after day, week after week, month after month, is gone. And what good would I be to you anyway if I couldn't even catch the guys who killed my wife?"

"I do feel bad, Tooth," Rockett said. 'I feel bad 'cause I know you're in pain and there ain't nothin' I can do about it. I feel bad 'cause you're in pain and I know I'm leanin' on you. I'm fully aware of that. But I came all this way, so let me just say my piece and then you make up your mind. Whatever you decide is cool with me. I mean what the hell, it's only a job, right?"

Troy studied his old friend lying there on the couch. Rockett's eyes were closed. The tough, forbidding expression he perpetually wore had disappeared from his face as though he had removed a mask, and he simply looked tired. Troy thought of all the times Rockett had come through for him, bending a rule, backing him up, putting his ass on the line. No matter how bad he felt, the least he could do was listen.

"Sure, Rock," he said. "Talk to me."

Rockett opened his eyes and propped his head up with a throw pillow.

"The federal agent in my unit who got himself killed was working a case up in Velvet," he said. "Two years ago, one of the psychics there was murdered. He was an old man named Leo Weiser who used images on photographic paper to do readings. The subject, or client . . . the psychee . . . would sit there and the old man would dip the paper in developing solution for a couple of seconds and pull it out. These black and white patterns would appear, swirls, blobs, whatever. The psychic would claim to decipher faces in them—dead relatives, long-lost loved ones, animal spirits watching over you, that sort of thing. The old guy was strange, but strange in that town is like Catholic in the Vatican. He was harmless and he didn't have any obvious enemies. No beefs with any of the other psychics, no feuds, nothin'. An old man who didn't bother anybody and kept to himself.

"Anyhow, Leo Weiser was shot twice in the back of the head,

execution style. The cottage he lived in was turned upside down but it sure didn't look like a robbery because whoever did it left a drawer full of valuable jewelry, some expensive stereo equipment, a couple of antique cameras worth a small fortune and over thirty thousand dollars in cash, which was pretty interesting considering Weiser bought his clothes at Goodwill and drove a twenty-year-old Corolla. The money was all in hundreds stuffed into a couple of half-gallon ice cream containers in the freezer. There were no suspects, no apparent motive and no leads. There was also apparently no Leo Weiser. There was a Florida driver's license issued to him ten years ago when he turned in a perfectly clean one from Kansas, or Nebraska, somewhere like that. He had automobile insurance in that name, a homeowner's policy, a checking account, a telephone. I mean, all the papers were there but when they went looking for next of kin everything came up empty. His records were all bogus. A Social Security card, but the man never made a payment or drew a check. Paid the doctor with cash. His history was a dead-end street. Leo Weiser the psychic photographer who showed up in Velvet, Florida, ten years ago and set up shop was somebody else.

"So all of the old man's worldly goods are impounded, the case lays there like a frozen fish for two years and would be layin' there still if Stan Erland, now deceased, hadn't received a phone call from a woman who knew Weiser, or whoever he really was. She's a psychic too. They were friends. They ate dinner together a couple of times a week. She thinks she knows who killed him, she tells Erland. He goes up to Velvet and talks to her. She gives him these composition books with notes Weiser kept. How come she had 'em I don't know. She tells him she goes over to Weiser's cottage, which is still vacant, once a week so she can sit there and commune with his spirit. She talks to him, he talks to her, she says to Erland. One night she's sitting there in the dark, communing, when two guys show up and start digging around in the backyard. They have no idea she's in the house. She hears one of them say something like, 'I don't give a shit whether you're sick of this or not, you fucked it up two years ago and you're gonna keep looking for as long as it takes unless you want to wind up like him.'

"It's possible she told Erland some other stuff too, but if she did he never had a chance to transfer it from his notes to his computer, so I have no idea what that might be. What I do know is that he came back from Velvet more agitated than a horny rooster, sayin' he was onto something big and was going up there again. He must've been right about the size of it 'cause the next thing I knew he was dead, all his files were gone, the old man's composition books were missing, and Erland's computer was rifled. But lucky me, I knew where he kept his back-up files. I gave those to the detective in my unit to go through while I was gone, and she called me last night in Virginia with some interesting information.

"She?" Troy said. It was the first time he'd spoken in several minutes.

"Yeah," Rockett said. "She. The other member of the unit, the one I picked, is a woman. Her name is Angela Becker. Damn good cop. Real smart. Does things her own way, stretches the envelope a little more than the bosses would like, but she gets the job done. In a way she reminds me of you. An eccentric. Only she's better looking. Matter of fact, she's even a neighbor of yours, or would be if you were still living on your land. She bought Lucky Painter's old place just after you moved up here."

"Lucky Painter's place," Troy said. "I'll be a son of a bitch. Stolen from old Lucky the moonshiner by John Varney, the dope-dealing banker. Now a woman cop owns it. A lot of history in that ground. Lots of ghosts in the swamp. Indians used to camp there five hundred years ago and fish the river. When I was a kid, I heard there was pirate's treasure buried somewhere in the woods. So what did she find, this Angela that you picked?"

"Well for one thing, Leo Weiser was a Holocaust survivor. He'd been in one of the death camps. For another, it looks like maybe the dudes who aced him were part of some neo-Nazi organization. I didn't know that when I decided to come up here and talk to you. I don't even know for sure if it was neo-Nazis that killed Weiser, and then Erland 'cause he came sniffin' around their den. What I am sayin' is that I'd like you to consider working with me for just this one case. Handle it any way you want. We got a little office upstairs in that old wooden garage, that place where they keep the tractors. Got everything we need there, computers, electronic tie-ins to any system in the country, you name it, so you wouldn't even have to show your face over at the main building unless you felt like it. I already took the liberty of talking to your old buddy Jack Ubinas. He made a couple of calls and if you say yes the feds won't send in anyone else. They'll cooperate with any assistance you want, but they won't step on your toes. And that's it. That's my pitch, Tooth. It's up to you."

"Let me think about it," Troy said. "I can't pull your car out until tomorrow. Well, shit, I probably could pull it tonight but tired as you look I'd make you stay here anyway. So let me sleep on it and I'll let you know in the morning. How's that?"

"That's fine," Rockett said.

Roland Troy awoke to the hooting of a barn owl perched on a limb of a sugar maple. The tree was twenty feet from where he lay in the bed of his pickup truck in the field behind his cabin. When he opened his eyes he could see the owl, backlit by the light of a full moon that hung high overhead.

Unable to fall asleep inside, Troy had tossed for hours until finally at around midnight he got up, got dressed and walked outside. Two deer were watering in the stream fifty yards from where he sat. Hearing him climb into the bed of the truck they paused in their drinking but didn't run off. He watched the deer for several minutes, then stretched out on his back, breathed deeply, and stared up into the sky. The next thing he was aware of was the owl.

There had been an owl in the tree outside his house in Florida on the night he and Clara lay in bed planning their trip to Europe. They had just made love and were discussing whether sex was better at home or in a far-off, exotic setting when a barred owl began to call its mate from a pine tree near their bedroom window. "Who who," it seemed to say. "Who are you?"

"The hooting of an owl is either good luck or bad luck, but I can never remember which," Clara had said.

"Depends who you ask," he told her. "The Indians say it's good luck. My grandmother said it was bad. Tonight I have to agree with the Indians."

That was the night she told him he should get his tattoo redone.

"That tiger's beginning to look pretty sorry," she said. "A faded old guy. It's out of character."

"I thought you didn't like tattoos," he said.

"I don't usually," she replied, "but I love yours. The prancing tiger. That's who you are. A man of honor. A man who sees opportunity where others see only danger. A man who never runs from either one. You have to be true to who you are, Roland. Painful as it is for you sometimes, you have no choice. You know that and so do I. And you have to give that tiger a new lease on life. He doesn't look sexy anymore."

Now this other owl stared down at him from the maple tree, a hundred years later, it seemed. A hundred years and a million miles from that night in Florida but it sounded the same. "Who, who. Who are you?" It hooted twice, then flew off across the field to hunt, leaving Troy alone.

"This woman detective, this eccentric Angela," Troy said to Rockett in the morning. "You make sure to tell her ahead of time not to go pushing her envelope in my direction. You tell her you got an old man on the way and his envelope days are over. You tell her to be cool and we'll catch us some bad guys."

"She's already cool," Rockett said. "Although I admit, in ten years on the job she ain't seen nothin' yet like you."

VI

As was his habit, Herbert Stiefel rose before dawn, put on his silk bathrobe, opened the sliding glass doors on the east wall of his bedroom, and walked out onto the long wooden deck to drink a cup of coffee and watch the sun rise. The bedroom was part of a spacious apartment located high above the television production facility Stiefel owned in the tiny town of Aurora, Florida, forty miles north of Orlando. At the other end of the apartment, on the west wall of the dining room, were a row of floor-to-ceiling one-way windows that looked down on the largest studio in the facility, the one with banked rows of theater seats that could accommodate an audience of five hundred people. A communications system was set up in the dining room so that Stiefel could not only observe what was going on in the studio, he could also listen to what was being taped and speak to the technicians both in the studio and in the control room. Those who worked for him, the worms as he privately called them, never knew whether or not they were being monitored by Stiefel, which was precisely what he intended.

Stiefel poured himself a second cup of coffee from the pot he'd brought with him from the bedroom and looked out past the various buildings of his complex, that was enclosed by six-foot chain-link fencing topped with barbed wire. He looked out over the small lake ringed by rows of orange trees to his landing strip running north and south for almost a mile and a half. It was one of the longest privately owned runways in the world and had been built by the man from whom Stiefel bought the property.

This man, a former fighter pilot in Korea, was an inventive genius who made a fortune with several patents on navigational equipment and then used the money to indulge his every whim. Among other

65

enterprises, he had flown wild beasts to this place from all over the world aboard specially equipped 707s for his personal exotic animal farm that once included elephants, crocodiles, zebras, and an entire building filled with poisonous snakes. Now all these creatures were gone, save for one 450-pound gorilla, which upon its death had been stuffed in an upright position and mounted on a platform where it was displayed in the lobby of the large reception hall. Shortly after moving to Aurora, Stiefel had the gorilla sprayed with a special, clear, weatherproof lacquer and moved to the shore of the lake. It stood poised there in a menacing stance ten yards from the paved road leading from the complex to the runway. He never mentioned the gorilla to anyone beforehand, preferring to watch the startled reactions of people flying in to the studio or stepping from the living room of his apartment onto the deck.

"Oh him," he would say. "That's just a nigger who used to work here. Made a pass at one of the white girls in the office. I told him he could either jump off the roof of the studio or go for a swim in that lake. That was two years ago. We're still waiting for him to make up his mind."

Herbert Stiefel especially loved telling that to the liberals who flew in to be guests on T. Bryce Atwood's talk show, *Survival of the Fittest*.

"It gets those mealymouthed faggots all shook up," he'd tell his wife. "Makes it that much easier for Atwood to rip them a new asshole."

Stiefel would move in close to the guests, almost leaning on them, and bring his large shaved head right up next to theirs. Then he'd slap them on the shoulder and give them his wide, toothy grin. "They're good jumpers," he'd say in a stage whisper, "but they're scared shitless of the water."

His second cup of coffee finished, Stiefel walked back inside, showered, and put on a pair of running shoes and one of the two dozen nylon jogging suits he owned. Once in a while Stiefel would wear slacks and a shirt, and on rare occasions he'd put on a suit, but he felt most comfortable in workout clothes that reenforced his self-image as a highly disciplined athlete.

In his youth Stiefel had been a circus strong man, performing such feats as bench-pressing a motorcycle and lifting two women over his head at the same time, one with each hand. He had been in superb physical condition in those days, standing a shade over six feet and weighing 220 pounds, most of it solid muscle. Now, at sixty-five, he was still quite powerful, lifting weights for an hour and running on a treadmill every night in his private gym to maintain his physique. Failure to do this, he was convinced, was a sign of weakness. It was the personal equivalent of the moral and physical deterioration afflicting society, a subject Stiefel never tired of expounding upon to everyone around him.

Stiefel first observed what he interpreted as this decay when he left the circus to become an actor in Hollywood and met with very limited success. He managed to land a few minor parts in low-budget films playing a thug, a bodyguard, and a demented homicidal maniac who drooled on his victims. He left Hollywood after three years, blaming his failure on "the pinko, backstabbing, Jew-boys who run the place." He returned to the circus where he got his show-business start and took revenge for this perceived betrayal by murdering the circus's owner, who happened to be Jewish. Then he swindled the man's bereaved widow out of the business.

Herbert Stiefel looked over at his sleeping wife, Dana, whose long, fine auburn hair was spread across her pillow. She slept in a pair of men's flannel pajama tops, her mouth open, a swatch of the hair clutched firmly in her fist. Stiefel first met Dana eight years earlier when she was seventeen. She had been a contestant in a beauty pageant at which Stiefel had been a judge. After four failed marriages and countless liaisons, he immediately declared that at last he had found the woman of his dreams. She was, he believed, the perfect female specimen, with whom he would grow old, upon whom he would bestow a lifetime of knowledge and experience, and to whom his empire would be left. Not only did she have the physical attributes he found appealing—large, upturned breasts that stood firmly away from her rib cage without need of support, muscular legs and a narrow waist, clear skin, shining hair, and an expression that combined little girl innocence with seductive coquetishness—she was totally uneducated, having left school at fifteen. She was therefore untainted by what Stiefel saw as the liberal garbage that passed for higher education, an empty vessel into which he could pour the truth.

Stiefel moved slowly at first with Dana, sensing a certain reluctance on her part to hook up with a man forty years older. In point of fact the reluctance was feigned; she was more than willing. Her mother, whom Stiefel had bought off for a hundred thousand dollars, had schooled her from an early age. You got the looks, her mother told her, use them. Marry rich and marry old, the older the better.

Stiefel was fond of telling anyone who would listen how brilliant Dana was, narrowing his eyes and exclaiming that not only was she the most beautiful woman in the world, she had a mind like a steel trap, adding that one day she was going to run the TV production facility. Actually, though she was quite clever and possessed a single-minded determination to accumulate a great deal of money, she was lazy and had no intention of ever running the TV studio or any other business. Dana would never come out and say this, however, since her mother had trained her in another area as well, instructing her only daughter to keep her mouth shut.

Now, though Stiefel would admit it to no one, he had begun to detect a number of unignorable signs that belied his grandiose proclamations. For one thing, at twenty-five, Dana was beginning to gain weight. The finely chiseled features that had captivated Stiefel eight years earlier were rounding off, blurring, and as he looked down at her he could see drooping flesh below her chin and a network of lines on the outside of her thighs that had the look, already, of a parched riverbed. Furthermore, no matter how hard he tried, Stiefel could not get her to take an interest in the studio, either as a performer, or as a producer behind the camera. She also seemed to have lost any interest in sex and absolutely refused to work out. The truth of it was, Stiefel's young wife slept considerably more than he did, and when awake, spent her time watching television, eating junk food, and driving her Porsche to the mall to shop for clothes.

Stiefel sighed. He had an important meeting on the gulf coast in two hours and had at first planned to have Dana fly over with him. Maybe it's just as well she stays here, he thought. She would only be a distraction and the man he was going to see did not like distractions. Moving quietly so as not to disturb her he put his wallet, sunglasses and keys in the pockets of his jogging suit, put his pistol in his briefcase and called down to the hangar to make sure the twin-engine Navajo was fueled and ready for his departure.

"What the hell is going on?" Novac DuCharme said.

Herbert Stiefel began to speak, but DuCharme silenced him with an upturned palm. "It was a rhetorical question, Stiefel," he said. "I don't need to know every single detail. What I do know is that things have not been handled in the most appropriate manner. Neither with the agent, nor with the other one, the one who was left lying in the middle of a highway like a raccoon. Things have become sloppy, and sloppiness is something I will not tolerate. No sooner in my business affairs than on this boat."

DuCharme and Stiefel were sitting in the bright March sunshine on the afterdeck of DuCharme's ninety-four-foot motor yacht moored two miles off Cedar Key in the Gulf of Mexico. Though Stiefel had removed the jacket of his jogging suit and wore only the pants and a T-shirt, he was dripping wet. DuCharme, wearing gray slacks, a white shirt with a blue-and-silver-striped tie, and a blue blazer was dry as parched bone. Du-Charme dressed this way year-round, and even when he visited Florida in the middle of summer Stiefel had never seen him sweat.

DuCharme rose from his canvas deck chair and walked to the polished teak railing. "Look out there, Stiefel," he said, pointing to a school of bottle-nosed dolphins cavorting fifty yards away in the blue-green water. "Look at those dolphins. If you jump into the water and swim towards them they will let you come within approximately thirty feet. Then they will move away, but they will not disappear. They will resurface and watch you. If you swim towards them again they will do the same thing. They will play the game over and over, all day long if you like, but they will never let you come closer than the distance they, in their dolphin minds, have decided is appropriate. It is a distance they have instinctively determined to be safe."

DuCharme paused, turned back toward Stiefel, and lit the pipe he kept clenched in his teeth. He was a tall man, a good two inches taller than Stiefel, lean almost to the point of being gaunt and, though he was seventy-one years old, stood without even the hint of a stoop. He had thick, silvery hair combed straight back and worn long so that it covered the tops of his ears, and dark shaggy eyebrows from under which eyes the color of lead stared with unflinching coldness. His cheeks were hollow, his jaw rigid, and even when he was smiling, his thin, bloodless lips seemed to be composed in a snarl. He was an investment banker with offices in New York and Zurich, but also spent considerable time in Washington, working in an advisory capacity with an agency somehow connected to the defense department. Stiefel was unsure just what that relationship was. In fact, there was a great deal about DuCharme that mystified Herbert Stiefel, but since Novac DuCharme was the only man Stiefel knew who truly frightened him, he was not inclined to ask questions.

Stiefel first met Novac DuCharme in 1986 in Eureka Springs, Arkansas, where Stiefel's circus was performing. It was at a time when Stiefel's fortunes were at their lowest ebb, and on more than one occasion he had contemplated killing himself. His televised wild animal show, *Jungle Kingdom,* had been canceled. His chain of three touring circuses and several smaller carnivals had been reduced to one anemic traveling ensemble that was in danger of going broke at any minute. He was deep in debt and, unable to get any more money from a bank, had been forced to borrow from a loan shark in Miami to keep the remaining circus afloat.

One night, after the show in Eureka Springs was over and he was walking from the big top to the trailer where he slept, Stiefel saw a flyer tacked to a tree. The flyer advertised a meeting the following Sunday morning of a group called the Church of the Militant Redeemer at a farm outside town.

"The time has come for the white Anglo-Saxon race to stand up to the pestilence and rot undermining our civilization," the flyer read. "The time has come for the rightful inhabitants of this nation to reclaim our land."

The meeting was held in an empty barn where folding chairs and a makeshift pulpit had been set up. It was attended by about fifty people with weather-beaten, angry faces. The meeting mixed prayer with typical racist diatribes against a conspiracy of Jewish bankers who controlled not only the politicians in Washington but the subhuman Black race as well. According to the evening's message, these Jews were manipulating both groups in a plot to take over the world. Near the close of the meeting, the man who was running things, a beefy fellow dressed in jungle fatigues who introduced himself as Pastor Jim Keller, "a true freedom fighter," called for anyone in the audience who wished to present a personal testimony, a firsthand account, as it were, of oppression at the hands of the conspirators, to speak his piece. One man told about how the local bank had encouraged him to borrow money and then took his farm when he couldn't pay. Another man told a similar story. There was applause all around and a chorus of amens. The fact that the bank in question was owned by a family in Fort Smith whose roots in the area predated the Civil War didn't seem to make any difference.

After the two testimonies, there was a lull in the meeting, and Pastor Jim Keller asked whether anyone else wished to speak. At that moment, something Herbert Stiefel would later describe as the spirit of the militant Lord gripped him and he rose from his seat. In a voice charged with passion and fury at his plight he told his story. Stiefel had years of practice working crowds as a ringmaster, and almost immediately the folks in the barn were mesmerized. Inveighing against those who had thwarted his show business career he soon had everyone shouting and clapping their hands, urging him on. It was all a plot, he said, part of the same conspiracy Pastor Keller was talking about, by Jewish bankers in league with the Jews who controlled Hollywood. It was those same men, he went on, who controlled all the nigger athletes and the nigger musicians—the minstrel monkeys, he called them—that they placed on TV to lull white people into passive submission. They were the same men who took their farms and businesses and were now about to take his circus. It was time to stop these vermin, he said, before they controlled everything. When he was finished, the crowd gave Stiefel a standing ovation and Pastor Keller rushed from the pulpit to embrace him. Afterward, he joined the congregants outside the barn for a good old country barbecue and returned to his circus feeling better than he had in months.

By late evening, when the circus had finished its final show in Eureka Springs and he was once more alone in his tiny trailer, Stiefel's euphoria had evaporated. If anything, he was even more depressed, because, standing ovations aside, he still owed a small fortune to the loan shark and didn't even have enough to pay his weekly vig. He was sitting on the edge of his bed, wondering what would happen to him if he didn't come up with the interest payment when there was a knock on the door.

The man standing on the hard-packed dirt outside Stiefel's door on that hot, humid summer night was dressed in a suit and seemed oblivious to the cloud of dust that hovered in the air. He had an unlit pipe clenched between his teeth and his cold, hard eyes bore into Stiefel's with unrelenting intensity.

"Mr. Stiefel, my name is Novac DuCharme," he said. "I heard you speak today at the meeting and was quite impressed. I believe that I can help you, and that you in turn can help me. May I come in?"

"Sure," Stiefel said. "There isn't a whole lot of room, but come on in." He didn't remember seeing the man at the meeting but frankly was glad for anything that would distract him from his troubles. DuCharme, despite his formal appearance and slightly stilted language, appeared at ease in the cluttered confines of the trailer. He sat on one of the chairs next to the small kitchen table and came right to the point.

"There is a war going on, Mr. Stiefel," he said. "It is a war for the survival of the white race. It was begun in Germany more than fifty years ago and is still being fought on various fronts. I believe you have the talent to occupy a key position in this war, a position of great importance, helping to counteract the filth and lies being shoved down people's throats by the mass media in this country. How would you feel about running a large television production facility whose purpose would be just that: to produce the truth?"

For several moments Herbert Stiefel said nothing. He had spent forty years of his life working in carnivals and circuses. During that time he had come in contact with just about every type of con artist and grifter who walked the earth, and, though dejected and depressed at the moment, he was far from gullible. He was also mean and ruthless. In addition to murdering the circus owner, whose death in a cage full of lions was judged accidental, he had killed two other men. The first one he shot in a bar fight, the second he beat to death in a fit of rage involving perceived advances made to one of his wives. Both were attributed to self-defense and up to that moment he had never spent a day in jail. As he now looked across his kitchen table at DuCharme it was not without a considerable amount of suspicion, but if this man was running some sort of scam its nature had Stiefel completely baffled. Furthermore, Stiefel didn't really care. What concerned him, he said, when he finally did speak, were his immediate financial troubles, the money he had to come up with if he planned to be around to run his little circus, to say nothing of a television studio.

"Your financial difficulties can easily be dealt with, Mr. Stiefel," said DuCharme. "The question is whether you are prepared to come forward and take a stand, not just in front of forty or fifty farmers in a barn, but in front of the entire nation. The entire world eventually. If you think I am joking then you underestimate both the power of television and me. That's no problem. I've been underestimated before. In any case, Mr. Stiefel, there's no need for a snap decision on your part. Think it over. It's a tall order. One that will demand relentless dedication and complete, absolute fealty to our cause."

"I'll think it over," Stiefel said.

"I understand completely," DuCharme said. "You're wondering just who in the world this man is who has appeared at your door and now sits at your table making you such a grandiose offer. You're wondering how someone like me happened to be in this out-of-the-way place at this time and why I chose to approach you. You, who are more concerned at the moment with whether or not the man you owe so much money to will have your legs broken, or worse. Do you mind if I smoke?"

Stiefel shook his head. "No, go right ahead," he said.

DuCharme lit his pipe and puffed silently for a few moments. Stiefel watched him and was silent as well.

"I'll tell you what," DuCharme said after a time. "As a gesture of good faith, I'll see to it that the interest you owe for the coming week is taken care of. How's that? Meanwhile, you travel with your circus to . . . Kentucky? Isn't that your next destination? I'll visit you there in a week and we'll talk again. That will give you time to think it over."

DuCharme rose from his chair, walked to the door, and opened it. "Oh yes," he said before leaving, "give the man in Miami, the one to whom you owe the money, a call in a couple of days. You will see I haven't made you a hollow promise."

After DuCharme left, it occurred to Stiefel that he hadn't given DuCharme the name of the man who'd loaned him money. In fact, he hadn't even told DuCharme the man lived in Miami. Two days later, when Stiefel called the loan shark's office, he was told by the woman who answered the phone that the man was out of town but that the interest on Stiefel's loan was up to date. At that moment, a chill ran up Herbert Stiefel's spine. He wasn't yet afraid of Novac DuCharme, but he soon would be.

"You have been chosen," Novac DuCharme told Stiefel a week later. "It is my opinion that you possess the attributes of someone I need, of someone I can use. If you tell me you aren't interested then that will be the end of it. You owe me nothing. If, however, you sign on, so to speak, then there is no turning back. The consequence of betrayal is something you don't even want to think about."

"I've thought about it," Stiefel told him. He was sick of the circus, sick of the travel, the hassles with local ordinances, the problems with employees and animals and his insurance company. He was, after all these years, sick of the smell. "I'm your man," he said.

"Are you sure?" DuCharme asked.

"Lead me to the TV studio," Stiefel said.

"Oh, I most certainly will," DuCharme said. "I have one picked out that's for sale. The funds will be provided for you to buy it. But first I want to lead you to something else."

DuCharme drove Stiefel in his rental car to a remote spot in the woods near Glasgow, Kentucky, where the circus was performing. A mile or so down a narrow dirt road they came to an old barn that appeared to be abandoned. DuCharme stopped the car and turned to Stiefel.

"There are demon souls alive in this world, Mr. Stiefel," he said. "Souls of those who throughout history have represented the Antichrist. The worst of them are alive today, reincarnated in Jewish bodies. These people are bent on destroying civilization as we know it. Although you have encountered them, you may not believe this yet, but you will.

My job . . . our job is to destroy them first. Come with me, I want to show you something."

DuCharme got out of the car and walked toward the barn carrying a flashlight. Stiefel, considerably uneasy but wanting to please his new benefactor, followed. As they passed through a wide opening in one of the side walls where there once had been a door, DuCharme stopped and raised the beam of his flashlight. Hanging with a rope around his neck from a beam ten feet off the ground was the naked body of the loan shark from Miami.

"There is one of those demons about whom you no longer have to worry, Mr. Stiefel," DuCharme said.

Novac DuCharme walked back to his chair on the afterdeck of the yacht, sat down, and puffed calmly on his pipe.

"I am not unlike those dolphins," he finally said. "What I mean by that, Stiefel, is that while I may be curious about various people and what they are up to, I insist on a certain distance between myself and anything I regard as a potential threat. That is where you come in. You're my thirty yards of ocean. You and several others. That is why you now sit in that lofty perch running your television studio. But then, when things become sloppy, I have to become involved. That is not good for me, Stiefel, nor is it good for you."

"Everything's taken care of," Stiefel said. "The agent. Viens—"

Once more DuCharme stopped him with his hand. "Don't say everything is taken care of," he said. "That is what you said two years ago after the death of the old man, the psychic photographer who was neither a psychic nor a photographer and could have destroyed both of us. You were wrong then, and you are wrong now. If you had been right, then agent Erland would have found nothing, but that was not the case. Agent Erland was one step away from discovering who that old man really was. So this time the South American is brought in, the one known as the parrot, to take care of the agent and also take care of Viens, the strutting peacock, the one who got rid of the old man."

"Which he did," Stiefel said. He wanted to add that bringing in El Papagayo was DuCharme's idea but thought better of it.

DuCharme puffed once again on his pipe and looked down and toward the bow of the boat. Stiefel followed his gaze and saw a man busily scrubbing the deck. Another man stood near the one who was cleaning. He was holding a telephone and glanced up in their direction.

"Yes he did," DuCharme said. "The parrot killed the peacock. Quite interesting, ornithologically speaking. And I'm reasonably certain that this new bird is better at keeping his beak shut than the first one was. But meanwhile, there are details concerning the way it was done that disturb me. Details that you should have prevented. Using the woman to lure agent Erland. Allowing Tito Pettibone to take the peacock's car, leaving the brother, whatever his name is, still alive. To say nothing of the nigger mechanic who I am sure got a very good look at our friend Tito. Your job is to see that things like that don't happen. You think you're still running a circus, Stiefel? A sideshow?"

"There was no other way," Stiefel said. "Peacock might have said something to the woman. The cop—"

"Don't interrupt me," said DuCharme. "I'm not finished. What I'm trying to impress upon you is that, whatever the reasons or excuses, we are still left with loose ends. One of them, Mr. Tito, I have taken care of personally."

DuCharme began to say more but heard steps on the staircase leading up to the afterdeck and waited. In a few seconds the first mate, who had been holding the telephone, appeared at the top of the stairs and came toward them. He was a powerfully built man in his early thirties with close-cropped blond hair, dressed immaculately in white deck shoes, perfectly creased white cotton slacks, and a white knit short-sleeve shirt. He came within six feet of the two seated men and stood with his hands behind his back. DuCharme nodded to him, signifying it was all right to speak.

"Nick Sharifi just landed back at the key," he said.

"Go get him with the whaler," said DuCharme. "And tell the cook he'll be joining us for lunch."

When the first mate was gone, DuCharme turned back to Stiefel. He smiled, but his eyes were as chilling as a snake's.

"Loose ends, Herbert," he said. "We have to wrap them up and move forward. There is far too much at stake. Your future, my future, the future of the white race. You understand what I'm saying? Everything must be in place. Every piece of the machine, from the least significant to the most important, must work in conjunction with every other piece."

DuCharme placed one of his large, bony hands on Stiefel's shoulder.

"You're doing a good job with the studio, communicating the truth, getting people to wake up to the plague running rampant in our society," he said. "But now the time has come to prime the pump, and I'm not talking about a bunch of kids in combat boots burning a cross on someone's front lawn.

"Sharifi has come to tell us he has made a deal with Rafiq Said and a group of Russians for certain weapons. If all goes well these weapons will be transferred by helicopter from one of Said's tankers to a fishing trawler. This trawler will arrive here, offshore, two weeks from today. The weapons will be brought ashore and trucked to your studio, where they will be stored in the bunker next to the airstrip. Meanwhile, thirty-million dollars in cash, in shrink-wrapped hundred-dollar bills, will be sent from a bank in New York to Russia in a perfectly legitimate exchange with a Russian bank for gold bullion. Only, this bullion that appears to come from a Russian bank will in fact be my gold, the last of the gold I brought here forty years ago. And the cash involved in this exchange will never reach Russia. It will be turned over to me, and I will bring it to your airstrip to pay for the weapons at a meeting with Sharifi and the Russians. All loose ends must vanish before then, Stiefel. All sloppiness. I want you to make sure that happens. I don't want any trouble from the brother of the peacock, or the woman who was Erland's partner, or the nigger who was Erland's boss, or Tito's blond girlfriend who seems to have disappeared into thin air. I don't want any more psychic photographers."

"I'll take care of all of it," Stiefel said.

"I hope so," DuCharme said. He rose, walked to the railing again, and relit his pipe. A gust of wind blew several sparks into the air and lifted DuCharme's hair so that Stiefel could see both his ears. The top third of the right one was missing. Stiefel had noticed it several times before but always looked away and never asked DuCharme about it. This time he didn't look away fast enough and DuCharme saw him staring.

"It happened when I was fourteen," DuCharme said. "An old man caught me with his young wife. He came after me with a straight razor. I am sure he intended to slit my throat but I was too fast for him and he had to settle for part of my ear. A week later he was found in his garden with a knife in his back. The authorities seemed to think his wife killed him but they were never able to prove it. The fellow who built the place where you live had a young wife too. Did you know that? His ran off with the man who took care of the elephants. He shoveled their shit, if I remember correctly."

DuCharme motioned for Stiefel to follow him and walked to the staircase leading to the lower deck and the stateroom, where they would dine. At the bottom of the stairs DuCharme turned and faced Stiefel.

"I almost forgot," he said. "Tell me about our friend Agent Calloway."

They were standing at the bottom of the staircase in a narrow passageway leading to the stateroom. It was dark and cool in the passageway, a marked change from the bright sunlight on the deck. The sudden change in lighting and temperature combined with the rocking motion of the sea was making Stiefel slightly dizzy. With the stairs behind him and DuCharme blocking his way, he felt cornered.

"There's nothing to tell," he said. "He got all of Erland's files and cleaned out his computer."

"I already know that," DuCharme said. "What I'm wondering is whether he's been up to anything else."

"I'm not sure I know what you mean," Stiefel said. "Calloway's a damn good man, devoted to our cause. You said so yourself."

Once again DuCharme put his hand on Stiefel's shoulder. His grip felt like the frozen talons of a giant bird. "I said that to *him*, Stiefel," DuCharme replied. "To you I'm saying that Agent Calloway is devoted to the money you're paying him. Be careful. Watch him. He's already demonstrated the willingness to sell out one colleague. Why wouldn't he be just as willing to sell out anyone else?"

At that very moment, as Novac DuCharme led Herbert Stiefel into the stateroom of his boat, where a sumptuous buffet had been laid out, Agent Reed Calloway, assigned to the central Florida office of the FBI, stood in the dining room of Stiefel's apartment. He watched as Dana

Stiefel pulled the knit dress she was wearing over her head and stood naked before him.

"Don't move," she said. "And don't get undressed. I want you to do it to me with your clothes on."

She walked to the far side of the room and opened the drapes covering the floor-to-ceiling windows that ran the length of the wall. Below her, the studio audience was responding appreciatively as T. Bryce Atwood verbally eviscerated a hapless professor of political science carefully chosen for his liberal views and whining, nasal speaking voice.

"Jesus Christ, Dana," Calloway said. He was a muscular man of medium height with short, dark hair, a swarthy complexion and a mustache. The other agents called him Pancho.

"Don't be nervous, baby," she said. "These windows are one-way. We can see them, but they can't see us."

She leaned forward, her palms on one of the windows, her legs spread. The dining room lights were off and the only illumination in the room came from the studio far below. She turned her head and he could see her face in the semidarkness, illuminated by the studio lights. Her mouth was open and as she ran her tongue over her upper lip she moved one of her hands from the window to her breast. Her long auburn hair hung loose, partially across the pale skin of her back and partially in front of the window. She took her hand from her breast, put it between her legs, and moaned softly.

"No one can see me but you, Reed," she said. "Come over here. Look at all of them down there. Look at those men. I bet they'd love to see me do this. I bet they'd love to see me fingering myself, but you're the only one who can. Come on, baby. Come here and do it to me right now."

As he grasped her hips and entered her she once again put both hands on the window to steady herself. "Look down there," she said. "Pick out a woman you'd like to fuck. Tell me which one it is. It's all right. That's what I want. Do it for me."

"I don't know," he said. "I don't know."

"Oh yes you do," she said. Her hips undulated slowly as she talked, moving, so it seemed to him, in rhythm with her voice. "Tell me now. Go ahead. I don't mind. I want you to tell me. It'll get me off."

"Last row," he told her. "The woman with the dark hair in the short dark dress. The one with her legs crossed."

"Oh yeah," Dana said. "I see her. She looks hot. I bet she'd really like you to fuck her. Watch her while you fuck me. Pretend I'm her. Pretend she's up here and you're lifting up her dress and putting it in her. You'd like to do that to her, wouldn't you? Tell me you'd like that."

"Yes," he said. "I'd like to fuck her just like this."

"You want me to go get her for you, don't you?" she said.

"Yes. I want you to go down there and get her and bring her back up here so I can fuck her."

"I'd do that for you, baby. I'd get her for you and bring her up here and then I'd finger myself while you fucked her." She moved her hips faster and began to moan louder. "Look at her face," she screamed. "Look at her face while you come. Tell me you want her. Oh God, I'm going to come. Tell me now."

"I want her," he said. "I want to come inside her just like this."

"This is a bad idea, Dana," he said to her ten minutes later. "We're gonna have to meet somewhere else."

He was sitting in a chair in her bedroom watching her comb her hair. She had put on her husband's silk bathrobe and was standing in front of a large oval mirror that hung above her dressing table. His instincts told him he should quit seeing her altogether but so far he had been unable to stop.

"For a guy with a badge and a gun you're one nervous individual, Reed," she said. She had finished with her hair but was still looking in the mirror, fixing her makeup.

"I have reason to be," he said. "What if he came home? What if he walked in on us?"

"He won't," she said. She turned from the dressing table, walked over to where he sat, and let the robe fall open. "But isn't it scary thinking he might? I like it scary, Reed. Scary makes me hot. You like it too. I can tell you do."

"No," Calloway said. "What I like is careful. Careful and safe."

"Oh sugar, you're a long way past careful and safe," she said. "Or you wouldn't ever be up here. For sure you know that. You're in the land of wildness and risk. What you gotta do is stay cool and run with it."

One more time, Calloway thought, as she loosened his tie and unbuttoned his shirt. Then I'm done with her. Let her play this game with someone else. He was walking enough of a tightrope as it was and had come to the conclusion that consorting with Dana Stiefel was every bit as dangerous as dealing with her husband.

VII

"I was traveling in California with my sister and brother-in-law when Leo passed over," Justine Fallon said. "When he was killed. We were in their motor home, driving up the coast from San Diego where they live. It was the first time I'd been to northern California. We were camped in Redwood National Park. It was so beautiful there. So peaceful, even with all the people. Early one morning I went for a walk by myself. I sat down under a magnificent redwood and Leo came over and sat down beside me and said let's have a talk. That's when I knew he'd passed over."

"Passed over," Angela Becker said.

"To the other side," Justine Fallon said. "To the spirit world. That's when I knew Leo was dead. The Indians believed those giant trees were inhabited by spirits. The Indians lived very spiritual lives, you know, which is why many of our spirit guides—our helpers from the other side—are Indians. Spirit guides can also be dead relatives or friends. They are the spiritualists' helpmates, our advisers, our counselors, those who bring us good and bad news. They can do this because they're in tune with the universal intelligence. Leo is one of my spirit guides. Would you like some more lemonade?"

Angela Becker nodded. She was sitting across from Justine Fallon on the screened front porch of Justine's cottage in Velvet. Justine rose and bustled into the house. In less than a minute she returned with a large earthenware pitcher and refilled Angela's glass.

"I can tell you're quite skeptical," she said. "Many folks are."

Angela started to protest but Justine laughed and dismissed her with a wave of the hand. Justine Fallon was a handsome, sturdy, motherly looking woman in her sixties with short gray hair and dark, sparkling eyes. When she was young she had no doubt been quite beautiful.

She was wearing a yellow silk shirtwaist dress, matching pumps, and a necklace and earrings made out of engraved sterling silver beads. Her laugh was deep and rich and completely without affectation.

"It's all right," she said. "Your skepticism is not what matters. What matters is that you're here. I knew you would come, by the way. Leo told me you would."

"Leo told you this while you were sitting under the tree?" Angela asked.

"Oh no," Justine said. "He told me that much later. While I was sitting under that redwood tree he told me not to worry, that it might take some time but that things would be all right."

"When you got back to Velvet why didn't you tell the police what you knew about Leo, about the concentration camp, about him being a survivor of the Holocaust?"

"The time wasn't right," Justine said. "There was no rush. You see spiritualists don't view death in the same way as other people. Naturally we miss the person's physical presence, but we don't feel that someone who has been close to us is really gone. They've just moved to a higher plane. They see things from a much broader perspective. Leo understood things in the spirit world that I couldn't comprehend. He told me to wait and so I did."

"Did he tell you why you should wait?" Angela asked, fully aware that she was talking about the motivations of someone who was dead.

"No," Justine answered. "He never said why, but my sense is that you'll find that out. Either you, or the man you're working with."

"I'm working alone," Angela said. "Agent Erland was murdered four days ago."

"I know that," Justine Fallon said. "I was speaking about someone else."

Angela sipped her lemonade and gazed out across the street where a woman in a multicolored smock was hanging wash on a clothesline in the bright sunlight. From the moment she had pulled off the winding county road onto a gravel parking lot at the entrance to Velvet an hour earlier she had felt as though she were in a time warp, transported backward forty or fifty years to the era of milk delivered to the doorstep in glass quart bottles and potluck suppers on the lawn in the town square.

She had let her Trans-Am idle down for a few seconds in the parking lot, tapping her hands on the padded steering wheel in time to the music on the tape deck. Then she turned off the ignition. Instantly the deep rumble of the car's engine and the pulsing rhythm of Eddie Palmieri's Latin Jazz Ensemble ceased, and except for the chirping of a single bird, she was enveloped in silence. It was midafternoon and she was parked in the shade of a giant water oak in front of the old wood-frame meeting hall in Velvet. Across the street was the Spanish-style church and the town's lone general store.

Velvet was exactly thirty-eight miles north of her property on the Coacoochee River. She'd driven there to talk to Justine Fallon, who had been a friend to Leo Weiser, the psychic photographer. Justine Fallon was a psychic too. She was the one who told Stan Erland about the two men digging in Weiser's backyard. She also told him that Weiser was a survivor of the Holocaust and that she thought the men in his yard were part of some neo-Nazi organization responsible for his death. What else Justine Fallon told Erland that was relevant to Weiser's murder and maybe to his own was unclear; Erland's notes concerning the rest of his interview with her were uncharacteristically garbled, a result, no doubt, of the deteriorating state of his mental health.

Still seated in her car, Angela had taken out the book about Velvet she'd purchased the previous day. She flipped to the section in the back with pictures and brief descriptions of all the mediums in town, spent a few minutes looking at several whose faces seemed interesting to her and studied the map showing where each of their houses was located. She noticed that most of them lived near one another in the center of town but that a number of the houses, including those of Justine Fallon and Leo Weiser, were on a road that looped around a lake on the outskirts. Probably there was nothing significant about this but Angela took note of it nonetheless.

On the surface Angela Becker affected a devil-may-care nonchalance that seemed to border on recklessness, but unless she had no choice, she never walked into anything unprepared. Her father had been a highly successful defense attorney on Long Island who repeated the old courtroom adage to her over and over again while she was growing up: never ask a witness a question to which you don't already know the answer.

From an early age she had tried to apply that philosophy to all areas of her life. In school, she was one of those children who never appeared to study for a test, yet she always wound up with high grades. Before she went out for the crew team at the fancy boarding school she attended in Connecticut she spent an entire summer getting up at five in the morning to work out in a single-person shell on a lake near her home. At the end of her senior year she announced to her astounded friends that she wasn't going to college but instead was moving to New York to become a fashion model. What she didn't tell them was that she had been approached by a major modeling agency and had already signed a six-figure contract. Ten years later in Orlando, when she showed up for an early morning meeting of the narcotics squad wearing a Smith & Wesson .44 magnum revolver, no one, including McKenzie Rockett, had any idea that she'd practiced with the gun for two months before strapping it on. She also never bothered to tell anyone she was using .44 special ammunition, which produced considerably less recoil than the full-power magnum rounds people assumed were loaded in the gun.

It didn't always work that way. There were times when in spite of all her cleverness and forethought she followed her heart instead of her head and her plans went awry, times when she leaped spontaneously into situations that caused her great pain. In general, however, Angela Becker lived her life dealing from a stacked deck.

Angela had never been to Velvet before but she'd heard about it and now knew a considerable amount of its history from the book she had with her. It was a slim volume and she'd already read it twice.

The town was founded in 1877 by a man named Arnold Olmondson, a spiritualist from Wisconsin, who reportedly had great psychic powers. To Olmondson, individuals who had died—who had passed over from the Earth plane to the spirit plane—were as real as the folks he met walking down the street. He claimed to communicate with them on a regular basis and one day declared that he'd been advised in a dream by a particular spirit—a North American Indian named Kumessik—to head south to a spot in Florida where the latitude and longitude were just right for receiving the universal vibrations of the spirit world.

Olmondson, along with his family and a number of devoted followers, took a train to Jacksonville. From there the group proceeded down the St. Johns River on a wood-burning steamboat to the end of the line just south of Orange City where they hired a wagon and a team of mules and headed east. The country was pretty rough, filled with snakes, alligators, insects and varieties of low growing palm that could slice a careless person to the bone, but Olmondson told everyone not to worry, Kumessik was guiding him. It took Kumessik a day and a half to get Olmondson and his party to the shores of a clear, spring-fed lake nestled behind several steep, wooded hills.

"This is the place," Olmondson said. It was early summer, and after a winter in Wisconsin the hot moist air felt to him like a blanket of velvet.

"I will call this the Velvet Spiritualist Encampment," he proclaimed. "In time it will become a center where spiritualists can live and others from around the world can come to study and put themselves in tune with the universal intelligence."

It took awhile, but Olmondson's prediction eventually came true. About two hundred spiritualists now lived within the eighty-acre tract Velvet encompassed, and hundreds more visited there every year. Between twenty-five and thirty of the residents were actual mediums who, so the spiritualists said, were conduits between the living and the dead. These mediums gave readings using various means to recreate a person's past and predict his future, and at the services in the church they delivered messages from the departed to various congregants. Some used psychometry—the picking up of vibrations. Some saw significance in different colors hovering around an individual's head. Leo Weiser used images that appeared on photographic paper for psychic stimulation. So, apparently, did Justine Fallon.

At first Angela was going to wait to go to Velvet until McKenzie Rockett returned from up north but she hadn't heard from Rockett in two days and she was getting fidgety sitting at her desk pouring through Erland's files. A born skeptic, made even more so by nine years in law enforcement, she regarded the notion of communication with the dead as ridiculous. At the same time she was drawn by natural curiosity and her fascination with the unusual to this village filled with psychics. Moreover, she felt the need for action, for a clue she could sink her teeth into, for something as simple as an interrogation that produced results. She'd been talking to skinheads for almost a year and getting nowhere. Her new assignment on the task force was thus far a joke. She believed she was due for a break. Who knows, she thought. Maybe this Fallon woman can tell me things that weren't in Erland's notes. Maybe she'll give me a lead I can run with.

She had rolled both of the car windows all the way down, started the Trans-Am's engine, and driven slowly through Velvet toward Justine Fallon's house, studying the landscape and architecture around her that was so different from anything she'd seen anywhere in Florida. The narrow, oak-shaded streets ran up and down a series of steep hills and were lined with small houses of two and three stories. The houses, packed closely together, had sharply pitched roofs, oddly angled dormers and cupolas, stained glass windows cut asymmetrically into walls at random, and brick chimneys covered with strange decorations. The whole town looked to Angela like an old New England fishing village without the boats, or better yet, something lifted from the pages of a children's book of fairy tales. Even the people she passed, raking leaves, talking to one another across a fence, tinkering with their cars, or simply rocking on their front porches, appeared somehow out of sync with the world as she knew it, as though they were moving to a rhythm all their own. No one's in a rush, she thought. Nobody here is in a hurry. It's as if they have no place special to go and all the time in the world to get there. Yet in spite of the unhurried atmosphere and the overwhelming stillness, Angela felt a certain tension in the air. Although no one whom she passed as she drove through the town looked her way, she had the distinct sensation of being watched.

Some of the houses were either vacant or terribly neglected, the screens on their front porches torn or missing, the rusting hulks of ancient cars resting on blocks in their weed-choked driveways. Others were meticulously kept with carefully manicured lawns, white picket fences, and brick walkways that looked like they were regularly scrubbed. Justine Fallon's immaculate cottage, painted robin's egg blue with white trim like a piece of Wedgwood china, was one of the latter. The interior was filled with porcelain figurines of American Indians and the walls were covered with paintings and photographs of Indian men and women. The porch where Justine and Angela sat in large comfortably upholstered wicker chairs, however, was devoid of any artifacts or decorations with the exception of a carved wooden sign hanging on the door that read, CERTIFIED MEDIUM, NO APPOINTMENT NECESSARY, WALK IN.

"How much do you charge for a reading?" Angela asked.

"Thirty-five dollars ordinarily," Justine said. "But if someone is experiencing financial difficulty I make an exception. I've never turned anyone away. Would you like me to do a reading for you?"

"Maybe later," Angela said. "First tell me about the two men you saw digging in Leo's yard. The ones you told Agent Erland about."

"Leo told me they'd come back," Justine said. "He told me they didn't find what it was they were looking for when they killed him and that after things quieted down they would return. The night I saw them wasn't the first time. They'd been there before, digging up the pipe."

"What pipe?" Angela asked. There had been nothing in Erland's notes about any pipe.

"Leo had a problem with flooding in his backyard every time there was a heavy rain," Justine said. "He installed a drainage pipe that went from the shed to the hill at the edge of the property so that the water would run down into the lake. He did the entire job himself, which was quite an accomplishment for a man his age. That pipe was more than fifty yards long and wide enough so you could roll a grapefruit through it. I have no idea what they wanted with it, but they dug it up. Then they reburied it. The night I saw them they were digging it up again."

"Can you tell me what they looked like?"

"It was dark. I couldn't see them very well, but I could hear them just fine. One of them was complaining about having to dig back there with all the mosquitoes. The other one told him to shut up. He said, 'If you'd done the job right the first time two years ago we wouldn't have had to come back at all.' "

"What do you think he meant by that? 'Done the job right.' "

"I think he meant if the first man had found whatever it was they were looking for in the pipe."

"And that's why you think those two guys were involved in Leo's murder? Because of what the second guy said."

"Oh, my dear, it's not only because of what the man said. I know they were involved. There's no doubt in my mind at all. Leo told me the one who was complaining did it. You see, since he passed over I've been going to his house two or three times a week. It's just down the street back in that grove of trees near the corner. I have a key. It's empty now, but Leo's spirit is very strong there. It's where we often talk. On the night I saw those two men in his yard I came right out and asked Leo and he confirmed it."

"He confirmed it?"

"Yes he did. He said, 'Justine, that man who walks funny is the one who killed me.' "

"I thought you couldn't see them?"

"I couldn't see their faces, but I could tell that the one who told the other man to shut up was taller, and the one who complained about the bugs had a strange way of walking. His chest stuck out and he kept his arms perfectly straight and swung them back and forth. He looked like a toy soldier."

"Whoever killed Leo didn't take his money, they didn't take his cameras and they didn't take his jewelry," Angela said. "So what else did he have that was important enough to get him murdered? What were those men looking for in the drainage pipe?"

Justine Fallon clasped and unclasped her hands and for a moment squeezed her eyes shut.

"I don't know the answer to that," she said. "I wish I did. You have to realize that I'm not perfectly clairvoyant. I don't see everything. Exactly why Leo was murdered has been a puzzle to me ever since he came and sat beside me in California underneath that tree. I've asked him again and again, but all he says is that it's in the pictures. He used psychic photography to read, and so do I. Initially, that was what drew us together."

"And you told all this to Agent Erland?"

"I certainly did. But Agent Erland was even more skeptical than you. He thought I was crazy. He didn't say it, but I felt it just as clearly as if he had. My impression was that Agent Erland didn't really care about Leo at all. I believe that a good deal of what I told him went in one ear and out the other."

A red Lincoln Mark VII turned onto Justine's street and came up the hill toward her house moving, like everything in Velvet, at a pace that was somewhat slower than normal. As it passed by, the man behind the wheel turned and nodded at them. He had a sharp-featured, corvine face with dark hair and a carefully trimmed beard and appeared to Angela to be in his mid to late thirties.

"Angus Elliott," Justine said. "He's one of the mediums here. In the six years he's lived in Velvet I've only spoken to him two or three times at the general store. He's not particularly friendly nor is he supportive of the spiritualists' association. It's my understanding that up north where he came from he helped the FBI locate missing bodies."

Justine Fallon poured herself some more lemonade and took a long drink. Angela watched her expression go from childlike innocence to a kind of feral wariness and part way back again. She took a sip from her own glass and waited, gauging the swing of the older woman's emotional pendulum. Angela had built a reputation as a first-rate detective by carefully cultivating her innate ability to read a witness or suspect. She would then elicit the most information possible by adopting whatever persona the situation seemed to require, playing the role of a hard-nosed interrogator, a coquette, a beer-guzzling yahoo or your warm-hearted best friend all with equal ease. After studying Justine Fallon's picture in the book about Velvet she decided to adopt a professional, ladylike, and nonthreatening approach. She had worn a simple beige pants suit, white stockings that obscured her tattoo, and a pair of tan Capezio loafers with low heels. She had also removed the diamond stud from her nose and left her .44 magnum at home, bringing a compact 9 mm Sig Sauer with her instead.

Thus far it seemed the tack she had taken was working fine but something had now put Justine on guard. Probably it was the appearance of Angus Elliott whom the psychic clearly didn't like, but just to be sure it seemed to her that letting Justine do a reading as she had suggested might be a smart move at the moment, a gesture of acceptance. Angela also had an instinctive sense of when to press her questioning and when to back off, and anyway she wanted to see what psychic photography was all about. She was about to propose this when Justine suddenly began talking again.

"I may have made a mistake," she said. "When I let Agent Erland read Leo's notebooks I thought he would use them to help solve his murder. Instead he went running around in a frenzy trying to solve something else, asking everyone in Velvet if they knew a woman named Michelle or a man named Tito. He was a very troubled man, Agent Erland. When I looked at him I saw a doorway opening into blackness. I never said a thing to him about it but I felt death surrounding him. That's why I wasn't surprised when you told me he'd been killed."

Justine stopped talking as abruptly as she had begun and gave a little shake of her head almost as though she had suddenly awakened from a snooze. She stared straight at Angela and smiled.

"You're wondering how you should act toward me," she said. "How you should behave in order to get me to tell you what I know. That's because you are suspicious of people's intentions. In your line of work that's understandable, and besides, you aren't a trusting person to begin with. There are probably good reasons for that. There are many people I don't trust too, but my spirit guide tells me your intentions are good and that you are a decent person, so you can just be yourself. Sit back and relax."

"I am relaxed," Angela said.

In point of fact, Velvet's otherworldly atmosphere and Justine Fallon's syrupy voice had made her feel downright somnambulant, and in spite of her desire to learn something pertinent from Justine, she was actually in danger of dozing off when the psychic startled her by reading her mind.

"I was just thinking about your offer to do a reading for me," she said. "I was thinking I'd like to try it."

Justine smiled. "I want you to understand something first," she said. "This is not a game for me. I consider it a great responsibility to read for someone. I feel a moral obligation so I always ask for the best and highest guide to assist me. Sometimes I can identify the spirit guide. Other times it's someone I've never met. I want you also to understand that I would not have picked up on your thoughts just then unless I knew you were going to ask me for a reading. I never pick up in the open, like at a restaurant or in a store. That would be an invasion of someone's privacy. It would be a total violation of what spiritualists believe, a violation of the sanctity of each individual's life. Come inside."

The young child's face was a screaming rictus below the eyes of a cat. The old man's skeletal jaw was set in a benevolent smile. The dog, or wolf, or whatever it was appeared to look right through her, and next to it was a leering, thick-lipped countenance that bore a striking resemblance to Mick Jagger. None of it was real, Angela told herself. It was nothing but a phantasmagoria, imaginary creatures lurking in the shadows of a street lamp, a vision of the Virgin Mary on a tree trunk brought on by the power of suggestion. But then there was the couple, the man and woman wrapped in blankets, swirls of light engulfing their feet as though they were standing beside a campfire. The man was unidentifiable, but staring at the shrouded image of the woman was like looking in a full-length mirror through a layer of fog. Angela took a deep breath and sat back in the easy chair. This is bullshit, she thought. Hallucinations. Nonetheless, she felt a sudden chill and shuddered involuntarily.

There were four pieces of photographic paper, each four inches by five inches, on the table between them. Justine Fallon had dipped them one at a time into a tray of developing solution for approximately ten seconds, then dipped them in a solution of fixer for ten seconds more. The images on the paper—swirls of white against a sepia background—resembled the billows of smoke from a burning oil well or the interlaced tendrils of cirrus clouds. Justine had instructed Angela to study the images carefully, turning the pieces of paper one way and the other, searching for faces the way one might look for animals hiding in a field of tall grass.

"You see them, don't you," Justine said. "Look at them carefully. They are the faces of your spirit guides. You don't believe that. You think it's just some coincidence or trick. I disagree, because I believe in communication from the spirit world. But in any case, sit back and let me read for you."

Angela felt a perceptible change in the atmosphere of the room, an ebbing of her control.

"No, I've changed my mind," she said. "I'm going to pass on the reading. Maybe another time."

"Something you see in one of the pictures has upset you," Justine said. "It's this one, isn't it?"

She pointed to the piece of paper with the two figures who appeared to be standing near a fire.

"You see the images of a man and a woman. You're very uneasy with this because you feel the strength of their involvement with you. I feel it too. There is a strong bond between both of them and you. They care for you a great deal. The woman is someone from far in your past, from your early childhood. The man . . . this is very strange . . . you see how the figure of the man has no face? I have the strong sense that this person is not really from the spirit world. I think he is still alive. I think this is someone from your past whom you think is dead but who in fact is not. Even so, this person has such a powerful interest in your well-being that his aura is with you. He wants you to know he is all right.

"The woman is someone who died when you were very young. An aunt, or a close friend of the family, or maybe your mother. She was very beautiful, like you. She is very proud of you. You were . . . at one time in your life you had something to do with the world of fashion. You were very successful at this but you left it. That was a good choice. She is proud of your independence. This independence will make your life very difficult from time to time, but in the end it will be the source of your triumph. What you are doing now . . . your work . . . it's very important . . . more important than you think.

"I'll stop," Justine said. "I can tell you want me to. But before you go let me tell you something about me that is not in Agent Erland's files. I moved to Velvet fifteen years ago after my husband died. Before that I worked for a large insurance company in Illinois, Mid-America Mutual. No doubt you've heard of them. My husband was one of their senior vice presidents. Ordinarily they had a strict rule against nepotism but I helped them solve a case that saved the company a great deal of money and after that they hired me to uncover fraudulent insurance claims psychically. It was a very conservative company so only two or three executives at the top knew that. Officially, I was employed as a consultant. During the time I was with Mid-America I saved them millions of dollars and they rewarded me well for my work, so, Detective Becker, you and I have something in common. Neither of us is doing what we do for the money."

"How did you know that?" Angela asked. "About the money?"

"The transference of thoughts from a higher plane," Justine said. "I think that if you believe in the immortality of the soul then you must believe in that kind of communication as well."

Justine Fallon had been right about the other things too, but Angela didn't want to discuss them. What she wanted was to get out of the woman's house and out of Velvet. She wanted to drive down the interstate with her windows open and the cool evening air blowing across her face and Stevie Ray Vaughan's guitar blasting from the tape deck and after that she wanted a long hot soak in the hot tub at her condo, far from the spirit world and thoughts coming from a higher plane, from people who were dead. She didn't want any more to do with death today but she couldn't leave yet because there was still something she needed to know.

"The police report never said a thing about Leo being in a concentration camp," she said. "Wouldn't they have seen the number tattooed on his arm?"

"There was no number," Justine said. "Leo had it removed many years ago. He wasn't ashamed. That wasn't why he did it. He was protecting someone but he never told me who that was or why."

"I don't understand," Angela said.

"I don't either," Justine said. "Not completely. He only told me part of the story, not long before he was killed. He's never mentioned it since and I've never asked. I assumed that when the time was right I'd know."

"What did he tell you?"

"He said he had once been someone else before he was Leo Weiser. At first I thought he meant in a previous life, but then he told me he was someone else in this life. He told me he had been a prisoner in a Nazi death camp. The night he told me that he was very agitated, very concerned. In fact, I'd have to say he was terrified. I'd never seen him like that before. It was because he saw a man here in Velvet who had been a guard in that camp."

"Someone living here?"

"No. Someone he saw riding past in a car while he was standing in front of the general store. I asked him if he was certain and he said there was no question about it. Then he said something in German or maybe in Jewish . . . Yiddish. I asked him what he'd said and he told me he was sure because there could be no one else on earth who looked like him. No one who had such evil eyes and was missing part of one ear."

VIII

On a cold autumn morning, Solomon Kessler walked out the back door of his home in Newton, Massachusetts, with the album he had taken from the dead woman in the alpine forest twenty years earlier carefully placed inside an expensive leather briefcase. He opened the trunk of his dove-gray 1965 Cadillac Sedan DeVille parked in the driveway and placed the briefcase, along with a matching leather suitcase, inside. He closed the trunk, waved good-bye to his wife, who was standing at the kitchen window holding their baby daughter, climbed into the car, and drove to Logan International Airport.

Solomon Kessler had prospered in the United States far beyond his wildest dreams. After crossing the Atlantic in the bowels of a tramp freighter he landed in Baltimore where he was met by his sponsors, a wealthy Jewish family from northern New England. This family took him into their home, gave him a job in a factory they owned, hired a tutor to help him learn English and, once he mastered the language, paid for his tuition at the University of Vermont. Kessler proved to be a brilliant student, graduating summa cum laude in three years with a degree in history, then going on to law school at Harvard, where he was a member of the law review. Now thirty-nine years old, he was a senior partner in a prestigious Boston law firm specializing in international relations. He was a frequent consultant to corporations in various parts of the world, an adjunct professor at Boston University Law School, and the author of a highly acclaimed book on multinational trade agreements. He had a beautiful wife, a child, and a summer cottage on Cape Cod in addition to the house in Newton. Not a week went by, however, that he didn't think about where he had been and how lucky he was to be alive. On this November day, he was flying first to New York to meet with a fellow survivor who had devoted his

97

life to tracking down former Nazis, then continuing on to Frankfurt where he would present his album as graphic corroborative evidence—proof positive, as Kessler liked to call it—in the trial of three former SS officers.

There was a message waiting for him when he landed at LaGuardia, an envelope left at the Eastern Airlines ticket counter. Inside was a sheet of paper with a single typed sentence. "It would be in the best interest of your family if you did not go to Frankfurt," it read.

This was not the first time Kessler had testified in a war crimes trial, nor was it the first time he had received a warning. No doubt word of his appearance in Germany had been leaked by a Nazi sympathizer to a contact in the United States who in turn was attempting to intimidate him. This same ominous tactic had been used twice before and in both instances it proved to be nothing but an empty threat. With a disdainful expulsion of breath he put the note back in the envelope and placed it in his briefcase alongside the album. No scum who had crawled out from under a rock was going to scare him off.

"You should notify the FBI," his friend said to him at lunch when Kessler showed him the note. The man was the same age as Kessler but projected a weariness that made him seem much older.

"It's meaningless," Kessler told him.

"Nothing is meaningless," his friend said. "If you don't call them, I will."

"Suit yourself," Kessler replied. "I have a plane to catch."

There was another message for him at the airport in Frankfurt, typed in English like the first. "It is not too late to turn back," this one said. "If you do not, you will have made a terrible mistake."

Kessler thought about mentioning the note to the German official who was driving him, but decided against it. For all he knew, the driver was the one who had left the message. When he got to his hotel, however, he did call his wife. She assured him she and their daughter were fine and said they were going to spend a couple of days at her sister's house in Weston.

"I'm going to leave the baby there on Friday as well," she told him. "When you come home we'll have a night alone in the house together. So now you have something to look forward to."

The usual kitchen light was on when Solomon Kessler pulled into the driveway shortly before eight o'clock on Friday evening. The testimony provided by his album had helped convict two of the three SS officers. The third, of whom there were no photographs, was acquitted. Tired from his journey, but satisfied by the results, he climbed from his car, took his bags from the trunk, and walked toward the house. It was then he noticed that the kitchen door was ajar and saw the trail of blood leading into the backyard.

The police found Kessler's wife as he had found her in the backyard. Her body was halfway down a leaf-covered slope, curled against the trunk of an old maple tree, a hunting knife protruding from her back. Her hands were bound behind her and her mouth was covered with duct tape. This was late on Saturday afternoon, by which time Solomon Kessler and his daughter had disappeared.

There was all sorts of speculation about Solomon Kessler's disappearance. His sister-in-law claimed he was perfectly rational when he took his daughter from her house. Based on this, and on the sighting of a strange man on Kessler's property the day of the murder by one of his neighbors, an early account insinuated that he murdered his wife when he found her with a lover. The police, however, immediately contradicted this notion saying she had been dead for hours before he returned home. It was more likely, officials speculated, that Kessler had been followed and that both he and his daughter met the same fate as his wife.

After all the furor around the case died down, the *New Yorker* did a long piece on Kessler's life. Although he projected a tough, unflappable image, the writer found evidence indicating that underneath this exterior Kessler was a suspicious, insecure man who trusted no one. A famous psychiatrist who dealt with people like Kessler suggested he was a man with a split personality whose dark fragile side was produced by the horror he experienced as an adolescent. Concealed behind a carefully constructed wall of success and self-confidence, it could indeed be brought into the open by a trauma such as his wife's murder and easily dominate his existence from then on. It was perfectly plausible, the psychiatrist said, for someone like this to appear rational and react by fleeing.

Regardless of whose theory people chose to believe, one thing remained indisputable: Solomon Kessler and his daughter had vanished. In spite of the massive efforts of the police, the FBI, and a team of private investigators hired by Kessler's law firm, they were never found.

"He was so calm," Solomon Kessler's sister-in-law would later say. "His voice never broke. His hands when he reached out and lifted up the baby were steady as could be. Even the knot of his tie was perfectly straight. You know how there are some men who can knot a tie just right? Solomon was one of them, and I remember clearly how he was wearing a dark blue tie with wine-colored stripes and how nice it looked against his white shirt. He gave me a hug and I asked him how his trip had been. He said it was fine, just fine. He said his testimony at the trial of the SS officers was crucial. I remember him using that word, *crucial*. Then he picked up the baby. She was wrapped in a blanket, sound asleep, and he scooped her up blanket and all, gave me a kiss on the cheek, and left. Can you imagine? Twenty minutes earlier he had been standing in his backyard right next to where my sister's body was lying and you would never have known. Never in a million years."

A psychologist she saw for several months afterward told her that what she observed in Kessler was undoubtedly a form of dissociation— the splitting off of a group of mental processes from the main body of consciousness. Dissociation, he said, could manifest itself as amnesia, or occur in conjunction with certain forms of hysteria.

"He knew who he was," Kessler's sister-in-law said, "and he sure didn't seem hysterical."

In fact, the psychologist was right, only Solomon Kessler's dissociation had taken place twenty-one years earlier when he was forced to watch the murder of his parents and his crippled sister on a railroad siding in southern Poland. In the instant that he saw their bodies topple into the ditch he had helped dig, a piece was ripped from the whole of him, existing from then on as though it had a life of its own. In his

mind, Kessler heard the rending. It sounded precisely like the screaming wheels of the train veering from the main line onto the spur that
led to the death camp at Birkenau.

From then on there had been two Solomon Kesslers. One was a
probing, sensitive scholar, a devoted husband and father, a passionate
idealist committed to seeing justice served. This side of Kessler was
determined to keep the silent promise to bear witness he made to his
dead family and friends and to the anonymous young woman killed in
the snowy alpine forest from whose dead body he had taken the album
of photographs he guarded with his life.

The other Solomon Kessler was cold and calculating with little
faith in the ultimate goodness of human nature. This side of him knew
full well the risks he ran by bearing witness against the former members
of the SS and, realizing the potential consequences of his actions, had
planned carefully for the day when he and his family might have to
disappear. Kessler had anticipated various scenarios, and using his ex-
pertise in international law and finance, he had made appropriate ar-
rangements beforehand to put the necessary plan into operation. On
the night he came home and found the body of his wife lying in their
backyard it was this side of Solomon Kessler, as devoid of any visible
emotion as the tree limb against which she lay, that retrieved his baby
daughter and vanished into the darkness. This side of him was aware
that his wife's murderers would kill his daughter next, preferably while
they made him watch, before doing away with him as well, and so
dispassionately contrived to hide her, even though that meant cutting
himself off from her, perhaps forever.

Solomon Kessler drove six hours that night to the home of the
one man in the world he trusted implicitly, a man he had known since
law school who had worked with Kessler behind the scenes helping
him bring former Nazis to justice. He knew all about the danger Kessler
was exposed to and the consequences he could suffer. When Kessler
telephoned him after finding his wife's body he simply said, "I understand," and hung up.

This man came from a Dutch family that had settled in America
in the early 1600s, made a vast fortune in lumber, real estate and
shipping, and then retreated from the public eye, preferring to exert
power quietly. He knew everything about Kessler's situation and had

helped him set up an untraceable repository for his assets. The wealth of Kessler's friend was so great that Kessler's own holdings, when blended with it, caused barely a ripple. Moreover, the insulation provided by his friend's position made the addition of a child possible without drawing undue attention. One day Kessler's daughter wasn't at this man's estate, the next day she was, and no one from the world outside asked any questions. She would be raised as a member of this man's family, never knowing the origin of her considerable inheritance or the true identity of her parents.

"I have no choice," Kessler said to his friend. "There can be no trail for them to follow."

Kessler's friend did not reply. He knew that in spite of all his money and connections Kessler was right; there was no way he could prevent harm coming to Kessler and his daughter. The best he could do was shield them as he was about to do. Solomon Kessler would go underground. He would secretly provide funds to Kessler as his friend needed them and make sure Kessler's daughter had every advantage money could buy as she grew up. Kessler's home and summer cottage were both deeded to a holding company controlled by a bank in the Netherlands. The bank in turn was controlled by a second holding company owned by Kessler's friend. Once the police investigation was through, the two dwellings would be sold, the money would be added to Kessler's hidden assets, and all of Kessler's possessions would be transferred surreptitiously to a vault on his friend's estate where they would remain in storage for Kessler's daughter. All of this had been discussed and plotted long in advance so that now there was nothing that needed to be said.

It was four in the morning. The two of them were standing in a dank old two-story garage on the man's estate. Kessler's daughter was asleep in the main house a quarter of a mile away. Kessler was dry-eyed, in the same state of detached equanimity observed by his sister-in-law. He had changed from his suit into old work clothes. A suitcase with more clothing and some toilet articles lay on the wooden floor beside him. Another suitcase filled with cash stood beside it along with a cardboard carton containing a few books, some jewelry, and a few other personal effects. Kessler reached down and lifted first one and then the other suitcase into the open trunk of an old Chevrolet sedan procured two years earlier in the event his disappearance became necessary. His friend did the same with the carton.

"All of the documents are in the glove compartment," Kessler's friend said.

"The new me," replied Kessler, climbing into the Chevrolet. There was no trace of humor in his voice.

Kessler's friend pressed a button on the wall and the overhead door of the barn opened. Kessler started the car, reached out the window and shook his friend's hand.

"Good luck," the man said.

And so began a period of twenty years during which Solomon Kessler wandered back and forth across America, living in rooming houses, small apartments, trailer parks, and tiny shotgun shacks in the low rent end of one town or another. The unadorned, impoverished lifestyle he adopted was out of choice, not necessity. All he had to do was make a phone call to his friend and any funds he needed would be wired to him immediately, but when he did call, late at night from a phone booth, it was only to find out about his daughter, not to request money.

Perhaps it was guilt that made Kessler live this way, or maybe he no longer cared about material things. No one would ever know, because soon after the night he left his daughter in the care of his friend, the side of him that was the repository for all the grief and conflict in his soul rose to the surface. It overwhelmed the cold, calculating side, driving Kessler deeper and deeper into emotional isolation from which he would never emerge. In the cryptozoic world he inhabited he grew old virtually overnight and bore little resemblance to the proud, influential attorney he had once been. He became obsessed with photography and spent days taking pictures of people's faces with a telephoto lens, developing them in a tiny portable darkroom he constructed. At night he spent hours comparing the pictures he took to the faces in the death-camp album, searching for similarities that might corroborate his growing belief in reincarnation.

He took jobs as a technician in a series of custom photo labs in various parts of the country, worked as a photographer in a number of small-town studios, and became an expert at repairing and restoring antique cameras. In time, the photographs he took started to assume symbolic meaning for him and he began to read Eastern philosophy and study the Cabala, the ancient Jewish mystical interpretation of scripture. From there he moved into the world of psychic phenomena and the occult. One day, while working in a camera shop in Kansas City, he happened upon a pamphlet written by a man who described an obscure corner of this world known as psychic photography in which the spirits of the dead manifested themselves on photographic paper. Reading this pamphlet he felt as though a divine presence were speaking to him. Psychic photography, Solomon Kessler concluded, was his true calling. Of course he had long ceased being Solomon Kessler, having lived by then for many years with his new identity. His name was now Leo Weiser.

On the night Solomon Kessler disappeared with his daughter, Novac DuCharme was planning a journey of his own. DuCharme sat in the master bedroom of his house that was built on a bluff overlooking Long Island Sound. He had pulled open the curtains and was watching a Panamanian tanker filled with Algerian oil make its way into Port Jefferson Harbor to unload. The room was redolent of his mistress who had left a half hour earlier, returning home to her husband, a man with whom DuCharme on occasion did business.

DuCharme had never married. He wanted nothing to do with children, and his only use for women was to indulge his sexual urges. For this he found mistresses the most satisfying. Unhappy at home for one reason or another, they were always more than willing to demonstrate their desirability by doing whatever possible to please him in bed. Furthermore DuCharme, who viewed women as nothing more than possessions, enjoyed dominating those who from his point of view, belonged to somebody else. This current mistress was by far his favorite. She was very beautiful and being nearly his own age had no illusions about an enduring romance. Outwardly she was haughty and cold, but in his presence she transformed herself into an abject, groveling slave, acting out whatever humiliating scenario DuCharme might concoct. On this night, after they had made love, DuCharme ordered her into the bathtub. He then urinated on her while she talked on the telephone to her husband, who was working late at his office.

Novac DuCharme watched the running lights on the Panamanian tanker, that formed an incandescent outline of the ship above the dark water. The husband of his current mistress owned the petroleum depot toward which the tanker was headed. The tanker itself was owned by another man connected to him, a man who had known him when his name was still Helmut Weber.

DuCharme had arranged the deal between these two men that now regularly brought oil from the Arabian peninsula into this harbor. All that remained to make the entire affair complete, he told himself, was for him to sleep with the tanker owner's wife as well. DuCharme smiled. He would visit this man before long and, if the opportunity presented itself, might in fact suggest it. Since the tanker owner, a former SS officer like himself, owed his freedom and perhaps even his life to DuCharme, he might actually bring that to pass while in the man's home.

The oil tanker disappeared from view and DuCharme turned his attention to his desk and the journey he was planning. On the desk lay the map he had taken from Konrad Stuebbe's satchel after his traveling companion had been shot outside the hunting lodge in the snowy forest near the border of Austria and Italy. Next to the map sat a small leather bag filled with gold teeth. For almost twenty years, while his wealth and influence grew, DuCharme kept the map and the leather bag in a fire-proof wall safe hidden behind a bookcase in his bedroom.

DuCharme had a particular attachment to the teeth, which came from the mouths of Jews murdered in the death camp where he was stationed. Though DuCharme hated Jews, imagining them to be agents of the devil, he nonetheless ascribed mystical powers to them. How else, he asked himself, could they have survived so long on earth? A secret devotee of the occult, he regarded the bag of gold teeth as a talisman from which he derived similar power.

Every month or so, late at night when he was alone, he removed both the map and the leather bag from the safe. He would set them on his desk side by side and tell himself to be patient. He would open the bag and empty it onto the polished wood, staring transfixed at the pile of teeth that gleamed in the light of his desk lamp. My little devils, he called them. They were but a trifle compared to the thousands of others that had been melted down into gold bars and secreted in waterproof steel chests along with tons of other gold and jewels. The chests lay at the bottom of an alpine lake in northwest Austria. The map pinpointed the exact location of the chests.

Not yet, DuCharme would tell himself as he dropped the teeth one by one back into the bag. The time is not yet right. Then he would put the map and the leather bag back in the safe and go on about his business running a small company that manufactured electronic components for weapons systems, trading currency on the international market, arranging deals like the one between his mistress's husband and the owner of the tanker, and providing the United States government with information about various operations in Eastern Europe and the Middle East made known to him by an underground network of former members of the SS.

In the fall of 1965 Novac DuCharme finally decided to retrieve the gold. He was fairly certain there were those in the American intelligence community who either knew about his past or at least suspected something, but the United States was getting deeper into the war in Southeast Asia and he was becoming a very valuable resource both for the technology and hardware he provided and for his information. No one in a position of power was about to impede his comings and goings or give him a hard time about anything unusual surrounding his affairs.

DuCharme waited until the following spring when the ice on the alpine lakes had melted. Then, along with two experienced salvage divers from Long Island, a truck driver from Munich, and a couple of Austrian laborers, he journeyed to the shores of a remote lake southeast of Salzburg. The stated intention of DuCharme's expedition, which took just over two weeks, was archaeological research. His actual mission was clouded in mystery since both of the divers were reported drowned in more than two hundred feet of water. Their bodies were never recovered. A car carrying the two laborers ran off a mountain road and plunged down a ravine killing both of them, and the truck driver was found shot to death in an alley three days after delivering twenty-one heavy steel boxes to a warehouse not far from the airport in Munich.

The gold DuCharme's crew hoisted from the bottom of the lake was worth close to $100 million, but gold wasn't all Du-Charme recovered. One of the steel boxes contained a master list compiled by the SS of all the people around the world to whom Nazi plunder had been funneled. DuCharme had no idea a copy of this list existed, but when he discovered it while cataloging the contents of his haul he was overjoyed. Having additional information to trade provided him with even more insulation from anyone attempting to run him to ground. Furthermore, it was always good to know where he could locate people in one country or another who would be more than willing to help him do business. There was no doubt in DuCharme's mind that those on the list would be glad to assist him, especially after he informed them of the manner in which they had been found.

DuCharme did not go directly home from Germany. Instead he flew with his gold in a cargo plane to Algiers to visit the former SS officer who was now a wealthy petroleum exporter living in a large villa outside the city on the Mediterranean coast. The man's name was Muller. He owned the tanker that floated past DuCharme's house on the night he decided to recover the gold from the bottom of the alpine lake. It was in a special compartment in the hold of another of Muller's ships that the gold would be transported to America, although the metal boxes were now encased in wooden crates believed by the oil exporter to contain automatic weapons.

"Hauling your cargo is the least I can do," Muller said to Du-Charme. "Two more of our comrades are in prison because of this Jew Kessler. It was only a matter of time before he led someone to me."

They were sitting in wicker beach chairs on a stone terrace bordered by a low seawall. Thirty feet away, in a pool lined with multicolored tiles, Muller's wife, a tall, angular blond, was swimming laps.

"He won't be leading anyone to you, my friend," DuCharme said. "He and his daughter have disappeared. The police have no idea of their whereabouts."

"But he is still alive and he has the album," Muller replied.

"As far as I know, yes, he is still alive," said DuCharme. "And no doubt he has the album. But I don't think we have anything to worry about. I believe this time he got the message."

"Undoubtedly he did," the man said, "and for that I am forever in your debt. Surely there is something more I can do for you than merely transport a few guns."

DuCharme smiled at the man, fixing him with his cruel eyes. Muller had done well in the oil business, and in dealing with the employees of his company and the servants at his villa he comported himself with considerable authority, but DuCharme could see that underneath the commanding exterior Muller was soft. Great rolls of fat hung over his belt, and his flabby double chin jiggled when he spoke. As DuCharme continued to watch him he could actually sense Muller quivering.

Muller's wife climbed from the pool and with a towel draped around her shoulders walked toward them. DuCharme's gaze swung from Muller to his wife. Muller was a secretive man and his much younger wife had no idea who DuCharme really was or what he had done. She looked back at him with icy disdain, as though he were a waiter who had brought her the wrong plate of food.

She was wearing a bikini that hid very little. DuCharme lowered his eyes to her flat, tanned belly still glistening with moisture. Slowly, he raised his head, pausing when he reached her small pointed breasts. Finally, he focused on the sharp, greedy features of her face. The woman stood as motionless as a slab of marble, never flinching while he inspected her. An iceberg, he thought, but she would do whatever Muller wanted because of his money. He stared hard once again at the oil exporter. The man was a bombastic weakling, afraid of him, just like everyone else.

"Since you are in such a magnanimous mood," he said, "I will have to think of something more you can do."

"I'm going into town to do some shopping," Muller's wife said to her husband. "I'll be back later." She turned to DuCharme. "Are you leaving today?" she asked with studied indifference. "Or will you be staying another night?"

"I'm leaving today," DuCharme said. "After dinner."

"I should be back before then," she said. "But in case I'm not I'll say good-bye now."

As DuCharme knew she would, Muller's wife came to his room in the late afternoon while he was waiting to be called for dinner. He was sitting in an easy chair reading when she knocked. She entered the room, closed and locked the door and turned to face him. She was wearing a white silk tank dress and open-toed high-heeled sandals and carried a matching white leather shoulder bag.

"Go over to the dressing table and brush your hair," DuCharme said.

She looked at him quizzically but said nothing as she walked across the room and stood before the mirror above the table. She hesitated for a few seconds, then took a brush from her bag and began to run it through her hair. After a moment or two DuCharme told her to stop.

"Now put on fresh makeup," he said.

She looked at him again and seemed about to speak but stopped herself. She was not a woman used to taking orders and DuCharme wondered what Muller had promised her in order to make her go through with this. Maybe it hadn't taken that much persuasion at all. DuCharme suddenly had the feeling that Muller's wife was not at all averse to playing this game. She took a silver compact and a small brush from the bag and applied blusher to her cheeks, darkened her lids with smoke-colored eye shadow from a smaller silver container, then took out a matching silver lipstick tube and carefully painted her lips a deep crimson that matched her long fingernails. She turned from the dressing table with the tube still in her hand, walked over to DuCharme's chair, put the open lipstick between her lips and then ran her tongue slowly up and down the length of it.

"What now?" she asked.

"Now take off your dress and walk slowly over to the bed with the bag on your shoulder," DuCharme said.

Muller's wife was wearing nothing under the dress. As she walked, the white shoulder bag bounced slightly against her firm, tanned hip. When she reached the bed she stopped and was about to set the bag down when DuCharme interrupted her.

"No," he said. "Keep the bag on your shoulder and lie on your back."

DuCharme rose from his chair and approached the bed. He unzipped his pants, and without removing any of his clothing knelt above Muller's wife and entered her.

"You're wet," he said to her. "You like this, don't you? Fucking a strange man in your husband's house. Made up for a day in the city with your bag on your shoulder."

"Yes," she said.

Her mouth was open and she began to groan with each exhaled breath.

He pushed deeply into her and took her nipples between his fingers. "Has Muller ever done this to you?" he asked, squeezing the nipples tightly.

"No," she gasped.

"Or this?" He squeezed harder still. Then, as he moved quickly inside her he began twisting her nipples, pulling and pushing on them at the same time so that she bounced up and down on the bed. "Tell me whether your fat husband ever did this."

"No," she screamed.

"And how about this?" DuCharme suddenly let one of her breasts go. As he squeezed the other nipple even harder he pulled out of her and using his free fingers as a guide, penetrated her other opening and began thrusting wildly into her ass.

"Tell me if your husband has been here," he said. As she screamed no again DuCharme withdrew, and holding his cock in his hand, ejaculated onto her face.

DuCharme stood up, straightened his pants, and walked over to the spot where Muller's wife had dropped her dress. He picked the dress up and with a quick, violent motion tore it in half. He threw the pieces of the dress on the floor, walked back to the bed, and lifted Muller's wife to her feet by the hair. Her carefully made up face, now twisted with pain, was flecked with gobs of semen. Still holding her hair in one hand, DuCharme dragged her to the door, opened it, and pushed her into the hallway.

"Perhaps I'll see you at dinner," DuCharme said to her. "But in case I don't I'll say good-bye now."

IX

"When I was a kid on Long Island we had a big swimming pool," Angela Becker said. "My stepbrother and I put two heavy wooden beach chairs on the bottom at the deep end. Then we'd dive down, sit in them, and stare at each other. The idea was to see who could sit there the longest. That's how I felt when I was in Velvet. Like I was sitting at the bottom of that pool."

"How you felt isn't important," McKenzie Rockett said. "What's important is whether you learned anything that wasn't in Erland's notes."

"I learned that if you listen to someone tell you about communing with the spirits of the dead long enough you start believing all sorts of things you know for a fact are bullshit," Angela said. "You stare at a piece of photographic paper that's been dipped in developer and see the monster that was hiding under your bed when you were six, or you see the faces of the Beatles who are watching over you. Obla-di, Obla-da, life goes on, yeah. I learned that the Indians believed redwood trees were inhabited by spirits."

"Don't discount anything you learn about the Indians," someone said from across the room. The voice, deep and resonant, had the courtly, mellifluous accent of the Old South. Even though the words were spoken softly they were perfectly distinct.

Angela had assumed she and Rockett were alone in the task-force office. The ancient wooden stairs leading up to the second floor creaked like a worn-out wagon wheel and neither of them had heard anyone ascending. At the sound of the voice she gave a jump and whirled in her chair. A tall, lean man in a pair of faded Levi's and a checked shirt with the sleeves rolled up was standing just inside the doorway to the office. He had large scuffed hands and powerful-looking forearms and his long curly hair and beard, both chestnut colored, were flecked with gray. Beneath the beard she could see a scar running from just below his left eye to his jawbone. What Angela noticed most though were his eyes. They were the color of sun-bleached slate, and in sharp contrast to his tough, weather-beaten face, they were kind and compassionate.

"Sneaking up on people who are armed can be bad for your health," McKenzie Rockett said.

"At my age everything's bad for your health," the man said. "Mexican food, apple pie, cigars, fast automobiles. I'll add sneaking up on people to the list."

"How long you been standin' there, you son of a bitch," Rockett said.

Angela turned part way around in her chair and saw that Rockett was smiling broadly. "You know this guy?" she asked.

"Yeah I know him," Rockett said. "He's your new partner. Say hello to Roland Troy. Roland, this is Angela Becker."

Troy crossed the room, shook her hand, gave Rockett a hug, and sat down in the old easy chair she'd bought for thirty dollars at a secondhand furniture store. Angela noticed he walked with a slight limp but still moved with the fluid grace of an athlete. Staring at him she was reminded of a book she had in her library about the legendary mountain men who'd blazed the first trails through the Rockies in the 1820s and '30s. There was one, a trapper and army scout, who had the same hard, craggy face and soulful eyes. She couldn't remember his name, but made a mental note to look through the book when she got home.

"There's an island not far from your property on the river," Troy said to Angela. "When I was a young boy my grandfather took me there in a canoe. It was full of cabbage palm and mangrove, and had one small stand of sycamore. My grandfather asked me whether anything about the place seemed unusual. I told him it was very quiet. 'That's because there is no wildlife here. Not a bird. Not a snake. Not a squirrel. Nothing,' he said. He told me the Indians claimed this was because it was a holy place, an ancient burial ground inhabited by the spirits of their ancestors. He told me I could come there to sit and think but that I shouldn't disturb anything, that I should always leave the island the way I found it.

"A little while after that a team of scientists from the University of Florida came and checked this island out. They came up with all sorts of theories but not one of them had an answer to the question of why no wildlife was on that island."

"And you believed the Indians," Angela said.

"I asked my grandfather whether he believed them," Troy said. "He told me he wasn't sure, but there were many things in this world that couldn't be explained. The older I get the more I see how right he was."

"So you think the psychics in Velvet really can communicate with the dead?" she asked. "And you think the shapes I saw on the photographic paper were really the faces of spirits watching over me? Is that what you're saying?"

"I don't dismiss anything," Troy said. "Not when I'm trying to solve a murder."

She was about to reply—maybe say something like oh, and I guess you're going to solve all the ones we've got here in the next three hours—but he was looking at her with an intensity that stopped her cold. It wasn't sexual, at least not in the way she was used to men staring at her, although for an instant she felt as though she were naked, but rather the way jungle cats she had seen on wildlife films locked on an animal that was potential prey.

"What happened to your shoulder?" he asked.

"What do you mean?" she said, aware of exactly what he meant.

"Your left shoulder," Troy said. "I thought maybe you'd hurt it."

"You hurt your shoulder?" Rockett asked. "You didn't tell me anything about hurting your shoulder."

"It was a week ago," she said. "I pulled something doing the overhead press machine at the gym. It's nothing. I don't even feel it unless I raise my left arm suddenly."

How in the hell had he known that? she wondered. She hadn't told anybody about the injury and not a person she'd talked to in the past week had asked her a thing. What was it he noticed that nobody else had?

Long before Rockett told her Troy was joining the task force she'd heard the stories about him. She'd heard the one about the tooth, and the other one they liked to tell late at night at the jazz club down on Orange Avenue where the lawyers who thought they were tough guys hung out with a few of the cops from homicide. That one was about the time just before Troy quit the department, when right in the court-room, in front of the judge and the jury and all the attorneys, he stuck the barrel of a .38 in the ear of a vicious killer who had murdered a young woman and just gotten off on a technicality, telling the man he ought to blow his brains out right there, telling the judge he hoped it wasn't his daughter the man killed next, then pocketing the gun and walking out without anyone even so much as trying to lay a finger on him.

"I know what you've heard," Rockett said to her when she asked him what Troy was like. "But let me tell you a story the rest of them don't know. I was there and I've never told this one to a soul.

"This young guy, not much more than a kid really, named Meredith Bouchard, comes home and finds his wife in bed with his best friend. He grabs a shotgun and kills them both. Then he disappears. Troy and I draw the case. A few days go by and I'm sitting by myself in the office when Troy comes in. 'I talked to Bouchard's mother,' he says. 'I think I know where to find Meredith.' I ask where that is and he tells me he's in New Mexico hiding out at his sister's. I ask him which one of us is going out there after him and he says, 'Neither one of us. I'm going to call him up.'

"I don't say anything. I just sit there and watch, 'cause by this time I've worked with Roland Troy for a good while and I've come to expect the unusual. So he picks up the phone and dials the sister's number and when she answers he asks to speak to Meredith Bouchard. 'You tell him it's Roland Troy,' he says. 'Tell him I just want to talk to him a minute.'

"The mother must've called first and said something to that boy because damned if he doesn't get on the phone. Troy says to him, 'Look, son, you and I both know you killed two people and you're gonna have to come back home and answer for that. You know I found you once, and if I have to I'll find you again, only the next time it'll be in person, I'll be pissed off, and you don't want to have to deal with that. So listen to me. Tomorrow morning you get on a Greyhound for Orlando and when you get here you call me up and I'll come get you at the bus station. Meanwhile, I'll talk to a couple of my friends over in the state attorney's office and I'll tell 'em all about the circumstances surrounding those killings and how cooperative you're being and how they ought to take all that into consideration.'

"Troy goes on for a while longer telling the kid how he knows he feels terrible about what happened and that it's gonna be a huge load off his conscience if he comes back, stuff like that, and then he hangs up. He looks at me, I look at him, and he says, 'Give him three days. He'll show up.'

"Angela, three days later we're sitting in the office when the phone rings and sure as shit it's Meredith Bouchard calling from the Orlando bus station. The world's full of guys who can stick a gun in someone's ear, but Roland Troy's the only person I've ever met who could talk a man seventeen hundred and fifty miles away, facing life in prison, into giving up on the telephone. I mean that kid could have hauled ass for Alaska, or Borneo, but he climbed on the Greyhound just like Troy told him to and came home instead."

"What's his secret?" Angela asked.

"He senses things other people don't," Rockett told her. "I don't know how he does it, but he does. He's in tune with things other people don't even hear."

She watched Troy now as he took a cigar out of the pocket of his shirt.

"Do you mind if I smoke?" he asked her.

"No," she said. "Go ahead."

"Listen," Rockett said. "I have a meeting in fifteen minutes with the chief, the regional director of the FBI and some other guy they sent down from Washington. Like I told you Roland, they're gonna leave us alone, at least for the time being. But bosses are bosses, so you know they're going to ask me if we have a plan. I am naturally going to tell them we not only have a plan, the two of you are putting it into effect even while the meeting I am in with them is taking place. What I'm hoping is that my eloquence won't be complete bullshit."

"Tell 'em we're peeling an onion," Troy said.

"We're peeling an onion," Rock repeated. "The chief will love that one."

"No, I'm serious, Rock," Troy said. "Tell 'em our investigation thus far has led us to believe we're dealing with a multilayered organization, configured much like an onion. Tell 'em we're going to peel it a layer at a time. Shit, you can even call it Operation Onion if you think they're in the mood for a themed investigation."

"Operation Onion," Rock said.

"Yeah," Troy said. "Tell 'em Angela and I are gonna peel us the outer layer this very afternoon."

"And what would that outer layer be?" Rockett asked. "Not that I'm going to divulge that to the aristocracy, you understand. I'm just curious."

"The outer layer is the skinhead. Jason Badger. Your old buddy," Troy said, nodding slightly to Angela and lighting his cigar.

"Jason Badger is as far underground as the creature who shares his last name," Angela said. "It'll take the two of us a month to find him, assuming he's still alive, and even when we do he won't tell us anything."

"I've already found him," Troy said. "And he'll talk. Come on, let's you and me take a ride."

"Operation Onion," Rockett said. "You know, Tooth, that isn't such a bad name. I could grow to like it."

"Should we take my car or do you want to drive?" Angela asked when they were out in the parking lot. She said it matter-of-factly although inside she was churning. She wanted to drive, to show him she wasn't some bimbo, some window dressing, at the same time furious with herself for feeling she had something to prove.

"He knows your car," Troy said. "He ain't never seen my truck."

They climbed into his four-wheel-drive Ford that was still caked with mud from the back roads of Vermont. Troy grabbed the New

York Yankees baseball cap that was hanging on the rearview mirror and put it on. As they left the parking lot and pulled onto the access road that paralleled the interstate he turned on the tape player.

"Early Miles Davis," she said.

He turned part way toward her and raised his eyebrows slightly. "Is that OK?" he asked.

"That's fine," she said, wanting to say I love early Miles Davis but feeling foolish.

" 'Kind of Blue,' " he said, around the cigar that was still in his mouth but had gone out. "Coltrane's on it. So's Bill Evans and Cannonball Adderley. It's one of my all-time favorites."

They rode in silence for a while, driving southeast, away from the city. She leaned against the passenger door, her long legs bent against the seat, her feet resting on the transmission hump, watching him. He was easy on the truck, she observed, shifting well below the redline, keeping it right around the speed limit, backing off to let other vehicles change lanes in front of them. His large hands hung loosely on the steering wheel. The knuckles of both his index and middle fingers were enlarged to the size of acorns and covered with thick calluses, the result, she assumed, of some kind of martial arts training. Over the years she'd known men who trained like that but all of them were wound tighter than the inside of a golf ball. In fact all the cops she knew projected the brittle synaptic ambience that came from a life of perpetual suspicion. Roland Troy, on the other hand, seemed completely at ease; he was watchful, but he was calm.

Eventually they left the main highway and headed down a beaten-up stretch of blacktop lined with run-down warehouses, body shops and junk yards. The road crossed a double set of railroad tracks and turned to dirt in a community of dilapidated shacks and off-kilter mobile homes so coated with dust it was difficult to determine their color. It was a desperate, futile place, a white trash ghetto filled with angry, hard-faced men and women and sullen, hollow-eyed kids.

"He's in there," Troy said. He had pulled over and was pointing to a tiny house resting cockeyed on cement blocks fifty yards up the road. An old battered Lincoln missing one of its front fenders sat in the front yard next to a rusty swing set. "There's a girl inside with him, and her kid. She works the two-to-ten shift at a Handy Way.

Drops the kid at her mother's." He glanced at his watch, leaned back in the seat, and folded his arms. "She ought to be leaving in about ten minutes. I figure we'll wait and talk to Jason after she's gone."

"I told myself I wasn't going to ask you this but I can't help it," Angela said. "How the hell did you find Jason Badger so fast?"

He took a book of matches out of his shirt pocket and started to light the dead cigar in his mouth but paused. "You mind?" he asked.

"No," she said. "I'd tell you if I did."

He smiled and struck a match. "I go back a long way in these parts," he said. "Back to when it was nothing but a sleepy southern town with a lot of pretty lakes and no Disney World, no Orlando Magic, no interstate highway running past a bunch of high-rise office buildings with the names of banks on 'em. There're still folks left who go back with me. Guys I played football with in high school. The sons and daughters of men my grandfather guided on fishing and hunting trips when there were more deer and bear and wild hogs than human beings up north of town where your property is. A few Indians that nobody even knows are still around. People like that. You'd be amazed how much I can find out from them and how fast. Without a cell phone or a beeper." He paused and puffed for a minute on his cigar.

"You know what this place is called? Where we're stittin'?"

"Yeah," she said. "It's called General."

"You know *why* it's called General?"

"No I don't," she said.

"It got the name back in the Depression when it was a hobo camp. One winter a leader of the hobos by the name of Jacob Coxey, the guy who organized the hobo march on Washington, stayed here. They called him the general. The men who built the camp named it after him. There's people living here today who are the grandchildren of those hobos. You could stand 'em up against a wall and put the barrel of that forty-four of yours between their eyes and they wouldn't tell you or any other outsider a thing."

"But they'd tell you, right? Even wearing that Yankees hat."

"Here comes the girl," Troy said. "Let's hope that Lincoln starts."

Jason Badger was stretched out on the couch, a plate of nachos and cheese balanced on his stomach, flipping the TV back and forth from *Days of Our Lives* to *All My Children* with the remote control, thinking what a better place the world would be if the ads were on at different times on the different stations, when he felt the cold barrel of Roland Troy's .45 press into the base of his neck.

"Don't move and everything will be just fine," Troy said, coming around where Jason could see him. He grabbed the remote control and the plate of nachos in one fluid motion and tossed them both into a corner of the room. There were two ratty chairs facing the couch; Troy sat in one of them and Angela, entering the tiny living room from the kitchen, sat in the other. There were children's toys and empty fast-food containers everywhere, and the whole place had the sweet stench of rotting fruit.

"Miz Beck—" Jason started to say, his eyes widening, but Troy stopped him with a wave of the gun.

"Nothing's gonna happen to you," he said. "Unless, that is, you don't cooperate. Now then, my name is Roland Troy and I'm trying to find out who killed your brother. To set the record straight, and so we don't waste our time, Detective Becker, who you think set your brother up, had nothing to do with his murder. Detective Becker is a cop. What she wanted from your brother was information and you don't ordinarily get information from dead people."

"You a cop too?" Jason asked.

"That's right," Troy said. He watched Jason's face relax and saw the tension go out of his body. At eighteen the kid was a pro at wheeling and dealing with the law.

"I ain't tellin' you nothin'," he said. "You both can go fuck yourselves. I want a lawyer."

Troy leaned over and flicked the barrel of his gun in the kid's direction. Angela wasn't really sure he had actually done anything until she heard Jason howl and saw blood running down the side of his face. Jason put his hand to the cut, examined his fingers and cursed softly.

"Here it is," Troy said, "and you better listen good 'cause I ain't gonna say it twice. You missed your meeting with Detective Becker day before yesterday in direct violation of the court order. That means you go to jail, no bond, no plea bargain, no nothin'. Now understand that I don't rightly give a fuck whether I take you to jail or they cart your sorry ass off to the morgue, so you make one move to get off that couch and I'll kill you. You go to jail, I'll see to it somebody in there fucks you over so bad you'll be screaming for me to come talk to you in less than two days. Tell me what I want to know now, I won't kill you and you won't go to jail. It's as simple as that, and while you're wondering whether I mean what I say, ask yourself how it came to be that Detective Becker and I are sitting here in this room without you picking up the phone and inviting us over."

Troy puffed on his cigar, saw it had gone out, struck a match with one hand and relit it. "This here ain't no intervention session," he said. "This ain't no rehabilitation program where you get to be an asshole for six months and Detective Becker has to play by the rules and put up with your shit. The party's over, Bubba. Start talkin'."

"What do you want to know?" Jason Badger asked.

"I want to know who your brother was working for," Troy said. "I want to know who put him in business making those radio commercials."

From the waist up Jason's body was relatively still but his feet were moving back and forth like a couple of runaway windshield wipers. He pulled a blue bandanna from the pocket of his jeans, held it against his cheek and looked desperately over at Angela for help. "I didn't know you were a cop," he said. "I never saw that diamond in your nose before either."

"You better tell him," she said. "He isn't nice like me."

Jason looked from one of them to the other and made a ratcheting sound in his throat. "The guy's name is Stiefel," he said. "Herbert Stiefel. He owns the television studio up in Aurora. He was a good friend of our cousin, Joe Didier." He took a deep breath, his eyes fixed on a spot somewhere on the ceiling, as though maybe it would magically open and he could fly away.

"You're doin' fine," Troy said. "Keep it up. What happened? After Didier's girlfriend killed him, this Stiefel offered your brother a job?"

Angela stared hard at Troy. The son of a bitch must have memorized the files, she thought. With everything else going on she'd almost forgotten who Joseph Didier was. She took a notebook and pen

out of her jacket pocket, wrote hastily for several seconds and waited
for Jason to continue.

"Stiefel came to the funeral," he said. "He and my brother got to
talking. A little while after that Ernie told me Stiefel called him with
a business proposition. The first time Ernie went by himself. He stayed
a couple of weeks. When he came back to Louisiana he said he had
this radio commercial deal and we were moving to Orlando."

"Was your brother runnin' from somebody? Did he fuck somebody
over bad enough so they'd want him dead? One of your skinhead
buddies maybe?"

"Ernie took care of the skins. They was all tight with him. White,
tight and right. He was family. None of them would've done him."

"What about Tito?" Troy asked. "Tell me about him."

Jason rubbed an index finger across his scraggly mustache,
scratched one of his forearms and opened and closed his mouth a couple
of times as though he were checking to see if his jaw still worked. "My
face is killin' me," he said. "I'm in need of medical attention."

"You'll live," Troy said. "Tell me about Tito."

Jason looked over at Angela again for help. She looked up from
her notebook, smiled at him and went back to writing.

"What are you doing?" he said to her. "What are you writing
down?"

"Hey," Troy said. "I'm asking you for the last time. What about
Tito?"

"He was a shrimper who went to work for Joe," Jason said. "He
piloted a crew boat to Joe's offshore rigs."

"Did Stiefel give Tito a job too?"

"I guess."

"You guess?"

"He was around. He worked with my brother some. I don't know
nothin' else about Tito."

"You don't huh? The dude sees your brother get nailed, climbs
into his car and drives off leaving you standing next to his dead body
and you're gonna protect his ass? Well, son, let me tell you what I
guess. I guess whoever shot Ernie was hired to do the job and paid
real well because people who can shoot that good don't come cheap.
If I were you I'd grow me another eye right in the back of that shaved

head of yours because what else I guess is that you're on the same list. Maybe you know something or maybe you're gonna want revenge. Even if neither one of those is true, they'll kill you anyway just to be sure. The other free advice I've got for you is that if you've got any more information you tell me now. In return, Detective Becker and I will see to it you get protection."

"You gonna protect me? I'm supposed to believe that after you crack my face open? Shit, I'll take my chances."

"Suit yourself," Troy said. "You change your mind you know where to find us."

"That's it? You ain't takin' me in?"

"Nope," Troy said. "You answered my questions." He rose and holstered his gun. "C'mon," he said to Angela. "Let's get out of here."

"That was wonderful," Angela said, climbing into Troy's truck and slamming the door. "Next time you plan on assaulting a witness I'd appreciate it if you tell me in advance so I can decide whether or not I want to be an accessory."

Troy put another tape into the deck—someone Angela didn't recognize playing the blues on a Hammond B-3—wheeled the truck around on the dirt road and headed back the way they had come. Even after they recrossed the railroad tracks and were on the blacktop he drove slowly, as though the tension he had created in the room with Jason Badger had taken place in another life.

"You danced with that little prick for six months and got so frustrated you were all set to go drag racing with his brother," he said calmly. "Maybe you were alone, but if you weren't, whoever you had with you could have been an accessory to all sorts of things. Me, I don't have no race car. And I don't plan to spend my time fucking around, especially with some sleazeball who's white, tight and right. I made him bleed a little. I didn't hurt him. I talked to him in the only language he understands."

Angela could feel a flush begin at the back of her neck and spread around to her cheeks. She brushed the hair back from her face and narrowed her eyes. "And what happens when he files a brutality complaint?" she asked stoutly.

"He won't," Troy said. "The next time we'll hear from Jason Badger is when he wants to trade information for a place to hide, and that won't be long, you can bank on it."

"Tell me," she said, "what's it feel like to always be right?"

He didn't answer her at first, but instead pulled into a small strip mall and parked in front of a tiny pizza shop. "You ever eat here?" he asked.

"No," she answered, still waiting for him to respond.

"Those narcotics guys," he said. "They don't know nothin' about food. This place has the best pizza in central Florida. C'mon, it's on me."

He had finished one slice and was halfway through a second when suddenly he stopped chewing and looked at her. "I was starving," he said. "That doesn't happen to me very often, or at least it didn't used to. Used to be I could go a whole day on the job and not eat, but no more." He took another bite, wiped some sauce from his mustache and sat back in his chair.

"You see how I walk?" he said "You see that limp I have? It's because I listened to a guy in the Mekong Delta thirty years ago when I should have known better. He was a guy I knew from right here in this town and he was a piece of shit from the time he was a little kid. But the thing is I did listen to him and he walked me into an ambush and got me shot. He may even have done it himself. That I'll never know for sure because he's dead. He became a big-shot politician, by the way. I followed him for the same reason you were gonna race your car against Ernie Viens. I wanted to show him something. I wanted him to see the person I thought I really was."

"And who was that?"

"The baddest cat in town. The Lone Ranger. The guy who knows the answer before you know the question. You know why I'm on this case? Why you got me as a partner?"

"For Rockett," she said. "You came back to help Rock."

"No, that isn't why. Rock's a wonderful man and a damn good friend and if I can help him out that'll be just fine, but he isn't the real reason I'm here. It's because of my wife. My wife who was murdered by the same kind of scum as Jason Badger and Ernie Viens and whoever was running them—the other layers of the onion we haven't

125

as yet peeled back. My wife of eight months who should have been my wife twenty years before I married her."

"I heard about . . ." Angela said, clearing her throat. "I wanted to say—"

"That's OK," Troy interrupted. "You don't have to say anything. But you should know that I still have bullet fragments in my hip from that night in the Delta, and a day doesn't go by that they don't remind me about how wrong I can be, not how right."

"I'm sorry," she said. "I shouldn't have said that. I'm just pissed is all. I see Jason Badger and I get even more pissed. I thought I could turn him around. I thought maybe he was different from the other ones."

"You got reason to be pissed," he said. "You're a good cop who got stuck in a no-win situation with those skinheads, and a political cesspool with this task force. But that don't mean you should be pissed off at me. What were you writing in your notebook?"

She took the notebook out of her pocket, flipped it open and put it on the table between them, turning it so he could read it. On the left-hand page were a series of names connected by lines like an airline route map. On the right neatly written notes that ran over to the next page. Troy studied all three pages while Angela munched a slice of pizza and sipped her Coke.

"How come you didn't say anything to Rock about those guys digging up the drainpipe in Weiser's yard or about Weiser seeing the Nazi?"

"I was about to," she said, "but I didn't get a chance. You crept up behind us and interrupted me with the parable about your grandfather and the Indians. You wanted me to see the person you think you really are."

Troy looked up from the notebook, smiled, and scratched absently at his beard. "So you think the two guys in Weiser's yard were Ernie Viens and his buddy Tito, both of whom were working for Herbert Stiefel, Mr. Television of Aurora, Florida," he said. "You think Stiefel hired them to kill Weiser. And one or both of them also shot Freddy Hatton, Stan Erland's obsession. Erland found out so Stiefel had him whacked along with Ernie and probably Tito as well."

"What do you think?" Angela asked.

"I think you're mostly right," Troy answered. "But I think Erland stumbled onto more than who shot Leo Weiser. I think he was onto the reason Weiser was killed. I think that's what got Stan Erland whacked."

"And you think there's a connection between that and what Ernie and Tito were looking for."

"I sure do," Troy said, pointing with the end of his spoon at two names connected by lines to Herbert Stiefel. "Tell me about these guys, Pastor Jim Keller and T. Bryce Atwood. What the hell's a minister and that newspaper columnist Atwood doing with Stiefel?"

"I guess you didn't have cable TV or a satellite dish up there in Vermont?" she said.

"I didn't have a TV set up there," he said. "I have one here but I haven't hooked it up since I got back."

"You have no idea what you're missing," she said. "T. Bryce Atwood and Jim Keller are Stiefel's star performers. Keller was a preacher from somewhere in Arkansas. He ran one of those hate-mongering white supremacist churches. Now he's the judge on a show called *The Common Folks' Court*. They put all sorts of people on trial, in absentia. Congressmen, judges, civil rights activists, environmentalists, lots of Jewish businessmen. They sit a dummy of the person in a chair and rant and rave about how they're traitors selling out America. Then Keller administers his brand of frontier justice complete with mock hangings and firing squads. Atwood still writes his column but he's added the boob tube to his repertoire. He does a talk show with pretty much the same agenda. Both of 'em are real good at getting the audience all worked up. It's a regular circus."

"Makes sense," Troy said. "Stiefel used to run a circus."

"You know him?"

"I never met him, but I know about him. When he first opened his studio a friend of mine went to work for him until she found out what kind of garbage he intended to produce. When she told him she was quitting he scared her pretty good so I checked him out for her. Stiefel's a mean, evil-hearted bastard perfectly capable of murder or any other crime you might imagine, but he's slick. He's never spent a day in jail. The thing is, I don't believe he's in charge of the show."

"Why's that?" Angela asked.

"It was a while ago so I don't remember all the details," Troy said, "but near as I can recall, one day Herbert Stiefel was eating cold beans from a dented can and the next day he was running that TV studio. I'd bet anything somebody else put up the money to buy that place. Stiefel was the perfect front man. He knew something about show business. He was a right-wing fanatic. And he was a thug with a clean record. No dirt tracks on the carpet."

"You think this somebody else is involved in our case?"

"I think that if the trail stopped at Herbert Stiefel's doorstep Stan Erland wouldn't be dead. Ernie Viens might be, and this Tito character too, but not Erland. I don't think Stiefel would have an FBI agent killed unless someone told him to do it."

"So now we go talk to Herbert Stiefel," Angela said. "You smack him with your gun barrel and he tells us what we want to know."

Troy took a large bite of pizza, chewed slowly, and swallowed. He took another bite and pointed at Angela with the spoon that was still in his other hand. "I'm beginning to like you," he said, his mouth half full, "in spite of your desire to keep me in line. I heard you're a woman who speaks her mind and doesn't take crap from anyone. I'm beginning to see that's true. But to answer your question, no, I'm not going to smack Herbert Stiefel with the barrel of my gun. Not yet anyway. What we're going to do now is drive back to the office. You're going to find McKenzie Rockett . . . excuse me . . . I would deeply appreciate it if you would find McKenzie Rockett and tell him what we're up to. I'm going home to finish pulling the boards off the windows of my house so the place can finally get aired out. Then I'm going to make a couple of phone calls. Herbert Stiefel ain't goin' anywhere."

"I have a question," she said.

"What's that?" Troy asked.

"How could you tell there was something wrong with my shoulder?"

Troy washed down the last of his pizza with a sip of Coke and looked at Angela for a moment without saying anything. He saw a flutter in the lightly freckled patch of skin at the base of her throat above the V-shaped opening of her blue silk blouse. The flutter lasted for only an instant, then returned to an even rise and fall. He saw the color of her cheeks deepen ever so slightly beneath the blush she was wearing and her almond-shaped eyes narrow at the corners. Like the fluttering of her throat, these changes appeared and were gone so quickly it was almost as though they hadn't happened at all, but to Roland Troy they were indelible. She's afraid I can see something she doesn't want anyone to see, he thought. She's afraid of being vulnerable.

"Lucky guess," he answered.

"You're full of shit," she said.

"C'mon," he said. "I want to get those boards off my windows while it's still light."

X

"I figured you'd call," Jack Ubinas said. "How do you like your new partner?"

"She's smart," Roland Troy said, smiling around his cigar. "And feisty. But that's not what you want to know. You want to know what she looks like."

"I heard she was very beautiful," Ubinas said.

Troy took a deep drag on the cigar, blew a smoke ring, and watched it float above the railing of his front porch. He was sitting in one of two rocking chairs mounted high on cement blocks that were set on the old wooden planks of the porch so that he could see above the railing out over the sloping ground that led down to his lake. In the fading daylight he could still make out the pair of great blue herons who had nested there for a decade. They took turns feeding in the marsh grass at the far side, one dipping its head, the other peering this way and that, ever watchful for the sudden appearance of the old female alligator who had hunted them unsuccessfully for years.

Everything in its place, he thought, everything so familiar—the herons, the gator, the ancient, creaky house that began life as a shack built by his great-great-grandfather. The house with its peeling yellow paint faded almost to white, and the large metal sign from the auto repair shop that covered a gaping hole in the porch and crackled like a line drive off a tin roof whenever anyone approached the door. The house with the third-floor room ringed with windows like the turret of a castle where his grown daughter had played endlessly as a child. The house where he had lived with his one true love, Clara, for six months before they went off to Europe and she was killed.

Everything in its place, including Jack Ubinas. Ubinas, the company man who looked like a college professor with his pipe and his frayed

Brooks Brothers shirts and horn-rimmed glasses. Ubinas who had re-cruited Troy out of Miyazato's karate dojo in Naha, Okinawa, taken him off to the border between Laos and Vietnam before hardly anyone in America even knew where those countries were, and turned him first into a silent, invisible scout—a shadow—and then into a deadly sniper, showing Troy a side of himself he had since been unable to escape. Ubinas, former king of the spooks, who now, from his farm-house in the Virginia countryside, sat alone for hours and hours in front of a computer crammed with data on every imaginable clandestine activity on earth, assessing, evaluating, speculating, working with gov-ernment agencies that on paper did not exist.

Troy blew another smoke ring. The breeze out of the northwest had died with the setting sun and this one crossed the porch railing and hung above the bed of impatiens Clara had planted beside the brick path. Everything in its place, he thought, but not the same, never the same.

"She ain't bad," Troy said. "For a horny old fucker like you she'd be heaven on earth. I hear you're snowed in."

"Got over a foot and a half since last night," Ubinas said, "but what do I care. I have a new computer to play with. Custom built by your old buddy Van Fleet. Better than twenty gigs on the hard drive, seven hundred fucking megahertz, two hundred fifty-six megs of ram, faster than a bum on a ham sandwich, roomier than the palace of Versailles."

"Let's put it to work."

"That'll be my pleasure, but first tell me how you're feeling."

"I'm fine," Troy said. "My hip made it through two Vermont win-ters. Cross-country skiing no less."

"It isn't your hip I'm talking about," Ubinas said. "It's your head. When McKenzie Rockett called me he wanted to know it I thought it was a mistake for him to contact you. He asked me if I thought he should just leave you be. I told him quite the contrary; leaving you be was the mistake. But now that you're there, in the house and all, I wanted to make sure you were OK. There's only a handful of us left, Roland. Johnny Dunshee killed himself last month."

"I ain't Johnny Dunshee," Troy said. "How about we ask your palace of Versailles a few questions."

"Ask away."

"I got a regular shopping list here Jack. Get out your pencil. First of all, I need the scoop on a psychic by the name of Angus Elliott who supposedly did some work helping the feds find dead bodies. Assuming he was on the payroll I'd appreciate a list of everyone he worked with. Then . . . let's see here . . . while we're on the subject of psychics see if there's anything on a woman named Justine Fallon, or a guy named Leo Weiser."

"The one who was murdered two years ago," Ubinas said. "The psychic photographer. Rockett told me about him. I ran his name. Zero. Dead end."

"It seems he was someone else before he was Leo Weiser. Maybe someone who survived a Nazi death camp. But you already knew that."

"I'll keep looking."

"Right. A bum on a ham sandwich. I haven't heard that one for twenty years. Next we have Herbert Stiefel who you checked out for me a few years back but maybe there's something new. And bringing up the rear there's a couple of cable TV personalities, Pastor Jim Keller and T. Bryce Atwood, who's also a columnist for the *Journal-Express* here in O-town. Oh yeah, I almost forgot. Check and see if you can find anything on a guy who's missing part of one ear."

There was silence on the line, an almost imperceptible pause that lasted only an instant but altered the rhythm of their conversation, and Roland Troy was a man who responded with uncanny sensitivity to rhythms.

As a defensive back in high school he set a Florida state record for interceptions in one season by honing in on the rhythm of the opposing quarterback and anticipating the pattern the receiver would run. In southeast Asia he lived in perfect harmony with the rhythm of the jungle, surviving in situations where others perished. Later, as a homicide detective his sensitivity to shifting speech patterns and body movement, or even the far less obvious changes he sensed in the atmosphere around a crime scene helped him solve cases that other investigators had abandoned. Earlier that same day, in fact, it had been a minute hitch in the rhythm of her motion as she turned in her chair to face him that prompted Troy to ask Angela Becker about her shoulder. Now he felt an extra beat in the ebb and flow between him and Jack Ubinas.

"You still with me?" Troy asked.

"Yup," Ubinas said cheerily. "Just bringing up a file."

Troy had continued his relationship with Jack Ubinas long after he returned from Southeast Asia, accepting assignments from time to time as a freelance covert operative in various parts of the world. In return, Ubinas provided Troy with the kind of information unavailable to all but a few government agents. Over the years, they had worked closely together, but at the deepest level Troy remained wary of the avuncular man in baggy corduroys he secretly referred to as the lethal teddy bear.

"I'm with you all the way, partner," Ubinas continued. " 'Man missing part of ear' just added to the list. I should have some information for you by tomorrow morning. Maybe even later tonight."

"I appreciate it," Troy said.

"Anything I can do to help," Ubinas said. "So now tell me, what does she look like?"

Four miles away, a little less if you were traveling up the Coacootchie by canoe, Angela Becker drove her Trans-Am slowly down the narrow dirt path between the main highway and her trailer. She was still on edge, unsettled, slightly out of focus, not because of the Jason Badger episode, nor because she had felt scrutinized by Roland Troy. She had a strong enough sense of herself—enough confidence in her ability— to brush everything that had happened during the day aside, get a good night's sleep, and start the next day feeling just fine. It was something else that had been gnawing at her for several days, ever since her meeting with Justine Fallon when she looked at the piece of photographic paper and saw, amid the swirling pattern of black and white tendrils, what seemed to be the face of the only man she ever loved.

She was twenty years old and one of the top young models in New York when she met him. He was a medical student at Downstate, a serious, intense young man who spent the week attending class and studying. He studied on the weekends too, but on Friday and Saturday nights when the weather was good and his telephone rang telling him a run was set he became someone else, a drag racer, the driver for a group of men who built and maintained a stable of street machines that ran for enormous stakes against cars from all up and down the East

Coast. His name was Bobby Maizell, and no one racing on the street from Bangor, Maine, to Miami Beach was better.

She met him one Friday night, one Saturday morning actually, since it was after two o'clock when the car in which she was riding with some friends was abruptly stopped on a Long Island parkway somewhere between Manhattan and Quogue. An incredibly tall man in a flowing black cape simply stepped into the road, held up his arms, and halted both lanes of eastbound traffic. Someone in the car with Angela cursed. Someone else asked what the hell was going on, but Angela, who could already see what was happening from her vantage point in the front passenger's seat, didn't answer. Instead she jumped out and sprinted fifty yards along the grassy slope beside the parkway until she reached the spot where two race cars, tires still smoking from their burnouts, hoods shaking from the monster motors that roared beneath them, waited for a signal from the starter.

As she watched the tall caped man move between the two bellowing cars, standing in front of them like a matador, readying them with hand signals for the race, she could feel the power of the unmuffled engines from the soles of her feet to the pit of her stomach. The deafening noise gripped her, pulling at her as though she were in a whirlpool, and without meaning to, she screamed. As she did, the driver of one of the cars turned and looked in her direction. He had long dark hair, chiseled features, and the most beautiful eyes she had ever seen. He turned away, the starter dropped his arms, and the race was on, but in that instant she fell in love.

She waited for him on the grassy slope, knowing he would come back. When the race was over and his car loaded onto a trailer and quickly towed away, he walked the quarter-mile he'd just driven in eleven seconds to the spot where she stood. Her friends were waiting too, but when Bobby got there she told them she'd changed her mind, she wasn't going to Quogue after all.

He had another car parked alongside the parkway's access road, and the two of them drove in it to her parents' estate on Long Island's north shore where she was living. They sat on the beach, on a blanket she brought from the house, and talked for more than two hours. Just before dawn they made love, looking wordlessly into each other's eyes, coming together. Afterward, lying in the sand, while he held her and they watched the early morning fishermen head out into the sound, she cried for the first time since she was six years old.

Within a week she had moved into the city to be with him and for nearly a year they lived together. For Angela it was a period of intense and absolute joy, the only time in her life when she had ever felt that rare combination of passion and trust, when her sense of peace replaced her need to always have the upper hand. Then it ended, violently and abruptly, because, she later told herself, she foolishly allowed her happiness to cloud her judgment.

There had been another man in her life when she met Bobby Maizell. He was the son of a wealthy clothing manufacturer, a wastrel who lived off a trust fund and featured himself a tough guy because he dealt cocaine. She went out with him once, found him repulsive, and refused to date him again, but he pursued her relentlessly, her rejection only intensifying his desire. He sent her flowers, jewelry, and perfume. She trashed the flowers and returned the gifts, but he persisted. When she did a runway show he would be there, sitting in the front row, applauding. He never did anything to her, nor did he ever say anything untoward, but he was always around.

One night, shortly after Angela and Bobby began living together, he ran into them at a small jazz club in the Village, and though his actions were cordial, he was incensed. Secretly he vowed to destroy the man he saw as his rival. He called Angela the next day, congratulated her, told her how delighted he was to see her so happy, and asked if they could still be friends. Angela, in a moment of weakness fueled by elation, said sure.

The man took his time, waiting the way a snake waits patiently beneath a bush for its prey. He began showing up at the street races, betting large sums on Bobby's car, picking up the tab for everyone at the diner where they went when the race was over. Then one night when Angela was in Paris on a modeling job he struck. The cops who pulled Bobby over as he drove from the city to the garage where the race cars were kept claimed his brake lights didn't work, but it wasn't brake lights that made them stop the car; it was the five kilos of coke they'd been told were taped inside the right rear fender.

The judge knew Angela's family; he had worked with her late

father, but he was up for reelection and gave Bobby twenty years. Bobby Maizell, however, never made it to prison. On the snowy night he was being transferred upstate from Riker's Island the van skidded off an ice-covered bridge and plunged forty feet into a river. They recovered the bodies of the driver, the guard, and two prisoners. They dragged the river for a week, but Bobby and a fourth prisoner were never found. There was no way, though, the two men could have survived. They were both handcuffed and had shackles on their legs, and the water temperature of the river was forty-three degrees.

A month after the accident Angela moved from New York to the condo she'd bought in Orlando as an investment, turning her back forever on a career that in the previous year had paid her more than $300,000. Inconsolable, she wanted nothing more to do with the world of modeling, the world of glitter and style. She didn't care about the money and furthermore didn't really need it since there was plenty in her inheritance to support her for the rest of her life.

For a while she did nothing, but then one day at a shooting range where she'd begun to spend some time, she met a man who had just joined the sheriff's department. He asked her out. She told him it was nothing personal but she didn't want anything to do with cops. He told her as good as she could shoot she ought to become one and take out her anger chasing bad guys. That's what he was doing he said. She laughed at him, but began thinking about it and after a time it began to make sense.

"How long will it take me to get into the narcotics unit?" she asked the burly black lieutenant who interviewed her after she'd passed all the preliminary tests. He had the improbable name of Rockett embossed on a tag that was pinned to his chest, and Angela had to keep from smiling as she thought about him being launched into space from the pad over at the Cape.

"I run the narcotics unit," Rockett said to her. "Put in a couple of years on the street, maybe a little less if you're a fast learner, and I'll talk to you."

Eighteen months later she went to work for him. A year after that she bought her first race car and began dragging it at Orlando Speedway on Saturday nights.

The face was an illusion, she told herself, a figment of her imagination brought on by the lassitude she'd felt while listening to Justine Fallon's singsong voice in that slow-motion town. Eleven years had passed since she'd walked off the plane from Paris and heard the news, eleven years since she'd seen Bobby's tortured face for real, staring at her through the wire mesh of the visiting room at Riker's, eleven years, and like Roland Troy and his hip, not a day went by that she didn't feel the pain, not a day she didn't blame herself for what had happened. We're alike, she thought, Troy and I. Maybe that's why his rap about the Indians annoyed her. Maybe that's why she reacted so strongly to the way he dealt with Jason Badger. Beneath the insightful parable and the sudden brutality, she had sensed Troy's pain that she knew was much more than physical. It reminded her of her own because like hers, it was masked by an aura of control.

She climbed out of the Trans-Am and leaned her arms on the open door, wondering where the hell her dogs could be. Usually they'd hear her the moment she came through the gate at the highway and would be bounding beside her car all the way down the path. They better not be in the river, she thought. She had trained them long and hard to stay out of the water, fearing the attack of an alligator or the bite of a cotton-mouth. She put her thumb and forefinger to her lips and whistled, waited for a few seconds and whistled again. Then she looked up and saw both of them, hanging by their hind legs from the limb of a tree.

XI

"Personally, I think moving back to the house and going to work with McKenzie Rockett was the best thing in the world for you," Roland Troy's daughter Katherine said. "That's why I told Rockett where to find you. You aren't a maple syrup farmer, Daddy. You're a detective. And don't be angry at me for saying so but that's what Clara would have wanted you to do."

"I hit a guy today," Troy said. "To get him to talk."

"He probably deserved it," Katherine said.

"That's not what my new partner thought."

"She doesn't know you yet. She's probably got you confused with all those cops and football players who beat their wives. Have her give me a call and I'll set her straight. I'll tell her how I lived in the same house with you for eighteen years and never so much as got a tap on the butt. Not even the time I ruined a model you'd been working on for about a week. You remember that, Daddy? You sure were pissed, but you didn't hit me. It was a model of an Irish pub, a Chinese restaurant, and what? A tire store. That was it. You had all those little tires you found arranged out in front in a little rack you built, and little cars and trucks and everything. And Janie Maloney and I got to fooling with it and the whole thing tipped over."

"I remember," Troy said. "I'm sitting across the room from that very model as we speak."

"No shit," Katherine said. "What are you doing in there?"

"I was dusting," Troy said. "And airing the place out."

"At eleven o'clock at night?"

"The house was boarded up for a long time. Everything was musty. I couldn't sleep on account of the smell."

"I thought Halpatter and you aired the place out last week."

Sheridan Halpatter was a Seminole Indian who lived on a cypress-choked tributary of the Coacoochee River not far, by water, from Troy's house. Among other unusual enterprises, he hunted alligators for a living and was Roland Troy's oldest friend.

"We started on it," Troy said. "But then we got to smoking cigars and reminiscing and before I knew it he talked me into going fishing with him instead and we never finished."

While it was true that he and Halpatter had indeed interrupted their housework to go fishing, Roland Troy, as his daughter well knew, had slept like a well-fed dog in places far less hospitable than a musty house. The fact was, Troy had done everything he could think of to keep from going to sleep because he was convinced that on this night he would have the dream again about his murdered wife. After he got the remaining boards off the windows and ate some dinner he carefully scrubbed and polished the wooden floor in the large open area of his second-floor bedroom where he did his yoga exercises and practiced the prescribed karate moves known as kata. Then he vacuumed every rug in the house, cleaned out the fireplace in the living room, and finally set about dusting the collection of crime-scene models he had constructed years before and kept in a large workshop off the kitchen.

It was late when Troy finished vacuuming the dust off the dozen or so models he'd saved, but the work had made him nostalgic. He still didn't want to go upstairs to bed, so in spite of the hour he decided to telephone his daughter. She was now a marine biologist living in Woods Hole, Massachusetts, with her husband, a commercial diver and underwater photographer.

Troy had raised his daughter himself after his first wife abandoned them and went home to Norway when Katherine was two years old. From the time she was a little girl, talking to Katherine had provided Troy with solace, even when the two of them disagreed. He would never tell her he was upset, or sad, or depressed, but of course she always knew, and no matter how low he felt, no matter how gruesome his work, she could always make him laugh.

"Hey Daddy," she said now. "You hear about the old Zen master who goes up to a hot dog vendor and says make me one with everything?"

Troy smiled and took a sip from the mug of tea he was holding. "That's good," he said. "Make me one with everything. I like that."

"I thought you would," she said. "I heard it a couple of days ago and it reminded me of you. So how's the case look?"

"Like a spiral staircase leading down into a sewer," he said.

"That's kind of what Rockett said. He sounded worried, but that was before you came on board."

"He's under a lot of pressure. It looks like we're dealing with neo-Nazis. Furthermore, somebody knew all about the dead agent's work habits. They knew about his computer files. Rock's pretty sure someone on the inside is involved. He can feel the point of the knife against his spine."

"And what about you? Are you still having those dreams?"

Troy hesitated and took another sip of tea. The window of the workshop was open wide, and beneath the sound of the wind he thought he heard the rumble of a car approaching along the narrow dirt road that snaked through his woods.

"Daddy?" Katherine said.

"Yeah," Troy finally replied. "I still have 'em. I think I also have me some company. There's a car coming down the road. Lemme go see who it is. I'll call you again in a couple of days."

"Listen to me," Katherine said. "What happened to Clara was not your fault."

"So you've told me," Troy said. "Any number of times."

"And will continue to do so," his daughter replied. "Every fucking time you call me up. Like *you* always told me, you want to know what I really think or you want me to co-sign your bullshit?"

"I gotta go," he said.

"I love you, Daddy," she said. "Be careful."

"I love you too," Troy said. "Give Turner a hug when he comes up for air. And tell him to get a job on the surface. Or better yet, on dry land."

Troy hung up the phone and sat listening. The rumble of the engine had ceased and all he could hear now were the night sounds of the forest and the wind. He got up, turned off the light in the workshop, and walked into the kitchen where the holster containing his .45 hung from a peg beside the sink. He had just retrieved the gun and turned out the kitchen light as well when someone stepped on the metal sign covering the hole in his porch. The sign gave out a resounding crackle and whoever was there halted.

"One more step and you're dead," Troy said through the screen door.

"It's me, Roland," Angela Becker said.

Troy lay the gun on the kitchen table, turned the light back on, and unlatched the door. Angela came inside holding her shoes and stood somewhat unsteadily, blinking in the light. She was still wearing the stylish outfit she'd had on earlier in the day but her clothes now looked disheveled and her face was streaked with dirt. There was a long scratch across her forehead that was still bleeding slightly, no doubt where a branch had hit her as she walked through the woods.

"I got a fucking flat tire," she said. "Can I have a glass of water please?"

"Sure," Troy said. "Sit down and I'll get it for you."

Troy filled a large tumbler with ice water and while she drank it he soaked a dish towel with warm water at the sink and wrung it out.

"Here," he said, placing the towel against her forehead. "Hold it there while I get you something to clean out that cut."

"Somebody killed my dogs, Roland," she said. "Somebody came on my land and killed my dogs and hung them in a tree by their legs."

"Did you call Rockett?" he asked.

"No," she said softly. "I didn't call anybody."

In the fading light she had stared up in silence at the two animals hanging from the limb of the tree, feeling as though she were having one of those dreams in which she was trying to run from something but was unable to move. Then finally she did move, flinging herself back into her car and driving fast up the long rutted driveway to the highway, forcing herself not to look in the rearview mirror even though now in the darkness there was nothing for her to see, fishtailing onto the blacktop, not thinking at all about anything but putting as much distance between herself and the tree as possible.

She drove blindly for an hour, leaving the blacktop, working her way north along the graded dirt roads of the national forest, stopping finally when she was nearly out of gas at a small café with a couple of pumps out front. She climbed from the car and looked around numbly, not quite sure where she was. A cold wind blowing out of the northwest helped to clear her head, but by the time she'd filled the Trans-Am's tank she was chilled, so she pulled the car around to the side of the café, parked next to a doorless pickup truck with a bed full of logs, and went inside to get some coffee.

Two skinny men with long hair were sitting at the counter drinking beer from the bottle. They were both wearing cowboy boots and checked flannel shirts covered with dirt and wood chips. Aside from the woman behind the counter they were the only people there. Angela paid for her gas, got a mug of coffee from the woman and took it to a booth in the far corner of the café. She could feel the eyes of the woodcutters on her as she walked past but she ignored them.

She sipped the coffee and stared at a large bass mounted on the wall above her. The fish reminded her of her dogs and though she clenched her teeth an involuntary sob escaped her lips. She cursed silently to herself, looked back down at the mug and saw that her hands were shaking. She felt she should call someone, but who? Rockett? Her friend Cortez the rug man, who'd spent years chasing animal butchers through the swamp? Joshua Gibbs, the defense attorney she'd dated for two years and actually thought about marrying until she started living with him? She had bought the dogs from a man he defended right after she and Gibbs broke up. They were littermates that she'd raised from tiny puppies. She was thinking she'd be better off calling Patti, the woman who cut her hair, than that lying son of a bitch Gibbs, when one of the woodcutters loomed over her, the beer bottle still in his hand.

"Hey," he said. "Want some company?"

"What?" she asked, looking up at him. The man appeared blurred to her and she blinked several times to bring him into focus.

"I asked if you wanted some company."

"No," Angela told him, setting down her coffee mug and gripping the edge of the table with both hands. "Go away."

"You ain't very polite," the woodcutter said.

He sat down across from her, put his beer on the table and took a cigarette out of his shirt pocket jailbird style without removing the pack. Angela could see him fine now, and smell him as well. He smelled like the inside of Jason Badger's house. Maybe that was what suddenly brought everything clearly into focus. She reached into her purse on the seat beside her, pulled out her badge and flashed it.

"I'm a cop," she said. "There's a magnum where the badge came from. Get lost."

The woodcutter held his hands palms up and rose.

"That's cool," he said. "I don't want no trouble."

He motioned with his head to his buddy and the two of them slid out the door into the night. Angela waited to leave until the sound of their truck had died away. She was back on the forest road five miles from the café before she realized she hadn't called anyone and didn't really want to. She thought about the fish up on the wall of the café. That had been her, a fish with a hook in its mouth that had swum as far as it could until the line ran out. Then the asshole in the flannel shirt had come along and though he didn't know it had done her a favor. Now she was the fish and the fisherman too, reeling herself back in. She gunned the Trans-Am up to seventy-five. She didn't know it but the woodcutter had driven a roofing nail into her right rear tire. Fortunately for her the tire wouldn't go flat until she was two hundred yards from Roland Troy's house, since she didn't have a spare.

"I thought about calling someone," she said. "But then I decided to come here." She looked up at Troy, who was sitting on the kitchen counter across from her. "I drove around and thought about it for quite a while, but then I figured you and I were in this together and I'd come talk to you first. I thought you'd be the one who'd know why they did it. Hanging them like that, I mean, instead of just shooting them or something. And I was hoping . . ."

She paused, lay the towel that she'd been pressing to her forehead on the table and took a long drink of ice water.

"The dogs," she said. "I can't go back there and look at them again. Somebody has to investigate the scene. Somebody has to cut them down."

At first light, Troy set out in a canoe across his lake, slipping through an almost invisible passageway on the far side that connected the lake to a network of swampy inlets, dark, cypress-filled ponds, and streams thickly overhung with branches, all linked to the smoothly flowing waters of the Coacoochee River. Other than Troy, there were only two or three people left in the region who could navigate this watery maze. One of them was Sheridan Halpatter who lived beside a tributary of the Coacoochee. It was to Halpatter's house that Troy now paddled.

Angela Becker had taken a shower, eaten some of Troy's home-made vegetable soup, and dressed in an old sweat suit Troy gave her, had fallen asleep on his living room couch. She was still there, out cold, wrapped in an old comforter when Troy came downstairs shortly before dawn. He scribbled a note, which he pinned to the comforter, informing her he had called McKenzie Rockett and telling her to make herself at home, eat some breakfast, and wait there for him until he got back from her property.

Troy paddled swiftly and without wasted effort, deftly avoiding the cypress knees and underwater vines that threatened to ensnare his canoe. In less than twenty minutes he rounded a bend and Halpatter's dock came into view. Halpatter was sitting cross-legged near the end of the dock working on the tip of one of his alligator poles with a rasp. Of medium height, but powerfully built, Halpatter was one of the strongest and most agile men Troy had ever known. Even now, in his late forties, he could scale a tall oak tree in less than a minute, a feat made even more remarkable since he had not once in the last thirty-five years worn a pair of shoes and therefore did his climbing the way he did everything else, barefoot.

Halpatter's name was derived from the Seminole word *halpatah,* which means alligator. Halpatter took great pride in this name, regarding it as a legacy. Because of this he hunted the beasts in the ancient Indian manner—by ramming a long sharpened pole down their throats. Using this method, he dispatched them quicker and more efficiently than any man in Florida armed with a rifle or shotgun. His broad, copper-colored face broke into a wide grin when he saw Troy's canoe and he stood up, raising the alligator pole above his head in a greeting. His large misshapen feet, so callused they could repel the fangs of a water moccasin, curled over the end of the dock like a pair of horny clamps, and his waist-length black hair, now streaked with silver, shone in the sunlight filtering through the trees. The temperature was thirty-eight degrees but all Halpatter had on was a T-shirt and a pair of bib overalls cut off at the knees. Troy, who was wearing jeans, a hooded sweatshirt, and thermal socks under his desert boots, looked at his friend and shivered.

"I know how you get in situations like this, Roland, which is to say you probably haven't eaten a goddamn thing today so I brought breakfast," Halpatter said, handing a large paper bag to Troy as soon as he made fast to the dock. "The minute I mentioned to my wife that you were coming she made plans for a three-course sit-down meal but I told her we had to make tracks so she settled on homemade bran muffins and a thermos of hot chocolate for the road. Be sure to eat one of those muffins or she'll be extremely upset. She won't say a word to you, but I'll have to pay."

Halpatter tied his hair into a ponytail with a leather clip, swung himself lightly into the bow of the canoe, stowed his sharpened pole, and picked up a paddle. Spreading his arms wide, he took a deep breath of the morning air, turned in his seat, and smiled broadly at Troy again.

"Let's hit it," he said.

They backtracked for a way along the route Troy had just traversed, then took a shortcut across a small shallow pond that led them to Deets's Creek, the Coacoochee branch that bordered Angela Becker's land. The trip took thirty minutes during which time they paddled in silence, both so familiar with the swamp and with each other that no words were necessary.

Halpatter roped the canoe to the old wooden dock that was partially submerged in the water and stood ankle deep in the creek. He had Roland Troy's Mini-14 with its folding stock and thirty-round magazine slung over his shoulder and the bag of food in his hand. Oblivious to the cold water, he watched Troy climb onto the dry section of dock, take his .45 out of the small waterproof pack he was carrying, and snap the holster onto his belt. Few people knew it, but many years before, Troy arranged for Halpatter to be officially designated a special deputy assigned to the state attorney's office. He was therefore legally empowered to handle evidence, make an arrest, and carry a weapon. Sheridan Halpatter, however, was uncomfortable with firearms, ordinarily arming himself in the woods with one of the longbows he fashioned from a seasoned length of yew. He was deadly accurate with these bows at distances of more than a hundred yards, and though he went along with Troy's preference for a gun when he accompanied his friend on investigations, he continually voiced his distaste for them.

"People aren't like wild animals," Troy told him. "If there's a bunch of them and you shoot one the others might not run away."

"I've been doing this with you for twenty years, Roland," Halpatter answered. "I haven't had to shoot at anyone yet."

"Well if you get lost, a gun makes more noise than an arrow," Troy said. "I'd be more likely to find you."

They had carried on this way with one another since they were teenagers, Halpatter claiming Troy was a pretty decent tracker but he wasn't any Indian, Troy countering that Halpatter wasn't any Indian either since he couldn't ride a horse. In truth, even Sheridan Halpatter, was no match for Roland Troy in the woods. When he was only ten or eleven years old Troy would calmly go out at night in his canoe deep into the pitch black swamp, to places even Halpatter's father avoided, more at home there than most people were in their own neighborhoods. As a scout in Southeast Asia, Troy honed these skills to such a fine point that eventually it would feel to him as though his heart were beating with the same rhythm as the jungle. He could stand as motionless as a tree, unseen by enemy troops passing ten yards away, or walk into a mountain village, make a detailed map of the place, and leave without anyone realizing he'd been there.

"I don't understand how he does it," Halpatter once said to his father.

"That boy moves like oil," his father replied. "He disappears like smoke. Roland Troy is a mysterious person."

"You know," Halpatter said now, "even with little sleep you look much better than you did the other day."

"Yeah?" Troy said. "That's nice to hear. I sure as shit don't feel no better."

"Other folks might not notice the difference but there's a certain brightness to your eyes. And the angle of your Yankees hat has improved. I'm encouraged."

Troy took a cigar out of the pack, stuck it in his mouth, but didn't light it. "I think maybe you ought to leave our breakfast here," he said.

147

When they reached the end of the path through the woods they saw the dogs hanging from the branch of a live oak at the far side of the clearing thirty feet from Angela's trailer. Two turkey buzzards stood on the ground below them and a third sat beside them in the tree. Without saying a word, Halpatter fanned out from Troy, staying inside the treeline. Troy leaned against a cabbage palm and waited. In a few minutes the buzzards flew off and he heard a low whistle from high in the live oak, above the dogs. He looked up and saw Halpatter sitting comfortably on a thick limb, his back against the trunk, the Mini-14 resting easily across his thighs. Halpatter's view of the clearing was unobstructed.

From decades of martial arts training and meditation Roland Troy was able to slip at will into an acute state of heightened awareness. This served him well while working as an undercover operative in remote parts of the world, or investigating a murder as a homicide detective in Florida, when he would sometimes sit for hours at a crime scene, shutting out everything but his immediate surroundings, re-creating a mental image of what had happened. At times like this his concentration was so intense he believed he could actually sense the violence still hanging in the air.

Now, almost as though he were in a trance, he moved slowly across the clearing, pausing every few feet to study the ground. In half an hour he found a cigarette butt, a piece of wrapper from a Snickers bar, two nickels and a penny. He saw the tire tracks of Angela Becker's Trans-Am crisscrossing those of another smaller vehicle, several sets of footprints, and the impressions in the dirt made by Becker's dogs. He took notes in a small spiral notebook but touched nothing. Then, as he was about to signal for Halpatter to join him on the ground he saw the tranquilizing dart lying in a tuft of grass still glistening with early morning dew.

"One of the dogs either shook it loose or pulled it out with his teeth before he collapsed," Troy said when Halpatter was beside him. He jotted down the location of the dart and without touching it slipped it into a self-sealing sandwich bag and handed it to his friend.

"Get this to Peiser," Troy said. "Don't give it to anybody else in the lab."

Halpatter nodded and put the plastic bag in the pocket of his overalls.

"They must have taken the other dart with them," he said. "There's nothing sticking into either one of those animals."

"So they knocked 'em out and cut their throats," Troy said.

"And then removed their hearts."

Troy looked at his friend, pushed his cap back on his head and raised his eyebrows. "Removed their hearts, huh?" he said.

"Clean as a whistle," Halpatter said. "Whoever did it was an expert. The other thing is there's a piece of wire wrapped around their muzzles, which is the reason their mouths are closed."

"Odds are that's where we'll find their hearts," Troy said.

"Some sort of symbolism, no doubt," Halpatter said.

"The Incas used to do something like that to people they thought were possessed by demons. Hang 'em upside down, cut out the heart and offer it as appeasement to the gods."

"I assume you've seen it before."

"Years ago," Troy said. "In South America. Only it wasn't a couple of dogs. A Convair 440 full of the most advanced surveillance equipment known to man, traveling from La Paz to Buenos Aires, went down in the mountains on the border between Bolivia and Argentina, up around thirteen thousand feet. The plane was still sending out a steady radio signal so they assumed the guy was alive. They sent me, this other character from San Diego, and a chopper jockey from Chile in after him.

"We get there and we see it wasn't no accident; an explosive device had blown out the tail section. The plane was stripped; all that sophisticated surveillance stuff was gone. The pilot was hanging from a tree limb by his feet with his throat cut and his heart sewn into his mouth, same as these dogs. I'm pretty sure he wasn't the one who turned on the radio. Whoever did the job turned it on so we'd find that Convair and get their message. The Chilean got it loud and clear. He turned white as a ghost, crossed himself about six times and just about pissed his pants trying to get us to leave."

"What was the message?" Halpatter asked.

"The Convair pilot was a Jewish guy from Canada working for

Mossad. The feeling was that South American guerrillas, or banditos, or drug runners, either from Bolivia or Peru, were hired by some wealthy ex-Nazis to do the job. Nobody was ever caught. It was the ex-Nazis who were sending the message. The guerrillas just wanted money, and of course all that surveillance equipment."

"So the message was 'stay off our trail,' " Halpatter said. "And you think perhaps the same sort of people have sent it here."

"What I think is I better call the guys from the crime lab and get 'em out here before the sun starts beating on those dogs and them buzzards come back," Troy said, taking a telephone out of his pack. "And I think you and me better eat us a couple of those bran muffins so we don't have to deal with the wrath of your wife."

"I'm impressed, Roland," Halpatter said. "A cellular phone. You're becoming a man of the nineties."

"It ain't mine," Troy said. "It's Becker's. I took it out of her car so I wouldn't have to open the trailer."

"In case there are fingerprints on the doorknob," Halpatter said.

"To tell you the truth I wasn't really thinking about fingerprints," Troy said. "I was thinking about that doorknob being wired to a bomb."

They were on their way back to Halpatter's house, paddling in silence across a small pond covered with water lilies, when the phone in Troy's pack began to ring. The pack lay amidships, halfway between them.

"I imagine it's for you," Halpatter said without turning around.

Troy lay down his paddle, unzipped the pack and took out the phone. Halpatter raised his paddle from the water as well and the canoe began to drift idly among the flowers.

"Hello," said Troy.

"I assumed it was you who took my phone," Angela Becker said.

"I didn't want to touch the trailer," Troy told her as Halpatter pointed with his paddle off to the left of the bow. Ten yards away, Troy could see the head and long, serpentine neck of an anhinga, the snakebird, swimming with a tiny fish in its beak. Anhingas could hunt for up to half an hour in the water, but then, because their feathers lacked the oil of true aquatic birds, they had to spend long periods of time on shore, drying out. The notion of drifting on this hidden pond,

watching the snakebird while talking on the telephone, at first struck
Troy as beyond incongruous, but then he thought what the hell, they
have phones on Mt. Everest, they take 'em down the Amazon, why
not here?

"No problem," Angela said. "In fact I'm glad you have it with you.
I got a buddy coming over with a wheel and tire so I'll probably be
gone when you get back. I didn't want you to think I'd been abducted
or something."

"I thought you'd still be asleep," Troy told her.

"I probably would be," she said, "only the phone woke me up. It
was sitting right next to the couch. I wouldn't have answered it but I
was so far under I didn't know where the hell I was. Anyway, I got a
message for you, which is why I'm calling you now."

"A message," Troy repeated.

"Your daughter called. We had a very nice conversation once I
gained consciousness. She's a lovely person. I'm impressed."

"I'm delighted," Troy said. "Is that the message?"

"Gimme a fucking break, Roland," Angela said. "You think I'd call
you out there just to tell you that? The message is from your daughter.
She said it was very important. If I'd known you had my phone when
I was talking to her I would have given her the number, but obviously
I didn't know until I went out to my car. She said to tell you she was
fine and so was Turner so you're not to worry, but that she wants to
talk to you as soon as possible. She'll be in the lab all day. Do you
know the number or should I give it to you?"

"I know the number," Troy said. "Did you eat some breakfast?"

"I'm eating it now. That raisin bread you had in the refrigerator
is outstanding."

"I made it myself."

"I know. You told me last night, remember?"

"I forgot," he said. "It's been a busy morning."

"I appreciate this, Roland," she said. She didn't mention the dogs.

"Yeah," he said. "Well whatever it is you're doing today you be
careful. And give me a call later. I got this portable phone now so I'll
be easy to reach."

Troy hung up and looked at Halpatter who had turned around in
his seat to face him and was washing down the last bran muffin with

a cup of hot chocolate. The canoe had drifted to the edge of the pond and come to rest against the aerial roots of a red mangrove tree.

"That was Angela," Troy said. "Katherine called her. She has an important message for me. I have to phone her at the lab."

"I have to say this is a new experience for me," Halpatter said, swallowing. "Most interesting I might add. Detached from things but yet connected. Unlike you, I enjoy modern technology."

"You don't wear shoes. You hunt alligators with a stick. What the hell are you talking about?"

"Guns and leather footwear have been around for centuries," Halpatter said. "What I'm talking about is new technology. Angioplasty, airplanes that navigate without ground control, microbes that eat old tires. You know Motorola now makes a portable phone that weighs less than four ounces. You can stick it in your shirt pocket. My new laptop computer linking me to the information superhighway weighs less than *Webster's Encyclopedic Unabridged Dictionary*. I can browse through the Library of Congress from right here on the Coacoochee. And it isn't a stick, it's a pole fashioned from the trunk of a live oak that was estimated to be two hundred and seventy-five years old. *Old Ironsides* was made from the same kind of tree. According to some accounts the hull of that ship could repel grapeshot."

"*Old Ironsides* fought against French men of war in 1798," Troy said. "What's that got to do with modern technology?"

"I learned about it while surfing the Internet," Halpatter said. "I've been doing research on wood. Don't forget about your daughter."

Halpatter leaned back against the bow deck, folded his massive forearms across his chest and smiled contentedly. Troy lit the cigar he'd been holding between his teeth, pulled his cap down over his eyes and punched some numbers into the phone.

"You want modern technology?" he said, holding the phone in the air so Halpatter could hear it. "I'll show you modern technology."

"Green Mountain CDs," a woman's voice said.

"Yeah, I was wondering if you had the Joe Sample CD in stock called *Black and White*," Troy said into the phone, holding it away from him once more so Halpatter could hear the woman's response. "If you do I'd like to order a copy."

"Let me check," the woman said. "Please hold. . . . We sure do," she said cheerily a few seconds later. "Please press the pound key and your account number so we can verify the order and we'll get that out to you right away."

Troy pressed another series of numbers, held the phone in the air a third time and puffed on his cigar.

"Nobska Point Marine Laboratory," his daughter said.

"Katherine it's me," Troy said. "Hang on just one second."

"There's the information superhighway," he said to Halpatter, "and then there's the underground railroad."

"Hi, Daddy," Katherine said when he got back on the phone. "Boy, we have a good connection. Like you're right next door. Are you at work?"

"I'm sitting in a canoe watching your godfather digest his breakfast and learning about modern technology," Troy said.

"What fun," said Katherine. "Listen, some guy called the house at ten minutes after six this morning. He sounded like a total redneck only he was far from dumb. He said he had a message for you. I was still half asleep. I think I said something to him on the order of, 'Why don't you call him yourself?' He just laughed, but in a way that gave me the distinct feeling he was someone who had his shit together in a big way. You know what I mean? So then he says, 'I think maybe this method might be smarter,' and by then I was awake enough to realize he didn't want to take a chance that your phone might be tapped. So I say, 'What's the message?' and he says to tell you if you ran up against a brick wall to remember you could go over it or you could go through it. He said you'd know what he meant."

"Bassai," Troy said under his breath.

"That's what I figured," Katherine said. "You know, I took the vase he gave me and Turner for a wedding present out of the bank vault and put it on the dining room table where it catches the morning light off the water. It really is incredibly beautiful."

"Be careful. That vase is worth more than your house."

"The guy who called said something else I think you'll find inter-esting. He asked me if I ever did research around any of the coral reefs in Florida. I said not since I was in graduate school, and then he said he never realized how dangerous those reefs could be until he heard about a ship that ran aground on one in a storm and sank. He said the ship went down with a whole load of horses."

"A load of horses," Troy said. "That is pretty interesting. Well thanks, baby. I really appreciate your calling right away."

"My pleasure," Katherine replied. "Can I say hi to Sheridan?"

"Sure can," her father told her chuckling to himself. She still hadn't said a word about talking to Angela Becker, no doubt trying to be discreet. He handed the phone to Halpatter, sat back and puffed on his cigar while they chatted. The conversation could go on for quite some time. When Katherine was young Halpatter had watched over his daughter like a second father whenever Troy had been called away from home on an assignment. Now that Clara was dead, the two of them were the only people in the world he trusted completely.

Troy looked out over the pond. The anhinga swam in slow circles among the lily pads, ducking under the water, popping up shortly fifteen or twenty yards away. Troy tried several times to guess where the bird would surface next but he was consistently wrong. The same as Bassai, he thought, vanishing from his life for years at a time but always there like a buried memory, reappearing suddenly from some unexpected location that might be anywhere on earth.

XII

It was seven in the morning and a cold March wind whipping off the Gulf of Mexico blew sand across the runway that ran almost the entire length of Isla de los Caballos, the Island of the Horses. The old pilot, a thin, grizzled man in his sixties known as Brownie, climbed from a Cessna 180 he had just landed. He turned up the collar of his leather jacket and tethered the plane in front of a semicylindrical steel hangar. Carrying an old canvas pouch, he walked quickly along a path bordered by sea grass and Australian pine. After two hundred yards the path ended in front of a large, two-story wooden dwelling built up on posts. A Bell Jet Ranger helicopter sat on a concrete pad next to the house. A Chevy Blazer and a four-wheel drive Toyota pickup were parked underneath, and in back was an enormous swimming pool flanked by a guest cottage. The only other structures on the island were a shed containing the primary generator and a backup, a boathouse on the opposite shore from the landing strip, and three good-sized cabins, post-mounted like the main house, and located down another path behind the guest cottage. A tall, muscular black man wearing a nylon windbreaker and a watch cap and holding an automatic rifle stood on the widow's walk above the second story of the house. He nodded when he saw Brownie but said nothing.

Brownie climbed the exposed wooden staircase to the first story and opened the door to the kitchen. He removed copies of the *New York Times* and the *Wall Street Journal* from the canvas pouch and lay them on the kitchen table. A beautiful Eurasian woman in her thirties dressed in jeans and a T-shirt stood at the stove cooking a vegetable and fish omelet. She turned and smiled at Brownie. A steady rhythmic pounding, as though someone were driving stakes with a padded mallet, came from another part of the house.

155

"He's finished his kata and is practicing *makiwara*," she said. "I think he's nearly done. How was your flight?"

"No sweat," he said. Long ago he had been an Air Commando pilot, flying out of a base hidden in the mountains of Thailand, providing cover for the secret war in Laos. After that he'd worked for a time as a lift-off operator, rescuing operatives from remote outposts all over the world. Compared to the conditions he'd faced back then a little buffeting from a stiff breeze was hardly worth talking about.

Brownie crossed the kitchen and walked down a hallway. At the far end he opened another door and entered a large room with a polished hardwood floor and a wall covered with mirrors. On the wall opposite the mirrored one were two crossed swords above an image of a tiger on its hind legs. Below the tiger was the Chinese character signifying both danger and opportunity. Three chest-high rectangular wooden posts, called *makiwara,* were mounted securely in the floor near this wall. They were four inches by four inches at the base and tapered to a thickness of half an inch at the top. This thin top section was wrapped with rice rope.

A lean, powerfully built Oriental, about five foot six or seven, with thick silvery hair, stood before one of these posts, his hard, angular face an impassive mask. Though he was past sixty, he had the body of an athlete thirty years younger. He wore a traditional white karate *gi* tied with a frayed and faded black belt. The room was unheated and the windows were open but still the floor at his feet was slick with perspiration.

The man stood with his back perpendicular to the floor. His left leg, bent at the knee, was in front of his right leg which was straight. His right arm was bent as well, the fist clenched and tucked tightly under his armpit, while his clenched left fist hung poised above his left thigh. With a fluid motion, so quick it appeared but a blur, his hips twisted slightly and his left arm drew back. At the same instant his right fist slammed squarely against the *makiwara*, the first two knuckles, covered by layers of thick callous, striking the rice rope with a loud thump. Again and again—twenty times in all—the man's right fist struck the post, each blow accompanied by a low growl. Then the man shifted his stance, placing his right leg forward, and repeated the exercise with his left fist.

When he was finished he stood for a moment with his arms at his sides. The callus on one of the striking knuckles of his left hand had split and a trickle of blood ran down his finger. It was impossible to tell whether he felt any pain by looking at his face. The man took several deep breaths and bowed slightly, as though he were saluting the post he had been striking. Then he pivoted and faced Brownie, who had been his pilot and confidant for more than twenty-five years.

"I assume my message was delivered," the man said.

"At ten after six, Bassai," Brownie replied. "From a phone booth in Fort Myers."

"Wait for me in the living room," the man called Bassai said. He walked to the far corner of the room, opened a sliding door that looked to be part of the wall, and disappeared up a narrow stairway to the top floor.

Bassai, a Japanese word meaning "to breach fortifications," was the name of a most difficult and advanced kata in the style of karate in which Roland Troy had been trained. It was also the nickname of Chotoku Nakama, a master in the same karate style. Nakama was so fast and so adept with the long wooden staff, known as a *bo,* that he once crossed a room and killed a man with it who had threatened him with a gun. Brilliant, ruthless, and willing to act on his instincts without hesitation, Nakama had risen from a childhood of abject poverty on the streets of Foochow, China, to become first a karate master in Okinawa and then a feared warlord with his own private army operating from a stronghold in the mountains of Burma. Not content to limit his interests to Southeast Asia he had branched out, extending his sphere of influence to the West until his power and wealth had become inestimable. His holdings, all carefully camouflaged, included a fleet of freighters, banks in Europe, the United States and Latin America, and a communications company that controlled numerous radio stations and newspapers. In addition, Nakama owned real estate on every continent and more than a dozen homes. Throughout his life, Nakama remained elusive and completely unpredictable, an international vagabond without roots, drifting from one place to another according to his whim. Allied to no nation, he lived completely by his own rules outside any system of law, yet in more than sixty years no government had been able to lay a hand on him.

The friend who betrayed Roland Troy in the Mekong Delta and led him into an ambush had been attempting to steal a fortune in drugs belonging to Chotoku Nakama. Troy had been seriously wounded in the ambush and would certainly have been left to die had not one of Nakama's men noticed the tattoo on his arm identifying Troy as a member of Prancing Tiger, the ancient, secretive martial arts society to which Nakama also belonged. Because of this Troy was flown to Nakama's sprawling fortress in the mountains of Burma not far from the Chinese border where he was nursed back to health. During Troy's convalescence he and Nakama spent much time together and the Asian came to admire the young American for his integrity and sense of honor. He also had great respect for Troy as a warrior, a man who embodied the characteristics of a true Prancing Tiger.

Nakama at first considered making Roland Troy a part of his inner circle, a knight in his kingdom, but recognizing Troy as a true romantic—a man who would spend his life in pursuit of justice—he chose to send Troy on his way, vowing instead to watch over him from afar. Nakama's largess was, however, double-edged, since he was also an arch manipulator, a master game player, a connoisseur of human frailty who enjoyed nothing better than throwing an assemblage of disparate characters together just to see what would happen. Though less susceptible than a number of others who found themselves within Nakama's sphere of influence, Roland Troy had still been made aware on more than one occasion of the warlord's ubiquitous control.

"I see our visitor has arisen," Nakama said to Brownie. "No doubt he's hungry."

The two of them were standing in the living room that overlooked the pool and past it, the gulf. A swarthy man, grossly overweight, dressed in baggy denim trousers with an elastic waist and a brightly striped rugby shirt, emerged from the guest cottage and walked along the pool deck toward the main house. Nakama, wearing a white dress shirt open at the neck, and perfectly creased khaki slacks, watched him intently.

"No doubt he's always hungry," Nakama said, turning from the window and picking up the business section of the *Times*. He said nothing more until the man had joined them but Brownie could sense his disdain. Lack of self-control was a trait Nakama despised.

"Ah, Mr. Sharifi, so nice to meet you," he said, offering his hand as the fat man entered the room. "You're just in time for breakfast. Come, sit down at the table with Brownie and me. I believe an excellent omelet is on the way."

"Please," the fat man said gesturing widely with his arms as he moved into the dining alcove and seated himself at the long teakwood table. "Call me Nick."

"Nick," Nakama said. "An interesting name for someone from your part of the world. Iran, isn't it?"

"Persia. I prefer to call my homeland Persia. My actual name is something difficult for Westerners to pronounce. Nick is my nickname."

Sharifi laughed loudly and Nakama joined him, though at substantially less volume.

"Nick it will be then," Nakama said, sitting across from him. "I trust you slept well, Nick."

"Quite well," Sharifi replied. "Quite well indeed." He spoke with a strong Middle Eastern accent blended with the inflections of an English boarding school. "The air blowing off the water was very fresh. Although to be perfectly honest I am a bit disoriented. You are a difficult man to locate, Mr. Nakama, if you don't mind my saying so. Extremely difficult. First I was told you were in the south of France, then in the jungles of Central America, and finally on a remote island in the Bahamas. But of course we are not in the Bahamas, are we? Don't misunderstand me. It is a magnificent place all the same, this island. A lovely place. Isla de los Caballos. I have never heard of it before."

"Do you know how it got its name?" Nakama asked.

"I do not," Sharifi replied, wondering if he had said too much.

"In 1801, a pirate named Juan Sanchez captured a ship crossing the gulf from Mexico on its way to Spain. Not satisfied with just the gold and jewels on board he took a number of horses with him as well. He thought they would make a fine diversion for his men here on this island that was his hideout. It was an excellent hideout. With the exception of one narrow opening, the unmarked channel through which you passed last evening, it is completely surrounded by a coral reef. By sea, it is therefore nearly invulnerable. In any case, a violent storm came up and the ship of Juan Sanchez, overloaded because of the horses, became unmanageable. It went aground on the reef and sank. Juan Sanchez and all of his men drowned, but several of the horses made it to shore, hence the name, Isla de los Caballos.

"The horses survived, by the way. There is a freshwater spring in the middle of the island and of course there was plenty of vegetation for them to eat. There were horses here a hundred years later when the island was purchased by the owner of a steel company from Pittsburgh. He was an expert yachtsman and so had no trouble with the narrow channel. Others, from the time Florida was acquired from Spain until the present, have not been so lucky."

"How long have you owned it?" Sharifi asked.

"Who said that I owned it?" Nakama replied with a smile.

The woman who had been in the kitchen preparing the food brought in a large silver platter brimming with omelet and another heaped with toast and English muffins. When she returned with a pot of coffee and a pitcher of orange juice she was accompanied by the muscular black man who had been standing guard on the roof. The black man, a former navy seal who had brought Nick Sharifi to the island on one of Nakama's boats, went into the living room, sat down in a leather easy chair and began to read the *Wall Street Journal*.

"Madeleine, will you join us?" Nakama asked.

"I've been picking at things in the kitchen all morning," the woman said. "I'm full."

"What about you, Tim?"

"No thanks," the black man said. "I ate earlier too."

"Well in that case it's just the three of us. Dig in gentlemen."

Sharifi had washed down several English muffins slathered with butter and strawberry jam with nearly a quart of orange juice and was halfway through his second plate of eggs when Nakama lay the piece of dry whole wheat toast he'd been eating on his plate, sat back in his chair and smiled broadly.

"So, Nick," he said. "Let's talk about why you've come to the island of the horses, the island that owes its name at least indirectly, to a pirate's foolishness and greed."

Sharifi was chewing a mouthful of eggs and had his fork poised above his plate for more. He swallowed, took a drink of juice, and glanced first at Brownie and then at the black man in the living room.

"It's all right," Nakama said. "You can speak freely. Tim and Brownie have been associates of mine for a long time. They know all about Novac DuCharme. He is the reason you contacted me, am I right?"

Sharifi lay down his fork and wiped his mouth vigorously with his napkin. He cleared his throat and took another drink, this time of water.

"You are a remarkable man, Mr. Nakama," he finally blurted out. "A remarkable man indeed. Yes, Novac DuCharme is the reason. To come right to the point, I am afraid to say that he has gone off the deep end. This . . . this uh . . . this mission, I suppose you would call it, that he is on. Ranting and raving about the Jews and the Blacks . . ."

He glanced again into the living room but Tim, the ex–navy seal, continued to read the paper without any indication that he was listening. Nakama watched his portly visitor closely but said nothing. There was some sort of food stain on the white collar of the fat man's rugby shirt and a small piece of onion or pepper from the omelet was stuck to his chin.

"I always had my suspicions about him," Sharifi went on. "I have my sources too you know, like you, Mr. Nakama. He has a past, Novac DuCharme. We all do, don't we? But now his has become an obsession. It appears that he is consumed by a need to personally alter the course of human history. To save his version of civilization. He believes in reincarnation, you know. He practices all manner of occult rituals. 'Demon spirits,' he calls the Jews. He wants to get rid of them all. 'Finish the job,' he says. The blacks aren't human to him at all. And then there is that maniac who runs his television studio. That fellow who formerly ran a circus. The one who keeps a stuffed gorilla on his grounds . . . a most unstable person . . . most unstable—"

"This is all very interesting," Nakama said. "But tell me, Nick, what does it have to do with me?"

"I'm coming to that, Mr. Nakama," Sharifi said.

For the third time Sharifi gazed off into the living room at Tim, who had finished with the *Journal* and was reading the op-ed page of the *Times*. He looked for an instant at Brownie, sitting at the far end of the table, who appeared to be sleeping with his eyes open. Then he sighed with resignation and continued.

"You see," he said, "there is a ship loaded with arms, with some of the most desirable and sensitive armaments available in the world. Very sensitive. It is scheduled to arrive from a port in the Middle East at a destination in the Gulf of Mexico very soon. In a matter of days actually. Ordinarily I would have given you much more notice but as I said you are a most difficult man to find. In any event, this ship is disguised as a tanker. In fact it is a tanker. But rest assured there is a portion of its cargo that is the furthest thing from crude. Novac DuCharme has agreed to pay thirty million dollars for the nonpetroleum contents of this ship. But as I said, in my opinion, he has, if you will excuse a bad pun, gone overboard."

"And so you want to sell this cargo to me," Nakama said. "Instead of consummating the deal with Novac DuCharme."

"That was part of my proposal, yes," Sharifi replied. "But I was thinking of an arrangement that was more of an alliance than a simple transaction."

"An alliance," said Nakama. "Indeed? So you want to sell me this cargo at a discount, but in order for me to take advantage of this discount you would like me to make Novac DuCharme disappear. Is that the sort of alliance you had in mind?"

"That is uh . . . that is more or less correct," Sharifi said. "A ten million dollar discount."

"Why come to me with this plan, Nick," Nakama asked. "Why don't you do it yourself and save the ten million?"

"I am an arms dealer," Sharifi replied. "A broker. A simple businessman who brings together a buyer and a seller. Novac Du-Charme . . . Novac DuCharme is very dangerous. In a word, he is a madman. He is bad for business. Mine and everyone else's. But he is a well-connected madman. He has some very important friends in certain places within the American government. I am not sure precisely what his usefulness is to them but he is well protected."

"This cargo Novac DuCharme intends to purchase," Nakama said, "where is it from?"

"Algiers," Sharifi answered.

PROOF POSITIVE

"You misunderstand me," said Nakama, smiling benevolently at his guest. "I wasn't asking you where the ship was coming from, I was asking about the origin of the cargo. The portion of the cargo that is not, as you phrased it, crude. Whose weapons are you selling, Nick?"

Sharifi took another drink of water and belched quietly into his napkin. He sighed again, closed his eyes and squeezed the bridge of his nose between his thumb and forefinger, feeling part of his breakfast rise in his throat. He had come to see Nakama with what he assumed would be an irresistible proposition—an enormous sum of money for a simple job. The man who put Sharifi in touch with Nakama had no idea how vast an empire the reclusive Asian controlled. He had led Sharifi to believe that the warlord whom he described as a yellow-skinned savage was willing to do anything for a price. Sharifi had done business with plenty of desperadoes, but all of them were either eager to sell weapons or anxious to buy them. Nick Sharifi, a man who loved making deals, worked the middle and kept everyone happy. He had approached Nakama certain his offer would provide him with considerable leverage and convinced the deal was already done. Instead, he felt he'd been quietly boxed into a corner, finessed into a totally defensive position. Worse still, he felt completely intimidated.

It began when Nakama's men, the black one who was paging through the newspaper as though he were in the reading room of a library, along with two tough-looking Orientals armed with Uzis, brought him from the west coast of Florida to the island on Nakama's fifty-foot Scarab. Traveling at high speed over rough water left Sharifi slightly ill. When they arrived at Isla de los Caballos Nakama was not at the dock to greet him. Sharifi was shown to the guest house and told to relax. Someone would call him for dinner at which time he and Nakama would talk. He lay down on a comfortable king-size bed and immediately fell asleep.

When the phone woke him an hour later he was completely disoriented, and at first had no idea where he was. The voice on the other end of the line was that of a woman who identified herself as Madeleine, Nakama's personal assistant. She informed him that regrettably the private meal he had been promised with Nakama had been postponed. Something urgent requiring Nakama's immediate attention had come up, she said. Nakama was nowhere to be seen when Madeleine served dinner to him and a tall, dour man with thick glasses. Madeleine told Sharifi he was Nakama's director of communications. While Sharifi stuffed himself with strips of sirloin steak smothered in onions, fried shrimp, and scalloped potatoes, followed by the richest chocolate cake he had ever tasted, the tall man, who ate almost nothing, immersed himself in a technical manual of some sort, answering Sharifi's attempts at conversation with a series of grunts.

After dinner, Sharifi went back to the guest house and immediately fell into a deep sleep, but twice during the night and again in the very early morning he was awakened by a plane taking off and landing. Why, he wondered, had he not been flown to the island? Although the black man running the Scarab had certainly been friendly, inviting Sharifi to join him in the cockpit, perhaps the pounding at sea had been intentional, as had the incredibly rich food and the hours of isolation.

"The weapons," Nakama repeated. "The weapons that are already on the high seas in the tanker that is more than a tanker. Where do they come from?"

"They come from Russia," Sharifi said with resignation.

"Ah yes," Nakama said. "And who owns the ship?"

"Rafiq Said. It was in fact Said who suggested I speak to you. He mentioned that he had done business with you in the past. He thought you would find this situation . . . quite desirable."

"Did he?" Nakama said. "And by desirable was this Rafiq Said referring to my need for a boatload of sophisticated weapons or my inclination to kill people for money?"

"No no, not you," Sharifi said, raising his hands as though he were trying to surrender. "He . . . we . . . no one was suggesting that you *personally* were going to kill anyone. Not at all, Mr. Nakama. It . . . Rafiq Said implied that this uh . . . this disappearance might be something you could arrange."

"Is that so?" Nakama chuckled. "I must say I am having difficulty placing your friend Mr. Said. Tell me, what does he look like?"

Sharifi hesitated for a split second and blinked two or three times.

"What does he look like?" he repeated. "What does he look like? He's a gray-haired man, like yourself, and of medium height and build I'd say. Thick eyebrows. A thick mustache. Dark piercing eyes. Dresses in Western clothes. Very well dressed, actually. Favors silk suits, as a general rule."

Nakama shook his head slowly and smiled sympathetically at Sharifi.

"Well," he said, "the reason I ask is that I'm afraid I can't recall ever doing business with this man who implies things. No, I don't remember him at all. But be that as it may, your Mr. Said, whoever he is, has misled you because I really have no use for a boatload of arms, even those of the most sensitive kind. You see, Nick, like you I am a businessman. My interest is in staying out of wars, not starting them. As for Novac DuCharme, during the course of my life I have seen men like him come and I have seen them go. They are like a fire in the forest. They cause much devastation but eventually they burn themselves out. He is your problem, I am afraid, not mine. Making people disappear is not my line of work."

"So I have made this trip for nothing," Sharifi blurted out.

"Apparently so," Nakama said. He was still smiling but his eyes, riveted on Sharifi, sent a rivulet of cold sweat down the fat man's chest.

"I was told . . ." Sharifi began, but his voice trailed off.

"Tim is going to the mainland for some supplies," Nakama went on. "He'll take you back to your hotel. By the way, how did you like riding in that boat? Quite exciting, I'll bet. It belonged to a famous politician I used to know. A United States senator no less. A man who unfortunately never learned how to control himself. He could control that boat, however, which as I'm sure you noticed is not all that easy. I'm sorry to be so abrupt but I have much work to do."

"I understand," Sharifi said. "But could I ask you one last question, Mr. Nakama?"

"Yes, you can ask me one question," said Nakama.

"How did you know beforehand that the purpose of my visit was to discuss Novac DuCharme?"

Nakama lifted the cloth napkin from his lap and busied himself for half a minute carefully folding it and placing it next to his plate. When he looked up at Sharifi he was no longer smiling.

"Twenty-five hundred years ago Sun Tzu wrote that an army without secret agents is exactly like a man without eyes or ears," he said.

"That is as true today as it was then. You have spent many years buying and selling weapons, Sharifi-san. In the old days, as I understand it, you also worked for the Iranian secret police, in the middle of things, between one side and the other. Apparently, though, you have never been to war."

Nakama's hands, protruding from the starched white cuffs of his shirt like two thick claws rested palms down on the table, the oversized knuckles of both index and middle fingers as menacing as the barrel of a gun. He continued to look directly at Sharifi who tried vainly to return his gaze. After several seconds of silence, Nakama bowed slightly, and seeing this, the black man rose from his chair in the living room and came toward them.

"Time for another boat ride, Mr. Sharifi," he said. "Let's go gather up your things."

"So now Rafiq Said owns tankers," Brownie said when Sharifi was gone. "Last time I saw him he was living in Cyprus selling women and hashish. He sure has moved up in the world."

"Rafiq Said remains what he always was," Nakama said. "A slippery eel. He works for the widow of an ex-Nazi named Jergen Muller who lived for nearly half a century in Algiers under the assumed name of Marcel Bergeron. Two years ago Muller had a heart attack while swimming and drowned in the Mediterranean Sea near his home. He owned a fleet of tankers flying flags of convenience, which the widow inherited. Perhaps she did not wish to draw attention to herself, or perhaps she thought that in the world of petroleum exporting a woman would not be taken seriously. Whatever the case, she pretended to sell her husband's company to Rafiq Said who was one of his assistants. Said does not own these tankers. She does. Other than some silk suits, some gold jewelry, a white Mercedes, and a quick tongue, Rafiq Said owns nothing."

"So that's where DuCharme comes in," Brownie said. "He was connected to this ex-Nazi, Muller."

"To both Muller and his wife," Nakama said. "DuCharme had an interest in Muller's shipping operation, just as he had an interest in many other operations run by ex-Nazis in various parts of the world. He also took an interest in his associates' wives.

"Sharifi knows the Russians, Said knows Sharifi, the widow knows DuCharme. DuCharme wants weapons, the Russians want cash, Sharifi makes the deal," Brownie said. "Only then Sharifi meets DuCharme and gets nervous so Said tells him about you. You think the wife knows about this?"

"That I do not know," Nakama said. "But what I do know is that at the moment our recent guest, Mr. Sharifi, owes thirty million dollars minus his commission to some very dangerous Russians. Imagine what would happen if all the sophisticated weapons on board the widow's tanker vanished along with Mr. Sharifi. These Russians would still want to be paid for their goods. That could result in a most intriguing situation, don't you think?"

Brownie sat back in his chair, stretched his arms over his head and let out a long breath. He still had on the old leather flight jacket and when he stretched, the sleeves rode up his arms revealing a gold-banded Rolex GMT Master worn on his left wrist since the old days in Laos. The watch and a battered pair of cobra-skin cowboy boots were the only signs of flamboyance he revealed. He dropped his arms, looked quizzically at Nakama and scratched his head, but said nothing.

There had been several women in Brownie's life but he never married, devoting himself completely first to his passion for airplanes, and then to Chotoku Nakama. He met the warlord in a mountain village in Thailand many years earlier when a friend introduced them and told him Nakama was in need of immediate transportation to Rangoon. At the time, a monsoon was raging but Brownie never flinched. Nor did he ask anything about the nature of the trip. Nakama, a consummate judge of human nature, recognized at once that he had found the perfect addition to his private army—a man who wanted only a plane to fly and someone to tell him when and where to fly it. Over the years Nakama came to trust Brownie as much as he would ever trust anyone, often confiding in his pilot, occasionally even asking him for advice.

"You're wondering why I sent you flying off to make a telephone call to Roland Troy," Nakama said. "You're wondering what Sharifi's visit had to do with him. Come upstairs to the library with me. There's something there I want to show you."

PHILIP SINGERMAN

Brownie followed Nakama up a spiral staircase at the end of the living room. At the head of the stairs Nakama entered a code into a security panel and a steel-clad door slid open admitting them into a large thickly carpeted room with a wall of windows looking out over the gulf. Shelves brimming with books lined the two walls perpendicular to the windows, but it was to the wall on the opposite side of the room that Nakama led his old companion. A half-dozen television screens were mounted in this wall, and below them, resting on a long shelf and stacked in open cabinets, were three computers, a digital color scanner, two printers, a copy machine, and a large assortment of radio communications equipment. The tall, bespectacled man who kept Nakama electronically linked to his empire and in touch with the rest of the world was crammed underneath the shelf fiddling with some wires. He gave a little wave, extracted himself, and without saying a word left the room by the same sliding steel door. Nakama sat down at one of the computers, turned it on, and waited for the machine to boot up.

"In a nutshell, Roland Troy was brought back to Florida because a federal agent working with a special hate crime task force was murdered," he said. "The head of this special unit is a black man under great political pressure to make the task force a success. He is an old friend of Roland's. An old partner in fact. He prevailed upon Roland to lend his help."

Nakama turned back to the computer and busied himself for a minute at the keyboard. He watched intently as a series of color photographs began scrolling slowly up the screen, continuing to talk to Brownie at the same time.

"You may recall our friend Sharifi-san mentioned that Novac DuCharme put a former circus owner in charge of his television studio located in Aurora," he said. "I believe Sharifi referred to the man as 'a maniac.' Inasmuch as I too am in the communications business I have, as you know, kept tabs on this operation stuck up there in the middle of nowhere."

"With a runway long enough to land a seven-forty-seven on it," Brownie said.

"Indeed," said Nakama, turning in his chair and smiling. "Your kind of place, Brownie. But now, take a look at this picture."

Nakama pressed a key and the scrolling stopped. On the screen was an image of a man and woman sitting on a couch. The woman was quite pretty, though just a trifle plump. She had very long hair that hung down over her shoulders, partially obscuring her exposed breasts. The man, wearing only a pair of brief undershorts, had his head turned toward the woman and a hand resting on her belly. He had dark hair and was very well built.

"The woman's name is Dana Stiefel," Nakama said. "She is the young wife of Herbert Stiefel."

"The man who runs DuCharme's television studio," Brownie said. "She ain't bad lookin', Bassai. A little chubby but as my mother used to say, at least you wouldn't have to shake the sheets to find her."

"No, I don't suppose you would," Nakama said. "Mrs. Stiefel's companion, who seems to be having no trouble at all finding her, is Reed Calloway, a federal agent assigned to the central Florida office of the FBI. Now look at this next picture."

A photograph of two men standing on a narrow concrete path bordered by palm trees appeared on the screen. One of them was the same federal agent, now wearing slacks and a short-sleeve knit shirt. The other was a large, brutal-looking man with a shaved head dressed in a nylon jogging suit.

"I'm sure you recognize Agent Calloway," Nakama said. "Even with his clothes on. The other man is Herbert Stiefel. Given the smiles on their faces I doubt they are discussing Agent Calloway's clandestine visits to Stiefel's wife."

"I'll be a son of a bitch," Brownie said. "You want me to go see Roland Troy? Maybe bring him back here?"

"No," Nakama said. "There is no need to bring him here. I only wanted to let him know where I was in case he decides that he wants to talk to me. However, it might not hurt to get copies of these photographs to Roland-san, don't you think?"

"All these years you been keepin' track of that boy, Bassai, ever since the day he was well enough to leave your villa in Burma and I flew him down to Thailand, and you've never done that before," Brownie said. "You've never reached out to him first. You always waited for him to come to you. Something's changed."

"We have all changed," Nakama said. "You, I, Roland-san. All have changed. He has lost the only woman he ever loved. He was unable to find the people who killed her, to solve the one crime above all others he wanted to solve. I haven't seen him since all that happened but he is not the same man he was before. There is no way he could be."

"Do you know who killed his wife?"

"No. If I did I would already have told him. In that case I would have made an exception and gone to see him."

"And in this case? The case of the murdered FBI agent?"

"A friend of ours in Orlando has looked into that," Nakama said. "The agent's name was Erland. He had been investigating the unsolved murder two years ago of a psychic who lived in Velvet, the village filled with psychics that is not very far, you may remember, from Aurora."

"You think there's a connection between the psychic's murder and the guy who runs the television studio?"

"The information given to me was that the murdered psychic was a Jew who survived a Nazi death camp," Nakama said. "Having seen what the former circus owner Stiefel produces at this television studio I would not be surprised. But then, Roland Troy is an excellent detective. In fact, I have never come across one who is better. If there is a connection I am sure he will find out."

"Then why would he need your help?"

"Ah, Brownie-san," Nakama said, "by this time you should know that finding out who did something and making them pay for it is not the same thing, especially when those in power who are supposed to make them pay have no intention of doing so. No intention at all."

XIII

Twice in his life Oliver Reavis didn't die because he went to get a gun. The first time was in Vietnam when his M-16 jammed and he crawled out of his hole to get another one off the new guy in a hole nearby who got his ass shot off before anyone even learned his name. He was in there with the dead new guy when a mortar round landed in his hole right where he'd been crouched like it had his name and address written on it. A load of dirt had landed on him but that was it.

The second time was half an hour after he got the call from Angela Becker about her flat tire. He was sitting in the kitchen of his house next door to the big old citrus-packing house that was now his garage drinking coffee and eating a chocolate-covered doughnut wondering whether to start the day on the Cutlass with the blown head gasket or the Dodge Diplomat with a seized AC compressor when she called. He scrounged around out in back of the garage until he finally found a wheel from an old Camaro that would fit. The tire on the wheel had seen better days but it held air, so it would do. As he was loading the wheel into his truck it occurred to Reavis that all things considered maybe he should bring a gun.

Since the night he drove off and left the skinny punk standing over Ernie Viens's dead body in the middle of the road he had kept his movement to a minimum and watched his back, but nothing out of the ordinary had happened. No one had shown up at the house or the garage to ask him questions, nor had he seen anybody following him when he looked in his rearview mirror. Still, he had an intuitive sense that being witness to the shooting of Ernie Viens was the beginning of something, not the end. Now that he was about to venture afield, a piece seemed like a wise idea.

Reavis closed the tailgate of the truck and walked back inside the garage. He unlocked the bottom drawer of the old wooden desk in the office, took out the loaded .357 Smith & Wesson he kept there, and stuck it in the side pocket of his coveralls. Smooth Lee, one of the two old men who sat outside his garage all day in rusty metal lawn chairs, commenting, yelled something to him but he couldn't hear what Smooth was saying.

Probably sayin' somethin' 'bout the woman, Reavis thought. Frankie Polite, the other old dude, probably said, "The girl done gone and got herself a flat tire and he's fixin' to bring her a wheel on account she don't mess with no spare." Actually Smooth Lee wasn't yelling about Angela Becker at all. He was yelling about Oliver Reavis's truck, which was still parked in front of the garage where Reavis had left it the night before and where it was now blocking the path of the snack wagon.

"Shit," Smooth Lee said to Frankie Polite. "He can't hear me all the way back in there. I'll move the motherfucker myself."

Smooth Lee opened the door of Oliver Reavis's 1986 Chevrolet pickup truck and climbed in behind the wheel. He took the key from above the sun visor where Reavis always left it, stuck it in the ignition and went to start the engine. Instead the truck exploded.

Angela Becker waited for an hour and a half before she called Oliver Reavis's garage. A recording said that the phone was temporarily out of service. She had no way of knowing that the explosion had blown the phone box off the side of the garage, but coming on the heels of what was done to her dogs she instinctively knew something was wrong. Oliver was a survivor though, she told herself. If he hadn't been taken by surprise he'd be all right. If he had been taken by surprise there was nothing she could do about it now. She took Troy's portable phone out onto the porch, sat down in one of the chairs mounted up on blocks and considered her next move.

The first thing to do was call McKenzie Rockett. She dialed his direct number but got only his voice mail and decided not to leave a message. She began to dial his pager but stopped in the middle, suddenly remembering Justine Fallon, who was probably in as much danger as Reavis had been. She went back into the house, got her notebook from her bag and found Justine's phone number, then decided that calling from Troy's house might not be such a good idea either and that what she ought to do was drive up to Velvet, warn Justine in person, and maybe even get some more information from the psychic. She could wait for Troy and the two of them could go up there together, but she had already told him she was leaving and for all she knew he might not come back to his house for hours. The debilitating horror that had gripped her when she came upon her dead dogs had turned to anger. Now she was energized and had no intention of sitting around all day when she could be doing something. This left her with two options. She could call a garage and hope someone would come out and fix her tire before midafternoon, or she could take Troy's truck. After all, she told herself, he took her cell phone.

Angela stared at the keys to the Ford pickup hanging from a peg on the kitchen wall. Borrowing someone's phone, she realized, and borrowing the sole means of motorized transportation from a person who lived out in the country weren't exactly the same. Before driving off in the truck she better make sure there was something else around that was running. There was a set of General Motors keys hanging from another peg. A third key on the same ring looked like it belonged to a padlock. Since the Ford was the only vehicle sitting in the yard Angela assumed that whatever the GM keys fit had to be out in the barn.

The padlock was rusty but after wiggling the key a few times she got it to work, and the double doors of the barn swung open blowing brittle oak leaves and dust into the yard. She saw the El Camino first. It was sitting off to the left near the front of the barn, its hood bathed in an angled shaft of sunlight filtering down from the slatted cupola. It looked to be either an '86 or '87, the last couple of years they made them, and was in almost perfect condition. Angela studied the El Camino and smiled. The wheels and tires on it were larger than those that normally came from the factory and the wide-mouth dual exhaust pipes poking out from beneath the rear bumper were definitely not standard equipment. She was about to see if it would start when the rustle a small animal made her jump.

The noise had come from the far end of the barn, way in under the loft where there wasn't much light. She took a few steps farther inside, peering into the darkness to see if she could make out what was there. Slowly her eyes adjusted to the dimness and she saw an old tractor, a wooden dinghy resting on a pair of sawhorses, what appeared to be an ancient lathe, and an engine block hanging by a chain from a rolling A-frame hoist. Behind all this, covered by a painter's drop cloth, was another car, a good deal larger than the El Camino and raised up off the wooden floor on jack stands. Angela walked back to get a better look, lifted one of the rear corners of the cloth and let out a low whistle. She was staring at the tail fin and trunk of a 1957 Cadillac Eldorado convertible. She pulled the cloth all the way off and whistled again. Judging from the faded gold paint, the cracked white leather interior, and the top that had once been white as well but was now torn and gray, the car looked to be in original condition. Even unrestored it was worth a fortune.

There was a Texas license tag from 1965 on the Caddy's rear bumper. Angela was about to open the door to see how many miles were on the car when she suddenly remembered Rockett telling her Troy's murdered wife was originally from Texas. She shuddered involuntarily and as quickly as possible replaced the drop cloth feeling as though she had peered beneath a shroud. She walked quickly back to the front of the barn, got into the El Camino and sighed with relief when it immediately roared to life. She listened for a minute to the powerful motor, which she could tell had been worked on, shut the car off, and was about to leave the barn when she was startled by the flutter of wings above her head. She turned quickly and saw a flash of white as a barn owl swooped down from the loft in a sudden graceful arc, shrieking once as it flew. The owl perched on the roof of the Eldorado, made two long hissing noises that sounded like escaping steam and fell silent. Angela could see the bird staring at her with its coal-black eyes. She looked back at it and had the sudden sensation that she had done this before. At first she thought it was simply déjà vu, but then remembered an incident from her childhood that was chilling in its sameness.

When she was a young girl there were a number of owls living on her parents' estate. She developed a great interest in them and would sit outside at night listening for their cries, hoping to catch a glimpse of one sitting on a tree limb or gliding through the forest of tall maples and cedars on the bluff above Long Island Sound. She read in a book on bird lore that the Amish believed if you placed a barn owl on a sleeping person the person would reveal his darkest secrets. She found this notion thrilling and extended it, imagining the creatures themselves held all manner of hidden information they attempted to divulge through the various eerie sounds they made. She enlisted her brother in the nocturnal search for owls and one summer night persuaded him to accompany her to the old barn that had been on the property since the War of 1812 to see if owls were nesting there.

This barn, several hundred yards from their house, was filled with rusting farm machinery left over from the days when a section of the land had been planted with soybeans and potatoes. It was also home to a number of old vehicles Angela's father was attached to and, since he was rich enough not to have to worry about such things as trading in a car, had decided to keep. There was a 1935 Auburn Speedster and a Pierce Arrow Custom Club Sedan that had belonged to his parents; his wife's 1950 Chrysler Town and Country coupe, 1953 Buick Skylark convertible and 1955 Lincoln Continental Mark II; a Studebaker pickup he drove back and forth to town until it threw a rod; and the '54 Austin Healey 100-4 with a roll bar and bashed-in front end that he had driven off the side of the mountain at the Mt. Equinox Hill Climb in Vermont. There was also a Cadillac, a '65 or '66, stuck off in one corner with an old canvas awning covering part of it and a bunch of wicker lawn furniture stacked on its hood and roof. That one, so the story went, was a lemon from the day it was bought. Finally, when it refused to start one winter morning, it was simply pushed way in, where it was out of the way, and left.

The barn was kept locked and boarded up and was considered off limits for the children, who were given strict orders never to go inside without the company of an adult.

"I bet I can find a way in," Angela told her brother.

"I bet you can't," her brother said, "unless you break in, and then we'll be in big trouble."

"Ten bucks says I can do it without breaking anything," Angela told him.

Naturally when she made the challenge she had already discovered a narrow hole big enough to slip through where the siding had rotted away on the back wall of one of the stalls at the rear of the barn. Her brother paid up and from then on the two of them would sneak in on rainy afternoons and sit in one or another of the cars pretending to be race drivers or escaping bank robbers or runaways heading for California.

On this particular night they crept into the barn with flashlights but turned the lights off once they had their bearings and crouched in the bed of the Studebaker to wait. They had been there for about twenty minutes when suddenly they heard the rapid beat of wings descending from the rafters accompanied by a shrill, haunting cry. In the confines of the barn the sound was paralyzing.

"Come on, Angie," her brother said. "Let's get the hell out of here."

"You go if you want," Angela told him. "I want to see if I can find it."

"You'll never find it," her brother said. "And anyway if you corner it, it might attack."

"It isn't going to hurt us," she said, but he was already scrambling toward the stall. He was thirteen, two years older than she, but timid and far more cautious. She was a born adventurer and basically fearless.

When he was gone she climbed out of the truck bed and began to thread her way through the maze of iron hulks. She had been in the barn so many times she could move through it without her flashlight as easily as she could cross her bedroom in the dark. She was squeezing between the Austin Healey and the Buick when she heard a metallic clacking that sounded like someone tapping two spoons together. This was followed by a low hiss. She turned the flashlight on, pointed it in the direction of the noise and saw a barn owl, its claws wrapped around the arm of an overturned wicker lawn chair that lay across the roof of the Cadillac. The owl watched her intently, its eyes two black dots against a snow-white face, its chest the shape and color of a speckled egg. She turned out the light so as not to frighten it.

"Tell me your secrets, owl," she whispered. "Tell me all the secrets of this barn."

With another hiss the owl flew off, back into the upper reaches of the barn. Angela stood perfectly still and waited for a few seconds, imagining herself to be an augur who had just been shown a sign. In the darkness she crept toward the Cadillac, feeling her way with an outstretched hand. When she reached it she groped around until she felt a handle, opened the door and climbed into the rear seat. The upholstery was slightly damp and smelled like wet ashes and moldy rags. It was the first time she had bothered to get inside this car since she and her brother had always dismissed it as the one vehicle in her father's collection that was completely devoid of panache. Furthermore it was nearly buried in junk.

She turned on her flashlight to inspect the interior and saw that the front window on the passenger's side was open and that there was a nest spread across the front seat. She played the light on the nest and began poking around in it, certain she would find something—an omen, a talisman, something symbolic linking her to the owl—so when she spied the piece of white material amid the twigs, leaves and skeletal remains of the owl's prey she was not surprised.

It was a small child's cotton sock. Angela picked it up and examined it in the beam of the flashlight. The sock was dirty and discolored with mold, but otherwise in good shape. This is it, she thought. This is the sign from the owl. Immediately she decided it would be her amulet. She took several tiny bones that probably came from a mouse, a dried leaf, a few little pieces of straw, and two feathers from the nest and put them in the sock. Then, approximating the owl's metallic clicking sound with her tongue, she crawled out of the barn and hurried back to the house.

"The sock belonged to a little girl who drowned at sea," she told her brother the next day. "It washed up on the shore and the owl brought it to its nest. It has magical powers."

"Yeah right," her brother said. "And how'd you find this out?"

"The owl told me." Angela smiled.

"You're crazy," her brother said. "You're totally insane."

"Maybe," Angela replied, "but at least I'm not scared."

The next day her father asked her if she'd been in the barn. She was one of those rare individuals who, when confronted, never lied, so she admitted that she had. Her father told her he already knew and praised her for her honesty. As he had many times in the past, he mentioned to her that a good lawyer never asks a question to which he doesn't already know the answer. She asked him how he found out and he told her a good lawyer also never reveals his sources. She knew it had to have been her brother who ratted but said nothing more.

Two days later she left for a French-speaking summer camp on Lake Champlain in Vermont. When she came home the barn had been turned into a shop where an old man her father hired was hard at work straightening the Austin Healey's sheet metal. The rest of the cars were parked in two neat rows, like customers at a barbershop waiting their turn. Bright sunshine streamed through the windows that were no longer boarded up and classical music came from a radio sitting on the hood of the Studebaker pickup. The Cadillac and the farm machinery were gone. The Caddy wasn't worth restoring, her father told her when Angela asked where it was. He needed the room, he said, so he scrapped it.

She looked upset, and when he asked her why, she told him about the owl's nest. He told her not to worry, barn owls were very adaptable creatures. This one had most certainly found another home somewhere nearby. They were standing outside the barn when he told her this. The doors were open wide and she could hear the tapping of the old man's pick hammer against the fender of the Healey. The noise of the hammer sounded just like the metallic clacking made by the owl. Night after night she sat in the woods near the barn listening for it, hoping to get a glimpse of it gliding between the trees, but she never heard the owl or saw it again.

That fall she went off to boarding school for the first time. The day before she left she buried the sock along with some of her other favorite possessions in a steel box out behind the barn. She told herself the box would be a time capsule that she'd dig up in twenty years, but then her father died and everything changed and after a while she forgot about the box and the sock and the owl too until that moment in Roland Troy's barn when she stood next to his El Camino.

Angela walked back to Troy's house tossing the keys to the El Camino from one hand to the other, wondering if she could still find the box she'd placed twenty inches underground and twenty paces back from the stall with the rotten board on the estate where her brother, now a cardiologist, lived with his wife and kids. It was twenty years ago this coming summer that she'd buried it, twenty years since she'd been gripped by an unexplainable sense of loss and loneliness that had really never gone away.

Angela Becker drove north to Velvet in Roland Troy's Ford pickup listening to a Billie Holiday tape she found in the glove compartment. There were a couple of Macanudos in there too. She unwrapped one, bit off the end and lit up using the cigarette lighter in the dash. Why not, she thought. She was driving his truck, wearing a pair of his daughter's old jeans, her tennis shoes and flannel shirt. Might as well try one of his cigars. She clamped the cigar between her teeth, moved into the left lane of the interstate, and took the truck up to seventy-five. In motion, with a purpose, she began to feel better. She was glad she hadn't gone over to her condo first to get some of her own clothes, or worse, gone down to the task force office to find McKenzie Rockett. She could talk to him later, and anyway, if he got upset and asked what the hell she was doing running up there on her own she'd tell him Troy's truck with the Vermont plates was the perfect cover. It made her look like a typical pilgrim, she'd say, down from the cold Northeast in search of psychic enlightenment.

In forty minutes she was back on the narrow hilly streets lined with oddly shaped houses. Even though she'd been telling herself since her first visit that all the spiritualist stuff was a load of crap—mumbo jumbo for the weak and vulnerable—she nevertheless felt drawn back to the strange little town where no one ever hurried and even the cars seemed to float noiselessly on a cushion of air. In spite of her cynicism about communing with the dead, she was also looking forward to seeing Justine Fallon again.

She parked the truck in Justine's driveway noticing that the curtains on all her windows were drawn and that all the furniture was gone from the front porch. Angela had spent enough time searching for people in the past ten years to know without knocking that Justine wasn't home and probably wouldn't be coming back anytime soon. All the same, she banged on the front door, waited half a minute, and banged again. When there was no response she walked slowly around the outside of the house twice looking for anything unusual but found nothing.

A light wind was blowing out of the south and the afternoon had turned quite warm. In the thick moist air the silence in Velvet became oppressive, closing in around Angela like a tight-fitting glove, draining the enthusiasm she'd brought with her. She was about to get back into the truck and leave when she heard someone call her name. She whirled around and saw a tiny old woman standing in the tall grass fifteen feet away. The woman was very tan and wore a brightly colored serape. She had a beatific expression on her deeply lined face.

"Angela," she said again, coming closer. There was no question in her voice, no surprise; it was as though the old woman had expected her to be there. Angela lifted the tail of the flannel shirt, wrapped her fingers around the butt of her gun and watched warily as the woman approached. The old woman smiled sweetly, ignoring the weapon.

"This is for you," she said, extending her hand from under the serape and handing Angela an envelope. "It's from Justine."

"Where is she?" Angela asked.

"I don't know, dear," the woman said.

"Who are you? What's your name?"

"Marie," the woman said. "Marie Calvert." She was still smiling benignly but it seemed to Angela that she was anxious to leave.

"How'd you know who I was?" she asked.

"Oh, Justine described you perfectly to me," Marie Calvert said. "I saw you walking around her house. I live back there, on the next street. I have to go now. I left someone right in the middle of doing a reading."

Angela began to say something more but the old woman, still smiling, shook her head and scuttled off. She moved quickly through the tall grass like a startled little animal and disappeared around the corner of a cottage painted an unusual shade of deep blue. Angela stood by the truck with the letter in her hand waiting for something else to happen but nothing did.

Leo and I had a long conversation last night, the letter said. *He told me that it wasn't safe to stay in Velvet right now and so I've gone away for a little while. Leo said you'd know why. He said you would be concerned and would soon come to warn me so I've written this note and given it to Marie Calvert, who will be watching for you. Marie is an old friend and a very spiritual*

*person. I can trust her. That isn't true for everyone else in Velvet,
which is why I have told no one, even Marie, where I am going.
You needn't worry, though, because I will be safe.*

*There is more to tell about Leo's story—some things I didn't
mention when you and I spoke. Now Leo thinks the time is right
for you to know about them. You and the man working with you,
the tall man with a beard who limps. But I don't think it's wise
to write these things down in a letter so you will have to wait
until someone else who knows all about Leo contacts one of you.*

*That's all I feel free to say, except to tell you that you must
be very careful. My thoughts are with you, Angela. So are those
of your spirit guides who are there to help if you are willing to
listen.*

The letter was signed, "your friend, Justine." Angela folded it and
put it back in its envelope. She was parked at the far side of an Exxon
station just off the interstate, having waited to read the letter until she
had put a few miles between herself and Velvet. She had the truck
backed up to a low chain-link fence separating the station from a
field where several head of cattle grazed, a spot affording her a clear
view of the pumps and the station's convenience store. Through the
window of the store she could see the cashier, a young woman who
was watching something on a tiny TV set. Other than the young woman
the station was deserted. Angela turned the ignition key on but didn't
start the truck. The side of the tape with Billie Holiday on it ended.
The player paused, switched to the other side, and Jimi Hendrix came
on singing "Red House."

Angela relit the Macanudo, blew smoke out the truck's window,
and listened as Hendrix did straight ahead blues. When he got to the
line about not seeing his baby for ninety-nine and one-half days, she
closed her eyes for a moment and shook her head. Longer than that
for me, she thought. A whole lot longer than that.

Her friend Cortez the rug man was a big Jimi Hendrix fan. One
night he came over to her trailer with three Hendrix CDs, an extra
set of headphones, and some weed he'd grown up in the Ocala National
Forest. Angela made him leave the dope in his car.

"Don't cops get high?" Cortez had asked her.

"You tell me," she answered. "You were one once."

"I weren't no cop," he said. "I was an undercover fish-and-gamer. A bad alley-gator. No light filtered down to where I lived. I did everything. Everything except trust people. And look, I still got chopped up and served for dinner. That's why I like Jimi. He had a sense of irony."

" 'Love all, trust a few, do wrong to none: be able for thine enemy,' " she recited.

"Where's that from?" he asked.

"Shakespeare," she said. "He had a sense of everything."

"Is that why you became a cop?" he asked. "To be able for your enemies? I would have thought all your money had that department covered."

"Money buys good lawyers," she said, "but people still fuck with you. Money just attracts a better class of enemies. Nobody fucks with cops. People see me coming and step aside. My blue light strikes fear in the hearts of the wicked and the mighty."

"Your blue light don't mean shit where I been," he said. "Just ask my missing hand. Or any other part of me that got took. Show up in the wrong place at the wrong time and it'll happen to you too."

Angela's eyes popped open at the sound of a car. A gray Mercedes pulled into the station, swung around the pumps, and came to a skidding halt perpendicular to the truck and twenty feet away. The front passenger door was directly in Angela's line of sight but the windows of the Mercedes were darkly tinted so there was no way for her to know how many people were in the car. She also had no idea what they were up to but assumed at once that she had been followed.

Instinctively she reached for the two-way radio and cursed when she remembered Troy hadn't gotten around to having one installed. Even if he had, what good would it do her out there in the boondocks, or a phone either, for that matter? All she had was her .44, which she pulled from the shoulder bag on the seat next to her, never taking her eyes off the doors of the car.

She wasn't boxed in; there was plenty of room to wheel the truck around the Mercedes and make a run for it but then she'd risk getting gunned down while she drove.

No, she decided, if this was it she'd stay right where she was and shoot the first one who stepped out of the car. Maybe the second and third ones too if she got lucky. She slid out of the truck, cocking the hammer of the .44 as she moved. Bracing her arms on the hood, she crouched and flattened her body against the fender, offering as little of herself as possible to anyone in the car.

The front passenger door of the Mercedes opened slowly. She could feel her heart pounding but her hands were steady; in all her years on the force she had drawn her gun five times but had yet to shoot at another human being. Not yet, she told herself, wait until the target is clearly in sight. Her finger tightened on the trigger which was slightly narrower than stock. In the half-dozen heartbeats that she waited, she was aware of the trigger's coolness and the roundness of its edges that the gunsmith had smoothed for her when he cut the width.

The car door opened farther. Angela saw movement and was about to fire when a little girl, maybe six or seven years old, jumped out and made a dash for the restroom on the side of the convenience store. The girl never saw her. Neither did the fashionable young woman in a long black skirt who extracted herself from the driver's side of the car and bustled after the child. Angela took a deep breath, and rested her head against the truck.

"Jessica, you wait for me," the woman shouted. "Don't you go in there by yourself. You know what I told you. Those places are dangerous for small children."

"I gotta make, Mommy," the little girl wailed, clutching herself between her legs and doing a bunny hop in a small circle. "If I don't go in there I'm gonna pee on the ground."

The fashionable woman caught up with the girl and the two of them disappeared into the restroom. Angela got back in the truck. She returned her gun to the shoulder bag, gripped the steering wheel with both hands and stared at the Mercedes that now seemed to exist in a dimension other than her own. The tape player was still running; Hendrix was singing Dylan's "All Along the Watchtower." " 'There must be some kind of way out of here,' said the joker to the thief," he sang. " 'There's too much confusion. I can't get no relief. . . . No reason to get excited,' the thief he kindly spoke. 'There are many here among us who feel that life is but a joke.' "

"Oh my God," Angela said aloud. "Oh my God." A single tear ran down her cheek and hung on the edge of her chin. It was the first time she had cried in more than ten years.

XIV

When Troy came home in his canoe from Halpatter's and found Angela's note he took the wheel with the flat tire off her Trans-Am and went over in his El Camino to the nearby village of Lake Monroe where a friend of his ran a garage and bait shop. There was no fixing the old tire his friend told him; in addition to the nail driven into the tread there was one embedded in the sidewall. The two of them scrounged around in the stack of tires beside the garage until they found something that would fit the rim. The new tire wasn't in particularly good condition but at least the car would roll on it. Troy brought the wheel back to his house, reinstalled it, and drove the Trans-Am into his barn, where it would be out of sight. He had just finished cleaning his hands in the kitchen when Jack Ubinas called.

"I saw a photograph of your new partner," Ubinas said. "You were holding out on me, Roland. She's absolutely gorgeous. I think I'm in love."

"She's too tall for you, Jack," Troy said. "And too young."

"I hear she's got a tattoo on her ankle and a diamond stud in her nose," Ubinas said. "I find that tantalizing."

"Sooner or later you hear everything."

"Oh my, you sound jealous. Or maybe protective is the better word. But then you always were a chivalrous fella. I, however, remain an unrepentant lecher."

Troy walked out onto his porch with the phone and sat in one of the rockers. A sheet of rain was blowing across the pond in his direction. The wind pushing it was already swinging from south to west. By morning the wind would be out of the northwest and it would be clear and cool again, but in a few weeks the weather cycle that lasted through the winter and early spring would end bringing six months of relentless heat.

The rain swept over the sloping ground between his house and the pond and began drumming on the porch roof. Troy could feel the fine spindrift from the storm on his hands and face but he stayed where he was. During the two winters he spent in Vermont he had listened to people bitch about the cold; in Florida they complained about the heat and the powerful thunderstorms, but Troy enjoyed all of it and only rarely let the weather drive him indoors.

"You still there?" Ubinas asked.

"I'm still here," Troy said. "I was just watching the rain come in off the pond. It feels nice."

"Aren't you going to ask me where I got her picture?"

"Somebody killed her two dogs yesterday, Jack. Cut out their hearts and stuck 'em in their mouths. Hung 'em by their hind legs in a tree next to her trailer. We've only been partners a short time but she's a woman of character and I'm taking it personally. You understand what I'm saying?"

"I understand perfectly," Ubinas said, the jocularity gone from his voice.

"As I recall you ran into something like that once before. On a job in South America, if I'm not mistaken."

"You've got a good memory," Troy said.

Jack Ubinas might project the rumpled locker-room bonhomie of an aging Ivy League jock, but underneath the disheveled geniality beat the stone-cold heart of a lifelong company man, a man who had ordered up death and destruction secure in the belief that he was doing the right thing. Few people had any idea who Ubinas was, which bothered him not a bit, just as long as he always knew the score. Information was his sustenance, his comfort. Doling it out to those in command was his source of power.

In the background, Troy could hear the clicking of his computer keyboard. No doubt Ubinas was already searching his files, checking to find what might be buried in the vast data banks of SIAC (situation actual) and SISPEC (situation speculative) on the ritual murder of animals.

"It's on automatic pilot," Ubinas said, reading Troy's mind. "Let me tell you what else I've got for you and by the time I'm done maybe we'll come up with something on the animals."

"I'm listening," said Troy.

"Leo Weiser, your psychic photographer, is still a blank," Ubinas said. "In fact it's too damn bad he got himself killed because that man could have taught both of us a thing or two about covering tracks. Hell, I'd have hired him in a minute. If he was getting money from somewhere it must have all been cash because the only checks he ever deposited were for whatever work he was doing. I ran his prints and came up empty. Same with his dental records. Your buddy Rockett already tried to trace his cameras and jewelry and got nowhere. You could dig him up and get a DNA sample but in my opinion it would be a waste of time because there isn't a damn thing to try and match it with. All I can tell you is that one day Leo Weiser didn't exist and the next day he did."

"What day was that?" Troy asked, lighting a cigar and walking back into the house. He took a pencil and a pad of lined yellow paper from a shelf in the kitchen, sat down at the table, and switched from the cordless phone to the one mounted on the wall. A green light glowing from a small plastic box attached to the phone indicated that the line was clean.

"That would have been April the twentieth 1967, in Des Moines," Ubinas said. "One Leo Weiser opened a checking account at the Central Iowa National Bank. Shortly thereafter he got himself a social security card, a driver's license, and a job in a camera store. He didn't make it down to your neck of the woods until eighty-five. In between he lived a solitary, prosaic life in a variety of places. Never got arrested, never protested against the war, filed a tax return every year. The strange thing is that for all Weiser's interest in photography the only picture of him on file anywhere is the one taken for his Florida driver's license. Obviously he was someone else, a man who ran away. Happens all the time. It's a big country, Roland. Easy place for a person to get lost if he knows what he's doing. Unless of course there's someone like you on his trail."

Troy leaned back in the kitchen chair, put his feet up on the table and listened intently. There was something unusual in Ubinas's tone, an uncharacteristic breathlessness, as if he were trying to talk while climbing a long flight of stairs. Troy was about to ask Ubinas if he was feeling all right but changed his mind. His instincts told him Ubinas's health was fine and that something else was going on, so instead he took a couple of long pulls on the cigar and said nothing.

"Weiser's friend Justine Fallon, by the way, is completely clean," Ubinas went on. "Worked for a large insurance company in Illinois before she moved to Velvet. Her husband was a big deal in the same company. Died and left her a bundle."

"What about everyone else on the list?" Troy asked.

"Ah yes," Ubinas said. "The others. Well, let's see. I don't have anything new about Herbert Stiefel, but I got something on the guy who hosts one of his shows, this Pastor Jim Keller you asked about. Keller was the founder of a right-wing extremist organization in Arkansas called the Church of the Militant Redeemer. The good pastor, once upon a time, served with the Special Forces. Did two tours in 'Nam. After that he kicked around a bit in the oil fields, joined a neo-Nazi group known as the Aryan Defenders and wound up in Louisiana working for a very wealthy oilman with similar political leanings named Joseph Didier."

"That figures."

"You know about him?"

"Yeah, I know about him," Troy said. "Right after his girlfriend shot him his cousin Ernie Viens went to work for Stiefel. I'm pretty sure cousin Ernie was one of the guys who killed Weiser but now he's dead too. What I don't know is how Stiefel, who was running a third-rate circus, got the money to become a media tycoon in not much more time than it took you to dial my phone number."

"From where I'm sitting it looks like Stiefel's TV studio was funded by Keller's church. Keller's church got its backing from Didier's oil company. Joseph Didier was one mighty rich coonass. Probably he funneled the dough for the studio through the church."

"Could be," Troy said.

"You got a better idea?"

"Not at the moment. Tell me about Angus Elliott."

"Ah yes, Angus Elliott, the psychic who knows where missing dead folks lie," Ubinas said. "You on a hard line or a portable phone, Roland?"

"I'm back in the house, Jack," Troy said. "Hard line. Green light. The coast is clear. I'm a little rusty but I ain't senile."

"That's reassuring," Ubinas said. "One can never be too careful. A moment ago you were out in the rain."

"Angus Elliott," Troy said.

"Don't get testy," Ubinas said. "Angus Elliott worked for naval intelligence for a couple of years and did indeed spend his time searching for dead bodies. It seems he was pretty good at it. He helped them find one guy who was at the bottom of a lake, another one in the New Jersey pine barrens, and a third who'd been buried under a land fill outside Moline, Illinois. After a while, however, Angus started getting a little too weird, even for a psychic. From what I can gather he began ranting and raving about reincarnation, demon souls from the past wandering the earth in the bodies of blacks and Jews, the coming war against the Antichrist, that sort of thing. He was deemed a liability and they decided to cut him loose. But here's something interesting. There was another guy working for naval intelligence at the same time, in the same place, named Reed Calloway. That name mean anything to you?"

"No," said Troy. "Should it?"

"Well," Ubinas said, "Reed Calloway is presently an agent with the central Florida office of the FBI."

"That's interesting," Troy said.

"I thought so," said Ubinas.

Troy scribbled a few notes on the yellow pad, took a look at the page filled with writing that he'd folded over, and puffed on his cigar.

"You done good, Jack," he said. "Now what about the guy who's missing part of an ear?"

The pause was shorter than a shallow intake of breath, but once again, as in his earlier phone conversation with Ubinas, Troy sensed it. It was a barely perceptible interruption in the flow of words between them, a break in the rhythm betraying Ubinas's unease. He would divulge information to Troy out of loyalty, out of friendship and trust, and because of a debt that went back thirty years, to the day Troy saved the life of Ubinas's brother in the mountains along the border of Laos and Vietnam. But for some reason there was a microsecond of silence before Jack Ubinas spoke. Ubinas, Troy knew, was holding something back.

"There's this guy by the name of DuCharme," Ubinas said. "Novac DuCharme. He came to this country after World War II. During the war he was a member of the French Resistance. At least that's what his file says."

"What do you say?" Troy asked.

"I say he made a bundle as an international financier, which is a fancy way of saying he's a money changer. I say he owns a little company that produces electronic components for weapons systems. Timing devices, controls, that kind of thing. Pretty basic stuff mostly, but he also supplies the big boys like Hughes and Martin with some highly classified technology. The other thing Novac DuCharme supplies is information. Quite valuable information. He has tentacles all over the world. Contacts from the old days. Eastern Europe, the Middle East, South America. But here's where it gets sticky, Roland, because I can't tell you where all his information goes."

"You can't or you won't," Troy said.

"Come on, Roland, you know me better than that. I don't know everyone he talks to."

"This boy's in deep is what you're telling me."

"Very deep." Ubinas said. "As deep as it gets."

"And he's missing part of an ear."

"So it seems."

"Well, well, well," Troy said.

"Indeed," said Ubinas.

"Where is he now?" Troy asked. "This fount of information with contacts from the old days?"

"I have no idea," Ubinas answered. "He's got a place in New York, a weekend house on Long Island, a condo in Zurich, a great big boat that floats hither and yon. You get the picture. He could be anywhere. But wherever he is, and whoever some old man may have thought he was, Novac DuCharme is impeccably protected. He's unassailable. His slate is clean. No matter what some psychic imagined he saw. No matter if what the old man saw was somehow connected to his murder. Nothing's going to get hung on Novac DuCharme. He's too smart to let that happen. And too valuable. From what I hear he was the guy whose connections helped infiltrate the Shining Path in Peru. If we'd gone all the way to Baghdad his contacts would have pinpointed the whereabouts of Saddam Hussein. You understand what I'm talking about here?"

"No one is unassailable," Troy said. "You should know that. You come up with anything on the animals?"

"Not yet. I'll get back to you as soon as I find anything."

"Much obliged. I'll talk to you later."

"Be careful, Roland," Ubinas said.

Troy hung the phone back on the wall and climbed the stairs to the single room with huge windows on all four sides that occupied the entire third story of his house. The turret, he and Katherine had called it, back in the days when his daughter had used it as a playroom. To the west you could see all the way across the pond where, amid a tangle of mangrove roots, the hidden creek began, leading to the waterways of the swamp. To the north and south the windows overlooked the thick woods that bordered the same swamp, while the view form the east window was of the sloping, weed-choked pasture dotted with huge oak trees and clumps of pine. The only visible structure was Troy's barn, fifty yards to the northeast.

"I'm surveying our kingdom," his daughter would say when Troy came up the stairs and found her standing on the wooden swing he had hung from the turret's ceiling. The swing was long gone, but the large replica of a compass he had painted on the floor for her was still there, as were the wooden chest he had made for her toys, and the table he had built where she sat for hours on end drawing pictures of animals and birds. Troy looked down at the shore of the pond at the spot where the two of them had seen a mama bear and two cubs drinking early one Sunday morning. That was fifteen years ago, but it seemed as though it were last week. Now Katherine was gone, a grown woman with a husband and a career, living in her own kingdom, and the land that had run through his blood for nearly fifty years no longer felt the same.

The driving rain had slackened to a light drizzle and the wind had picked up. Troy opened all four windows and let the cool, moist air blow through the room. He checked his watch. It was twenty after three, still early enough to drive down to the task force office, check in with McKenzie Rockett, and let Rock know what he'd learned from Ubinas, but first he wanted to clear his head. Working murder cases for so long had taught him that no matter how similar one might appear to another, each was unique and demanded its own plan of attack. After his conversation with Ubinas it seemed that the pieces of the puzzle relating to this one were beginning to fall into place. He should have been elated, but instead he felt weary and terribly sad.

He tried to focus, but all he could think about was Clara. He wondered what had gone through her mind in the instant she saw the blue-white flame of the shotgun blast that killed her. He wondered, as he had a hundred times before, what it was that Bruno Schleifer, the filmmaker she was working with, had stumbled across, only this time he wondered whether, by some strange chance, there was a connection between Schleifer and the psychic, Leo Weiser. That was foolishness, he told himself, emotions obscuring reality, useless speculation interfering with a logical approach to the case.

For a few minutes he sat cross-legged on the floor in the center of the painted compass, facing northwest into the wind, breathing deeply, but then his hip began to ache, no doubt from the dampness, and he stretched out on his back. He looked up at the wooden beam from which the rope of Katherine's swing had hung. Here in my kingdom, he thought. The kingdom of a thousand ghosts. He closed his eyes and almost immediately fell into a deep sleep.

"Cops are used to being in control," McKenzie Rockett said. "When they feel that control slipping away . . . that's when they can get themselves in trouble . . . that's when they have to be very careful."

"And you think that's me?" Angela Becker asked. "Slipping out of control?"

"We're all in danger of it," Rockett said. "You in particular though, you want me to be straight with you."

"Why? Because I'm a little upset that someone mutilated my dogs?"

"It isn't just the dogs. There's something else going on."

"And what might that be?"

"I don't know, Angela. Do you?"

"I think I'll take a ride over to your house and see Carolyn," Angela said. "I'm tired of talking to men. I'm tired of hearing what they have to say. I need another woman's point of view."

She was sitting in the old easy chair she'd lugged up to the task force office when Rockett brought her on board, still wearing the tattered jeans, flannel shirt, and worn-out sneakers that she'd found in the closet of Katherine's old bedroom at Roland Troy's house. She had driven straight to the office from her gas station encounter with the Mercedes, telling herself the best move for her sanity was to keep working. She had printed out Stan Erland's notes and wanted to go over them one more time with McKenzie Rockett to see whether there was something they had missed. It seemed to her that she was handling things just fine, given all that had transpired in the past ten days. She looked down, saw she had been unconsciously shaking her right foot, and made herself stop. Nervously shaking and wiggling body parts was completely out of character for her. She had never done that, even back when she was in narcotics on dangerous stakeouts when all hell was about to break loose. She thought about telling Rockett what had happened at the gas station but decided against it. She was afraid he would think she was crazy.

McKenzie Rockett had his tie unknotted and his feet propped up on his desk. He had been trying, without much success, to explain why, in light of the recent turn of events, Angela should quit driving her Trans-Am, and why she should stay in her condo where she would be less exposed instead of out in the woods in her trailer, at least for a few days, until they had a better grasp of the situation.

"My wife is on a plane to Ohio to visit her sister for a spell, even as we speak," he said. "The only female you'll be talking to in my house is the cat."

"You sent her out of town?" Angela said. She was duly impressed. McKenzie Rockett was neither a paranoid nor hysterical man. "You think it's that bad, huh?"

"Ask your dogs," Rockett said. "Ask Smooth Lee. Or Stan Erland, for that matter."

A can of Diet Pepsi and a plastic plate heaped with Jimbo's ribs sat on the desk in front of him. He took a sip of the Pepsi, picked up one of the ribs, and studied it as though it were a laboratory specimen.

"You look hungry," he said, still holding the rib aloft. "Help your-self. Eat something. You'll be easier to reason with."

"A woman would not have said that to me."

"Listen, I can call this whole thing off, you know. Pull the plug. The feds'll send in thirty fucking agents in windbreakers who'll comb the woods for weeks. They won't turn up anything, but we'll be out of business. Roland Troy can go back to Vermont and boil syrup, they'll put me in charge of the Community Relations Division, and you'll wind up behind a desk at the Women's House of Detention or better yet, down on the Trail helping to bust ten-dollar hookers. And notice, by the way, what course your friend the psychic took. She split."

"She's a frightened old woman. I'm a cop. Cops don't split."

"I'm not asking you to split. I'm asking you to be careful. You go somewhere potentially dangerous, such as your trailer, go with backup."

"You give that same advice to Troy?"

"Sheridan Halpatter called me, just before you got here," Rockett said. "He's the guy Troy took with him when he went to your place this morning." Rockett paused and began eating the rib, which he held between the thumb and index finger of one enormous hand. He waved his other hand over the plate, signaling her to join him. She took one from the pile and stuck her tongue out at him before biting into it.

"You meet Halpatter yet?"

Angela shook her head and continued to eat. Rockett had been right; she was famished and the ribs were, as usual, delicious.

"Well, I'm sure you will," Rockett said. "He's a most remarkable man. One of the last full-blooded Indians in these parts. Hunts alliga-tors. Ain't had a pair of shoes on his feet in forty years. Him and Troy been friends since they were kids. They'd die for one another, Angela. I mean that literally. Anyway, while Troy was checking out your prop-erty Halpatter was up in a tree with a mini-fourteen. The same tree where they hung your dogs."

"Why'd he call you?" she asked.

"He was looking for Troy, actually. Said there wasn't any answer at his house. He wanted us to know he got the dart to Peiser over at the crime lab. He should have something for us by tomorrow."

"The dart?"

"I thought you knew. Troy found a tranquilizing dart on the ground near your trailer. He figures it was used on one of your dogs. Peiser and Troy are old buddies. He'll tell us what chemical they used on the dart, and he won't tell anyone else."

Angela threw the rib bone into the wastebasket and took another. "Where's Troy?" she asked between bites.

"That's the same question Halpatter asked me," Rockett said. "He's going over to Troy's house in his canoe to see what's up."

"Climbing trees, paddling canoes," she said. "It's starting to sound like *The Last of the Mohicans.*"

"Humor me, Angela," Rockett said. "It's been another long day. Leave Troy's truck here. Take the Crown Vicky from the motor pool. The dark blue, unmarked Crown Vicky, with a radio in it and a phone. It's parked around back. Drive it to your condo and stay there tonight. Take a hot shower. Get some sleep. Tomorrow morning meet me and Troy at Jimbo's for breakfast, eight o'clock sharp."

"Is that an order?"

"The part about breakfast is," Rockett told her. "The rest is simply good advice. Don't go to that trailer tonight. You hear me, girl?"

"I need to think," Angela said. "I think a whole lot better out there."

She stuffed the printed copy of Erland's notes into a manila envelope and stood up. McKenzie Rockett sighed. She was going to her trailer, he knew, to confront the demon, to prove to herself that whoever had butchered her dogs could not scare her off.

"Don't go alone," he said. "And take these damn ribs with you. I gotta lose some weight. I gotta lose some weight and you need to watch your ass."

This time the dream began on a winding mountain blacktop in northern Vermont. Roland Troy was driving a large luxury car, a Lexus it seemed to be, although he'd never driven a Lexus in his life. There was someone with him, sitting in the front passenger seat, but it was unclear who that was. Suddenly, the car crested a short incline and plunged down an almost vertical section of highway on the other side. The man with Troy—it was a man, that much he knew—told him that they were now descending the steepest road in the country, the steepest, in fact, known to man. Troy could see where the hill, or more accurately, the cliff ended, curling like the bottom of a ski jump, blending seamlessly into a smooth, flat surface that stretched to the horizon.

Faster and faster the car went. Its wheels were no longer touching the pavement, and the landscape, streaking by the windows, became indistinct flashes of darkness and light. Still, Troy somehow knew he would make it safely down this precipitous drop, that his wheels would regain contact with the pavement like a jet plane landing on a runway. Then suddenly the paved surface turned into a raging torrent of blood strewn with jagged boulders. He pivoted in his seat to look at the man in the car with him, but no one else was there.

The car plunged through rapids, the blood splashing up over the hood and against the windows, the rocks scraping against its undercarriage. The river of blood tossed the car now as though it were a cork, but it was almost in the clear, almost into a calm, crimson pool shaped exactly like Troy's pond. He turned on the wipers to clear the streaks of blood from the windshield and saw his wife Clara and Bruno Schliefer floating on their backs in the pond. Rolling down his window he tried to cry out to them, but was unable to utter a sound. Then the car turned sideways and struck a jagged outcropping. There was a loud, metallic crack of steel banging against rock, and with a jolt, Troy awoke. It was dark in the room, and through the open windows he could see a first-quarter moon and a sky filled with stars. Obviously, he had been asleep for hours.

He had rolled in his sleep. No longer was he lying on his back on the painted compass, but instead was on his side, almost directly beneath the west window of the turret. He heard another loud metallic crack and was awake enough to know that it had come from directly below where he lay. Someone had stepped on the old wheel-alignment sign covering the hole in the floor of his porch. Before Troy was able to completely clear his head and react, he heard sounds of a scuffle, the blast of a gunshot, a cry of pain, and the splintering of wood. He leapt to his feet, reached in the darkness for the .45 he'd left on Katherine's old desk, and peered out the window, positioning himself flat against the wall so as not to provide a silhouette to anyone outside.

In the moonlight, he saw movement on the sloping ground leading to the pond. There was a second cry that came from near the water's edge, a loud splash, and then the noise of a car starting up and driving off along the dirt road that snaked through the woods. The car hit something, no doubt a tree, but kept going.

As the sound of the car faded Troy thought he heard Sheridan Halpatter calling to him, but Halpatter's voice, normally deep and robust, seemed weak and distant, as though his friend were trying to shout from the other end of a long tunnel.

"Roland," Halpatter cried. "Roland, are you in there? Roland, I'm lying out here in the yard. I've been shot."

Gun in hand, Troy bounded down the stairs and went outside through the side door in his workroom, avoiding the porch and the metal sign. Noiselessly, he crept around the corner of the house and knelt beside Halpatter who lay sprawled in the tall grass. A piece of the porch railing he crashed through when he was hit lay next to him.

"It's my leg," Halpatter said softly. "My thigh."

He was losing blood. Troy could see it soaking Halpatter's pants and spreading along the ground. The bullet was probably a hollow point that had exploded inside Halpatter's leg. Troy tore off his flannel shirt, probed as gently as possible with his fingers until he found the entry wound, then wrapped the shirt around Halpatter's massive thigh.

"There were two of them," Halpatter whispered. "I came by canoe so they didn't hear me. I surprised 'em as they were about to go into your house. I'm pretty sure I got the one who shot me with my pole, Roland. I heard him fall into the pond. I think the other one got away."

"You can tell me about it later, Sheridan," Troy said. "I'm gonna go call for help. Hang in there, buddy. I'll be right back."

XV

Cortez the rug man lay on his back on the couch at the front of Angela's trailer where her female Rottweiler used to sleep. A twelve-gauge semiautomatic shotgun with an extended eight-shell magazine was propped against the wall beside him. He was watching the Magic game on the small TV he'd brought over, but he had the volume turned off. The windows of the trailer were open so he could hear the night noises coming from the river and the woods. From his years of tracking poachers he had no problem distinguishing the difference between the sound of an animal and a man.

Angela sat cross-legged on the bunk bed, reading through the copy she'd made of Stan Erland's notes for the third time.

"The old man was suffering from dementia," she said. "I'm sure of it. Isaac, the old man was imagining things."

Cortez turned from the game and looked down the dark, narrow length of the trailer to where she sat, bathed in the light of the wall-mounted lamp above her head. She was losing weight, not that there was all that much to lose. Her shoulders, under the old crew neck sweater she wore, looked bony, as did her wrists, protruding from the sleeves. She tilted her head and smiled at him. Backlit, the edges of her hair appeared translucent.

"The old man?" he asked.

"Leo Weiser," she said. "You know, the guy who was murdered and got all of this shit started. The man who's indirectly responsible for you being here tonight instead of curled up at home watching on a proper big-screen. The psychic."

"You don't mind me saying so, Angela, a dude like him imagining things ain't no revelation. He firmly believed that blotches on photographic paper were spirits. Didn't you tell me that?"

"That's not what I'm talking about. I'm not talking about . . . his calling . . . what he saw in his pictures. What I'm saying is that he thought the blond woman who came to see him . . . this real flesh-and-blood person named Michelle, who Erland was obsessed with . . . I finally figured it out, Isaac. Leo Weiser thought she was someone else."

"So what? Why would you expect anything he thought to make sense? The old man was obviously crazy, Angela."

"He wasn't murdered for being crazy," she said. "He was murdered because of something he had, or something he knew. In the midst of lunacy sometimes you find the thing that makes sense . . . the answer to a question. You know that. You know things aren't always black and white. You were a detective once."

"Yeah, I sure was," Cortez said. "I detected people who poached wild animals and ran drugs. Only time any of them ever imagined anything was when they were dead drunk or stoned. The rest of the time their grip on reality was as black and white as it comes. There were no gray areas. Take that fucker who walked into the bar and recognized my face, for example."

"And what about you?" she asked. "What about your grip? Did you ever live in the gray area back then, when you did what you did, in the places you had to go? Back when you were pretending you were somebody else? Did you ever wonder what was real and what wasn't? Did you ever wonder who you really were?"

"I wondered that all the time," Cortez said.

"See, I had to deal with that problem when I was a little girl," Angela said. "When I found out I was adopted. 'Who am I, really?' I would wonder. One day I realized it didn't matter where I'd come from. What mattered was who I became . . . what kind of person I made myself into. From then on I never had that problem again. No matter how weird things got I always had a grip. I was planted."

"Until you talked to that woman. The psychic. The old man's friend."

"She knew about Bobby," Angela said. "In the ten years I've lived down here you're the only person I ever told about him. She looked at that picture, or whatever you want to call it . . . that image . . .

and it was like she saw into the secret corners of my life. The places where I go to hide."

She brushed the hair from her face and looked at him from the small pool of light in which she sat. That was where he had found her when he arrived at the trailer two hours before, sitting with papers spread all around her, looking like a schoolgirl studying for a test, except for the assault rifle resting across the arms of the deck chair next to her and the .44 hanging from the peg behind her on the wall.

"Come here," she said. "I want to show you something."

She gathered up the papers, put them into a manila envelope, reached down past her toes and removed a book from the shelf above the foot of the bunk. She opened the book and took what appeared to be an old photograph from between the pages.

"Did I ever show you his picture?" she asked. "I don't think I ever have."

"No," he replied. "You never showed me any picture." He lifted the rifle from the arms of the chair, put it on top of the counter next to the stove and sat down. "You never told me you had one."

"Here," she said, extending her hand.

The man in the picture looked to be in his mid-twenties. He was lean, skinny almost, but sinewy, with long dark hair and a handsome, angular face. He was wearing jeans and a T-shirt and stood with coiled energy next to an old Chevy Nova that had obviously been set up to race. Cortez could see a large exhaust pipe dumping out just below the Nova's door. He studied the picture for a moment, feeling Angela's eyes on him.

"You're surprised," she said. "You expected him to be taller."

Cortez looked from the photograph to her face.

"Yeah, I guess," he said. "How'd you know that?"

"All the time I've spent with men," she said. "I know how they think."

"That's the car he raced?"

"One of them. He could drive anything. He had the touch."

"And he was a doctor?" Cortez asked, looking back at the picture. The young man looked more like a rock musician or maybe an actor.

"Almost," Angela said. "Almost a doctor. Almost my husband. Almost the father of my children. Then the van he was riding in went off a bridge and exploded. You've heard that part of the story before."

She stretched out on the bunk and stared at the ceiling. Cortez placed the picture back in the book that lay beside her. It was a scuffed, leather-bound volume called *The Mountain Men*. The book was about the guides, traders and adventurers who blazed the trails through the Rockies to the Pacific Northwest. It was open to a full-page photograph of a craggy old fur trapper and army scout named Amos Watson. There was something vaguely familiar about his tough, weather-beaten face.

"I always saw myself as strong and invulnerable," Angela said. "You know, able to leap tall buildings in a single bound. When we were kids it was always me, not my brother, who climbed up and got the cat down out of a tree when it was stuck. My brother was afraid of the tree *and* the cat, both. Even after Bobby died and I came down here that's how I felt. I knew who I was. My heart was broken but I knew who I was. And I was never afraid. Not even when I had to go undercover in narcotics. Until I came home and found my dogs hanging in the tree, fear and vulnerability were not part of my working vocabulary."

"They weren't part of mine either," said Cortez. "Until the dude with the knife separated me from my right hand."

"So what do I do?" Angela asked. "Now that I'm scared."

"You could find a new career," Cortez said. "You could move to the south of France and quit working altogether. I mean it isn't as though you need the job. But see, I'm thinking no matter whether you're scared or not, you'd never forgive yourself if you bailed while this case was still open. Afterwards . . . afterwards it all depends how much you need the juice. Ain't no juice layin' carpet. Sometimes, I admit I miss it. But then I look at where my hand used to be.

"You have to watch out though, Angela. No more drag racing. No grandstand plays. No leaping off buildings in a single bound just to prove to yourself you really ain't scared after all. And the other thing is you gotta learn to reach out. Asking for help ain't a sign of weakness."

"I'm reaching out to you," she said.

"That's different," he said. "That ain't no reach. You proved all you ever have to prove as far as I'm concerned and you know it. You saved my life."

"Well, I reached out to Troy. I asked him to deal with my dogs. I couldn't bear to do it so I asked him."

"And I'm bettin' he don't think the less of you for it."

"It's hard to tell what he thinks."

"Well what did he say?"

"He told me to take a hot bath and eat some soup. No problem about the dogs. He and his friend took care of them. He insisted I stay at his house."

Cortez raised his eyebrows and smiled.

"I had no choice, Isaac. My tire was shredded. It was pitch black outside. I slept on the fucking couch. *He* slept upstairs. And anyway, I didn't want to be alone."

"The guy in the book, on the page where you stuck Bobby's picture, he looks kind of like Roland Troy. I forgot his name already. The army scout."

"Amos Watson," Angela said. "He lived to be ninety-six. Made a fortune mining silver in Leadville, Colorado, in his seventies. At seventy-five he married a woman thirty-eight years younger. They even had a kid. When he was eighty he helped run the campaign of Colorado's first governor."

Cortez chuckled. "Troy might look like the dude," he said, "but he don't act like him."

"No, I don't think Roland Troy will ever own a silver mine," she said. "I don't think he'll get married and have a kid when he's seventy-five either. In fact, I don't think Roland Troy will ever get married again."

"I wasn't talkin' about the gettin' married part," said Cortez. "When it comes to the human heart you can never be sure. But from what I've heard, Roland Troy would never help a politician. I think he's had to shoot a couple, but he'd never work for one."

"I don't imagine he would," Angela said.

"The guy in the book," said Cortez. "Amos Watson. He's got these eyes . . . does Troy have eyes like that?"

"Yeah," she said, wondering how Troy would react when she told him what she'd found in Stan Erland's notes. Based on what he'd said to her about the Indians when they first met, she doubted that Troy, unlike Cortez, would dismiss as irrelevant anything the old psychic might have imagined.

"Troy's eyes are what made me think of the picture," she said. "It's like they're hard and soft at the same time . . . like they know what you want to hide but they understand. It's like you can look into them and see a mirror of your own soul."

"You fallin' in love?" Cortez asked.

"Gimme a break, Isaac," she said. "You asked me a question, I answered you is all. He's an old man."

"He ain't that old," said Cortez. "Amos Watson was older."

McKenzie Rockett saw Roland Troy sitting alone at the table known as the wheelhouse in the back of Jimbo's Restaurant. There was an untouched plate of food in front of him and an unlit cigar in his mouth. He was reading a book and didn't see Rockett come in. Roland Troy was the only white person Rockett knew who could sit in the wheelhouse by himself with Jimbo's blessing. Years before Rockett had asked Jimbo why that was.

"You remember the Debra James murder?" Jimbo asked.

Rockett had nodded. Debra James was a fourteen-year-old black girl who was found dead beside the railroad tracks in Winter Park in 1976. Her throat was slashed and she had been raped. Her uncle, a man named Houston McCray, was tried, convicted of the crime, and sentenced to death. It was all nice and tidy, wrapped up, trial and all, in a matter of weeks. But Roland Troy knew the uncle well and didn't think he was the killer.

"There wasn't a cop in all of Florida who believed Houston McCray was innocent," Jimbo told him. "Or if they did they weren't goin' do anything about it. Except for Roland Troy. It took him a year and a half, working on his own time, to find the man who did it. But he did find him. Got him to confess too. It was that minister, the one who cut a record up in Nashville."

"Yeah," Rockett said. "I remember."

"Houston McCray was my cousin."

"I never knew that."

"Uh huh," Jimbo said. "That Roland Troy come to my house he can sit anywhere he wants, anytime he wants."

Rockett got a mug of black coffee from Jimbo's wife, Bernice. She asked him what he wanted for breakfast and he told her he wasn't hungry.

"You should eat something, McKenzie," she said in a motherly tone, no doubt prompted by the knowledge that his wife was out of town.

"Maybe later," he replied.

Several people said hello but Rockett only nodded to them and kept moving. He knew what all of them wanted to talk about. The fragmentation of Smooth Lee had galvanized the black community, and though McKenzie Rockett had never witnessed an avalanche he had the distinct sensation of being in the midst of one. It was a good thing, he thought, that his kids were grown and far away so they wouldn't have to deal with any of this. A split second later he wondered whether the distance would make a difference.

When Rockett reached the wheelhouse he took a long sip from the mug and sat down. Troy stopped reading, looked up and smiled. There were dark circles under his eyes and spots of dried blood on his flannel shirt. He had spent the night at the hospital waiting while Halpatter underwent surgery to remove the bullet from his thigh. Rockett saw that the book was a bound soft-cover monograph on right-wing extremism published by the Anti-Defamation League. He had no idea how Troy had gotten his hands on it.

"I called Angela and told her what happened," Rockett said, looking at his watch. "She should be here any minute. What's the word?"

"Halpatter's going to be all right," Troy said. "His leg's pretty well tore up, but he won't lose it. Ain't gonna be climbing trees for a while though."

"The shooter wasn't so lucky," Rockett said, unbuttoning the top button of his shirt and loosening his tie. "They found him at the edge of your pond. Halpatter's pole caught him in the lower back, punctured a kidney and severed his renal artery. He bled to death."

"Too bad Sheridan's so fucking accurate. I'd like to have had a chat with that boy."

"You ain't the only one."

"Any idea who he is?"

"Not a clue. Didn't have a bit of ID on him. Looks to be around thirty or so. They're running his prints. Got his gun though. Walther P-eighty-eight."

"I'm impressed," Troy said, lighting the cigar.

"Yeah, well I don't think he was planning on using it," Rockett said. "At least not on you. He had the timing device for a bomb in his jacket. His buddy probably had the works. My guess is they were fixin' to wire your house. They were gonna blow you up, Tooth."

"One of 'em stepped on my sign. That's what woke me up. They wouldn't have gotten a whole lot of wiring done."

"Kind of sloppy of 'em," Rockett said.

"They didn't think I was home," Troy said. "Where's my truck?"

Rockett had his coffee cup halfway to his lips. He paused and set the cup back down. "It's sittin' outside the office," he said. "Right where Angela left it."

"Speak of the devil," Troy said.

He looked past Rockett and nodded. Rockett turned and saw Angela Becker coming toward them. She was wearing a clean pair of jeans, a dark green turtleneck jersey and running shoes. Her hair was loose and swung across her shoulders as she walked. Troy and Rockett rose slightly from their chairs as she approached.

"Chivalry," she said, as she sat down. "And so early in the morning too. How's Halpatter?"

"He's going to be fine," Troy said.

"Any leads?" she asked.

"Not a thing," Rockett said. "Nothin' but dead bodies and dead ends. Got an ID on the woman in the motel room where one of the calls to Erland was made. Same gun killed both of 'em. Her name was Linda Bernard. She worked for an escort service in Atlanta. Once upon a time she was an actress. Had a minor role on a soap opera. Then she found cocaine. Arrested four times, twice in New York for possession, twice in Georgia for prostitution. No record of how she got to Orlando or who brought her here. Escort service says it was her day off. Says she must have been freelancing. No known next of kin.

"Smooth Lee, on the other hand, had lots of kin and I've been hearing from 'em pretty much nonstop. Every one of 'em has a theory about the bomb in Oliver Reavis's truck. Look around. Everyone in here has a theory too, you can bet your sweet ass on that. Everything from a direct strike by voodoo space aliens to a Klan hit on account of Oliver Reavis's close relationship with a certain tall, blond, female cop. Somebody in the neighborhood laid that one on the guy who's got the cops-and-robbers beat at the *Journal-Express*. Same writer's been doing some digging and guess what? He found out Stan Erland, the tall blond's partner at the task force, was mysteriously murdered—those were his words . . . 'mysteriously murdered.' He left a message on my machine which I haven't as yet returned saying he'd appreciate my comments for his story. As you might imagine, I'm now getting pressure from on high, which is royally pissing me off because I was specifically told we would be left alone until we asked for help."

"Maybe we need some help," Angela said.

Rockett got up, took off his suit jacket and hung it on the back of his chair. "I need some food," he said.

"Eat mine," Troy said. "I ain't hungry."

"I don't know if I am either," Rockett said, sitting down. "I went and shipped my wife off to Ohio, Tooth. Can you imagine that? I mean she's been wanting to visit her sister up there for a while, but all three of us know why she made the trip at this particular time. And there are other people in this restaurant who know why too. In all my years on the job I've never done something like that. I'm more than pissed off. I'm incensed."

Seeing Rockett stand up, one of Jimbo's nieces who was waitressing came over. "Y'all looked like you didn't want company," she said. "That's why I waited to come over."

Angela ordered toast and coffee. Rockett studied the plate in front of Troy. "What the hell *is* that?" he said.

"Potatoes and onions," Troy said, "with some of Jimbo's Cajun sauce."

"I want bacon and eggs," Rockett said. "Scrambled on the eggs, crisp on the bacon. And buttered toast. I will take my fury out on my arteries."

When Jimbo's niece was gone he turned to Troy.

"So what do you think, Tooth?" he asked. "You agree with Angela? Do we need help?

"I wasn't serious," Angela said. "We can handle it."

Troy relit his cigar, which had gone out again. He puffed on it a couple of times, then removed it from his mouth, set it down on the grooved corner of the ashtray and stared at Angela. She had obviously paid careful attention to her hair and makeup and looked absolutely radiant, yet at the same time she seemed in turmoil, as though she were at war with herself, fighting desperately to remain calm. He noticed that her fingers were tightly gripping the arms of her chair. She caught him looking and smiled uneasily.

"What?" she asked.

"Nothing," he replied. "I agree with you. You and I can handle it. Anyway, the kind of help they'll send in would just muddy the water. Long as the local crime lab is still in business we're OK. They're all the help we need. Speaking of which, did they get any prints off Oliver Reavis's truck?"

"They're working on it," Rockett said.

"If they find any, I'll bet we get a match with the dead guy on the end of Halpatter's pole. And I'll make you another bet. I bet the tire tracks at Angela's trailer match the ones they're gonna find out at my place. Put a spin on it if the big boys start twisting your arm. Call it progress." Troy turned to Angela. "You feel like taking a ride?" he asked.

"Sure," she said. "Where to?"

"To get my truck. I'll go home and take a shower, you drop the company car off and bring the truck up to my place."

"Then what?" she asked.

"Then we go look at the dead guy. The one Halpatter harpooned. We talk to Peiser at the lab. We keep our eyes open and see what develops."

"I've got a meeting with the big boys in an hour downtown," Rockett said. "Then I'm going out to Reavis's garage to talk to the guys from the bomb squad. After that I'll be in the office. My faithful pager will be at my side throughout. Do me a favor. If something does develop, let me know."

"Stay cool, Rock," Troy said, standing up. "Face those assholes with steel in your eye and certainty in your voice. I'm gonna get moving. Eat some breakfast. Breathe deeply. And don't worry. Just make sure those fellas from the bomb squad take a look at my truck before anybody tries to start it up."

XVI

Late the previous night, while the bullet was being removed from Sheridan Halpatter's thigh and Roland Troy dozed in the hospital waiting room, Nigel Fullerton, captain of the crude oil carrier *Honoria G*, sat in the drawing room of his suite on the captain's bridge deck sipping brandy and leafing through a book on kitchen and bathroom renovation. Fullerton was in excellent spirits. He had won his nightly game of chess with the ship's chief engineer, taken an invigorating walk twice around the circumference of the main deck, and was now contemplating the expansion and improvement project that he would soon begin at his home on the Isle of Wight. Since going to sea more than forty years earlier he had spent very little time there, but now Fullerton was about to retire, and each night before going to sleep he would pour through the stack of books on home design he had brought with him on this trip.

The *Honoria G* was moored at the giant tanker terminal off Lafourche Parish on the Louisiana coast. It had begun its journey from the Persian Gulf more than a month before, following the ancient trade route known as Carriera da India around the Cape of Good Hope. Fullerton, an avid student of maritime history, derived great pleasure knowing that this, his final voyage, retraced the same route around the tip of Africa taken centuries earlier by Chinese clippers, East Indian merchant schooners, and the ships of Portuguese traders who sailed back and forth from southern Asia. It gave Fullerton a sense of closure, a feeling of belonging that prior to his last few journeys had been torn from him like a signal flag ripped from a mast by a gale-force wind.

Nigel Fullerton had been employed by the same illustrious shipping company for his entire working life, but three years earlier the company was acquired in a hostile takeover by businessmen from Hong Kong.

In short order they dismantled this firm that had been a fixture in sea-going transport for more than two centuries. Fullerton, after forty-two years of service, found himself out of a job. At sixty-three, it was unlikely that anyone else would hire him. Furthermore, there appeared to be discrepancies in the handling of the firm's pension fund, leaving Fullerton and dozens of other former employees without any retirement benefits.

Devastated and despondent, Fullerton returned to the Isle of Wight and took a job driving a small tour bus around the island. Fullerton was a frugal man but most of his savings had been spent caring for his wife, who had recently died after a long illness. It appeared likely that even with this new job he might have to sell his beloved home high on a bluff overlooking the English Channel in order to make ends meet. Then one day a well-dressed man with piercing eyes and a thick mustache, who was a passenger on his bus, approached him at the end of the tour. The man's name was Rafiq Said. He told Fullerton he was the operator of a small fleet of tankers and tramp freighters flying flags of convenience. He was in need of a captain, he said, a man with plenty of experience who was willing to pilot ships with more than simply crude petroleum on board. Fullerton had been recommended to him, but he would not say by whom.

"What exactly might this additional cargo consist of?" Fullerton asked.

"For the amount you will be paid, that should not be an issue," Said replied. "The special cargo will always be stowed in either sealed wooden crates or steel containers. It will be loaded and unloaded by a separate team of men, not by anyone in your crew. The proper authorities will all be taken care of. Customs officials will never be a problem. Your risk will be minimal. Work for me for two years and you will never have to worry about money again. You will be able to keep your home here on this lovely island and will have no difficulty spending the rest of your life pursuing whatever interests you."

Nigel Fullerton made his decision at once. Running contraband, which is what he assumed Said meant when he referred to special cargo, appealed to him far more than either driving a tour bus, or jumping in front of one, an option he had recently begun to consider. He didn't bother to ask how Rafiq Said had known about his house.

The primary tanks of the *Honoria G* contained crude oil that had not yet been pumped from the ship. That process would take place once the special cargo, stowed in another holding container, known as a clean ballast tank, had been off-loaded at dawn on the following day. The reason for this is that fully loaded oil tanks are far safer than empty ones. Once emptied, a ship's oil tanks soon become chambers of highly volatile hydrocarbon gas, the result of oil residue left when the tanks are pumped. The presence of this gas greatly increases the possibility of an explosion. With the safety and cleaning procedures employed on modern tankers, explosions almost never occur, but Nigel Fullerton was taking no chances. As usual, Fullerton did not know precisely what the clean ballast tank held but he did know it was something of great value, since he was being paid a substantial bonus to haul it. He had been paid a very generous salary for the past two years, and with the addition of this bonus he would have no problem retiring in comfort and affording the renovations to his cottage. His despondency had long since disappeared and he had no intention of blowing himself or his cargo to kingdom come.

Upon docking at the tanker terminal, Captain Fullerton sent almost all of the *Honoria G*'s crew of thirty-four men ashore on leave. At the moment, the only men on board other than Fullerton were the chief engineer, with whom he had played chess, and the electrical officer, who ran the computer controlling virtually every operation on the ship. Like Fullerton, both of these men had been well paid to ensure the safe passage of the special cargo.

Nigel Fullerton set his book on the coffee table in the drawing room. He rinsed his brandy snifter in the sink located in his suite's tiny kitchen, went into the bathroom and brushed his teeth. Then he did a few stretching exercises and climbed into bed, satisfied that all was in order. Shortly before dawn he would arise, get dressed, go down to the main deck and await the arrival of a transport helicopter capable of lifting heavy loads. The pilot of the helicopter would give the electrical officer a code word for the computer, allowing the sliding steel door of the clean ballast tank to open. A second code word would activate the tank's elevator platform, raising the wooden crates containing the cargo to the level of the deck. The crew of the helicopter, working quickly and with precision, would then fasten the chopper's external cargo hook to the stainless steel webbing surrounding the crates and the helicopter would depart with the cargo. Its destination was unknown to Fullerton, who intended, upon its departure, to go back to his suite and have breakfast with the chief engineer and the electrical officer. The chef of the *Honoria G* was in New Orleans, but Fullerton himself was an excellent cook. Since he would be hauling no more special cargoes he anticipated whipping up something out of the ordinary for him and his colleagues. He fell asleep reviewing the ingredients for a ham and cheese soufflé.

Two hours later Nigel Fullerton was awakened by the sound of the helicopter. His mind still clouded by sleep, he listened to the percussive thudding of the chopper's blades, that seemed to be coming from almost directly overhead. He rolled over, checked the clock on his night table, and saw that it was two-thirty in the morning, a full three hours before the helicopter was supposed to arrive. Quickly, he threw on some clothes and opened the door to his suite. The chief engineer, whose suite was on the same deck as the captain's, was standing in the hall. The two of them looked at one another, both listening intently. The noise of the rotors diminished and then ceased. Obviously the helicopter had landed.

"Did anyone contact you?" the chief engineer asked. "Is there some change in the schedule?"

"Not that I am aware of," Fullerton replied. "We'd better go down to the main deck."

"Shall I call Holmquist?"

"Yes," said Fullerton, "but there's no need for him to join us. Tell him to repair to the computer room and wait until we find out what's going on."

As he and the chief engineer descended on the ship's elevator Fullerton decided he would call Rafiq Said's associate in Grand Isle before meeting the crew of the helicopter. There was a phone he could use mounted on the bulkhead in the passageway between the elevator and the main deck. He told the chief engineer to wait with him and was about to lift the receiver when a large, muscular man holding an automatic rifle came through the door that opened onto the deck.

214

"You don't want to do that, Captain," the man said. He had a ski mask over his head, but Fullerton could see by his exposed arms that he was black. He was immediately joined in the passageway by a smaller man, also wearing a ski mask, and also carrying an automatic weapon.

"We've come for the nonpetroleum merchandise you're carrying, Captain," the black man said. "We can do this the easy way or the hard way, but rest assured we are going to do it."

"I don't have the code," Fullerton said. "There's no way to get the tank open without it." No one had ever pointed a gun at him before and he felt slightly sick to his stomach. He could hear his heart pounding in his ears and feel sweat running down his back. He hoped the chief engineer, who was a rather belligerent fellow, wouldn't do anything stupid. But then, what actually could the man do, trapped in this narrow passage with two weapons pointed at him?

"We have the code, Captain," the black man said. "We have everything necessary to make the transfer, including your friends' Sikorsky out there on deck. Nice chopper considering its age. Now what say we get on with it."

Fifteen minutes later Fullerton stood watching as the stack of wooden crates—his final special cargo—enclosed in steel mesh netting and dangling from the helicopter's cargo hook swung out over the water and was lowered onto the deck of an oil rig tender bobbing in the water seventy feet below. He watched as the powerful tender disappeared into the darkness, followed by the helicopter and its heavily armed crew, knowing there was nothing he could do to stop either of them. There were men standing watch in the terminal's control platform six hundred yards away, but they had already been notified that a transport helicopter would be landing on the *Honoria G* that morning. Since no one aboard the tanker had sounded an alarm, they no doubt assumed the chopper simply arrived earlier than planned.

And even if Fullerton had been able to alert the terminal guards, what then? Surely, in the ensuing confrontation the special cargo would have been exposed. Then he, Nigel Fullerton, captain of the *Honoria G,* would have been implicated in God knows what kind of smuggling operation. The muscular black man obviously knew this, which is why no harm had come to either Fullerton or his two crewmen. Even so there would be no celebration for the three of them now, no gourmet breakfast. Nor would there be any bonus for delivering the goods. Fullerton sat down beside the clean ballast tank that was still open and dangled his legs over the edge. He peered down into the dark hole thinking that now there would be no renovations or additions made to his cottage by the sea. On the other hand, he did have enough money to keep the house and live in reasonable comfort. He would bear that in mind when he made his explanation to Rafiq Said, assuming of course that Said was still around to receive it.

XVII

From where he was sitting in the kitchen, Roland Troy saw the woman climb out of a white Chevy Lumina, come up the steps of his porch and approach the back door. She was of medium height and thin, with shoulder-length black hair and Eurasian features. She wore a charcoal gray tailored suit and had an athletic, supple walk, even in her high heels. When she got closer Troy could see that she was quite beautiful. Something in the way she carried herself and in her fine, sensitive features reminded him of someone but he couldn't yet identify who it was. She had a leather briefcase in her hand and he assumed she was another reporter. He had already talked to three of them—one from the *Journal-Express* and two from local television stations—out on the porch while the crime scene technicians went about their business, making tire-track molds, dusting for fingerprints, and generally nosing about.

Troy would rather have been left alone to take care of things but decided his best bet was to let them do their job. The head of the crime-scene unit and the chief homicide detective were old colleagues whom Troy had worked with and helped on many occasions. Though both of them had read Troy's statement detailing exactly what took place, they were more than willing to go along with his account to the press of the previous night's events on his property: Two armed men, obviously thinking Troy's house was unoccupied and probably looking for cash and jewelry to buy drugs, had been attempting to break in when they were surprised by Troy's close friend, Sheridan Halpatter. One of the men fired a shot that struck Halpatter in the leg. Before collapsing, Halpatter had struggled with the shooter, who was impaled on a piece of splintered wooden railing when the two of them fell to the ground. The man, who was thus far unidentified, had bled to death on the shore of Troy's pond. Troy saw no point in turning the episode into a media circus by mentioning such things as the timing device found in the dead man's pocket, the sharpened pole Halpatter used to hunt alligators, or his friend's perpetually bare feet.

He had been patient and cooperative with the reporters, but emphatically denied there was a connection between this incident and any other crimes. When the police beat writer from the *Journal-Express* asked him about Stan Erland he said all he knew was that the case was under investigation.

"Is it true that you've come out of retirement to help your old friend McKenzie Rockett solve it?" the writer asked.

"I'm just doing a little consulting," Troy answered.

The Eurasian woman stepped on the metal sign covering the hole in the porch and jumped slightly at the loud cracking noise it made. Gingerly, she took another step and then, seeing Troy sitting at the kitchen table, rapped lightly on the door.

"You're a little bit late," Troy said to her when she was inside. "Everyone's gone home and I'm about all interviewed out. But please sit down. You want a glass of iced tea?"

The woman's laugh was rich and throaty, not at all what Troy would have expected from someone so delicate.

"Oh Mr. Troy," she said, sitting in the chair he offered across the table from him, "I'm not a reporter, I'm an attorney. I must admit that broken porch railing and the yellow crime-scene tape in your yard has made me somewhat curious, but strictly from a personal standpoint. I'm here in an unofficial capacity, not to ask you questions. I've just come to deliver something to you from an old friend. My name is Madeleine, by the way. And yes, I'd love some iced tea."

"It must be pretty important if my old friend sent this something with you instead of sticking it in the mail," Troy said, pouring a glass of tea and setting it in front of her.

"He seemed to think so," Madeleine said. "But here, take a look and see for yourself."

She took a manila envelope out of her briefcase and handed it to Troy, sat back in her chair and took a sip of iced tea. Troy opened the envelope and removed three eight-by-ten color photographs. One was of a woman with long auburn hair and a man with dark hair and a thick mustache. They were sitting on a couch and the woman was wearing nothing but a pair of panties. The other two were of the same dark-haired man standing on a paved path talking with another man who was considerably larger and had a shaved head. By the looks on the faces of the two men and the way they were standing it appeared that the conversation was congenial.

"Recognize any of them?" Madeleine asked.

"Can't say as I do," Troy said.

"The big bald guy is Herbert Stiefel," she said. "The woman is Stiefel's wife, Dana. The other man's name is Reed Calloway. He's an FBI agent assigned to the central Florida office. It's your old friend's opinion that Mr. Stiefel is unaware of Mr. Calloway's intimate relationship with his wife."

"What do you know," Troy said. "What *do* you know. Well, that sure is mighty interesting."

"Your old friend thought so too," Madeleine said, laughing again. She took another sip of tea and stood up.

Troy knew from the first words this woman named Madeleine spoke—from the cheerful yet confident tone of her voice and her easy, self-assured manner—that the man she referred to as his old friend, the man who sent her to deliver the pictures, was none other than Chotoku Nakama, the powerful, secretive Asian warlord who had been a shadowy presence in his life for thirty years. Something was now different, however. Something in their long relationship had changed, since this was the first time Nakama had made an overt rather than surreptitious effort to contact him.

Troy didn't even stop to wonder how Nakama had gotten hold of the pictures. The warlord's resourcefulness was without equal. Instead, his initial reaction was to assume that for some reason Nakama's self-interest would be served by offering them to him. But perhaps, Troy thought, there was more to it. Maybe even Bassai, the impenetrable fortress, the arch manipulator whose ruthlessness was unparalleled, had finally mellowed.

Mellowed or not, Nakama's choice of emissary made perfect sense. Troy had no doubt that this woman was not only an attorney but a very good one, someone who would have no difficulty dealing with any sort of unforeseen interrogation that might have arisen in regard to the pictures. Her beauty was also not surprising, for Troy knew Nakama loved good-looking women and had a series of them as companions since the death of his wife. It suddenly occurred to Troy that in fact the woman Madeleine reminded him of was Nakama's late wife, a gorgeous French model Troy met while recuperating at Nakama's mountain retreat. Madeleine had the same grace, the same lithe movements, even the same slightly formal yet congenial way of speaking.

"You got a long drive ahead of you, and a boat ride after that," Troy said to her. "Assuming you're headed where I think you are. You sure I can't fix you something to eat before you go?"

"Oh, I'm sure you know exactly where I'm headed," Madeleine said, laughing for the third time. "But I'm not driving. That's a rental car. I flew a Cessna one eighty into Sanford. It's a lovely day to be up in the sky."

"An attorney and a pilot," Troy said. "And a mighty cheerful person to boot. My old friend is a lucky man. Tell him I'll come see him before too long."

Madeleine took a pen out of her briefcase and scribbled a phone number on the manila envelope. Troy glanced down and saw that the area code was in western Massachusetts.

"Give a call first," she said. "As I'm sure you know, he likes to move around. You never can tell where he might be."

McKenzie Rockett's beeper went off in the middle of a meeting with two congressional aids, the regional director of the FBI and an emissary from the mayor's office. He checked his pager, saw the call was from Roland Troy and excused himself, saying it was urgent and would only take a couple of minutes. The meeting was in a tenth-floor suite of a downtown office building. There were at least three telephones in the suite but there was a pay phone in an old-fashioned booth with a door in the lobby and Rockett made for it, choosing privacy over the irritation he was causing. On the way down in the elevator he realized he was drenched in sweat.

"I hope this is good news," he said when Troy answered. "I'm pissing off some very important people."

"Don't worry about 'em," Troy said. "I just had a conversation with my old buddy up in Virginia. I told him that contrary to our best interests we were being leaned on by the assholes he told you would leave us alone. You got a guy in your meeting named Esterhouse? Esterline? Something like that? Works for senator dumbass?"

"Yeah," Rockett said. "He's up there. He's twenty-seven years old with a degree in international relations from Georgetown. Magna cum laude, he was. He made sure to tell me that. He thought it was essential that I know. I just got done listening to his plan of attack. Among other things it involved flying in a federal strike force complete with snipers. I say, 'What the fuck you gonna do with snipers? Who you gonna snipe? There ain't nobody to snipe.' I say, 'You got off at the wrong stop, man. This ain't Waco. This ain't Ruby Ridge. This ain't Entebbe.' He never heard of Entebbe, Mr. Magna Cum Laude. He says, 'That isn't important. What's important is the public's perception of the seriousness of our intent. The people need to know we're prepared for any contingency.' Can you believe that? The people. What's that motherfucker know about the people? The dude's from Mars, Tooth. They're all from Mars. I'm holding court for a bunch of fucking Martians. Good thing they didn't hear about the dogs or I'd have the ASPCA up there with me too."

"You can relax, Rock," Troy said. "The Martian's cell phone is probably ringing as we speak. Those boys won't be bothering us for a good while."

"That's wonderful," Rockett said. "I've had enough of their horse shit to last me a lifetime. I got my good suit on and I've sweated right through it."

"There's more good news," Troy said. "I believe I've found where the roof is leaking."

"And where might that be?" Rockett asked.

"Where might *you* be?" Troy replied.

"I'm in a phone booth," Rockett said. "The door's closed and the line's clean."

"The guy's name is Calloway," Troy said. "He's a federal agent. Works out of the same office that Erland was in before he came to you."

"I'll be a son of a bitch," Rockett said. "Calloway, huh? I don't know him. Well, at least he isn't one of ours. How you want to handle it?"

"I could be wrong but I think he ain't nothin' but an errand boy. We bring him out in the open you know damn well what'll happen. His face'll be all over the paper and the TV and whoever's really throwing the party will disappear. If it's all right with you I want to deal with him personally. Squeeze him a little and see what drips out."

"That's the reason I went all the way up there and slogged through the mud to find you, Roland. So I'd have somebody I could turn loose. Do your thing, Mr. Tooth. Do it any goddamn way you see fit. You need me, just holler. What about Angela? She gonna get in your way?"

"On the contrary," Troy said. "She's going to be of considerable help. There is something bothering her way down deep, something other than what happened to her dogs, and I'm not sure yet exactly what it is. I don't even know if *she* knows what it is. But you were right about her. She's a tough woman. I believe she'll work her way through it. I got no problem with Angela Becker, Rock. None at all. You go kiss those hacks upstairs good-bye and get yourself a little rest. Give Carolyn a call. You'll feel better."

"You really want to know why I'm so fucking mad?" Rockett said.

"Because Esterline, the Martian, is black," Troy told him. "Because he's putting on a show for the white people up there, lettin' 'em know he ain't gonna cut you no slack just because you're a brother."

"How'd you know that?" Rockett asked. "Ubinas must have said something about him, right?"

"Ubinas didn't tell me anything," Troy said. "You did."

222

XVIII

There was a hill at one end of Isla de los Caballos, a geological anomaly covered with saw palmettos and pines, that sloped upward to a promontory almost forty feet above the gulf. Near the crest, on the windward side of the hill, the trunks of the pines were twisted and bent at odd angles from the constant lashing of the wind. At the very top the vegetation had been cut away to make room for a wooden platform on which a gazebo with a wide swing inside had been built. The swing, sheltered from the sun by the gazebo's roof, overlooked the far end of the island's runway and the blue-green water beyond. Chotoku Nakama, sitting in the swing, paused in his midafternoon meditation and watched as a Cessna Citation flown by Brownie, his pilot, landed and taxied toward the hangar at the far end of the airstrip. The jet engines shut down and once again the only sounds Nakama could hear were the cries of the gulls and the wind in the trees.

Ordinarily, no one living on Isla de los Caballos would interrupt Nakama when he was in the gazebo. So vast were Nakama's holdings, so widespread his sphere of influence, that an hour rarely went by during the day in which any number of important decisions had to be made, but it was clearly understood that when Nakama climbed to the top of the hill he wished to be alone, undisturbed. Even if the problem at hand were deemed serious, it would have to wait until the warlord left the gazebo and returned to the main house. Still, Nakama was not surprised when he saw Brownie coming up the path through the pine trees at a fast trot. Judging by the elapsed time between the Citation's landing and Brownie's appearance the old pilot had obviously dashed from the hangar to the main house and then, when he discovered Nakama wasn't there, come running straight from the house to the

223

hill. By the time he reached the gazebo he was too out of breath to speak.

"Sit," Nakama said, motioning to a wooden chair perpendicular to the swing. "Relax. Since both of us are still alive, whatever it is you have to tell me can at least be delayed two minutes while you catch your breath. You know, Brownie, if you don't mind me saying so, you are getting a little old for this. You could as well have walked. The world would not have changed that much in the time you lost."

"This ain't the kind of news that can wait, Bassai," Brownie said. His breathing had slowed somewhat, but a slight whistling sound still came from down in his chest. Nakama looked at him intently but said nothing.

"Matter of fact," Brownie went on, "if I thought I could've radioed it in code I would have called from the plane. It's about the shipment we intercepted over in Louisiana. There's something you have to know about it, and the sooner I tell you the better."

"And what is that?"

"The *Honoria G* wasn't just hauling Stingers and RPG-sevens. You're currently the proud owner of about forty pounds worth of weapons-grade plutonium."

"No doubt in pit form," Nakama said. "Pit form is what Sharifi would have specified. He would not have wanted to deal with either metallic plutonium or plutonium oxide. Plutonium pits are safer and cannot be dismantled. We can determine where this plutonium came from by examining the steel casings in which they are sealed. These casings have an inner coating of either silver and tungsten or copper and tungsten, depending on whether the plutonium was produced in Krasnoyarsk-twenty-six or Tomsk-seven. There should be a stamp on them somewhere indicating their origin."

"You already knew," Brownie said, his breathing normal now and the whistling in his chest almost gone. "How? Sharifi never told us. Said is dead. The Russians . . ."

Brownie's voice trailed off. He knew Nakama would never have communicated with the Russians who stole the plutonium. He was far too crafty to have exposed himself like that. Nakama gazed out over the gulf, saying nothing for over a minute. Brownie watched him, wondering whether the conversation was over. After all these years the warlord was still a complete enigma to him, totally unpredictable, impossible to figure out or second-guess. Brownie spent more time with him than anyone else, yet he had no idea where or how Nakama accumulated so much information.

"Have I ever told you how I became a businessman?" Nakama finally asked. "I was quite young when I did . . . still a boy actually."

"No, Bassai, I don't believe you have," Brownie said, trying to conceal his surprise. Nakama almost never spoke about his childhood, and on the rare occasions when he did, it was only in a cloudy allusion.

"After my father's death I was sent from Foochow where I was born to live in Okinawa with my mother's cousin Shoshin Myazato. It was with Myazato-san, as you know, that I began my study of karate. Then, a year after I arrived, the Japanese and the Americans fought a great battle for control of the island. One hundred and fifty thousand casualties in three months. The typhoon of steel it was called. To avoid being killed, we hid in caves in the hilly jungle on the northern end of the island. While hiding in the jungle I met a man who paid me and several other boys for weapons and other equipment we took from dead soldiers. It didn't matter to him whether they were Americans or Japanese. 'I am Okinawan,' he told us. 'They are all invaders here.'

"It was extremely dangerous work that we did, even though we went out at night, but we were starving and this man paid us with food. He stored the weapons and equipment in a huge, underground bunker—a hidden cavern the size of an airplane hangar—deep beneath a mountain east of Toguchi. He sold these weapons and equipment to agents sent by Ho Chi Minh, who was at the time fighting against the Japanese in Indochina.

"One day this man and the five other boys I worked with vanished. I never discovered what happened to them, but what I did know was that fate had smiled on me. The bunker with all the weapons and equipment was concealed by incredibly dense vegetation and I was the only one left who knew how to find it.

"Now it was 1946. World War Two was over. The Americans controlled Okinawa, and I returned to Naha where I studied and continued my training with Sensei Myazato. Myazato had a freight-forwarding business and to pay for my room and board I worked for him loading and unloading the trucks that brought goods to and from the docks. One night we made a delivery to a warehouse in Koza. Two men were there. One had been a high-ranking OSS officer. The other had been a commander in the Japanese navy. They were speaking openly because they did not know I understood English. These men were discussing the acquisition of arms they intended to sell to Ho Chi Minh, who was now fighting yet another war for independence, this time against the French.

"I was with my cousin Ansai Shima that night. Shima was a few years older than I and was driving Sensei Myazato's truck. When we were done unloading and ready to leave I told him to wait for me and went back inside the warehouse. I walked up to the American OSS officer and told him I could help supply him with weapons. I was then thirteen years old, and you might think that for this reason the American officer would have laughed in my face and told me to get lost but he didn't. Instead, he asked me where he could see the weapons. I said I would bring them to him, at that warehouse, one week from that night. I also told him that I had friends all over Okinawa and if he tried to cheat me, or torture me, or throw me in prison he would regret it. Instead of becoming angry with me, he patted me on the back and said he liked my style. That was when he laughed.

"Since I could not drive and the bunker was many miles north I enlisted my cousin Shima to help me. Actually, I hired him. He became my first employee, the first soldier in my army. As you know, he continued to work for me until he was murdered many years later in Miami by assasins working for a Chinese tong."

Nakama paused and once again stared impassively out over the water. The wind had died down completely and the only sounds now were the cries of the gulls. Brownie waited uneasily, saying nothing.

"Shima was a loyal, honorable soldier," Nakama said at last. "Like you, Brownie. It was Shima who discovered Roland Troy when I sent him to Florida to buy land. Roland-san was only fourteen when he and Shima met on the river near the place where Roland-san now lives. Shima trained him. It was he who made him a Prancing Tiger. Did you know that?"

"No, Bassai," Brownie said. "I always assumed it was Myazato."

"There were more than two thousand rifles in that cavern," Nakama said. "There were machine guns, flamethrowers, mortars and hand grenades. There were two-way radios and cases of ammunition. There was even a jeep, although it was not in the best of shape since it had rolled down a ravine. I was thirteen years old and all of that was mine.

"Shima and I brought only fifty rifles and one case of ammunition to the warehouse a week later. The American officer paid me five dollars apiece for the rifles and I gave him the ammunition as a gift. Two hundred and fifty dollars, as you well know, was an enormous sum to a boy my age at that time, especially in a place like Okinawa, but that was nothing compared to the amount I wound up with when I finished dealing with these two men.

"At first I sold only a little at a time because I thought if they saw the entire contents of the cavern they would try to take it from me. I told the American officer I was only a messenger, a middleman. I knew the American would not believe that someone as young and insignificant as I could control so many weapons. The American and the Japanese commander wanted to meet this man, but I said he wished to remain unknown. They chose to believe me because they were making money. In the end I sold them everything in that cavern. One month before my fifteenth birthday I had seventeen thousand American dollars hidden away where all those weapons had been stored.

"But you must understand that in addition to making that money I had learned a most important lesson. A lesson, Brownie, that I have never forgotten to this day. I began my career as an entrepreneur dealing with two men who had recently been mortal enemies, an American and a Japanese. Now these recent enemies were allies in the arms trade. They were selling weapons to the Viet Minh who had recently been mortal enemies of Japan and would soon be mortal enemies of the Americans. The Viet Minh were fighting against the French who were the Americans' allies. The lesson I learned was that ultimately none of that made any difference. What mattered, Brownie, was the bottom line. Alliances might change, rulers of nations might come and go, political doctrines might shift like the sands of a desert, but business would always be business.

"So now we have the breakup of the Soviet Union, the crumbling of the fearsome evil empire, and everyone scrambles to do business with the Russians. New alliances appear. Doctrines shift this way and that. One power-hungry politician is replaced by another and it is open season for plundering, much of it done by the men who ran the former Soviet regime. Nothing has changed from the time I was thirteen years old, Brownie. Instead of carbines picked from the bodies of dead soldiers, the new arms merchants are selling Stinger antiaircraft missiles supplied by the United States to the Pakistanis to shoot down Russian fighter planes. They are selling these missiles back to the American government for a hundred twenty thousand dollars each. Not a bad deal when you consider that the Americans supplied them for free.

"The Russian mobsters, however, know where the real money is to be made, and so when Mr. Sharifi came calling and spoke about weapons of the most sophisticated kind, I knew at once he was not talking about Stingers, or RPG-sevens. It was clear to me that his Russian friends had finally managed to get their hands on a supply of weapons-grade plutonium. Given the chaotic state of affairs in the former Soviet Union it was only a matter of time before that happened.

"Sharifi is a greedy pig but he was no terrorist. Fear dripped from him like water from a leaky faucet because he realized that money aside, he had involved himself in a deal with someone as unstable as the merchandise he was moving. This Novac DuCharme who was buying the plutonium is a madman. He patterns himself after Adolf Hitler, an earlier madman. In fact, he believes he is the previous madman's rightful successor. Frightened though he was, Sharifi-san spoke accurately when he said to us that DuCharme is bad for business."

Nakama folded his arms behind his head and leaned back in the swing and turned to look out over the water for a third time.

"So that's why you took Sharifi's cargo, Bassai? Because in DuCharme's hands it would be bad for business?"

For a long time Nakama continued looking out to sea and did not speak. The muscles in his hard face were relaxed and there was a smile on his lips, almost as though he expected something familiar to appear over the horizon.

"Madeleine flew this morning to see Roland-san," he finally said. "We should be hearing from him quite soon I think. Where is the cargo now?"

"At the retreat in North Carolina, Bassai," Brownie said. "Tim and I stored it in the underground shelter."

"And who knows where it is besides the two of you?"

"Only the forklift."

Nakama nodded in satisfaction. "I have been in the business of making my fortune for more than fifty years," he said. "Of ensuring that I would never have to peddle pots and pans like my father. I am getting tired of that business. There is another kind of business to be taken care of now and that is why I am, as you say, the proud owner of this plutonium." He rose from the swing and stretched. "You must be hungry, Brownie," he said. "I know I am. Let's go see what unusual dish Madeleine has cooked up for us this time."

XIX

"There's your trespasser," Dr. Arnold Peiser said.

He unzipped the black vinyl bag and folded it back, revealing the naked body of a man about six feet tall with a dark, purplish wound on the left side of his chest. The man's lips were parted slightly and his eyes were not completely closed. In the glare of the lab's fluorescent lights it looked almost as though he were awakening and was about to speak.

"Not a bad looking fella," Peiser went on. "Good muscle tone. Nice head of hair. Your friend the Indian really hit the bull's-eye with that pole, but the thing is, Roland, he would have died anyway. He had the same chemical in his system that killed Detective Becker's poor dogs. You want to sit down, Detective Becker? Want a glass of ice water?"

"I'm fine," Angela said. "He isn't the first dead man I've seen."

"No, I don't imagine he is," Peiser said. "I was only trying to be polite."

"That's nice of you," she said. "You can call me Angela."

"Tell us about the chemical, Arnold," said Troy.

He and Angela were standing on one side of the rolling table with the dead body on it. Peiser, a short, thin man with wispy brown hair and a pale, scholarly face, stood on the other side. Troy noticed that Peiser was wearing an Orlando Solar Bears sweatshirt under his lab coat and smiled. In the freezing room where the medical examiner worked, the souvenir of a semitropical hockey team seemed quite appropriate to him.

"This is very strange, Roland. Very strange indeed," Peiser said. "When I first examined the dogs I of course thought ketamine. You can knock down a fairly good-sized hippo with the proper dose of that stuff, to say nothing of a dog. The thing about ketamine, though, is that by itself it causes convulsions in dogs, so in a humane, veterinary situation it would ordinarily be mixed with a tranquilizer like xylazine. That would eliminate the possibility of convulsions. In this case, however . . . it didn't seem to me that the people who killed Detective Becker's . . . Angela's . . . dogs would be all that concerned about convulsions, so I was initially looking for a straight shot of ketamine. But that isn't what I found at all. What paralyzed your dogs, Angela, was curare."

"I've heard the name before," Angela said, "but I don't really know what that is."

"It's a very powerful poison," Peiser said. "A resinlike alkaloid, actually, that causes almost immediate paralysis. Certain Indian tribes in South America use it on the tips of their arrows. They get it from the bark of various trees, or from the root of the moonseed vine known as pareira. In twenty-two years at this job I've only come across it once before, when I was doing my residency out in San Diego. A couple of Bolivians were found on the beach in Coronado shot full of it. The police assumed it was some kind of vendetta, the way the bodies were laid out, but they never solved it."

"And curare, which took out the dogs, also did the trick on our friend here," Troy said.

"That it did," said Peiser. "There was enough curare in the guy to kill a horse. Here, take a look at this." He turned the dead man's head to the right and pointed with a gloved finger to a tiny discoloration on the man's neck. "Someone hit him right there with a syringe, probably when he was already on the ground. If it had happened up by your porch he never would have made it as far as the pond."

"Where are the dogs?" Troy asked.

"I got 'em on ice," said Peiser. "Nobody's seen them but me."

"Can you get rid of them?" Troy asked. Beside him he felt Angela's body tense slightly but she said nothing.

"That won't be a problem," Peiser said.

"And as far as we're concerned this guy bled to death, right?"

"That is my preliminary finding, yes. There could of course be any number of drugs or toxins in his system, but it might take a couple of weeks before we'll know for sure. You understand that at that point I might have to adjust my initial conclusion."

"I understand completely and I appreciate your thoroughness, Arnold," Troy said. "You take as long as necessary. And thanks."

"Anytime," Peiser said.

"So the men at your house were the ones who killed my dogs, and maybe even my old partner Erland. And the one who got away injected the other one just in case he didn't die from Halpatter's spearing," Angela said, when they were sitting in Troy's El Camino. "Then there's no chance he can talk. He injects him instead of shooting him because he hears you in the house and doesn't want to draw attention to himself with a gunshot. That all makes sense. That I understand. But the only South Americans I ever dealt with were either running coke or smack, and all of them had automatic weapons. I never met any who were packing syringes full of curare. You think we're dealing with some kind of international cult here? Ritual murder? Animal sacrifices? What's going on, Roland? And assuming Erland's murder was done by the same guys, how come there wasn't any curare in him, or for that matter in the hooker they found in the motel?"

Troy started the El Camino, stuck an old Jazz Messengers tape in the deck, and pulled slowly out of the parking lot behind the lab. "The hooker was bait," he said as he eased into traffic, heading south toward the city. "She wasn't part of anything. Erland was full of bullet holes. I doubt if they ran any chemical tests on him, but even if they had he probably would have come up clean. Whoever killed him wasn't trying to send a message. They just wanted Erland dead. The message began with your dogs."

"And what's the message?" Angela asked.

"I don't think the dead guy we just looked at got hit with curare to make sure his mouth stayed shut," Troy said. "If that's all the killer wanted to accomplish he could have cut his throat. That would have been quicker and less risky. You start fucking with a syringe in the dark you run the risk of sticking yourself. I think the man who did it knew we'd find the drug, just like he knew we'd find it in the dogs. Sort of like a calling card. He wanted us to find it."

"Why?"

"Maybe to demonstrate his power. To strike fear in our hearts. To let us know who he was. I'm not really sure yet, but I can tell you this, we ain't dealing with a bunch of primitive tribesmen swinging through the trees with poison-tipped arrows in their quivers. These dudes here use curare by choice, not necessity."

"Maybe we should go find Agent Calloway and see if he knows why."

"We'll deal with him in a bit," Troy said. They were about to get onto the interstate but instead he swung into a Handy Way just before the entrance and pulled up in front of the outdoor pay phones. "I have to make a quick call," he said. "I'll only be a couple of minutes."

He climbed out of the El Camino, leaving the engine running, and walked to the phone. He punched in the code for his long distance credit card and was about to reflexively dial the familiar number of Jack Ubinas in Virginia when a feeling as palpable as a hand on his shoulder stopped him. Instead, he dialed the number in western Massachusetts Madeleine had given him.

"Mountain View Inn," a woman's voice said on the other end of the line.

"This is Roland Troy calling," he said. "You have any vacancies for tonight?"

"I'm so sorry, Mr. Troy," the woman said. "We are completely booked for this evening. Let me transfer you to our other hotel."

Troy waited for almost a minute and then the same woman picked up again. "I'm having just a bit of difficulty forwarding your call," she said. "Let me have your number there and someone will be right back to you."

In thirty seconds the pay phone rang.

"If I had known you were planning a visit so soon, Mr. Troy, I would have offered you a ride with me," Madeleine said. "Seat-of-the-pants flying, like the old days. Now you'll have to settle for a ride in the jet with Brownie. Just tell me where and when."

"I have to pay a visit to a friend in the hospital," Troy said. "How about in two hours up at Sanford? I'll be in the FBO's office."

"That should be fine," Madeleine said. "Your partner is welcome as well. We'll expect you both for dinner."

"I'm sorry," Troy said as he climbed back into the El Camino. "Took a little longer than I thought."

"No problem," Angela said. "But there's something I have to ask you."

"What's that?"

"Why aren't we going straight after Calloway? Why do you want to put him on the back burner?"

"There's no doubt in my mind that Reed Calloway is getting paid by Herbert Stiefel, but Calloway has no idea we're onto him," Troy said. "He's ours whenever we feel like springing the trap. The question is, what do we want to do with him? He can probably hand us Herbert Stiefel, who more than likely is behind the murders of Erland and Leo Weiser, but maybe we can get even more."

"And the more we know . . ."

"The better use we can make of Agent Calloway."

"What if he does something dumb in the next few days and winds up full of holes like Erland?"

"That's the chance we take. But what the hell, we're gamblers, right? We drag race late at night and smack scumbags upside the head. Whatever it takes to grab an edge."

She stared straight ahead, looking through the windshield at a grimy man in hideous yellow shorts who climbed out of an old Buick with Ohio plates and shuffled into the store with several pink and white lotto slips clutched in his hand. Another gambler, she thought. Some poor soul without a prayer. They came here in droves, sick of winter, searching for comfort in the sun, starting over, just like her. She didn't need to play the lottery but in the end she was no different. The reference to the aborted race with Ernie Viens made her stomach churn. Even with the frustration of dealing with the skinheads she'd felt in control then, like she had the edge. It seemed like that had been years ago even though it was only two or three weeks. Disheartened, she thought about her dogs. She had felt so protected by them. By them, and her guns, and her badge. What a joke, she thought. There was no protection, especially not from herself. Justine Fallon had shown her that.

"So where do we go from here?" she asked. "What edge are we looking to grab now?"

"I want to check on Halpatter and see how he's doing," Troy said. "Then we're invited to dinner with a man I've known for a very long time."

She turned in her seat and looked at him, pulling the hair away from her face and cocking her head slightly. "Is that right?" she said. "And will I be required to dress for this dinner engagement?"

"No, the jeans are fine," Troy said. "This isn't any kind of formal occasion. Listen, if you've got plans or you want to go home and get some rest that's perfectly all right. But you were invited."

"Is this business or pleasure?" she asked.

"Does it make a difference?" he asked.

"Well I . . ." she began. "Hell, I don't know, Roland. It sounded for a moment like you were asking me for a date."

Troy hesitated for a few seconds before he spoke. In the closeness of the El Camino's cab her presence was suddenly intoxicating. He looked over at her and saw that she was grinning at him.

"Tough guy," she said, and winked.

"This man's name is Chotoku Nakama," Troy said. "He's one of the most powerful men on the face of this earth but very few people have ever heard of him. You'll never read about him in the paper or see his face on the evening news. Anonymity is an art form to Nakama. He's a fascinating man, brilliant, articulate, incredibly well read. He could charm the bark off a tree. But I ain't gonna lie to you, Angela. He's a totally ruthless outlaw, a desperado of a magnitude that's difficult to comprehend, the last man in the world you want to cross. Life is a game to him, a game where he makes the rules and people are nothing but pieces that get moved around on a giant board."

"And this guy is your friend?"

"I'm not really sure if friend is the right word. A long time ago he saved my life, when he could just as easily have let me die. Since then he's . . . I guess kept in touch is a good way of putting it."

"So you're one of the pieces on the board."

"I don't like to think so but sometimes I'm not sure."

"And he lives around here?" Angela asked.

"He doesn't have a permanent home," Troy said. "Countries, borders . . . they don't mean the same thing to him they do to most folks. He moves from place to place the way other people pick new restaurants to eat at. When I first met him he was living in a castle in the mountains of Burma. I'd been shot up pretty bad. He kept me there with him until I recovered. The only other time I saw him face-to-face was three years ago in Costa Rica. In between he's lived in Spain, France, Mexico, Chile, various places in the United States, the Caribbean. Those are the places I know about. There may be others. It's sort of a migratory instinct he has that makes him impossible to pin down. At the moment he's in the Gulf of Mexico on Isla de los Caballos, the Island of the Horses. I have no idea why he's there. Maybe somebody gave it to him to fulfill a debt. Maybe he just took it.

"The fact that he's invited me to visit him is very strange. He's never done that before. The fact that he's invited you to come with me is stranger still. In all the years I've known Nakama I've only talked about him to two other people but since he did invite you I figure you ought to know. I'm trusting you to keep it just between us, whether you go with me tonight or not. His pilot is picking me up at the airport in Sanford in two hours. It was Nakama who sent me those pictures of Calloway. Anything else he knows and is willing to tell me I can find out on my own. I just thought you'd find it interesting. You're my partner. And I'd like your company."

"I'd like to take a shower and change my clothes," she said. "My mother always told me if you're going to meet a desperado you should at least look clean and well dressed."

"Your mother told you that, huh?"

"Actually I never knew my real mother," Angela said. "My adopted mother was a drunk who fell off a balcony in our house and broke her neck when I was six. I lacked female guidance."

"So did I," Troy said, "until my daughter grew up. Now I've got it coming out of my ears. I'll drop you at your condo and pick you up on my way back from the hospital."

"Thanks," she said.

"I don't really have a choice," he said. "Your car's still in my barn."

"That isn't what I meant," she said. "I was thanking you for trusting me."

"Your partner is very beautiful," Chotoku Nakama said. "Is she a good detective?"

Roland Troy lit a cigar and propped his feet up on the low railing of the gazebo. "Is Madeleine a good lawyer?" he asked.

Nakama sat back in the swing and laughed. "Roland-san, when you lay in my house in Burma, full of bullet holes and morphine, I asked you how you felt and you said 'like a cross between a boat anchor and a piece of Swiss cheese.' You made me laugh then and you make me laugh now. I don't laugh much anymore and I suspect neither do you. It is something else we two old Prancing Tigers have in common."

"No," Troy said. "I don't laugh too much anymore, Bassai."

At sunset a wind had come up out of the northwest blowing away the thick cloud cover over Isla de los Caballos and the night turned clear and cold. Angela, who had worn a cotton knit dress, stayed behind at the house after dinner with Madeleine and Brownie while Troy and Nakama walked to the top of the hill at the far end of the island. There was no moon and the sky was brimming with stars all the way to the horizon.

"There I think is Spica, the centerpiece of Virgo," Nakama said, leaning forward in the swing and pointing. "But then again I am not sure. Dominique knew about the stars, not me. As you may remember she was a dreamer. She liked you a great deal, Roland-san. She asked about you frequently. 'Il passe comme une ombre,' she used to say. 'He moves by like a shadow.'

"She understood why it was necessary for me to send you on your way once you were recovered. She understood that your path was different than mine, but still it made her sad. When *Time* magazine wrote about that famous case you solved—the one in which you found the tooth—she cut the article out and put it on the refrigerator. We were still living in Burma then. I thought she would be glad when we left and moved to the coast of Spain, but I believe that she was happiest there in the mountains, teaching the children in her school. She's been dead seven years now, but still it seems as though it were last week.

In her case it was an illness, a genetic aberration about which nothing could be done. In the case of your wife, Clara, it was something altogether different. An unspeakable horror. I know you searched very hard for her killers, Roland-san. I heard. I want you to know that if I could have helped you I would have."

Troy puffed on his cigar and for a time was silent. In spite of the cold clear air and the vast, dark expanse of sky and water before him he felt as though he were slowly being drawn into a narrow enclosure, encircled by a thick stifling web. He had sought Nakama's help only one other time, when he traveled deep into the Costa Rican jungle to find him. A man's life hung in the balance, but Nakama toyed with him nonetheless. Now, even though Nakama's recent actions seemed to indicate a complete turnabout in his behavior, Troy couldn't keep from wondering whether the old warlord was engaged in yet another of his manipulative games.

"You are suspicious," Nakama said, reading Troy's mind. "You sit there with your cigar thinking what can the old man be up to? Out of the clear blue sky he contacts me offering his help. Instead of having to paddle a dugout canoe up a jungle river to find him he sends his jet plane to pick me up. Are his kind words some sort of subterfuge? Is there a trick up his sleeve?

"I don't blame you for being wary, Roland-san. Were I in your shoes, I would be wary too. Nevertheless, you are here and I suspect it is for more than a taste of Madeleine's delectable cooking. Tell me what has brought you to Isla de los Caballos."

"Angela had two dogs," Troy said. "A pair of Rottweilers. One day last week she came home and found them hanging from a tree limb. Their hearts had been cut out and stuffed in their mouths. Before they were butchered they were paralyzed with curare.

"Night before last my friend Halpatter surprised two guys who were trying to wire a bomb to my back door. One of them shot him in the leg. He killed the shooter. The other one got away, but before he left he injected his buddy with curare."

"And you are wondering who might take the trouble to use curare, which is not the easiest substance in the world to obtain, and also cut the hearts from animals and plant bombs," Nakama said.

"That's precisely what I'm wondering," said Troy.

Nakama rose from the swing, walked out of the gazebo, and looked up at the sky. "I'm getting stiff sitting in the cold like this," he said. "Come. We can continue talking where it is warmer."

They descended the hill in silence and worked their way through the deep sand back toward the lights at the other end of the island. Fifty yards before they reached the cluster of buildings Nakama motioned with his hand down a wooded side path that ended at the rear of the main house. They walked under the house, threading their way between the thick poles on which it rested until they came to a rectangular wooden shaft directly under the center of the structure. Nakama took out a set of keys, fumbled around a bit in the darkness, and finally found the one that opened a heavy steel door faced with wood that blended perfectly into the side of the shaft. As the door opened, a light came on illuminating a spiral staircase.

"This way we can go up to my study without disturbing anyone," Nakama said as they climbed the stairs. "Or, for that matter, without having anyone disturb us."

"You take the couch. I'll take the chair," Nakama said when they were in his study. "Stretch yourself out if you like. I can see that your hip is giving you some trouble."

"My hip's all right, Bassai," Troy said. "I'm tired is all. I don't sleep much these days."

Nakama turned off the bright overhead light that had come on automatically when the study door was opened, switched on a small desk lamp and sat down in an old leather armchair. "You lie awake thinking about your wife, no doubt," he said, shaking his head. "Her case is still open, né?"

"Unsolved murder cases are never closed," Troy said. "Even in Austria."

"So there is still hope that her killers will be found and brought to justice of one kind or another."

"There's always hope."

"What do you know about mushrooms?" Nakama asked.

"What do I know about mushrooms?" Troy repeated. "I know they taste good in spaghetti sauce."

"Indeed they do," Nakama said. "Indeed they do. Assuming of course that you do not have the misfortune to eat the wrong ones.

And among the wrong ones the worst of all is the white mushroom, amanita bisporigeia. One bite can be fatal. In certain parts of South America it is known as *el angel destructor,* the destroying angel. The portion of it that you see above ground—the reproductive organ of this fungus—is but the tip of the iceberg, so to speak. The invisible network of roots that grows beneath the ground has been known to extend for miles.

"There is a small group of far-right-wing extremists that is based in Argentina. The members of this group believe they are directly linked through the practice of various occult rituals to the former leaders of Germany's Third Reich. They call themselves El Hongo Blanco. The white mushroom. They are fanatics, sworn to secrecy, and are therefore extremely dangerous. It is my understanding that curare is the signature of their assassins. That, and mutilation.

"I am sure that in the course of your current investigation you have spoken to your old friend Ubinas-san, the man who first made you a scout. I would think he is one of the very few who is aware of El Hongo Blanco's existence, this man who lives alone in the country with his computer and seems to know everything. I am surprised he didn't mention it to you."

"I didn't ask him about the curare," Troy said.

"Instead, you came to me, *né?*" Nakama smiled and nodded his head slowly. "You are a clever man, Roland-san, a man who listens to his instincts. Law enforcement is fortunate to have you on its side."

"Ubinas didn't send me any pictures," Troy said.

"No, I am sure that he didn't," Nakama said. "Just as I am sure he didn't tell you that one of the members of El Hongo Blanco is a man by the name of Novac DuCharme."

Troy sat up on the couch and stared hard at the warlord who sat calmly in the easy chair, still smiling slightly.

"What else do you know about DuCharme?" he asked.

"I know that he is considered to be a valuable commodity by certain people connected to your government," Nakama said. "And I know that he is not quite as safe as he imagines, now that he has two Prancing Tigers tracking him instead of only one."

"There's something else you can do that might make the tracking a little easier for this Prancing Tiger," Troy said.

"And what might that be?" Nakama asked.

"Put me in touch with the man who took those pictures of Calloway," Troy said. "Or the woman."

"You realize that in the old days that would have been unthinkable," Nakama said.

"In the old days I ran faster and jumped higher," Troy said. "I didn't have bad dreams in the old days. And you never invited me over to dinner."

Nakama rose from the chair, went over to his desk and scribbled something on a yellow legal pad.

"Be very careful Roland-san," he said, tearing the top sheet of paper from the pad and holding it out to Troy. "The next time you need my assistance I may not be so easy to find."

XX

It appeared to Angus Elliott that Novac DuCharme's eyes were glowing and that radiant beams were emanating from his snow-white hair. It was not the first time Elliott imagined he was witnessing this phenomenon, which he took as physical evidence of DuCharme's transcendence, a sign that he was the direct agent of Christ militant. Elliott was convinced it was yet another indication of DuCharme's destiny as the ultimate savior of the human race, the true leader of the kingdom of light. Of late, however, DuCharme's kingdom appeared to be under siege. Links in the chain he had carefully wrought were either seriously weakened or in some cases completely broken. As Elliott saw it, DuCharme's progress was being impeded by agents sent from the kingdom of darkness, where the demon souls dwelled, waging war against the rightful heirs for control of the earth. These dark forces, Elliott believed, were either Jews, or various other vermin—Blacks and Asians mostly, but even certain lower orders of white people—who were controlled by Jews. That was the problem they had to confront. It was the same problem confronted by Adolf Hitler, the leader DuCharme had valiantly served and whose sacred mission he had inherited. That was what the voices from the other side told him night after night while Elliott, a chronic insomniac hooked on cocaine, drove in his red Lincoln Mark VII along the back roads near his home in the village of Velvet.

One of the voices Elliott heard exhorting him to counsel and assist the new führer was that of his late father, Werner Froelich who served in the same SS unit as Novac DuCharme. Like DuCharme, Froelich escaped capture by the allies and, after spending some time in Argentina, lived for more than thirty years in California as the businessman Wallace Elliott. His much younger wife gave up a promising career as

243

an actress to become a successful astrologer consulted by numerous movie stars and other wealthy Hollywood figures.

Angus, their only child, showed considerable interest in his mother's second profession and from an early age demonstrated what appeared to be remarkable extrasensory talents. When he was only eleven he gained local notoriety by leading police to a remote valley east of Santa Monica where a kidnapped infant had been abandoned. A year later he astounded his father by telling him there was a small tattoo just below his right armpit indicating the older man's blood type. Like all SS officers, Werner Froelich, or Wallace Elliott, did in fact have a tiny blood-type tattoo but until that day had never shown it to his son, nor told the boy about it.

Assuming something of great significance had been revealed to him, a sign presaging his son's extraordinary powers that would be vital to his cause, Froelich soon began a careful process of indoctrination, instilling in Angus a belief in an Aryan master race and filling him with virulent hatred for Jews, Blacks and Asians. In the following years he took him to underground gatherings of ultra–right wing fanatics in California, brought him to rallies deep in the woods of Oregon and Idaho, and introduced him to a cadre of retired military officers living out in the Arizona desert who were sympathetic to Froelich's extremist political views. Infiltration of the military, Froelich told his son, was an essential element to the triumph of what he referred to as the fourth and final Reich.

When Angus was seventeen and a senior in high school Wallace Elliott traveled to Argentina on business. The night before this trip Angus was sitting in his room doing homework. Suddenly, he was gripped by an overwhelming sense of doom, a feeling that something terrible was going to happen to his father. He raced downstairs and found his mother sitting at the kitchen table drinking a whiskey sour. It was immediately apparent to him that the drink in her hand was not her first.

"Your father is at an important meeting," she told him. "It has to do with the trip to Argentina."

"I have a bad feeling about his trip," Angus said. "A premonition. I think you should tell him not to go."

His mother looked at him with a strange, slightly quizzical expression on her face, as though she were trying to see inside his head.

"I've already spoken to him," she said in a voice that seemed to come from someplace far away. "There's nothing either of us can do to stop him. What will happen will happen."

A week later they received word that Wallace Elliott had died in the crash of a small plane taking him and two other men from Buenos Aires to the southern Paraguayan border town of Encarnación. Not long afterward, his mother told Angus about a man living in New York, a business associate of his late father named Novac DuCharme, who would one day lead a worldwide uprising culminating in the realization of his father's dream.

"When it seems to you that the time is right, seek him out," she said. "He already knows about you and will welcome you into his inner circle. You will be of great assistance to him, Angus. You will be a beacon for him, a valuable link to the world most believe does not exist."

"Do you know him?" Angus asked.

"Yes," his mother said. "I've met him twice. I did a reading for him . . ." Her voice trailed off. Angus waited for her to continue but she didn't say anything more. After studying her face for several seconds he decided not to question her further.

Angus Elliott observed carefully as the glowing eyes narrowed and the taut skin of Novac DuCharme's face became luminescent. The two of them were sitting across from one another in matching burgundy leather armchairs in the semidarkness of the stateroom on DuCharme's boat, which lay at anchor in the Gulf of Mexico eighty miles northwest of Isla de los Caballos. Between them was a low table on which a candle-burning hurricane lamp rested. Smoke from DuCharme's pipe, clenched tightly in his mouth, curled around his head. As usual he was impeccably dressed in a dark suit, white shirt, and wine-colored tie. Elliott's sharp, crowlike features were obscured by a hooded black sweatshirt. He looked from DuCharme's eyes to the small leather pouch on the table next to the lamp. It seemed to him that within the bag tiny embers glowed with the same incandescence that inflamed DuCharme's eyes.

"You have begun to doubt even me," Elliott said. "I can feel it."

"I have been robbed," DuCharme replied, picking up the leather pouch and caressing it with his right hand. "I have been betrayed. Our cause has been betrayed by one or more of those entrusted to uphold it. When my cargo worth thirty million dollars disappears without a trace I have reason to doubt everyone, don't you think, Herr Elliott?"

"Everyone but me," Elliott said.

"And why is that?" DuCharme asked. "What makes you different than the others? The members of the council who wait for me in Denver with news about the organization. The *kameraden* in Buenos Aires and Asunción. The South American cowboy with the nose of a Jew tied up out there in the dinghy and the other one who parades around the television studio like the circus performer he used to be. Do you suppose that any of them would declare his disloyalty if I were to confront him? Why are you the one among all the rest whom I should believe? And do not tell me it is because of whose son you are. Traitors have come from far greater lineage than yours."

"The reason you should believe me is because I am the only one other than you who speaks to those who came before us," Elliott said. "Because I can close my eyes and see things the others are unable to see, like the whereabouts of the sniveling half brother of Ernie Viens who's looking to make a deal with the police, or the apartment in New York where our Russian friends are staying. I can even close my eyes, *mein führer,* and see the gold teeth inside that leather pouch."

DuCharme looked down at the pouch in his hand for several seconds before putting it in the pocket of his suit jacket. Until very recently he had never taken it out of the study in his house on Long Island, but the voices he heard advised him that he was now passing through the most critical period since the end of the war. For good luck, and because he believed it brought him closer to the world inhabited by the spirits of the dead, the world from which the voices came, he had removed the pouch from his safe and carried it with him since hearing the news about the hijacking on the *Honoria G.* During the plane ride from New York, and while he waited on his yacht for his latest orders to be carried out, he periodically fondled the pouch as he considered his course of action. Not once, in all the years he'd kept it, had he ever shown its contents to anyone, nor had he spoken to anyone about it.

DuCharme puffed on his pipe and smiled through the smoke at Angus Elliott. From the day Elliott appeared in the offices of his electronics company, DuCharme was convinced he was a most remarkable man, a man with extraordinary powers who sensed things others were unaware of. The question he now asked himself was whether, at this crucial turning point, he was a valuable asset or whether, like his father before him, he had become a dangerous liability.

"Words are one thing," he said to Elliott. "Deeds are something else altogether. I have a test for you, Herr Elliott. A test of your absolute loyalty to me and to our cause."

"What test is that?" Elliott asked.

"You don't already know?" DuCharme chuckled. "You cannot close your eyes and see. I'm surprised. Come up on deck and I'll show you."

He led the way from the stateroom up the narrow staircase to the open deck. The April night was unseasonably chilly and Elliott thrust his hands into the pouchlike pocket of his sweatshirt. DuCharme, his hair ruffling slightly in the light breeze, appeared oblivious to the chill. He walked to the railing and Elliott followed.

There was a spotlight mounted on the corner of the railing. DuCharme turned it on and pointed it downward at the dark water. Below them, Elliott could see a small white dinghy, tied fore and aft to the larger vessel, tossing in the waves. El Papagayo, the South American killer, was seated on the dinghy's center seat. His hands were handcuffed behind him and his ankles were bound with heavy rope that was also wrapped several times around the seat. He had been stripped of his clothing and his pale, naked body, covered with a fine matting of dark hair, shook uncontrollably from the cold. In the bright beam of the spotlight he appeared to be some creature hauled from the deep. He looked up, squinting into the light, and spit in their direction.

"You want to kill me go ahead," El Papagayo shouted. "Kill him too while you are at it. Your lackey who thinks he can talk to *los muertos*. Then kill the big blond one who does your dirty work. You can't kill everyone, Helmut. You see, you don't think I know who you really are, but I do. I was told by others who also know. You think you are so powerful. You think you are more powerful than anyone or anything on earth, but I tell you and your slimy, hooded friend, *El Hongo Blanco es más poderoso que tú.* More powerful and more dangerous as well. Your time is growing short, Señor Savior of the Fucking Universe."

"Klaus," DuCharme said in a low voice that nevertheless seemed to carry for a considerable distance.

A very large muscular man with short blond hair emerged from the shadows. He was wearing crisply starched white pants and a dark windbreaker over a white turtleneck jersey. In his right hand was a Ruger Mini-14 assault rifle with a folding stock.

"Give him the gun," DuCharme said.

The blond man smiled slightly and handed the rifle to Angus Elliott. DuCharme nodded to Elliott. "The test," he said, gesturing over the railing with an upturned hand.

Over the years, in his service to DuCharme, Elliott had been required to do many things, among them arranging the disappearance of several of DuCharme's enemies, but this was the first time he had been asked to kill someone himself. Shooting a man in front of his führer was one thing. Shooting him in front of a second witness whom he considered little more than a brutal thug, a footsoldier in the army in which he served as the commander's aide-de-camp, was something else altogether. But Elliott, though hallucinatory and no doubt quite mad, was still a crafty, quick-witted man, one who prided himself on his clever and unconventional methods for taking care of business. They were anchored just beyond the outer limits of the continental shelf, and as the yacht rocked hypnotically in the waves, he closed his eyes momentarily and saw an image of El Papagayo one hundred and fifty feet below the surface, still sitting in the dinghy that rested on the ocean floor. El Papagayo was surrounded by schools of inquisitive multicolored fish that nibbled delicately at his body, unblemished by bullet holes.

Elliott opened his eyes and peered down along the rifle barrel at El Papagayo, who was now rocking back and forth and mumbling in Spanish. It seemed to him that he could see through El Papagayo's quivering flesh to his bones, which were vibrating in the blue-white glare of the spotlight. Elliott began to hum softly in rhythm with the vibrating bones as he raised the gun to his shoulder and fired three rapid shots into the floor of the dinghy in front of El Papagayo's feet. Still humming, he waited until the sound of the gunshots had died away, then fired several more rounds into the decking behind the center seat. El Papagayo shuddered involuntarily with each shot and tried, despite being bound hand and foot, to curl his body into itself. As water from the bullet holes began to pour into the small boat he let out a long, mournful howl. Angus Elliott wiped down the Ruger with the front of his sweatshirt and handed the gun to Klaus.

"Untie the ropes," he said.

Klaus glanced at DuCharme who nodded. The large blond man lumbered over to the stern of the yacht. He set the gun down, unfastened the lines to the dinghy that were wound around two chromed cleats, and threw the lines into the sea. The dinghy, half filled with water, bobbed listlessly and began to float away. El Papagayo, his legs completely submerged, turned his head and looked up once more.

"Fuck you, shit-eating Kraut," he yelled.

"Pleasant dreams," Klaus replied and turned off the spotlight.

"People are no different than other animals," Novac DuCharme said to Angus Elliott sometime later as they sat in the yacht's stateroom. They were making for shore, and the rumble of the ship's powerful engines underscored DuCharme's low voice.

"If, for example, you are raising dogs for a certain purpose," he said, "and you have a litter in which some are suitable and some are not, what you do is cull the inferior ones and keep the rest. But sometimes, in spite of all your efforts to breed correctly, all the care you have taken to ensure a good crop, you may produce a litter that is completely unacceptable, useless, contrary to your best interests. Then, of course, you simply dispose of it. You eradicate it and start over again. You understand what I'm saying? People need culling like anything else."

DuCharme smiled at Elliott around the stem of his pipe.

"Now there is only Stiefel, the ringmaster, to attend to," he said. "And Calloway, our friendly FBI agent."

"And the Russians," Elliott said.

"I've already attended to the Russians," said DuCharme. "I'll leave Stiefel and Calloway to you and your fertile imagination."

"I'll need access to the television studio," Elliott said. "I assume you have the keys."

"I have the keys to everything," DuCharme said. "You should know that by now."

XXI

Running camera high, Phelps watched through the lens as Herbert Stiefel bounded up the steps of the main sound stage at his television studio, raised both hands high in the air, and opened his mouth in a wide, toothy smile. At that moment it seemed to Phelps that Stiefel turned into a giant lizard, the wrinkles and bags on his face going from parchment to green and back in quick flashes, his thick, rubbery lips opening and closing, pulling in all manner of insects that had somehow made it past the security guards and gotten inside the studio while the guards were busy checking out the audience filing past the metal detectors. Actually, Phelps thought, it was the head of a lizard he saw, grafted onto the body of a man wrapped in an American flag.

Firing up a joint before coming to work was a risk, Phelps realized, inasmuch as Stiefel packed a gun and made no bones about his desire to shoot every pot smoker on earth. This, however, was special homegrown product given to him by Segovic, the tape editor. Clean as a whistle, Segovic told him. You could drive to Alaska smoking this stuff, he said, leaving out the fact that you wouldn't even need a car. So Phelps decided to take the chance, because he wanted something to blunt the negative aura of the place.

Anyway it was the same old three-camera shoot with the addition of a hand-held that mercifully had been assigned to Jarvis, the little fascist with eyes like a white rat. Phelps knew all about hand-held but didn't let on. He'd worked *Monday Night Football* for three seasons with one, slipping and sliding through Kansas City mud and Buffalo snow. Now he liked it just fine sitting on his ass behind the big old antique RCA with its piece of crap Angenieux lens that was softer than a roll of cotton if you knew what you were looking at, and Phelps knew.

Let someone else race around the studio grabbing reaction shots from the losers they got to fill the seats: old folks from dirt-road trailer parks who stared vacantly, their heads tilted slightly upward; flaccid middle-aged men and women with ignorant, defeated faces; mean-ass roofers and landscapers with ponytails, suspicious eyes, and stars-and-bars decals in the back windows of their trucks—guys with girlfriends who were made up like hookers because now they were going to be on TV, or so they thought. There were regular-looking folks mixed in too. Clean-cut men in knit shirts and Dockers next to stiff-looking women in high-necked dresses, vice-gripped to their children. Lord knows what they all made of this side show that passed for educational entertainment.

Maybe they believed the shit Stiefel and his buddies spewed at them about the secret council of Jewish bankers and their conspiracy to rule the world, about the overpowering desire of Black men to fuck all their women, about the slant-eyed Asian immigrants taking a bead on their jobs. Phelps didn't know and really didn't care. What concerned him was that he had a gig behind a camera, which was all he ever wanted out of life. That was no small matter after the fiasco in California when he caught his wife on the set with some two-bit actor and went berserk. The director had him arrested, telling him that whereas his wife was worth millions he wasn't worth a pound of piss and would never work in the business again.

Then a man came to visit him in jail, dangerous in appearance, who looked like he would rather chew his way through a door than turn the handle and open it. This man said he knew Phelps had talent and if he thought he could keep his eyes and ears open and his mouth shut, except late at night on a special telephone line, there was a cameraman's job for him in Florida. The ultimate destination of the information Phelps provided remained a mystery to him, but the consequences waiting for him if he divulged what he was up to were not.

"You make the calls from your house and only from your house," the man told him. "The phone there is secure. You make the calls only when you are alone. The individual interested in what's going on at that studio brooks no bullshit. Zero. You ever run your mouth about what you're doing, this jail will seem like paradise compared to what's in store for you."

"I understand," Phelps said.

"We may need some photographs. I'll see to it you get the right equipment but you'll have to rig it . . . conceal it. It could be tricky. You up for that too?"

"No problem," Phelps replied.

Phelps's head cleared somewhat and the insects flying in and out of Stiefel's mouth were replaced by words. Phelps had his headphones plugged into his Walkman and all he could hear was Bruce Springsteen singing "The Ghost of Tom Joad." He switched over to the studio sound system and Stiefel's big-blast carnival voice reverberated through his brain.

"Let me hear you say *aaha,*" Stiefel shouted to the audience. His usual nylon jogging outfit had been replaced by a double-breasted white suit, a blue shirt, and a bright red tie. In high-heeled white cowboy boots with red and blue stars, his huge bald head glistening with sweat, he pranced back and forth like a foppish Goliath, wielding a cordless microphone as though it were the handle of a bullwhip. The studio audience, jammed into the banked rows of theater seats in front of him responded, but without the kind of enthusiasm Stiefel was looking for.

"If we're gonna win this war against the Antichrist y'all are gonna have to yell louder 'n that," he said, leaping one way, then the other, finally coming to a halt facing forward like a pitcher looking in toward the catcher for the sign. "Now come on. On the count of three. One, two, three, aaha!"

This time the sound level in the packed studio was significantly greater, but still not at all to Stiefel's liking.

"One more time," he shouted, bouncing up and down on the balls of his feet, causing the carpeted stage to tremble. "One more time for unity and the salvation of the white race. Y'all gimme an aaha I can hear down in the soles of my feet. An aaha they can hear all the way down in Orlando. An aaha that sends shivers up the spines of all the cowards and traitors up there in Washington, D.C."

The noise in the studio increased dramatically and Stiefel now began pointing at the audience, swinging the microphone over his head with exaggerated sweeps of his arm as though he were casting a fishing line into a pond. With each successive cast the cry of the multitude became increasingly frenzied.

"Aaha!" they shrieked. "Aaha! Aaha! Aaha!"

"All right then," Stiefel finally said. "Y'all know what aaha means? What it signifies?"

Phelps heard a low voice through his phones coming from up in the control room. "It's what your wife said when she found out two nickels equal a dime," the voice said.

Phelps smiled and his eyes widened in surprise. Everyone who worked for Stiefel knew he had the entire facility wired so he could hear every peep in the place from up in his apartment. Everyone knew about the mirrored window too, the one that looked down on the main studio affording a one-way view of what was going on below. Florida was a right-to-work state and without the benefit of a union you could have a job today and be out on the street tomorrow without so much as a cursory explanation. Stiefel was there in the studio now, but you never could tell who might be upstairs listening, watching, taking notes.

All sorts of bone-chilling characters showed up in this place at all hours, either flying into Stiefel's private little airport or pulling up to the chain-link security gate in cars with darkened windows. Sometimes they would appear on the TV shows Stiefel produced. Sometimes they would be a forbidding presence in the audience. Sometimes, from the moment they arrived until the moment they departed, you would never see them at all.

Faceless behind the camera, Phelps observed their comings and goings in petrographic silence, like the ominous stuffed gorilla poised beside the concrete path. Then, from the phone in his cottage on the outskirts of Aurora, he made his periodic calls. Just the night before, he had been working real late in the editing suite, and as he was getting into his car, he noticed the sinister-looking dark-haired dude, the one who told fortunes over in Velvet, going in the back way with a giant-sized blond guy he'd never seen before. Who knew what nastiness the two of them might have been up to? Word had it that Stiefel was organizing a conference of right-wing militia leaders from around the country. Maybe the fortune teller and his buddy were part of that.

Phelps shot a quick glance up at the mirrored window. For some reason, instead of a reflection he was able to see beige-colored drapes that were pulled across it on the apartment side. It was probably because of the angle of the studio lights, Phelps thought, or maybe the dope he'd smoked was producing more phantasmagoric visions.

"What *aaha* means," Stiefel said, "is that you've discovered something important. You've learned the truth about an issue. Aaha! So that's what it's really all about! But tonight you're about to learn that *aaha* has an additional meaning that's closely related to learning the truth.

"Seated right here behind me is our special guest, Pastor Jim Keller, spiritual leader of the Church of the Militant Redeemer. But Pastor Keller is also a dedicated researcher who's the director of the Association for the Advancement of Historical Accuracy. That, my good friends, is what AAHA stands for—advancement of historical accuracy. AAHA! Lemme hear you say it one last time, with real emotion. On three. One, two, three."

"AAHA!" the audience shouted.

Phelps heard Segovic, who was up in the editing suite directing the shoot, tell the cameraman on Keller to zoom in, and saw the pastor's florid, puffy face fill the screen of the giant studio monitor. As usual, Pastor Jim Keller was dressed in combat fatigues and jungle boots. "If you're fighting a war," Phelps had heard him say maybe fifty times, "you better come dressed for a war."

Phelps pulled back into a standard two-shot as Herbert Stiefel turned and walked over to Jim Keller, shook his hand, and took a seat facing him. The two of them were on a set designed to look like a manly study, complete with shelves filled with books, a coffee table made from a slab of rough-hewn oak, and a fake fireplace.

"Dr. Keller—Jim—it's real good to see you," Stiefel said. "Why don't you tell all of us in your own words what your association for historical accuracy is all about."

"Herb, I'll be delighted to," Keller drawled, and looked meaningfully out at the audience. "Folks, those of you here in our studio audience, as well as all of you out there in America who are watching this on tape, are about to embark on a learning experience that's gonna have every last one of you sayin' *aaha* to yourselves. Some of you may be shocked by what you're about to learn, because it's a little different from the propaganda that you've been listening to for a long time. But let me assure you, what I'm about to tell you is carefully documented fact. Make no mistake about that.

"Let me start by telling you-all that there's a foreign government taking millions of dollars right out of your pockets every year. Robbing you, in the form of foreign aid, like a common crook. That common crook, that thief in the night, is the corrupt government of the illegitimate country of Israel. How do they do this, these crooks? It's really pretty simple. They operate undercover in this God-blessed country of ours with the help of hundreds, maybe even thousands, of secret agents—Jews and their paid flunkies in Washington. And do you know how they get away with this highway robbery? You know how they're able to slide their hands right into your pants pockets and your purses and make off with your hard-earned dollars? It's a very clever way, my good friends, because as you know, Jews are very clever, crafty individuals. What they've done, these clever Jews, is made people feel sorry for 'em by perpetrating an incredible hoax. The biggest hoax ever devised in the history of mankind. That hoax is the so-called Holocaust—the completely fabricated story about six million of their people being put to death in gas chambers that never even existed.

"The reason that I, and other like-minded white, God-fearing, patriotic citizens of this great county of ours founded the Association for the Advancement of Historical Accuracy was to inform the American people, through carefully researched scholarship, about this hoax. We're gonna push this hoax back into the darkness where it belongs and bring the truth out into the light. Let me hear you say AAHA!"

"AAHA!" yelled the audience.

Phelps thought he heard an echo coming through his headphones, only it sounded more like aah than aaha. He figured he was getting a dose of déjà vu from the dope and shook his head quickly to clear it, but then he heard the sound again and realized he wasn't listening to an echo at all, but rather to a single voice, an unmistakably female voice, this time saying "Aah, aah, oh baby do it just like that."

Phelps pulled off the phones. Now he could hear the woman's voice loud and clear through the studio sound system. "Do it to me, baby. Oh God, do it. Don't stop," she screamed.

Pastor Jim Keller was no longer lecturing. Instead the woman's passionate shrieks reverberated through the studio, mingled with tittering, a few guffaws, and several low cries of dismay and outrage from the people in the audience, some of whom were looking skyward in the direction of the large mirrored window thirty feet above the studio. Phelps saw a couple of the ponytailed roofers shaking with laughter as they pointed up at the window. The mouths of the women with them hung open in complete amazement.

Phelps raised his eyes and stared in astonishment along with them, realizing in a microsecond that the drapes he'd seen earlier, instead of a mirrored reflection of the studio, had been no illusion, that in fact the mirrored window was no longer there. In its place was a regular sheet of glass, five feet high and twenty feet long. On the other side of this glass, for all in the studio to see, was Dana Stiefel, completely naked, being fucked from behind by Agent Reed Calloway of the FBI. She was leaning forward, parallel to the floor from the waist up, her hands, with their long, pointy fingernails, splayed against the window. Her face was contorted in ecstasy, and her long auburn hair and pendulous breasts swung from side to side. Calloway, his hands on her hips, stood over her pounding away. Sweat dripped from his face onto her back as he grunted in syncopated rhythm with her cries. Obviously, no one had told the couple about the change of windows, nor about some fancy rewiring that had been done to the sound system, reversing its direction.

"Fuck me in the ass," Dana screamed, as the audience gasped. "I want you to come in my ass. See my fat old husband down there? That pig. I never let him do that, but I want you to, baby . . . do me in the ass . . . oh . . . oh . . . that's it . . . like that . . . oh Jesus . . . that's it . . . that's it, baby . . . you're gonna make me come . . . don't stop . . . don't stop!"

Phelps was mesmerized by what he was witnessing. He was plenty turned on as well, but managed to tear his gaze away from the scene and look into his camera. On the cozy, richly appointed set, Herbert Stiefel and Pastor Jim Keller sat with their heads tilted up, momentarily as transfixed as everyone else. They were as motionless as a freeze-frame, a still-life portrait of disbelief that lasted for perhaps thirty seconds and ended when Stiefel's face turned from tan to red to deep purple and he stood up, reaching into one of his cowboy boots as he rose and coming out with a short-barreled pistol.

The shrieks of pleasure continued to fill the studio as Herbert Stiefel disappeared from the lens frame. Phelps glanced up and saw him dash off the set and into the wings. There was a private staircase at the back of the building leading directly to Stiefel's apartment. It was accessible only to those with the key to a heavy steel door. Phelps hesitated momentarily, then unlocked his camera, swiveled it around and pointed it up at the window. He had a pretty good idea about what was coming next because he'd been there, but when he looked through the lens again the sound system had been turned off and the drapes on the window were pulled closed.

"We have a rather delicate situation here, Jack," the man from NEST said to Jack Ubinas. "I don't doubt that you've run into any number of 'em like it. Probably a lot more than I have, at least back in the old days, when you were out in the field instead of manning a computer all day."

NEST was an acronym for the Nuclear Emergency Search Team. It was a highly secret agency with serpentine connections to the Federal Energy Department, whose mission was to prevent any nuclear threat. The man from NEST, who was short and wiry, had on a hip-length parka over a bright tartan-plaid flannel shirt and khaki pants. He wore rimless glasses, and a fringe of pale, lank hair hung on either side of his otherwise bald head, making him look somewhat older than he actually was. His name was Jablonski, and Jack Ubinas recognized him at once as one of the new breed who were loyal to no one but themselves. Ubinas had never met the man before and though he didn't show it, was irked by his familiarity.

The two of them were sitting on a fallen tree limb next to the south fork of the Shenandoah River a quarter-mile down a narrow dirt road from Ubinas's farm. Jablonski had driven there from Washington very early that morning, ostensibly to do a little fishing for small-mouth bass. He figured as long as he was in the neighborhood he'd just stop by, he told Ubinas, to run his little problem by him. Nothing official, mind you. Just an informal visit. Very few people in Washington actually knew where Ubinas lived, but he decided not to ask Jablonski who'd given him his address.

"We've been tracking this group of Russians for nearly a year," Jablonski said. "We've been tracking them because some weapons-grade plutonium produced at the Krasnoyarsk-twenty-six nuclear facility apparently is missing. I say apparently, because, as I'm sure you know, everything over there involved with the production and storage of fissionable material is a complete mess these days, including the record-keeping. No one is even certain exactly how much of the stuff *is* missing.

"In any case, we had reason to believe these Russians were the guys who took the plutonium. We were waiting for them to make their connection, at which time we planned to grab them, their customer, or customers, and the plutonium, assuming, of course, that our hunch was correct. Then, shortly after New Years, they went underground and we lost contact. It was distressing, to say the least. I mean we can't have people running around with weapons-grade plutonium in their possession now, can we?"

"It could cause problems," Ubinas said.

"You bet your ass it could," said Jablonski. "Well, sure enough, three days ago we got a tip. A source who has, over the years, provided our agency and others with excellent information told us the deal was going down at a farmhouse near New Paltz, New York, at ten o'clock the following night. The Russians, their customer, the plutonium, along with thirty million dollars would all be there. To make a long story short, when our agents arrived at the scene, there was no plutonium, no thirty million, and no customer. Only the Russians, and they were dead."

"And now you have to find the customer and the plutonium he made off with," Ubinas said, "before someone takes out a full-page ad with a list of demands in the *Washington Post* and the *New York Times*."

"No," said Jablonski. "We don't think it's that kind of move. To the best of our knowledge, the customer's an Iranian arms merchant named Nick Sharifi. His agenda is monetary, not political. What we think is that he made a deal for the plutonium somewhere in the Middle East. Probably with Iraq. What those boys are up to is no secret to anybody. We think that's where Sharifi and the plutonium went. If so, both will be taken care of quietly."

"So no one's gonna set off a nuclear bomb at the World Series or the Super Bowl, or during Yom Kippur services in Jerusalem. At least not this year. It's just this Sharifi character who stole the goods from the Russians and made himself a shit-pile of money selling it to the Iraqis," Ubinas said. "Is that what your source told you?"

"That's the curious part," Jablonski said. "I tried to contact him to see what else he knew and the man had flat out disappeared. Poof! Vanished into thin air. It's very strange, Jack. He's been dealing with various agencies since the Bay of Pigs crisis, steady as she goes. I mean this guy's a reliable international businessman, not some junkie trading information for a fix."

"I don't imagine he would be," Ubinas said.

Jablonski gave him a curious, sidelong glance. He had no sense of humor at all, Ubinas decided. He looked at the wedding band on the man's finger and wondered what kind of woman would be attracted to him.

"This is an extremely valuable guy," Jablonski said. "A very useful individual to many. I'd hate to think he met a tragic end."

"It's a big ole' world," Ubinas said. "Individuals who appear to be reliable vanish in it all the time. Even reliable international businessmen who are useful to many. I'm sure you know that as well as I. Maybe his disappearance is self-imposed. Maybe he and this Sharifi have something going on. But I'm sure you've thought about that aspect too, so let's cut to the chase here, Jablonski. You want me to find him, this valuable guy. That *is* what brought you out here, isn't it?"

"Find him and assure him he'll be well taken care of . . . well protected, as he always has been," Jablonski said. "Assure him that the friends of Nick Sharifi have been . . . attended to . . . and that he can resume business as usual. I'd appreciate that, Jack. Other people would too."

Jablonski broke a small branch off the tree limb they were sitting on and threw it into the river. The branch caught for a second on a protruding rock, then the current pulled it free and swept it downstream. Jablonski watched it disappear and smiled slightly, as if he had just told himself a joke.

"You know," he said, "It could be that he thinks someone else is on his trail. Someone in addition to the friends of Nick Sharifi."

"Why would he think that?"

"Well, Jack, I was hoping that might be something you'd know. Or something you could find out and perhaps take care of."

"What's his name?" Ubinas asked. "This valuable source that people care so much about?"

"Novac DuCharme," Jablonski said.

"You don't say," replied Ubinas.

"Oh by the way," Jablonski said. "Your old colleague, Roland Troy . . . if it turns out that he's the one who's developed a particular interest in Novac DuCharme, you could do us another favor and call him off."

"What exactly do you know about Roland Troy?" Ubinas said.

"I do my homework," Jablonski said. "I know all about him."

"I don't think so," Ubinas said. "Because if you did, you'd know Roland Troy isn't someone you call off."

"Just do your job, Jack," Jablonski said, the convivial tone now gone completely from his voice. "This isn't the old days. This isn't Yellowstone Park either. Lone wolves are not considered an endangered species here. They're considered a nuisance. They're fair game."

"Unlike ex-Nazi informers," Ubinas said.

"I haven't the slightest idea what you're talking about," Jablonski said.

XXII

Wrapped in a blanket, Angela Becker slept on the plane ride back from Isla de los Caballos. When the Cessna Citation landed in Sanford shortly after midnight it was cold, and she began shivering as she and Troy walked to his El Camino. He found an old flannel shirt stuck behind the seat and she put it on over her dress. She told him she wanted to stay at her trailer and waited for him to tell her that was a bad idea but he didn't.

"My jeep's there, so I won't be stranded," she said. "I can get my car tomorrow if that's all right with you."

"That's fine," he said.

They drove from the airport in silence. He assumed she'd gone back to sleep and was startled when she suddenly spoke just as he pulled into the clearing, thirty yards from the trailer.

"Did you ever wonder what your life would have been like if you'd stayed with Nakama instead of becoming a cop?" she asked.

"I know what it would've been like," he said.

He was about to say more when he saw a figure dash across the penumbral fringe of light cast by the El Camino's headlamps and disappear into the underbrush between the clearing and the river. Troy gunned the engine and sped across the clearing, skidding to a halt at the far edge. Before Angela could ask him what was going on he leaped from the car and disappeared into the darkness.

It had been many years since Roland Troy walked through this section of forest once owned by his grandfather's friend, the old bootlegger Lucky Painter, but all the land for miles around, every animal trail, every spit jutting into the swamp, every tributary leading to the Coacoochee River, was embedded in his memory. From the time he was a boy Troy could traverse all of it, at night as easily as in broad daylight. Now he moved noiselessly along the only path to the river, a winding ribbon of hard-packed dirt treacherously overlaid with exposed roots, listening for the snap of a twig or the rustle of disturbed leaves. He had gone less than thirty yards when he heard a thump followed by a muted curse just ahead of him. Troy raised his forty-five to head level and eased forward. He rounded a sharp bend in the path and saw a human form—a man, judging by its size—on his hands and knees. The man was wearing some sort of loose-fitting jacket and had a watch cap pulled over his head.

"Move and you're dead," Troy said, and then he tripped, landing awkwardly on his side in a shallow depression filled with mud. As he hit the ground his pistol discharged into the branches overhead.

The man scrambled to his feet and began running toward the river. Troy stuck the gun in his holster and sprinted after him, ignoring the sharp pain in his bad hip. Whoever the guy in front of him was he had to be nuts to get up and run after the noise of the gunshot less than ten feet from his back. Just as that thought occurred to Troy, the man stumbled again, this time pitching sideways off the path into the razor-sharp branches of a saw palmetto. He let out a howl of pain followed by a rapid string of curses.

"Don't fuckin' shoot me, man," he said, as Troy stuck the .45 against the side of his head. "I ain't goin' nowhere."

"Jason Badger, my favorite skinhead," Troy said. "As I live and breathe."

"I cut my hand, man," Badger said. "It's bleeding all over the place. Every time I run into you I end up bleeding."

"It's only been twice," Troy said, handing him a handkerchief that Badger wrapped around his hand. "Couple more times you might not have any blood left. Now let's you and me go on back to the ranch so's we can have us another productive conversation."

"The ranch?" Badger said. "What fuckin' ranch?"

"It's a figure of speech, son," Troy said. "Now move before a gator smells that blood and decides you're dinner."

"What I want to know first," Roland Troy said, "is how you were able to find this place and why you're here."

The three of them were in Angela Becker's trailer. Angela had turned on the small kerosene heater in the back and put up a pot of tea. She was still wearing Troy's old flannel shirt over her dress and sat with her legs stretched out on the bunk, sipping from a steaming mug. Troy sat parallel to the door, facing her in the canvas director's chair. His clothes were caked with dried mud. He held his tea mug in one hand and his .45 in the other, waiting for the four Advil he had taken to kick in. Jason Badger sat cross-legged on the floor between them tightly gripping a can of Coke in his good hand. He was clearly terrified.

"You told me if I needed help or somethin' to come see you," he said. "That's what you said, didn't you?"

"That answers the why part," Troy said. "What about the how?"

"Don't be pissed, man. I wouldn't 'a run if I'd known it was you," Jason said. "But I seen it wasn't Miss Becker's Trans-Am or your truck. I thought it was them. That's why I ran."

"Who's them?" Troy asked.

"The dudes that brought me here the first time," Jason said. "The South Americans that killed Miss Becker's dogs. They were cool dogs, Miss Becker. What those fucks did to 'em was inhuman. They made me watch, man. They said I was next unless I told 'em what they wanted to know. See, they thought I knew somethin'. Like my brother told me somethin', you know? Otherwise they would've iced me for sure. How I got away was I fuckin' jumped out of their car when they was slowin' down for a stop sign. That's how I tore up my leg. Here, look, you think I'm shittin' you or somethin'."

He pulled up the leg of his baggy jeans revealing a nasty abrasion that ran the length of his calf.

"See what I mean?" he said, his eyes darting back and forth from Troy to Angela. He took a sip of Coke and began wiggling one of his legs. "And I got more on my back and shoulder. I'm a fuckin' mess, but at least I ain't dead. Not yet."

"Tell us about the South Americans, Jason," Angela said. Her voice was soft and soothing, a mellifluous counterpoint to Troy's deep, rumbling growl. "How did they find you? What is it that they want?"

Jason Badger took another sip of Coke, wiped the back of his bandaged hand across his mouth and sighed. "Kevin gave me up," he said. "The South Americans went to the clubhouse and Kevin was there. He knew I was down in General stayin' with my old lady. We were blood brothers, man. We took the fuckin' oath and everything, and wham bam that motherfucker gave me up. Nobody in the house tried to stop him either. Blood brothers my ass."

Angela nodded sympathetically. Kevin Arthur was the clean-cut, polite skinhead who had been sent to her by the state attorney's office at the same time they'd referred Jason Badger. The two of them, along with six or eight other skinheads, had been living in an old two-story building in southwest Orlando—their clubhouse—doing odd jobs for Ernie Viens.

"What about the South Americans?" she repeated. "How many of them are there? What did they want from you?"

"There's two of 'em," Badger said. "The shorter one has long dark hair. His name is Enrique. Not a bad looking dude. The other one is tall and thin with a big nose. Enrique called him Parrot on account of the nose, I think. I don't know his real name. I thought I'd seen bad, but these dudes was somethin' else altogether. They're into torture big time. That's what they did to Tito. They'd have done it to me too if I hadn't gotten away. They get off on it. They cut Tito up and fed him to the sharks. Tito was alive when they started cutting. They said the fish were getting their revenge. They thought it was funny. They even drank some of your dogs' blood after they killed them."

"You saw that? Saw them kill Tito?"

Badger shrugged, sniffed nervously a couple of times and wiped his mouth again. "Yeah," he said. "I saw it. Why do you think I'm so scared?"

"What do they want, Jason?" Angela asked for the third time. "What are these South Americans after?"

Troy watched her with great interest. Her face was completely placid and her voice remained soft and calm, even at the mention of her dogs. He was about to speak but restrained himself. She was obviously a masterful interrogator, even better than Rockett had let on, and he didn't want to interfere and break her rhythm.

"They're lookin' for some pictures they say the old man had. The old man up in Velvet that Ernie and Tito killed." Badger finished off the Coke and crushed the can, his feral eyes darting around from one of the trailer's windows to another, as though he expected to be shot through one of them at any moment. "I don't know a damn thing about no pictures but that wouldn't've stopped these motherfuckers from feedin' me to the sharks too."

"Who do they work for?" she asked. "Who brought them here from South America?"

"Could be Stiefel," Badger said. "Could be that spooky dude, Elliott, up in Velvet. That fuckin' psychic who thinks he talks to Jesus. Could be someone else I ain't even met. I never did get to see who-all was in the inner circle, you know. I was nothin' but a grunt. A fuckin' foxhole grunt, man. They said the skins was the foundation for the new temple they was building. Said we was the mortar that would hold the bricks together. Shit like that. But we was all nothin' but grunts. Tattooed circus freaks. I see that now."

Troy caught Angela's eye and she leaned back against the pillows on her bunk. "Take a look at this, Jason," he said, removing a small photograph from the flapped pocket of his shirt and handing it to Badger. "This look like anyone you know?"

"Where'd you get this?" Badger asked. Both of his shoulders began twitching and his legs fluttered like the wings of a moth. "That's one of 'em. That's the one named Enrique."

"I got it at the morgue," Troy said.

"Who did him? You?"

"Who did him ain't important. The thing is, he's done and you don't have to worry about him no more."

"Yeah, but there's still the other one. He's more dangerous than this one. He's the one who killed Ernie. He killed the cop too. Maybe some more. It'll be my turn next and that's for goddamn sure if he ever finds me."

"Don't worry," Troy said. "He ain't gonna find you."

"Yeah? You sure about that?"

Troy reached out and took the picture back. "I'm sure," he said. "And I've been right so far. We'll hide you real good just as soon as you tell me another thing or two."

"What thing or two you want to know?"

"How do you know the one with the big nose killed Erland, the FBI agent?"

267

"I heard him talking about it to the other one. See, they thought I was just some dumb fuckin' coonass didn't know nothin' about nothin'. What they didn't know was that down in Saint Bernard Parish where I was born and raised, Spanish is what they been speakin' since Spain owned the place. They speak Spanish down there still. My grandmother on my mother's side was Spanish. Not no Puerto Rican or Mexican either. I mean her people went all the way back to the dudes that came from Spain. I lived with her for seven years. I don't speak Spanish very good myself, but I understand it just fine. That's how come I knew the dude with the big nose was called Parrot. Papagayo. That's what the dead dude called him."

"You hear either one of 'em say anything about white mushrooms? *El hongo blanco?*"

Badger thought for a few seconds and shook his head. "No. I don't remember them sayin' anything about mushrooms," he said. "Why?"

"So Tito's dead," Troy said, ignoring his question. "What about Michelle Cornel?"

"Jesus. You know about Michelle too? Well yeah, I guess you would. Michelle the dancer. Fine-looking woman, man. Not as good-looking as you, Miss Becker, you don't mind me sayin' so, but fine enough. Michelle's long gone, man. Very long gone. She saw the way the wind was blowing and split right after the old dude up in Velvet got iced. She could be anywhere. Alaska. Australia. Anyplace they got a need for dancers, she'd find work. She was good, man. And she ain't no fool. Cut her hair and dye it red or somethin', get that busted tooth fixed, nobody'd recognize her, know what I mean?"

"Fisherman over in Indialantic claims he saw her at a party on a boat about six months ago," Troy said.

Badger stopped shaking his legs but now began moving his fingers as though they were playing an invisible piano while at the same time opening and closing his mouth. Angela stared at him, wondering if he were going to have some sort of seizure.

"Oh man, I don't know," he said. "I gotta get someplace safe. My old lady's up off the road there in her car probably sleepin'. That parrot dude comes along, wham! Hit her with that poison-dart gun of his. Do her like he did those dogs. Cut her poor heart out or somethin'. Oh Jesus, you got someplace for me to hide or what?"

Troy took a small notebook and pen out of the shirt pocket where he'd placed the picture from the morgue. He scribbled a number on one of the pages, tore it from the notebook and handed it to Badger.

"Where's your girlfriend's kid?" he asked.

"With her mother," Badger said.

"All right then," Troy said, glancing at his watch. "It's now ten minutes after one. What you're going to do is take four forty-one to highway nineteen, make a right on nineteen and go up past Umatilla, almost to Altoona. Think you can manage that? There's a motel on the left way back off the road just before you hit town called the Oak View Lodge. You stay there tonight. Tomorrow, you call this number. It belongs to a good friend of mine who lives up in the forest. He'll tell you how to get to his place. Ain't nobody gonna find you there. I guarantee it. But you listen here, Jason, and you listen good. This friend of mine spent nine years in special forces and he don't stand for no shit. You do precisely what he tells you to do or he'll run you off and then you can dodge Mr. Papagayo all by yourself. Is that clear?"

"He won't have no problems from me, Mr. Troy. No way. You got my word on that."

"I'm glad to hear that, Jason," Troy said, " 'cause he's got him a sawmill up there and he's gonna put you and your girlfriend to work."

"That's cool," Badger said, standing up and squeezing between Troy and the door. "That's cool. I ain't afraid to work. Jolene neither."

"One more thing you should know," Troy said, as Badger eased himself down the trailer's steps. "My friend is black."

Angela turned to the wall and buried her face in a pillow. Troy could see her shoulders shaking. "You all right?" he said.

She rolled over to face him and he could see, even though she had a pillow pressed against her mouth, that she was laughing.

"Is he gone?" she asked.

Troy nodded.

"Oh my God," she said, falling onto her side, "I can't . . . I can't . . . Mr. Parrot . . . a black guy . . . he looked . . . Jason . . ."

Whatever it was she was trying to say was lost in shrieks of un-controllable laughter. Troy started smiling and shortly, although he wasn't quite sure why, began laughing as well.

"I'm sorry," she finally managed to say. "Oh Jesus . . . I could see the reflection of his face in that mirror on the closet door. When you told him your friend was black . . . Oh God, Roland, I haven't laughed that hard in years. I hope this friend of yours knows what's coming his way."

"Oh yeah," Troy said. "He knows. It'll be like one of those movies you showed 'em come to life. Shock therapy. That boy will never be the same. By the time Russel's through with him Jason Badger'll be working for the NAACP."

Angela wiped her eyes with the sleeve of the flannel shirt and shook her head. "You're too much," she said.

"Not really," he said. "I fell flat on my ass and fired off a round at the gods. That ain't very slick at all. Matter of fact, I can't ever remember doing that before."

She got up, took a clean washcloth out of the cabinet above the bunk and soaked it with warm water from the sink.

"What are you doing?" he asked.

"Relax," she said as she wiped the dried mud off his forehead. "I won't bite you. You have all this mud on your face. From when you fell flat on your ass and fired off a round at the gods."

He looked up at her, no longer laughing, his slate-gray eyes a mirror of her own loneliness. She heard the low, steady hiss of the kerosene heater and the metallic trill of a tree frog just outside the open window above the sink. She looked down at his large, battered hands resting on the arms of the chair and touched the oversized, callused knuckles on one of them with the tips of her fingers. She raised her eyes and looked into his again. He said nothing but it seemed to her that something in him softened. She lowered her head and gently pressed her lips against his. When he responded and put a hand behind her head she gave a tiny cry, opening her mouth to his.

He rose, still kissing her, and took her in his arms. Under the thick flannel shirt she felt fragile; he could feel her ribs and the bones of her shoulders. He let one hand drift through her long, fine hair and placed the other in the small of her back, pulling her to him. They stood this way for a minute, maybe more. It was she who finally pulled away.

"This wasn't supposed to happen," she said.

"A lot of things weren't supposed to happen," he said. "You ask me, this was one of the better ones. At least in my recent memory."

"I . . . well, I uh . . . I feel sort of foolish, Roland," she said. "Help me out here. What should I do now?"

"You can turn that heater off and close the windows. Then you can come home with me. You don't want to stay here alone."

"I don't?"

"I don't want you to," he said, placing his hand behind her head again and pulling her mouth against his.

"The heater," she said after a while. "And the windows."

He kissed her again when they were in his car, and a third time after they climbed the stairs to the large bedroom that occupied most of the second floor in his house. She ran her hand over his beard, saying wait when he began to unhook her dress, take off your clothes and lie down. He looked at her, his eyebrows arched, but did as she asked, lying on his back and folding his arms behind his head, watching while she walked to the armchair over by the wall, turned off the reading lamp next to it and turned on the small radio sitting on his dresser. The radio was tuned to the local college station that played straight-ahead jazz all night long. An old blues piece was playing featuring someone on vibes but Troy couldn't identify who it was.

The room was dark now except for the glow of a small electric heater and the moonlight coming in through the large windows that had no shades. Angela walked over in front of one of them, and standing there, backlit, took off her dress. Her face was hidden by shadows but Troy could see the arch of her neck as she reached around to unhook her bra, and the outline of her small, firm breasts as she bent over to remove her panties. He saw the outline of her long legs and the curve of her hips. She ran both hands along the length of one leg and up her belly, in time, it seemed, to the plaintive runs of the vibraphone, then cupped her breasts in her hands and came slowly toward him. When she reached the bed she leaned over and let her hair fall against his legs, moving her head so that it brushed along them.

"Tell me you want me," she said, running her tongue up the length of his penis, putting the head of it in her mouth for an instant, then sliding catlike upward and kissing him on the chest and neck.

"I want you," he said, taking her in his arms. She felt his hands slide along her back and over the back of her thighs, drawing her to him, and felt his fingers between her legs, touching her gently there, then more firmly as she gasped and pressed herself against them. She felt the strength in his hands as he rolled her over, and as he entered her she wrapped her legs around his and clung to him, saying his name, pulling his mouth down against hers.

He moved slowly at first, sliding in and out of her, listening to her cry out softly in rhythm with his thrusting, listening to her cries grow louder as she began moving with him, saying do it, do it, do it just like that. Oh, like that. He felt her wetness increase as she opened herself to him in the darkness, felt her long fingers press into his back and then reach down to touch him as he pushed deeper inside her, her hips rolling under him now, her voice in his ear drowning out the music from the radio.

"There's something I forgot to tell you," she said later as they lay next to each other under Troy's old down comforter. "I meant to, but with everything going on I simply forgot."

"What's that?" Troy asked.

"I was going through the old psychic's notes again and I found something interesting. He was obviously having some problems with reality—the early stages of dementia maybe—I don't know. Anyway, he imagined that Michelle Cornel was someone else, someone he could trust, so he opened up to her, told her something. Then he realized he'd made a mistake but it was too late. I just now thought about it because . . . well . . . I feel so fucking stupid asking you this, Roland, but I was lying here thinking have I just made a big mistake too? I mean I don't go around doing this sort of thing. You realize that don't you? I haven't slept with anyone for . . . a long time."

Troy reached over and ran his hand along her cheek, then dropped his hand down to her shoulder and drew her close.

"Don't worry," he said.

"So what happens now?" she whispered.

"Now we stop thinking about old psychic's notes and young skinheads on the run and dead FBI agents and the yellow crime-scene tape flapping in the breeze down there in my yard. Now we go to sleep."

"That isn't what I meant," she said.

"I know what you meant," he said. "You didn't make a mistake."

Roland Troy soon fell into a deep sleep undisturbed by any dreams. When he finally awoke he could tell by the quality of light in his bedroom that it was late morning, probably close to noon. He was alone in bed, but he could smell food cooking and could hear Angela down in the kitchen singing along with an old Bob Marley tape that his daughter had left on her last visit. Troy pulled on his jeans, grabbed a clean T-shirt from the dresser and walked downstairs. Angela was doing some sort of hip-shaking dance in front of the stove where two frying pans steamed and sizzled. She was waving a large fork and a spatula in the air while she danced and didn't hear him come into the room. She had on flip-flops, a pair of his old tan corduroy Levi's that Troy hadn't seen in ten years and one of Katherine's bright red high school swim team T-shirts with the words TRAIN, TAPER, SHAVE, DESTROY printed across the back.

"Nice dance," Troy said.

Angela jumped and whirled around. "You scared me," she said, reaching across the counter to the small portable stereo and turning down the volume. "I was just making us some breakfast. I hope that's all right."

"Why wouldn't it be all right?" he said.

"I don't know," she said. She was still holding the fork and spatula aloft. She set them down and took the frying pans off the stove. One was filled with scrambled eggs, the other with hash brown potatoes. "I guess . . . I didn't want you to think I was being . . . you know, because of last night. I didn't want you to think I was moving in or anything."

"That food looks real good," Troy said, sitting down at the table, "and I'm real hungry."

"Me too," she said.

They ate quickly, washing down the eggs and potatoes with large glasses of orange juice. After they finished, Troy poured them both a mug of tea and lit a cigar.

"I have to make a couple of phone calls," he said. "Then I'm going to take a ride. Do some detecting. You want to come along?"

"I don't think so," she replied. "I'm going to go home and change my clothes and then go downtown. I have some paperwork to do."

She began to clear the dishes from the table but Troy stopped her with a hand on her arm. She paused, two plates stacked in her hand, and looked quizzically at him. Her full lips were parted and appeared to tremble slightly but she didn't speak. His old corduroys hung low on her hips and a band of smooth, pale skin was visible beneath the bottom of the T-shirt. He wanted to lean over and kiss the spot just below her naval where her belly rounded slightly, wanted to unhook the clip she'd used to tie up her hair and let it fall against his face while he reached under the T-shirt and caressed her breasts, but he was unable to move, feeling paralyzed by the familiar sight of everything around him—the stove, the old wooden table, the stained-glass pelican sitting on the windowsill—that had been nothing but vague shadows the night before. Instead of touching her he released her arm and leaned back in his chair.

"I'll clean up," he said. "You go ahead. Key to the barn's on that hook."

"I know. I already used it once when I took your truck," she said. "I wanted to make sure you weren't stranded. Your El Camino was in there. And an owl." And an old Cadillac convertible too, she almost added but stopped herself. She walked over to the sink and stared out the window at the pond. For a few seconds she watched the herons feeding on the far side but the brightness of the sunlight reflecting off the water's surface made her eyes tear and she had to look away. She reached up to wipe the tears away and touched the tiny diamond in her nose, which she had decided, after some thought, to wear when they visited Nakama. "Shit, I almost forgot my dress and shoes," she said, turning in the instant Troy reached her and took her in his arms.

"Don't go yet," he said. "Please don't go."

They went upstairs and made love in the bright sunlight that streamed in through the bedroom windows, stroking each other gently at first, sliding together and apart, together and apart, in slow motion, almost as though they were in a trance. Then suddenly, without speaking a word, their pace quickened, quickened even more, and she drew him deep inside her. She felt him grow larger, and as he began to come, felt herself lifted by a hot, undulating wave. "Come to me," she said, pressing tightly against him, letting the hot wave wash over her. "Oh baby, come to me."

"Tell me about the tiger," Angela said, as they lay naked on the bed and she traced the outline of his tattoo softly with her fingernail.

"It's the symbol of a very secretive and very old martial arts society called Prancing Tiger," Troy said. "It began in Okinawa nearly five hundred years ago. The original members protected the ships of merchants on the high seas from pirates. As time went on some of them bought ships and went into business on their own. Others became professional warriors, political advisors, scholars, you name it. A few went over to the other side and became pirates themselves, but even those remained true to the society's code of honor and loyalty. Above all else, one Prancing Tiger would always come to the aid of another. If necessary he'd defend him with his life."

"It sounds very romantic," she said. "Is it true?"

"As far as I know," he said. "Hard to believe, isn't it? Here in the age of the plea bargain and the drive-through divorce."

"How'd you get to be a member?" she asked.

"It's a long story," Troy said. "One day, when I was just a kid, thirteen, maybe fourteen years old, I met a man who was fishing on the Coacoochee not far from your trailer. He'd come here from Okinawa. We became friends and he taught me karate, which at the time hardly anyone in this country knew anything about. He was a Prancing Tiger. After I studied with him for several years he made me one."

"To protect people from pirates?"

"I was eighteen years old at the time and very self-destructive. I had enough trouble just protecting me from myself."

"And your old buddy, Nakama, he's a member too, isn't he? That's why he saved your life."

"You're a smart woman," Troy said.

Her fingers moved from the tiger to the scars on his left shoulder and then down to the ones on his hip.

"I've always wondered what getting shot would feel like," she said.

"When I was a little girl, before I ever had any idea I'd become a cop, I used to think that was how I was going to die. I had dreams about it. When I worked narcotics I thought about it all the time. Not when shit was going down, but afterwards, you know, when I was home in bed. I talked to one guy who'd been wounded and he told me it was like getting hit with a white-hot sledgehammer."

"I walked into a dark room in the middle of the night and suddenly there was incredible noise and flashes of light and I was flying through the air," Troy said. "The next thing I knew I was lying in a bed and a beautiful little girl was staring at me through an open window. She was holding a bouquet of flowers. I could see the side of a mountain and a waterfall behind her. The little girl was Nakama's daughter. She's a doctor now."

"I wouldn't have thought he'd have children," she said.

"Someone once said the same thing to me. I was very hurt."

"Whoever said that didn't really know you."

Troy got up, put on his jeans and T-shirt and walked across the bare expanse of polished hardwood floor where early in the morning he stretched and practiced kata—the formal, dancelike karate exercises composed of prescribed blocks and attacks. He stopped in front of one of the large open windows and sat down on the wide sill, resting his back against the window frame. Outside, a hawk circled above the field on the far side of the barn, saw nothing to eat, and disappeared into the woods beyond the field.

"I like to think I'm pretty good at figuring out what motivates people," Troy said. "I like to think I understand what makes them do the things they do, what their agenda really is. But sometimes I wonder whether anyone really knows another person. I really thought I knew my first wife. I thought because she was an artist she would be a nurturing mother filled with compassion. I was very naive. She abandoned her own child."

"Katherine? Your daughter?"

"That's right. Katherine, my daughter. I raised her myself from the time she was two years old. People were surprised. A number of them actually told me so."

"I'm not," Angela said. "I'll admit I would have been at first . . . when I first met you . . . but now I'm not."

She put on the red T-shirt, ran her fingers through her hair and crossed the room to the window where he sat. He reached up and held her hand in his. For a time neither of them spoke.

"Maybe I should sell this place," he finally said. "There are too many ghosts here."

She was about to say no, it's a beautiful place, it's where you belong, I can feel that, but she didn't get the chance because the phone rang. Troy got to it on the third ring.

"Where's Angela?" McKenzie Rockett asked.

"She's right here," Troy said. "You want to talk to her?"

"No. That's OK," Rockett said. He spoke slowly, his voice unnaturally calm. Troy had the sense that he was not alone. "I couldn't get either of you on the phone last night is all. I was beginning to worry. You really ought to get an answering machine, man."

"Tell you what," Troy said. "If it'll make you happy I'll go out and buy one today, right after I have a meaningful conversation with agent Reed Calloway."

"Any conversation you have with Calloway is going to be heavily one-sided," Rockett said, "seeing as how he's dead. So's Herbert Stiefel. I'm going out to the airport to pick up Carolyn. I'll leave a copy of the report for you at the office so you can read all about it. A couple of hotshots are flying in from Washington tonight. They want to meet with us tomorrow morning. I told 'em nine o'clock."

"I'll be there," Troy said.

"Things keep gettin' stranger and stranger," Rockett said, "but at least I can bring my wife home."

"Count your blessings," Troy said.

XXIII

"It's over, Tooth," McKenzie Rockett said. "The case is closed."

"What the hell are you talking about, Rock," Roland Troy said.

There were two other men in the task force office along with Rockett, Troy and Angela Becker. One of the men was large, the other small, and both were wearing gray suits. They had carefully barbered hair and cold, impassive faces that were easy to forget. Troy had never seen either of them before but over the years, on special assignments for Jack Ubinas, he'd met others like them.

"You heard the captain," the small one said. "The case is closed. Solved. You all did a fine job. Everyone locally and up in Washington is completely satisfied."

"What the fuck is going on here?" Troy said. "What do you mean 'solved'? The case ain't solved. It's wide fuckin' open."

"On the contrary, Mr. Troy," the large man said. "Last night, Herbert Stiefel, along with approximately one hundred and twenty-five other people, saw his wife having sex with another man—with Agent Reed Calloway of the Federal Bureau of Investigation, to be precise. In a rage, Stiefel shot and killed his wife and Calloway, but not before Calloway was able to return fire and kill Stiefel."

"I read the report," Troy said.

"In that case you know that the weapon Stiefel used was the same one used to murder Agent Stan Erland. It was also the one used to kill the hooker who lured Erland to the boat dock. As they say in Hollywood, it's a wrap."

"Herbert Stiefel might have shot his wife and Calloway but he didn't kill Stan Erland," Troy said.

"We think otherwise," the large man said.

Troy took a cigar out of his shirt pocket, lit it, and stared at the two men in suits. "So that's the way it is," he said.

"That's precisely the way it is," the large man said.

"And what about Leo Weiser?" Angela said.

"Stiefel paid Tito Pettibone and Ernie Viens to kill Weiser," the small man said. "Just like he paid Pettibone to get rid of Freddy Hatton. Then he hired the South Americans to get rid of Pettibone and Viens."

"And anyone else who was nosing around," said the large man. "Which resulted in the unfortunate death of your dogs, Detective Becker, and the injury to Mr. Troy's friend, Mr. Halpatter. Not to mention Mr. Lee, the African American gentleman killed in the explosion at his friend's garage. He was a bad fellow, that Stiefel. Responsible for a considerable amount of carnage. But now he's gone, and Operation Onion, as I believe you termed it, Mr. Troy, is concluded. Captain Rockett will brief the media later today. There'll be stories for a day or two and then life will return to normal."

Troy stared hard at the man for several seconds but was silent.

"What about the South American hit man who's still at large?" Angela asked. "The one they call El Papagayo. The Parrot. We have a witness who'll testify that he was the guy who killed Erland, not Stiefel. Don't you think we ought to find this Mr. Parrot. Maybe we can teach him to talk."

"Your witness wouldn't be a skinhead named Jason Badger, would it?" the large man asked. "Because if it is, you're going to have a problem getting him to testify. Badger ran his car into a tree at eighty miles an hour very early this morning in a little town called . . . what's the name of that place Captain Rockett?"

Out of the corner of his eye Troy saw Angela shudder and put her hand over her mouth. She was wearing a wine-colored double-breasted silk jacket with a skirt that came to just above her knees. In her matching heels she was almost as tall as Troy and looked absolutely gorgeous. Neither of the men in gray suits seemed to notice.

"Eustis," Rockett said, in a barely audible growl. His muscular neck strained at his shirt collar and he looked as though he wanted to leap out of his chair and strangle both of the gray-suited men.

"Right," the large man said. "Eustis. For some reason Mr. Badger decided to leave the safety of his new accommodations in a big hurry. The accident killed him and his girlfriend. You want to go looking for Mr. Papagayo, you and Mr. Troy will have to do it on your own time. This case is officially closed. Now if you'll excuse us, we have a plane to catch. Captain Rockett will fill you in on the rest of the details."

"I should have called it Operation Squeegee," Troy said. "The motherfucker running the show just took one, cleaned all the bugs off the windshield, and drove on down the road."

"Herbert Stiefel isn't driving anywhere," the small man said. "He's dead."

"I ain't talkin' about Herbert Stiefel, partner," Troy said. "Herbert Stiefel was a fucking stooge. A minor-league front man for an international underground group of neo-Nazis. What about the man he was working for? The man who picked him up off the street and set him up in that TV studio? What about Novac DuCharme?"

"Never heard of him," the large man said, rising from his chair and picking up his attaché case. "Have you, John?"

"Can't say as I have," the small man said.

"They're pulling the plug on the task force," Rockett said, when the two men had left. "The feds and the politicians have determined that it wasn't a feasible operation. The same goals could be accomplished through other means, is how it was put to me."

"What goals are those?" Troy asked.

"That was never articulated," Rockett said. "I'm being transferred to a new gang-intervention unit. Angela's going with me."

"Gang intervention?" Troy said.

"Dealing with the growing presence of street gangs in central Florida," Rockett said. "The Crips and the Bloods invade Disney World. Nobody wants to see that now, do they? They're starting to come into the hospitals to finish off rival gang members who were only wounded. Evidently that's considered to be a barometer."

Troy, seated in the old thrift-shop easy chair, puffed on his cigar. Across the room from him, Angela still appeared to be in a state of semi-shock from the news about Jason Badger. Rockett leaned back, put his feet up on the conference table and stared silently out the window for close to a minute, watching the traffic whiz by on the interstate in the distance.

"Tooth, I'm real sorry for dragging you into this," he finally said. "I had no idea it would go down this way."

"You don't have to apologize," Troy told him. "It wasn't your fault. And anyhow, you got my motor running again. I was in full retreat when you showed up at my front door."

"You want to go up to Jimbo's? Grab a bite?" Rockett asked.

"I'm not really hungry, Rock," Troy said. "I'll take a rain check. I'm going to go over to the hospital and see how Halpatter's doing."

"You want some company?" Angela asked him.

"Sure," Troy said.

"That OK with you, Rock?" she asked.

"No problem," Rockett said. "Take the rest of the day off. Meet me here tomorrow morning at eight. I'll show you where our new office is."

" 'An impeccably protected source of valuable information' is what I recall telling you about Novac DuCharme," Jack Ubinas said. "A young little prick came all the way out to my farm from Washington and made that very clear to me. He wants me to find DuCharme and wrap a thick, warm blanket around him. Keep him out of harm's way."

"I'll find him for you," Roland Troy said. "I can't make any promises about the blanket."

"The little prick knew all about you. He told me to exclude you from the hunt for that very reason. 'Call you off,' was the way he phrased it."

"What did you tell him?"

"I told him folks like you weren't so easily called off. Nevertheless, I think you're pissing up a rope. Even if you did find Novac DuCharme you wouldn't be able to pin so much as a parking ticket on him."

"I ain't talkin' about pinning, Jack. What I'm interested in is the extraction of information. Maybe even a confession. Interrogation is my specialty, or have you forgotten?"

"I haven't forgotten anything," Ubinas said. "But I'm not sure what you've got in mind is a wise idea. If I were you I'd forget it."

"DuCharme's a very bad guy, Jack."

"It's a matter of degree. He just fingered some Russians who were dealing weapons-grade plutonium."

"You sure he wasn't in on the deal?"

"Go back up to your cabin in Vermont, Roland. Enjoy the summer before the Florida heat sets in. If anything changes I'll contact you."

Troy was sitting on his porch, his feet propped up on the newly repaired railing. He held the phone in one hand, a cigar in the other, and had a steaming mug of tea resting on the arm of the chair beside him. In spite of McKenzie Rockett's assurances that they would be left alone, the sudden disbanding of the politically expedient task force hadn't really surprised him at all, and in the wake of its demise he actually felt liberated instead of angry. Now, free of the scrutiny the task force engendered, he could operate patiently, carefully, as silent and invisible as the old gator gliding beneath the surface of his pond.

"What is it you're telling me, Jack?"

"I'm telling you to watch out. You're a marked man."

"That must've been some little prick who paid you a visit."

"He was an ant. It's the people who sent him that concern me."

"How come you didn't tell me about El Hongo Blanco?"

"Where'd you hear about El Hongo Blanco?"

"From an old friend," Troy said. "Like you."

"There are some things I don't know as much about as I should," Ubinas said. "El Hongo Blanco's one of them. I've heard rumors, but nothing that was ever confirmed. It's like Santeria. Someone finds a dead chicken and next thing you know everyone is yelling voodoo."

"Angela's dogs weren't just dead. They were full of curare. So was the South American Halpatter harpooned. That's the signature of El Hongo Blanco, so I've been told."

"I've heard that too, but frankly it could just as well be a myth. A fantasy bought into by militia fanatics and hit men like the two jokers who showed up at your back door. They hear the tales and decide to join the party. In any case, there are people already out there digging for the roots of the white mushroom. Some of our guys, some Israelis, even some Germans. The situation is being thoroughly checked out. If something's really there, eventually they'll find it."

"That's what they told me about my wife and Bruno Schleifer, the filmmaker. In those very words, Jack. 'If something's there,' they said, 'rest assured we'll find it.' I felt neither assured nor rested."

"You're going to make yourself nuts driving down dead-end roads," Ubinas said. "When your buddy Rockett first called me up and said he was going to try to talk you into working with him I told him that was a good idea. I said you'd been off stewing by yourself for too long. I didn't know the whole story then. I should've done my homework first. Rockett got me to keep the feds off the case, and you see how long that lasted. You're going to make yourself nuts, Roland, and probably wind up dead."

"Which is why you decided not to mention El Hongo Blanco."

"How's your partner?" Ubinas asked. "Or should I say ex-partner."

"She's in the living room reading a book," Troy said. "You want to say hello?"

"Well what do you know?" Ubinas said. "That's nice. I really mean it. That's good news. You've had more than your share of loneliness. Take her with you, Roland. Get the hell away from there and take her up to Vermont with you."

"I'm not goin' anywhere, Jack," Troy said. "I like it in the heat. You know that. I ain't goin' back up to Vermont."

In 1842, Roland Troy's great-great-grandfather, fresh from fighting in the Seminole Indian War, camped on the banks of the river a half mile from where Troy's house now stood. Early one morning, as he stepped from his tent, he saw a wildcat drinking from the crystalline water and was so inspired by the sight he gave the river the wildcat's Indian name, Coacoochee. A month later he bought more than a thousand surrounding acres from the federal government. Since then, five generations of Troy's family had lived on the land he owned.

A hundred and forty years after his great-great-grandfather named the Coacoochee River, the sale of two hundred acres made Roland Troy a wealthy man. Judging from his life style it was impossible to tell, but he was then worth nearly seven million dollars. Selling off even a small portion of the property, though, was not an easy thing for Troy to do, since he drew sustenance from this land. The essence of it—the mysteriousness of the fecund swamp, the network of the Coacoochee's tributaries he could navigate in the dark, the wildlife and the plants, and the shell mounds and burial sites of the long-departed Indians—ran through his blood, providing him with a sense of continuity, a feeling of purpose when his job or his life seemed futile. But the money meant that Troy would from then on be a homicide detective and an undercover operative not out of necessity but only because he wanted to. It also meant that his daughter, who loved the wilderness as he did and wanted to spend her life helping to preserve it, could pursue her dreams without any financial concerns. So he made the deal, vowing as he did, to never leave the place nor to sell another inch.

Then with the murder of his wife the spell was broken, and suddenly for Troy, the magic of the land was gone. Instead of comforting him, the house, the Coacoochee, the centuries of history buried in the swamp all became unbearable and he moved away, far to the north, to a region with its own stark beauty, and where for him there was no history at all.

Of course there is nowhere to run from memories. Troy's dreams taught him that. But maybe now, he thought, with a trail to follow, it would be different. Maybe now the presence of this beautiful and independent woman, so full of life despite the demons from her own past, would chase his hideous dreams for good. Maybe the memories and the pain would fade, and things would once more be the way they'd been when the house and the land and the river fortified him while he raised his only child and hunted killers all alone. Troy had seen far too much to be naive and harbored few illusions but still at heart he was a romantic and thus had hope.

In the room where he had built and stored his crime-scene models Troy cleared a space and went to work, meticulously pouring through every note taken by Stan Erland, every entry in Leo Weiser's journals, every lead he and Angela Becker had run down, searching for a detail overlooked, a fragment of evidence that would connect Novac Du-Charme to the murders McKenzie Rockett had brought him south to solve. He contacted other government operatives he'd worked with through the years, spoke with detectives he knew in various parts of the country, and even traveled to Chicago where he'd tracked down Phelps, the cameraman who took the pictures given to him by Chotoku Nakama. He was hoping Phelps might have other photographs, a piece of incriminating videotape, or a recording of a conversation, but there was nothing.

Time after time Troy drove north to Aurora hoping to find something at the TV studio that would prove to be a clue, but on each successive trip he found the place as barren as before, a deserted ghost town with padlocked doors, sagging chain-link fences, and a profusion of weeds sprouting in the parking lots and on the runway. All the electronic equipment was gone, auctioned off along with the theater seats, the elaborate sets, and the furniture from Herbert Stiefel's apartment. Only the menacing presence of the stuffed gorilla remained. Half-hidden amidst the unattended tangle of bushes, the lacquered, grotesque creature had somehow been left behind, a bizarre and hollow reminder of the studio's former days.

More than once Troy drove to Velvet looking for Angus Elliott, but came up empty there as well. No one he asked had seen Elliott in months and the psychic's tiny cottage was as vacant and bereft of evidence as the studio.

Abandoned too was Nakama's retreat on Isla de los Caballos; nor could Troy locate Nakama anymore by phone. The number he had been given in Orlando was disconnected, and the one in Massachusetts was now just a recording saying all of the hotels were temporarily closed for renovations. Ubinas, at least, was home when Troy called him, but he might just as well have been away since he had no news about DuCharme, or so he claimed.

"Give it a rest, Roland," Ubinas said. "Let it go." But Troy couldn't.

He stayed on his land by the Coacoochee for nearly four months after the special task force was disbanded, and at first Angela stayed there with him almost every night. After spending the day with McKenzie Rockett in the new gang-intervention unit she would drive to Troy's house where she would usually find him pouring over notes, or listening to tapes. Occasionally he would be sitting on his porch deep in thought when she drove up, but when he saw her his face would brighten. He would smile at her, stand up and stretch, and when she climbed the steps to join him he would hold her in his arms and say her name. He loved the sound of it, he said. It reminded him of the bell on a buoy ringing in the fog.

Sometimes in the evening she would go with him by canoe to visit Halpatter who had returned to hunting alligators in the swamp. Halpatter had recovered fully from his wound but had a slight limp now, somewhat like Troy's. When she watched the two of them walking together down Halpatter's rickety old dock, or up the path to his house, she thought they looked like a pair of slightly skewed toy soldiers. Wind-up warriors, she called them to herself. Then she and Troy would run together along the serpentine trails through the woods, mile after mile in the summer heat, the sweat running off them like rainwater from a roof, and she would realize that though his joints crackled audibly and there was a hitch in his stride, his endurance and determination hadn't waned.

Sometimes she would simply join him on the porch and read a book, or show up with a load of groceries and cook something while he worked, but she never actually moved in. She had told him that she wasn't going to, and she kept her word, returning some nights to her trailer or her condo after they had finished making love. He never tried to stop her from going and never asked her why she did. He assumed it was her way of feeling free and independent and he respected that. He didn't realize that his obsession was the cause.

It wasn't that they didn't talk; in fact in the beginning they talked all the time. He told her about the history of their land: how it was taken from the Indians who used to live on the river, and how Lucky Painter, the bootlegger who once owned the parcel where her trailer stood, lost it to a crooked banker who was himself gunned down by a Mexican drug dealer.

"They say, though it's never been confirmed," he told her, "that there's a pirate's treasure buried near here, somewhere in the swamp. This pirate was an Englishman known as One-Eyed Jack because he lost an eye in a bar fight back in England. Legend has it that he fell in love with a beautiful young Indian woman. The young woman was murdered and the pirate went crazy searching for her killer. I heard the story from Sheridan Halpatter's father when I was a kid. He said the treasure will never be found because the ghosts of the pirate and the young woman are not at rest."

"You believe stories like that," she said. "I can tell."

"Well, I never went hunting for the treasure," he told her. "Lucky Painter did and so did that banker and look what happened to them."

She told him about her childhood on her parents' vast estate, about the boarding school she went to, and the world of high-fashion modeling that she abandoned when the man she loved went off a bridge in a van and was killed. She told him about her brother, who was a doctor and still lived on the estate with a wife who pushed him around and spent his money, and two kids, six and eight, who were already both on Ritalin.

He had a brother too, he said, a professional musician and collector of fine art. She was astounded when he told her how he'd once lived in New York City when he was very young and how his mother had tried to steer him and his brother to the world of music and art, taking them to the theater and the opera and museums when they were less than ten years old.

"You're making it up," she said. "That never happened. It can't be true."

"Oh yes it is," he told her. "She took me and my brother away from here after my father died. I was a little kid. I had no choice. She came from a very cultured family and was determined beyond belief that we'd become refined. She succeeded with my brother. He's a cellist with the New York Philharmonic. She failed miserably with me. We lived in an apartment on Fifth Avenue, on the twenty-third floor, with a balcony overlooking the park. I used to throw grapes down at the taxicabs late at night. Then I started running away. I ran away three times. After the third time my mother sent me here and my grandparents raised me. My mother and my brother hated this place, but it was heaven as far as I could tell."

"A detective and a cellist," she said. "My father was a lawyer and an investment banker. I guess you never can tell. Do you ever see him?"

"Who, Lansford? My brother? For a long time I didn't," Troy replied. "But he came to Katherine's wedding. Brought some of his musician buddies too. A string quartet. They played, right here, on the grass between the porch and the pond. It was quite a show."

"How'd you get him to do that?" she asked.

At the time, they were coming back from Halpatter's in the canoe. She was in the bow and he was in the stern. For a while he didn't say anything and she could tell from the way they'd begun to drift that he'd stopped paddling. She turned in her seat and saw him staring up at the canopy of oak and cypress branches above them. His hands were draped over his paddle which lay across his thighs.

"You all right?" she asked.

"I didn't get him to do it," he said. "It was Clara who did."

Their lovemaking was the most intense she'd ever known, but as the weeks wore on and nothing came of his investigation, she felt him disappearing, withdrawing to some remote private place she couldn't reach. She tried to talk to him about it but he said nothing was wrong, it was just the case.

"There is no case anymore," she told him. "You're looking for something that doesn't exist."

"Like the pain you had in your shoulder when I first met you," he said.

"Oh come on, Roland," she said. "That was different. With my shoulder there was concrete physical evidence—the way I was holding myself, or the way I moved. You saw something."

"You're wrong," he replied. "I didn't see anything. I felt it."

It was strange, she thought, how, after all the time she herself had spent delving into the case and all the heartache it had caused—her partner's murder, the deaths of Smooth Lee and Jason Badger, the emotions dredged up by her trips to Velvet, the horrible mutilation of her beloved dogs—she had been able to put it behind her while he had not. She told her friend Cortez the rug man about it when he visited her at her trailer.

"Well for one thing, you got a new job," Cortez said. "So you've got someplace else to channel all your cop energy. But there's something else you have to understand. That's why they used to call him Tooth. It wasn't just because he found the tooth in that junked car, it's because he *is* a tooth. Like a tooth on a pit bull. He bites down and he don't let go. The way I heard it, Roland Troy ain't never left a case unsolved."

Sometime in July, Troy began waking before dawn and walking silently from the bedroom, down the stairs and out the back door into the yard. When Angela reached across the bed for him one time and found him missing she arose, went over to the window, and saw him in the semidarkness on the grass between the back porch and the pond. He wore no shirt, only the pants from his karate *gi,* and was performing the dancelike moves she now knew were called kata over and over again with ever increasing intensity. She watched, transfixed, as the blocks and kicks and punches became a frenzied blur that ended with a short, sharp cry. For a moment he stood motionless, breathing deeply. In the moonlight his face was a twisted mask of fury that belonged to someone whom she didn't know.

Then on a hot Saturday night, after they had finished off a bottle of wine and made love twice, Angela fell into a deep sleep. Just past midnight she awoke with a start and found him gone. Even though it was far too early for his predawn exercise routine she went over to the window and peered out across the grass. Troy wasn't there, nor was he downstairs in the kitchen having something to eat, nor in his study working. Angela was suddenly quite thirsty and opened the refrigerator to get herself some juice. As she did she looked up and noticed that the key to the barn wasn't hanging on its hook. She found this very strange because since they'd been together Troy had left his El Camino and his pickup in the yard and never once gone inside the large old wooden structure filled with junk. She slipped on a pair of moccasins that were under the kitchen table and with the juice glass in her hand walked slowly down the path that led from the house to the barn.

An old hurricane lamp sat on the workbench about thirty feet from the open sliding barn door. It didn't cast much light, but there was enough so that she saw him. Troy had taken the drop cloth off the Eldorado convertible resting on jack stands at the back of the barn and had lowered the convertible's top. He was sitting in the driver's seat with his feet up on the dashboard and his arms folded behind his head. He had brought the AM/FM tape player he kept in the kitchen with him. It was sitting on the Eldorado's hood. A country-western tape was playing softly. Angela thought the singer was George Jones but she didn't know for sure. She watched him for nearly a minute before he sensed her presence and turned with a start.

"Hey," he said. "I didn't hear you come in. I must be losing my touch."

"I'm going back to the trailer," she said. "I think maybe . . . I think I need a little time to be by myself."

"OK," he said.

A week later, just before sundown, he pulled up in front of her trailer in his truck. She came outside and stood with one foot on the ground and the other on the trailer's metal step. He stayed inside the cab. She thought he looked tired and told him so.

"I'm going up to Vermont for a while," he said. "I've been thinking a change of scenery might jog my brain . . . maybe give me some fresh ideas. I came to say good-bye."

"Will you be gone long?" she asked.

"I'm not sure," he answered.

He wanted to ask her to come with him, but couldn't bring himself to say the words. She wanted to jump into the truck next to him, but couldn't move.

"I'll miss you," she said.

"I'll miss you too," he told her. "I'll stay in touch."

On his way north Troy stopped off at Woods Hole to see his daughter.

"Daddy, how the hell can you be so smart about so many things and still not know a goddamn thing about women?" she said to him.

"What do you mean?" he asked her.

"What do I mean?" Katherine said. "I'll tell you what I mean. In the first place you should have gotten rid of that car. Don't say anything. Just listen to me. You should have ditched that car because women respond to symbols . . . to symbolic gestures . . . much more than men do. To tell you the truth, you probably should clean all the old shit out of the barn because the way it is now it's a damn fire trap.

But be that as it may, the Eldorado should have been gone. See, you can tell her a thousand times that you'd chase *any* son of a bitch to the ends of the earth if you thought he had gotten away with murder—that it's just your nature. And I could call her up and assure her that it's true. But as long as that car is there, and anything else of Clara's you got hanging around the place, then she won't believe you."

"That's kind of melodramatic," Troy said. "I'm not sure you're right."

"Of course it's melodramatic," Katherine replied. "That doesn't make it less true. But I'm not surprised you don't think I'm right. After all, Daddy, I'm your kid."

XXIV

Summer became fall. The leaves turned color and fell from the trees. Roland Troy lay on the couch and listened to them whispering to the ground outside his cabin in the northeast kingdom of Vermont. During the day he cut and split wood, or dug rocks with a pick from the hillside above the cabin. The wood was stacked to dry under an overhang outside the cabin's western wall. The rocks he loaded into his truck and brought to the growing pile beside the shed. It was his plan to build a large addition to the cabin out of stone, using as his guide the chapter, "We Build a Stone House," from Helen and Scott Nearing's book, *Living the Good Life,* which he found in a little bookstore in St. Johnsbury. He thought the book was too didactic and the lifestyle they espoused extremely rigid and completely humorless, but in a moment of bleak self-examination decided that perhaps the couple were a lot like him. Then, after reading almost an entire page extolling the joys of eating various kinds of leafy green vegetables, he had jumped in his truck, driven straight to the little bakeshop in Barton, and bought a dozen assorted homemade doughnuts, seven of which he consumed on the ride home.

As he bounced along the dirt road to his cabin, munching contentedly and listening to a Rolling Stones tape, it occurred to him that the authors weren't like him at all. Anyone who claimed to never tire of eating cabbage and had no use for the processed filling of a jelly doughnut couldn't possibly have appreciated the Stones. Furthermore, the Nearings had fled from civilization to the boondocks without ever having had to shoot someone or inform a person that a loved one had been butchered. Or, for that matter, having to accept the fact that the killers of a loved one were running free and were likely to stay that way.

When Troy got home from the store he sat for a while on the tailgate of his truck. It was a cold morning in late October. The sky was the color of pewter and the air was still. Troy thought there was a chance that it might snow. It would be the first snowfall of the season, a soft and still reminder of something coming to an end. Sitting there he missed Angela so badly that his throat ached. He had called her several times and once or twice she called him, but their conversations were strained and remote.

Even though Troy's manual labor left him bone tired at the end of the day, he listened to music and read or worked late into the night hoping to fall into a dreamless sleep. His efforts, though, were futile. Again and again the dream about the river of blood returned, only now it was even worse. Now, as he was swept along through the canyon on the boulder-strewn river, he would pass under a narrow wooden bridge. It looked very much like the one leading to a Costa Rican jungle hideout owned by Chotoku Nakama. Troy had visited this hideout years before, except Nakama's bridge had been guarded by men with machine guns, while the only person on the bridge in his dream was Angela. As he passed under it, borne along by the raging, bloody torrent, she reached for him, stretching her arm as far over the side as she could. He tried to lift his arm from the river and grasp her hand in his but he never could. She called out to him; he saw her mouthing words, but in the churning roar of the river her voice was lost.

In spite of his dreams and lack of progress, Troy had by no means given up on the case. On the drive north, however, he decided to listen to the instinctive warnings he'd received in his first phone calls to Jack Ubinas and hadn't called him once since moving back to Vermont. Instead he pursued other avenues of information. He contacted an old, trusted friend who lived in Baja California—an undercover operative and former air-commando pilot, whose life Troy saved in Laos thirty years before. At this friend's suggestion Troy bought himself a computer, joined an online service, and began spending time probing the internet at night while working his way through the history of jazz. Troy gave himself the screen name Chuanfa, the ancient form of unarmed self-defense brought to Okinawa from China during the Tang dynasty thirteen hundred years ago.

Troy's friend was part of an underground network of undercover agents not formally aligned with any government organization. These freelance operatives understood the cold and treacherous nature of those who periodically employed them and had formed an alliance, of sorts, dedicated solely to helping one another. Through this network Troy learned how to access files that had previously been classified and spent hours delving into the labyrinthine archives of various government agencies with the same focused intensity he used as a tracker creeping silently through the jungle. Nevertheless, he was unable to find any information about Novac DuCharme nor anything referring to an organization known as El Hongo Blanco.

"I'll give you a list of screen names," Troy's friend wrote. "You can e-mail them and find out what they know. As you well know, there's sometimes gold in the most unlikely places."

"How about you e-mail them," Troy wrote back. "Then you can tell me whether anyone has something I can use."

"You're a cautious dude," his friend replied.

"That's why I'm still alive," Troy responded.

"I'll be in touch," his friend typed back.

A few days later Troy got an e mail message from his friend. "Help is on the way," was all it said. Then for more than two weeks Troy heard nothing.

It had snowed an inch or two and then turned warmer, making the hillside behind his cabin slick. Troy slipped twice while loading rocks into the bed of his pickup and decided to drive down to the cabin with what he had before he fell and really hurt himself. As he came around the corner of the shed he saw a Ford Explorer parked just off the road that ran in front of his house. Because of the angle of the slope the vehicle's plates weren't visible, but he could see the driver, who appeared to be a pleasant-looking older woman. She was bundled in a heavy coat and had a thick knit ski hat pulled down around her ears. When she saw him she waved and smiled cheerfully although he had no idea who she was.

"Mr. Troy, Mr. Troy," she called, extricating herself quite nimbly from the Explorer and bustling up the incline to the cabin as fast as her ponderous coat and fur-trimmed boots allowed. She continued waving to him as she walked. "Don't drive away. Don't drive away. I have to talk to you."

"I ain't goin' nowhere," Troy said, turning off the truck's engine and climbing from the cab. "This is where I live."

"Well," she said breathlessly when she was less than ten feet from him. "That climb is steeper than it looks."

Now that she was closer, Troy could see that she was indeed in her sixties, with an innocuous demeanor betrayed by clear, penetrating blue eyes. He had the distinct feeling she wasn't as benign as she looked. He also thought she looked familiar; he had seen this woman somewhere before, but not in the northeastern corner of Vermont.

"Listen," Troy said. "If you're selling pies for the volunteer fire department I gotta tell you that I already bought enough from Mrs. Safford to last me until the Fourth of July. Not to be rude or anything, mind you, but I don't even eat pie all that much."

"Oh, I'm not selling pies," the woman replied with a rich, throaty laugh. "I should have immediately introduced myself. My name is Justine Fallon."

"Come on inside," Troy said.

"It was quite a coincidence, actually," Justine Fallon said cheerily. "Leo and I had just spoken at some length when not more than an hour later your friend called me all the way from Baja California. Leo and I talk all the time, which I'm sure you've already heard from Detective Becker."

"Leo Weiser," Troy said.

"Yes, of course," said Justine. "You would be surprised what I've learned from him since he passed over."

Troy had taken off his boots and was sitting on the couch with his stocking feet up on the rough-hewn coffee table. Justine Fallon sat across from him in the easy chair holding the mug of hot cocoa he had made for her. Troy sipped from his own mug and studied her carefully. He still couldn't remember where he'd seen her before.

"In any case, I was sitting on the bluff overlooking the water, which is where we usually talk, and Leo said to me, 'Justine, it's almost time for you to go back and tell everything you know.' I asked him whom

I should tell it to and he told me I'd be getting a phone call and that call would make it completely clear. Of course I knew Leo didn't mean go back to Velvet. That would be too dangerous. I've always loved New England though. The coast of Maine is lovely, especially in winter when the crowds are gone. It has a stark, desolate beauty. It's so very cleansing. I think I'll give that a try for a while, after I nose around these parts, that is. I found a charming bed-and-breakfast place in Crafstbury Common. I would have been here sooner, by the way, but the weather was pretty bad on the island. Fog and rain. Not a plane flew in or out for nearly a week."

"Which island is that?" Troy asked.

"Oh, the Isle of Lewis off the coast of Scotland," Justine Fallon said. "The Callanish Standing Stones are there. Perhaps you've heard of them. It's a very spiritual place, the Isle of Lewis, not unlike Meditation Woods in Velvet, or the Indian burial island on your land." Justine's eyes smiled at him over the rim of her mug. She was one smart cookie, this psychic who learned things from the dead. "Or, for that matter," she went on, "Htee Pa Wee Cho . . . Sleeping Dog Mountain . . . in Burma."

"You were there," Troy said, remembering in a flash where he'd met her. It was in 1976 at a burned-out factory near Rangoon owned by an American businessman with ties to an Asian crime family. She was investigating the fire for an insurance company. He had been sent with his friend, the air commando who now lived in Baja California, to fly a defecting Chinese scientist out of the country. She had the scientist in the trunk of her car. He only saw her for thirty seconds but he remembered her benevolent smile and her piercing blue eyes. You didn't see eyes like that too often in Rangoon.

"Yes," Justine replied. "I was there. Twice, in fact."

"You can call me Roland," he said, wondering exactly how far she was intending to take her instructions from the late Leo Weiser to tell him everything.

"Roland," she said. "The romantic French military hero. One of Charlemagne's commanders. *Le Chanson de Roland*. You must have heard all that a thousand times. Please call me Justine."

"Actually, Justine, I only heard it three times. Once from my mother, once from my daughter when she read about it in European history class, and once from the French wife of a warlord who lived in the mountains of Burma. I was there too."

"Yes, I know," she said. "When I was there for the second time. I believe that's the trip you have in mind."

"Small world," Troy said.

"Isn't it?" said Justine. "Communication, of course, is what makes it so. Communication is so very important, but few people ever open themselves up to its limitless possibilities. They think they do, what with cell phones and cyberspace, but they rarely go beyond what's staring them in the face. They have no idea what is truly possible. Leo and I were discussing that very thing the day your friend called."

Troy took a cigar from the box on the table and removed the wrapper. "More cocoa?" he asked. "Cigar?"

Justine Fallon laughed heartily. "Oh, Roland," she said. "You're too much. A cigar indeed. I will have some more cocoa though. It's quite good."

Troy took her mug into the kitchen and refilled it. He handed it back to her, sat down and lit his cigar. "Well, Justine," he said, "would you like to tell me what you know now, or would you like to have some dinner and talk after that?"

"Thank you for the offer, Roland, but I'm not hungry," Justine said. "You go ahead though. You've been working hard and must be famished."

"Don't worry about me," Troy said. "I'm fine."

Justine Fallon set her mug of cocoa down on the coffee table and folded her hands in her lap. Her startling blue eyes, as unblinking as an owl's, had taken on a feverish glow, and two circular spots of color the size of quarters appeared on her cheeks. She suddenly looked twenty years younger.

"Leo Weiser had an album filled with pictures," she said. "They were taken in Auschwitz. Some were of the prisoners. Some were of the guards . . . the men and even some women who murdered the innocent . . . the helpless . . . children . . . even children. Leo never learned who took these pictures or why. The Nazis, you know, only allowed two men—Walter Kroner, the chief of identification, and Rolf Gorman, his assistant—to carry cameras in Auschwitz. Kroner had a photography studio in the camp, but none of the pictures in the album originated there.

"Leo got this album in 1945, after the death camps had been liberated, from a woman fleeing, as he was, across the border between Austria and Italy. She was trying to escape being sent to the east . . . to Russia . . . just like him. He found her lying in the forest, high in the mountains, in the snow. She had been shot through the back. She had been a prisoner, like he was, in Auschwitz. Leo knew that. But he never knew how she came to have this album, because she died before she could tell him. She had survived the horrors of the death camp only to be shot and killed trying to reach freedom.

"Leo vowed, as he stood next to the body of that poor woman in the snowy mountain forest, that if he managed to reach America he would bring as many of these murderers as possible to justice. And indeed he kept that vow, Roland. But not as Leo Weiser. That wasn't his name back then. Back then he was Solomon Kessler, a famous attorney who worked all over the world. He became wealthy. He had all the comforts that money could buy. He had a beautiful wife and a child. But he never forgot his vow. He used the pictures in that album as incriminating evidence in war crimes trials. But before his vow was complete—before all of the men could be brought to trial and convicted by the photographs that were irrefutable evidence of what they'd done—Leo's . . . Solomon Kessler's wife was murdered. He had been warned something like that might happen but he paid these warnings no mind. He had a mission and was compelled to see it through to the end. I think that's something you can understand. And then it did happen, and Leo . . . Solomon . . . took his baby daughter and ran, because he feared the monsters who had killed his wife would kill his daughter next.

"He had planned for it. He was a brilliant man and had planned everything in advance, just in case. He left his daughter with a trusted friend and disappeared."

"But he kept the album," Troy said.

"Yes," Justine replied.

"And Novac DuCharme's picture was in it."

"Novac DuCharme's real name is Helmut Weber. He was one of

the worst. One of the most brutal of all the murderers, if in fact there are degrees for such hideousness. There is a picture of him shooting an infant in its mother's arms."

"So DuCharme found out that Solomon Kessler was alive and still had the album," Troy said. "And that's what got Kessler killed."

"Leo had not been well," Justine continued. "His memory was slipping. When he saw Helmut Weber in Velvet, after all he'd been through, it was devastating to him, the final straw. He began having flashbacks, lapses. Then the dancer—Michelle Cornel was her name— came to see him, purely by chance. Her boyfriend, Tito, was working for Herbert Stiefel, whose television studio was only a few miles away from Velvet. Leo confused Michelle with his dead wife. He told her about the album. He told her about Helmut Weber, the SS officer with the mutilated ear that he saw in Angus Elliott's car. You're a very intelligent man, Roland. Very good at uncovering hidden information and solving puzzles. I'm sure you can piece together most of what happened after that."

"You loved him a great deal," Troy said.

"Oh yes," Justine said. "I still do. He's a wonderful man. But he suffered so. Not as much anymore though. Not nearly as much."

Justine Fallon's full, resonant voice had faded to little more than a whisper and tears ran down her cheeks. Troy brought her a glass of cold water from the kitchen and puffed his cigar silently while she drank.

"Leo realized what he'd done," Justine said after a minute or two. "When the dancer came back with her boyfriend, he knew. He said it was only a matter of time before they caught up with him. I offered to help him hide. I still know people from the old days—people like your friend in Baja California. People who later warned me to leave Velvet. But Leo refused to budge. There was no way I could convince him. So in the end he was murdered too, like those whose memories he had honored. Like his parents and sister. Like the woman in the forest. Like his wife. Spiritualists don't view death the way other people do. For us it isn't the end. Still, I wish I could have spared him the pain."

"What happened to the album?" Troy asked.

"Leo told Michelle Cornel it was hidden in a drainage pipe. That's why those men—Tito and the strutting one, Ernie—dug up Leo's yard. They dug up every inch of pipe there but they didn't find a thing. I knew they wouldn't. Leo told me the album was hidden in an old pipe laid with the blood and sweat of slaves. He said you could see a railroad siding from the spot, a siding like the one in the death camp that led to the crematorium. Leo lay all the pipe in his backyard himself and there wasn't any railroad track within twenty miles of his house."

Justine took another sip of water and smiled at Troy. "You're going to ask me where the album is now. The answer to that question is I don't know. I've asked Leo about it numerous times since he passed over but all he'll say is that when the time is right it will be found."

"You knew all about DuCharme. You and Leo, or Solomon. You both knew," Troy said.

"I knew about the album," Justine said. "Leo showed it to me. But I didn't know about DuCharme until Leo saw him in Velvet in the car with Angus Elliott. That's when Leo told me."

"Where is he now, DuCharme?"

"I don't know where he is," Justine said. "But I believe I know who does."

"Who's that?" asked Troy.

"Your old friend," she answered. "The man we both worked for when you saw me that time in Rangoon. Jack Ubinas."

Troy leaned back on the couch and scratched his beard. His cigar had gone out and he began to reach for a match to relight it, then changed his mind and held it, unlit, between his teeth.

"As you observed earlier," Justine said, "small world."

"Why didn't you tell Angela any of this?" Troy asked. "What made you wait so long?" He decided to relight the cigar after all and puffed deeply, raising a cloud of smoke above the couch as he waited for her to reply. He was expecting another elaborate explanation involving a conversation with Leo from the spirit world advising her not to talk, but Justine surprised him.

"You know what these people will do," she said softly. She began to rub her hands together and tears once more ran down her cheeks. "I was afraid."

"I understand that," Troy said. "And I'm not saying your fear wasn't justifiable. What I don't understand is why you didn't say something before you left Velvet."

"Oh, Roland, don't you see?" Justine said. "I wasn't afraid for myself. I was afraid for Angela. Solomon Kessler was her father."

XXV

There was a letter in a brown manila envelope waiting for Leo Weiser when he came home from his usual Saturday afternoon trip to the library. He took the letter from his mailbox, along with an electric bill, a flier advertising an upcoming chamber music series at Carlton College, and a copy of the *National Geographic,* and climbed the steps to the apartment he was renting above a garage on a quiet, tree-lined street in Northfield, Minnesota. He set the mail down on the kitchen table, hung up his coat, opened the kitchen window to let in some fresh air, and put a kettle of water up for tea. The apartment was not large, but there was a spacious walk-in closet off the kitchen that Weiser had determined would be perfect for a darkroom when he'd rented the place. While he waited for the water to boil he went in there and studied three eight-by-ten sheets of photographic paper hanging by clothespins from a length of cord strung between two of the walls. The three sheets of paper were covered with wavering gray shapes against a sepia background and looked, at first glance, like fields of wheat, or billows of smoke and tentacles of flame from a brush fire.

The water boiled and Weiser made his tea. He sat down at the table and gazed out the open kitchen window, breathing the clean, crisp November air. A group of boys was playing football on the large expanse of lawn between the garage and the house owned by the people renting him the apartment. Weiser reached across to the kitchen counter and grabbed a camera—a Nikon FTN with a 200mm lens and a motor drive—and quickly took a half dozen shots of the boys. He took pictures only with black and white film and always of human subjects, specifically faces. Photos of children of all ages were his favorites. He would look at them and think of his own child, a grown woman now, whom he had not seen since she was two years old. He was hoping one of the shots he'd just taken might have captured the wild exuberance of a twelve-year-old leaping for a pass or evading a would-be tackler. The letter in its manila envelope lay before him on the table but he was in no hurry to open it. Weiser was certain he knew what was inside. It would require an important decision from him and he was unsure what course he should take.

He continued watching the boys while he sipped his tea. One of them, short and wiry, but quick as a squirrel, reminded him of Lev Aronstam, a gifted soccer player from the town in Hungary where he was born. He closed his eyes momentarily and sighed. Of late, his mind had been flooded with childhood memories, most of which reduced him to despair. Weiser saw Lev Aronstam die at eighteen of a gunshot to the forehead as he stood in a grave he had been forced to dig on the outskirts of their town.

When he finished his tea, Leo Weiser rose and went back into the darkroom where he once more studied the three sheets of paper hanging from the cord. The ethereal shapes on the paper had not been produced with a camera and film, but by dipping the paper in developer, removing them after several seconds, and placing them in a solution of fixer. They were, he believed, graphic representations of the spirit world swirling around him, capturing images of his spirit guides from the world of the dead. He had hundreds of these pictures filed in expandable paper folders. They were his solace, his consolation, his catalog of otherworldly communiqués proving to him that he wasn't alone.

In one of the psychic photographs he stared at now he saw a woman's face peering through the waving field of wheat. She was smiling broadly and had on a jaunty feathered hat. Weiser believed this face belonged to the spirit of his murdered wife. Her image had appeared in four separate pictures he had made in the last week, and the previous night, while he walked through the streets of his neighborhood bundled in a long overcoat, he heard her voice. Very soon, she told him, he would have the opportunity to see their daughter. If he took this opportunity, she said, he would have to be extremely careful since the forces of evil responsible for her murder were still at large, waiting to strike.

Leo Weiser sat down again at his kitchen table. He took a steak knife and slit open the manila envelope. Inside was the usual monthly sheaf of thirty hundred-dollar bills wrapped with a thick rubber band. Since the death of his friend Peter Becker, the man who had raised Weiser's daughter, the money had been transferred from a special fund attached to Becker's estate to a Swiss bank. From the bank it was sent to one of Becker's associates in New York who mailed the cash to Weiser. The three thousand dollars was only a small portion of the interest from Weiser's investments that had been merged, twenty years earlier, with Peter Becker's own holdings. The bulk of this money went into a trust fund for Weiser's daughter.

In the manila envelope, along with the hundred-dollar bills, was a folded sheet of white paper. Weiser removed this paper from the envelope, unfolded it and read the single sentence typewritten on it. "Angela Becker has moved from New York and is now living in Orlando, Florida," the letter said.

As he had been for some years, Leo Weiser was presently employed in a photo-processing lab that doubled as a portrait studio, but as he slipped deeper and deeper into the world of spiritualism it seemed to him that his true work was as a psychic photographer. The more he studied the subject, the clearer it became that he was destined to live in the community of Velvet, Florida, a place imbued with spiritual vibrations, where he would be surrounded by fellow spiritualists and could pursue this calling. He had spoken to the head of Velvet's village commission by telephone several times and had already made a down payment on a cottage in Velvet that had recently become available. The typewritten message in the manila envelope in front of him was not a surprise; it was what Weiser had expected. Now he had to make a choice.

For twenty years Leo Weiser had kept track of his daughter and knew all about her through coded messages sent by Peter Becker and then, after Becker's death, by his associate. Fearing for his daughter's safety, however, Weiser had never attempted to make contact with her and had lived his anonymous, secret life in small cities far removed from her world. What should he do now, Weiser wondered? What course should he follow?

That night, Leo Weiser couldn't sleep. After tossing and turning for several hours he finally arose and went into the kitchen. The table where he sat was bare; he had destroyed the letter after reading it and put the cash in a plastic film bag he kept in the freezer. He looked out the window at the lawn where earlier he'd watched the boys play football. It was empty now and dark except for one far corner dimly lit by a nearby streetlight. There was no wind and the few remaining leaves, brown and brittle in the trees, hung motionless, lifeless. Like me, Weiser thought, like what is left of me, and then he saw something—a shadow, an animal perhaps, or a small person—move across the grass in the far corner where there was light.

Weiser reached for the Nikon, still on the kitchen counter, and peered through the 200mm lens to get a closer look but whatever had been there was now gone. He put the camera down on the table. It was then that he heard his dead wife's voice. "Go, Solomon," her voice said to him. "See our daughter. Be near her. In the end it will turn out all right."

He saw her four times in ten years but she never saw him. Each time, he marveled at her beauty and her poise. Once, he heard her speak and his heart stood still because she sounded so much like her mother. Often, late at night, he thought of going to her, of telling her who he was, who she was, but he knew it was too dangerous so he refrained. Maybe some day, he thought. Then it was too late.

Three days later and twelve hundred miles away, several men were sitting in the conference room on the top floor of a high-rise in Houston. On the surface there was nothing unusual about the meeting, nothing that would have appeared to be out of the ordinary. A single member of the group, perhaps the only man who might have attracted attention by his arrival, wore combat fatigues, but he had come up to the conference room by way of a private elevator and was not seen by anyone in the building's lobby or on the floors below. He was the head of an ultra-right-wing survivalist community based in the Ozark Mountains of northern Arkansas. The others were wealthy businessmen, fanatically committed to a far-right racist ideology. One of those in the room, a tall, well-built man in his early forties, wearing an impeccably tailored suit and custom-made cobra-skinned cowboy boots, was the owner of the high-rise. This man had considerable real estate holdings in Houston and several other cities and also owned a giant petroleum company with oil and natural gas leases in fields around the world. It was he who had brought the others in the room together.

All had been carefully screened by the oilman who had convened the meeting. They had met numerous times before and had taken a blood oath of absolute secrecy, vowing nothing that transpired in their meetings would ever leave the room. With the exception of the man in fatigues, each had contributed a million dollars in cash to the furthering of their cause, as a demonstration of good faith. The oilman wasn't worried about the intentions of the survivalist who looked as lean and hard as a combat marine. He had personally seen this man slit the throat of a Jewish civil rights lawyer whose body had never been found. The oilman was certain the survivalist would gladly hunt down and kill anyone who betrayed the others and defected.

At precisely 10 A.M. the heavy double doors of the conference room swung open and Novac DuCharme strode into the room accompanied by three other men in dark suits. Head erect, his cold, cruel eyes looking straight ahead, DuCharme walked to a low lectern at the end of a long table, turned abruptly, and stood with his hands clasped behind his back. Like his companions, DuCharme wore a dark blue suit, a crisply starched light blue shirt, and a silver-colored tie patterned with tiny black checks. His thick white hair was perfectly combed, his tanned face was free of any razor nick or blemish, and not a speck of dust could be seen on his highly polished black shoes. His eyes glinted as though stoked by some inner fire, but otherwise he displayed absolutely no emotion.

"You who have met with me in this room before are my inner circle," he said. "Jesus Christ had an inner circle. My predecessor Adolf Hitler had an inner circle. You are mine. As I have mentioned in the past, you are the men with whom I will build a kingdom of heaven on earth. Today, we welcome three comrades from South America, two from Argentina and one from Brazil. They are trusted allies, imbued with the spirit of our dream, and so part of that same circle. I'm sure that after this meeting some of you will want to speak to them individually and they have assured me they will be happy to oblige."

DuCharme nodded in the direction of the men who had entered the conference room with him and they nodded back. Like DuCharme, they were perfectly groomed and appeared to be in their late fifties or early sixties.

"Now then," DuCharme went on. "You are familiar with the intricacies of oil and gas production. You know about cattle, and steel, and electronics. You know about shipping and about the construction of large buildings, of whole cities in fact. And at least one of you knows a great deal about waging war. Today I am going to tell you about mushrooms, specifically about the white mushroom, amanita bisporigeia, an organism that may not be something you know very much about."

All the men in the room were accustomed to giving instructions, not listening to them, to lecturing others, not being lectured, but each of them, including the three South Americans, sat attentively as he spoke. In spite of their wealth and power, these men had all willingly acknowledged, as part of their blood oath, the absolute leadership of Novac DuCharme.

"There are two aspects of the white mushroom that are significant for us," DuCharme said. "The first, is that the mushroom itself—the portion that appears above the ground—is so poisonous that a single bite can be deadly. One bite is all that it takes to cause paralysis followed by a painful death. The second important feature of the white mushroom is that its roots may extend for miles beneath the ground. This support system, this life-giving network, is unseen, undetectable, but under the proper conditions it will grow steadily, becoming ever stronger.

"The purpose of this meeting, the reason you are here, is to increase the scope of our organization, our brotherhood, our common cause: the ultimate ascendance of the Aryan race to its rightful position as the ruler of the earth. With this ascendance will come the destruction of those forces that have opposed this rule. Because these forces have opposed our true destiny, for hundreds, even thousands of years, it will require, as I have said before, some time to accomplish this goal, and so we must all have patience. It may take some sacrifice as well. But believe me it will be achieved, for that is my mission. That is why I am here with you today. That is why I am alive."

DuCharme paused and looked around at the men in the room. His eyes were now on fire and his face was slightly flushed. When he continued speaking, his commanding voice rippled in powerful waves through the conference room, enveloping the occupants in a hypnotic cocoon. Each man felt as though the words were intended for him and for no one else.

"All of us have heard through the years that Adolf Hitler, who had this same goal, this same vision, was the agent of the devil," DuCharme exclaimed. "That blasphemy was propagated by the devil's very own agents on earth, the Jews, along with those who have been swayed by them.

"The truth, my brothers, is that Adolf Hitler was the agent of none other than Christ Militant, the almighty, powerful, forceful God. The God who has inspired me. The God who has spoken to me. The God whose true posture is neither meek nor defensive and who has ordered me to lead this crusade through the Church of the Militant Redeemer, to which all of you have sworn allegiance.

"What, you may ask, does this have to do with mushrooms? I will tell you. Our South American comrades who have flown here to be with us today have pulled together their considerable resources, just as we have, and created a support group for our noble cause, a support group for our brotherhood. They have named this group El Hongo Blanco, the White Mushroom. Its root system extends from South America to Europe and now to the United States as well. Until the day we take control and are able to use the police and armed forces of the state to squash our enemies, we will need this support. Until that day, whoever rises up against us, whoever stands in the way of our holy mission, will feel El Hongo Blanco's wrath. It will be as though they took a bite of the fatal white mushroom. They will be instantly destroyed.

"None of us will ever speak about El Hongo Blanco outside this room. None of us will even mention the name. Once we leave this room, it will be as though El Hongo Blanco does not exist. But be assured, my brothers, it does, and its root system will continue to grow. El Hongo Blanco will be ready whenever and wherever we need it."

Once again DuCharme paused, and this time when he began to speak his voice was soft, soothing, comforting.

"We have the funds and the will to succeed," he said. "Now, with

309

your help, it is my intention to build a communications network second to none. We will educate the people, slowly at first, then with ever greater intensity. They know virtually nothing and will believe whatever we choose to tell them. That is the next step in our ascendancy. Communication of the truth. Of our truth. The media is now controlled by the Jews and their lackeys. In the future it will be controlled by us. Are there any questions?"

"Where do you plan to build this network?" asked a man seated at the far end of the conference table. The other men in the room showed varying degrees of surprise at this question, which had the ring of insolence and disbelief. Several turned to look at the man who asked it, and though the oilman who owned the high-rise didn't show it, he was shocked. The questioner had been one of the first to throw his money and considerable resources behind the mission of Novac DuCharme and was the last one the oilman expected would create a problem.

The man who asked the question was tall and thickset, with broad shoulders, a florid face and gnarled hands. At one time, before he made a fortune in the oil patch, he had obviously done manual work outdoors. His western-style suit was set off by a wide leather belt with a large, oval-shaped gold buckle. A string tie with a gold bolo shaped like an offshore drilling rig hung around his neck, and on the little finger of his right hand was a diamond pinkie ring the size of a small olive. He had a white ten-gallon hat on the table in front of him, and a .380-Walther in his boot. He came from the bayou country of Louisiana and his name was Joseph Didier. He had been listening to Novac DuCharme's speeches for quite some time and unlike the other men in the room was beginning to have his doubts.

DuCharme smiled at Didier benevolently but his eyes were cold as ice. DuCharme was incensed at being questioned; he detested ever having to explain himself, but did so now for the benefit of the others in the room. "I plan to build it in central Florida," he said. "An ideal television production facility will soon become available. It's out of the way, yet fully equipped. Why do you ask?"

"A communications network costs a lot of money," Didier replied. "You're gonna need a pretty damn good one to counteract what all's goin' on these days. The Jews, the niggers, the spics, even the gook fishermen down along the gulf, they all have plenty of support these days. It ain't like it was in times past."

"You don't think so?" said DuCharme. "You think human nature has changed in the last hundred years? The last thousand? The last ten thousand? It hasn't, my comrade. First we will create our network, of communications and of other things that are necessary. We will mold peoples' minds to our will. Then we will create chaos, which will be blamed on the Jews and their allies. We will strike terror in people's hearts and then we will assume control and bring about order. Our order. It is only out of utter chaos that ultimate order is made possible. As far as the Jews are concerned, no one did anything to stop us the last time, and no one will do anything the next."

"Hey, brother, you're the man and I'm on your side," Joseph Didier said. "I just don't think it's gonna be all that easy. And it's gonna cost a fuckin' ton of money. The million each of us just put up is chicken shit compared to what you're gonna need."

"I think what Mr. Didier means is that we have to plan every move we make with the utmost care," said the oilman who had convened the meeting. "I don't think he's questioning anyone's intentions. Isn't that correct, Joseph?"

"I'll tell you one damn thing," Didier said. "That white mushroom idea is a fuckin' good one. We need some business taken care of, it's better to have the caretakers already locked and loaded. Specialists ready for special delivery. I like that."

The meeting ended moments later. Waitresses entered with platters of food and beverages and the men chatted quietly among themselves.

"I don't know what the problem is with Didier," the oilman said to Novac DuCharme. "That was out of character. He should have waited and spoken to you privately if he had a question."

"Don't worry about it," DuCharme said. "Joseph will be fine."

The woman who knocked on the door of Novac DuCharme's hotel suite that night was in her late twenties, tall and thin, with straight black hair that fell over her shoulders. She wore an expensive gray silk suit, matching heels, and had a thin gold chain around her neck. A gold pendant, shaped like an offshore drilling rig, hung from the chain.

"Where's Joseph?" she asked when she was inside the suite.

"Joseph is with his other girlfriend," DuCharme replied. "The one he intends to marry instead of you."

"What the hell are you talking about?" she said.

DuCharme walked over to the small table in one corner of the room and picked up a manila envelope. He removed several photographs and handed them to the woman.

"This is what I'm talking about," DuCharme said.

"That son of a bitch," the woman said. "That motherfucker."

"And to think all that money will be hers instead of yours," DuCharme said. "I don't blame you for being upset."

"I'm more than upset, partner," the woman said. "I ought to kill them both."

"Well, I have a little something for you that may help to ease the pain," said DuCharme, taking an attaché case from the table where the pictures had been and placing it on the bed. "Open it."

The woman snapped open the case and stared, speechless, at the wrapped bundles of hundred-dollar bills inside.

"It's a half-million dollars," DuCharme said. "There's another half-million waiting for you."

"You ain't just handing me a million bucks for nothin', sugar," the woman said. "What-all do I have to do for it?"

"Two things," said DuCharme.

"What's the first one?" asked the woman.

"Take off your skirt and your panties," DuCharme told her. "Leave your shoes and jacket on."

If someone had studied the videotape very carefully, which the police had not, he would have seen the leader of the survivalist community—the man dressed in fatigues at the meeting with the South Americans—react an instant sooner than he should have, and then hesitate an instant longer than he claimed. The tape was shot by the surveillance camera mounted above Joseph Didier's swimming pool. It shows Didier and the survivalist, along with two attractive young women, sitting next to the pool. Suddenly the dark-haired woman with the gold-drilling rig hanging from her necklace appears and draws a pistol from her bag. As she does this, the survivalist rolls off his lounge chair, but his roll begins before her bag is fully open. And when he comes up on his knees, a .45 in his hands, it seems he waits a second or two more than he might have, until the dark-haired woman has finished what she came to do and has emptied her pistol into Joseph Didier's reclining body. Then the survivalist shoots her, once between the eyes and twice more in the chest.

Angela Becker was reading through files that lay spread across her desk in the office of the gang-intervention unit and didn't hear Roland Troy come into the room. McKenzie Rockett had managed to install the unit in the same place where the task force had formerly been, in the converted attic above the barn that housed the department's lawn-mowing equipment. The old armchair was still there—the one Angela had bought used—and Troy sat in it and watched her narrow back, curved in concentration over the desk. In spite of the sunlight streaming in through the windows it was chilly in the office and Angela was wearing a dark blue cardigan over her dress. Her blond hair, contrasting sharply with the color of the sweater, cascaded over her shoulders giving her an air of schoolgirl innocence. She looks like a kid doing homework, Troy thought, remembering at the same time the fine lines at the corners of her eyes and mouth, and the eyes themselves, deep and haunted, that belied any trace of unworldliness. A lump came into his throat; he wanted to leap up and take her in his arms, but he waited. Now that he had proved his stealth he didn't want to frighten her. He considered leaving as silently as he had entered, then coming back and knocking on the door.

After Troy returned to Vermont, Angela seriously considered quitting the department, getting out of law enforcement, and moving far away. She had a place picked out, an island off the coast of Washington where there was a small bookstore for sale. The store was combined with a gallery specializing in Indian art of the Northwest and had a small apartment upstairs with a view of the water. A broker faxed her some pictures and she made plans to fly out and have a look, when early one morning the lawyer she had lived with years before called her at her trailer.

"It's about Karen," the lawyer said. "She killed herself last night."

"Oh my God," Angela said. "Oh shit."

"She did it with a shotgun," said the lawyer. "I always thought women were more . . . you know, wrist slitters or pill takers. A shotgun's kind of a guy thing, don't you think?"

"Go fuck yourself," Angela said, and hung up.

She went to the funeral. It was at a tiny church out in the woods. The people there, Karen's family and some childhood friends, were from another time, another era. None of the models from Karen's agency showed up. Neither did the man she was once married to, who had treated her terribly. Angela was the only person in the congregation from Karen's other life.

After the funeral, Angela drove quickly back to the office and went to work. She felt safe and secure there, with the birds chirping in the wild cherry tree outside the window next to her desk, and the sun streaming in, filtered by the tree's branches, and Rock popping his head in the door on his way to some meeting, asking her if she was all right.

She worked until well after dark and then drove home listening to the chatter on the police radio in her car. Two cops caught a guy trying to rob a convenience store. Another one broke up a fight in a bar. It was no big deal, just routine stuff, but she found it comforting all the same. It made her feel that she belonged to something that had meaning, to something that was flawed but still took care of business, still accomplished something worthwhile. That night she called the broker out in Washington and told him she was staying where she was, at least for now. The summers were too long, the crime rate was going up, and the traffic was getting worse by the week, but she loved her little piece of land by the river, and she'd already gotten through to some of these gang kids. They weren't like skinheads whose lives were based on hate. The gang kids were only scared, like everybody else.

"You're still favoring that shoulder," Roland Troy said.

Angela leaped six inches off her chair and whirled around. Her mouth flew open and the pen she was holding fell to the floor.

"Oh Roland," she said, and started to say more, but by then he'd crossed the room and was holding her in his arms.

"Come on," he said after a few minutes. "Let's get out of here. I'm going to take you canoeing."

"You're going to take me canoeing?" she said. "Now?"

"Right now," he replied. "Come on. There's a place I want to show you that you've never seen."

He was still holding her, but she moved back, grasping his arms and looking him in the eye. She took a deep breath, or maybe it was a sigh, let go of him, and sat down once more in her chair.

"You didn't come all the way from Vermont just to take me canoeing," she said. "What's going on?"

"I missed you," he said. "I missed you very badly. I wanted to see you."

"You forget I'm a cop," she said. "You're going to have to do better than that. Sit down and tell me why you're here, Roland."

His plan had been to wait until that night, go over to her trailer or her condo, wherever it was she was staying, and tell her there. But what he said was true. He had missed her terribly, and the farther south he drove, the more desperately he wanted to see her face and hear her voice and feel her heart beating against his chest, so instead of waiting, he had come straight to her office from the road, not even stopping at his house. Still, she was right; he was dissembling. If Justine Fallon hadn't shown up at his door, he'd still be chopping wood and digging stones out of a stubborn hillside. He had arrived at the notion of a canoe ride because he didn't want to tell her there, in that office. If he could take her somewhere calm and peaceful, he thought, somewhere away from everyone else, it might somehow make it easier.

He sat down in the old stuffed chair and took a cigar out of his shirt pocket, wondering if he'd wanted to make it easier for her or for him.

"You mind?" he asked, holding up the cigar.

"You know I don't," she replied.

He unwrapped the cigar slowly, bit off the end and lit it, feeling her eyes on him. He took two puffs and looked at her, knowing there was only one place he could go.

"Justine Fallon came to see me," he said.

She swiveled her chair around when he finished talking and stared out the window. Troy couldn't see her face and thought she was crying, but at first she wasn't. She stared out at the trees, and at a group of jailbirds in their orange jumpsuits bagging trash, and at the traffic speeding by beyond them, but saw instead the long driveway on the estate where she was raised, and the barn where she and her brother—still thinking of him that way—had played. That was his car, she thought. That big old Cadillac with all the wicker furniture piled on top of it and the nest inside was my father's car. God, how he must have suffered. Then she did begin to cry. When she was done she got up and went into the bathroom and washed her face.

"Let's go," she said to Troy when she returned. "I want to go canoeing. I want to breathe some fresh air."

"You sure?" Troy asked. "You sure you don't want to be alone?"

"Alone is the last thing I want to be," Angela said. "I want to be with you."

"I know where you want to take me," she said when they were driving in his truck. "It's to that island you told me about the first time we met, the island that was sacred to the Indians, the place they buried their dead, the place where no animals or birds go and it's perfectly still. You probably thought I forgot."

"I know you better than that," he said. "You're a cop."

"I'm going to get him, Roland," she said. "I'm going to get DuCharme if it's the last thing I ever do."

"We'll get him," Troy said.

They paddled north, then west, along a winding stream, Angela in the bow, Troy in the stern. Her long blond hair hung loose, shifting from one side of her back to the other with every stroke. The ends of it flowed over the gunwales and as she ducked her head to avoid an overhanging branch it brushed the water. She lay her paddle down for a moment, grabbed her hair in her hand and swung it around her neck, showering him with droplets. The drops of water roused him from a trancelike state in which he had drifted back in time, back more than thirty years, and was paddling on this very stream, in this very same canoe. There was a young woman with him then as well, tall and thin like Angela, paddling in the bow. This was before he went off to college at Alabama to play football for Bear Bryant, before his grandparents suddenly died and he quit school, before he went to Okinawa, and then to Laos, and Cambodia, and Vietnam, before he learned to kill. This was way before all that, when he was young, unscarred and filled with dreams. The woman in the bow was seventeen. Her hair was also long, but dark, and when she paddled with him on this stream it brushed the water too, and he fell in love.

He stopped paddling for a second and wiped the water off his face.

"I got you wet," she said. "I'm sorry. I should have tied my hair up but I forgot. At least I had the sense to change. That dress would not have made it in this swamp."

"I'm glad you didn't tie it up," he told her. "I like it better down."

The stream let out into another pond larger than the one near Troy's house, but hidden deep in the forest, so that even now few people knew it was there. In the middle of this pond was a small island ringed with red mangrove, the walking tree, its aerial roots jutting into the water like a thousand marching legs. They could see a sandy gap in the tangle of the roots, a beach of sorts, maybe thirty yards wide. They made for it, pulled the canoe up on the shore, and sat on a small blanket Troy had brought.

"Don't say a word, just listen," Troy told her. "What do you hear?"

"Nothing," she said after several minutes. "I don't hear anything. I only hear the beating of my heart. Can we make love here, Roland? Do you think the spirits of the Indians will mind?"

"I don't think so," Troy said. "I don't think they'll mind a bit."

The cool November wind had aired out his house by the time they returned in the canoe. Angela drove to the supermarket six miles away to get some food while Troy cleaned up the kitchen and threw in a wash. She hadn't said a word about Justine Fallon's story since they left her office except to ask one question while they were paddling back across his pond.

"Is there any proof that I'm his daughter?" she asked. "Is there something I can see?"

"I asked Justine the same thing," Troy told her. "She said your birth certificate is in a vault in the New York office of Peter Becker's associate. Your baby hand- and footprints are there too. You can check it any time you want, but if I were you I'd wait. You don't want to tip your hand. It's all true Angela. I kept that woman up half the night telling me everything she knew. She has a convoluted delivery, to say the least, but believe me, the story's true."

They were both famished and polished off a bowl of tomato soup with hunks of whole wheat bread, a vegetable lasagna ready-made but very good, and almost half a store-bought pumpkin pie. They talked about the island while they ate, and Troy told her what his grandfather had told him; there was no scientific explanation for why the animals and birds aren't there, no reason why the place should be so still.

"My grandfather said it simply proves that there are things on earth we just don't understand and never will," Troy said. Then he brewed up some tea and they took it out on the back porch to drink.

"I'm in a state of shock, you know," Angela said as they sat there on the porch. "I mean there I was working with those skinheads and all the time . . . my father was a survivor of the Holocaust . . . my mother . . . they were Jewish. I guess you have a thing for Jewish women, huh? I'm sorry . . . I'm sorry . . . that wasn't very funny . . . I remember when I was in boarding school I used to hear all the comments about Jews, you know, what the girls would say when they didn't think there were any Jews around, and all the time I was . . . at least I didn't join in . . . I didn't do that. Or say things about blacks or Puerto Ricans or gay people . . . I always hated that shit . . . so my brother isn't really my brother . . . well, he was my stepbrother so that's the same, sort of . . . Oh my God, Roland, I don't know who I am."

"The Indians have a saying," Troy said. " 'Who you are is who you are.' Halpatter told me that a long time ago. I think it loses a little bit in translation, but all in all it's pretty accurate. You're a force for good in this world, Angela. You're decent and kind and loving. I don't think any parent could ask more than that from a child. And speaking of Halpatter, we have to pay that man a visit."

"Tonight?"

"Tonight, tomorrow, it doesn't matter."

"I'm very tired, Roland. And now I think I do want to be alone. Let me take your truck over to my trailer. I'll come get you in the morning."

"No problem," Troy said. "You going to be all right?"

"I'll be all right."

"You call me if you're not, no matter what time it is, OK?"

"How are we going to get Novac DuCharme?" she asked. "How are we going to find that album so we can nail that son of a bitch and make him pay for what he's done?"

"That's the reason we're going to see Halpatter," Troy said. "When it comes to the interpretation of obscure references in this neck of the woods there's no one better."

"Well, well, well," Halpatter shouted when he saw Troy and Angela paddling toward him. He was sitting on his dock in a bright red coverall, barefoot as usual, dressing an alligator that looked to be at least ten feet long. "I had a funny feeling last night that I'd be seeing you, Roland, but the sensation did not include a lovely companion. How are you, Angela?"

"You notice he didn't ask how I was," Troy said, making the canoe fast to the dock.

"You're old and ugly," Halpatter said. "And you haven't written or called in over a month."

"I'm actually fine, all things considered," Angela said. She and Troy had already decided to tell Halpatter her story.

"Oh, I see," he said, nodding. "Let's go inside where we can sit and talk. It's a bit early in the day, but I have some very fresh and tasty marinated gator tail you might want to try. Not you, Roland. I was offering the meat to Angela. Does it strike you that 'fresh' and 'marinated' constitute an oxymoron? I wonder."

"How's your leg?" Troy asked.

"I'll never outrun my son, the linebacker, again," Halpatter said, "but it feels pretty good. I climbed a tree yesterday, in fact."

He covered the eviscerated gator with a tarp to keep the vultures off, unclipped his ponytail, and shook his head. Hanging free, his glistening black hair, streaked with silver, was longer than Angela's.

"Did you know my son plays for Minnesota?" he said to her. "The Vikings. There's an oxymoron for you. The Indian Viking. I would rather he had been drafted by the Jaguars or Panthers, but they weren't in the league yet. At least he isn't a Redskin. Come on, let's go in."

"So now we have to find the album," Halpatter said, when he'd heard the entire story. "And to find it we must decipher the reference to drainage pipes running with the blood and sweat of slaves, and determine how that coincides with a nearby railroad siding. Sit here for a minute or two. I'll be right back."

He rose from the kitchen chair and, favoring his bad leg slightly, went out into the garden his wife kept on the east side of their house. Troy and Angela could see him standing there surrounded by flowers, his arms outstretched, his head tilted up toward the sun. He stood there motionless for what seemed like a very long time.

"What is he doing?" Angela asked.

"He's praying," Troy said. "Probably for guidance and also for the souls of your parents. When Halpatter gets involved he doesn't screw around."

"He's a remarkable man," she said.

"You don't know the half of it," Troy said. "You're part of his circle now. He would die for you if necessary, and that's no melodramatic bullshit. It's the truth."

They watched him turn and walk back in through the screened kitchen door. He was smiling rather sheepishly. "You have to forgive me," he said to Angela. "I'm just a foolish old guy, stuck in the olden ways. But a thought came to me while I was standing in the garden. I think I know where we will find the album. I think it's in a clay field, Roland."

"That crossed my mind," Troy said. "But the clay fields are gone. They're all built over. The last one was where they stuck that Auto

Nation place up off forty-six. Thirty-five acres of used cars where all there used to be was muck. Ain't no more clay fields that I know of."

"It was only a thought that came to me," Halpatter said. "Though I will say it was a strong thought."

"What's a clay field?" Angela asked. "I thought all the clay soil was north of here."

"It is," Troy said. "This land we're talking about was drained river bottom. They started tilling it way back before the Civil War. The landowners had the slaves dig ditches all around the fields and then lay clay tiles under the dirt. They called 'em tiles. Clay pipes is what they were. They'd lay long, horizontal sections with short vertical ones connected to 'em, like inverted T's. The water would drain down through the muck into the vertical pipes and then run off along the horizontal ones into the ditches. It was brutal, backbreaking work diggin' those ditches and layin' that pipe, but it produced some of the finest growing soil in the south. They called 'em clay fields because of the clay pipe, but the soil wasn't clay at all. It was muck, thick black muck so rich with decomposed organic matter you could grow three crops a year on the same piece of ground.

"My grandfather told me he remembered when they hauled the vegetables from those farms to market on mule trains. They probably hauled 'em on the backs of slaves before that. Now that land's all been sold off and developed. You really couldn't blame the farmers. A million bucks for a thirty-acre cabbage patch is tough to turn down."

Angela looked hard at Halpatter, who still appeared flushed from standing in his garden. "What if there were a clay field the developers missed?" she asked. "What if it were too small to be of any use to them?"

"It would be way out of the way somewhere," Halpatter said. "It wouldn't belong to a white man. Nothing at all comes to my mind. What about you, Roland?"

"Like I told you," Troy said. "The last one I knew of got turned into a used car lot."

"It was only a thought," Halpatter said again.

"C'mon," Angela said after she and Troy had paddled back to his house and pulled the canoe up on shore. "Let's take a ride."

"Where to?" Troy asked.

"You aren't the only one who has friends," she said.

The large dog tied to an oak tree let out a low growl and Oliver Reavis came rolling out on a creeper from under an old Ford van.

"I could pick the sound of that Trans-Am motor out of an automobile lineup from a hundred yards away, maybe further," Reavis said.

"Good to see you, Oliver," Angela Becker said.

"I been hearing that a lot," Reavis told her. "People say I been blessed. Damn fools want to touch me. I say I got lucky. Who's your friend?"

"This is Roland Troy," she said.

"So you're Roland Troy," Reavis said. "I heard about you. Lemme get a rag and wipe this grease off my hands."

He got up and grabbed a rag from the pile on his workbench. "Have a seat," he said, gesturing to the old couch set against the wall. "You want a cold one? How you like my new place, Angie? And my new dog? Got him from the dudes up front. He's a retired bomb sniffer. I ain't takin' no chances. No, sir. Got good teeth too."

"I don't think you've got anything to worry about Oliver," Angela said.

"Smooth Lee don't got nothin' to worry about," said Reavis. "I ain't so sure about those of us who are still upright."

Reavis's new place was a two-bay cement-block garage off a dirt road many miles from where his family now lived. The garage was at the rear of a compound enclosed with six-foot chain-link fencing topped with coiled razor wire. Off to one side were rows of used cars headed for the auction. Near the front of the compound was a larger cement-block building that housed a guard-dog training facility.

"At night they lock the gate and turn four or five of 'em loose," Reavis said. "They all been trained to only eat out of their dish. They been trained not to bark either. You come in this yard after dark, first thing you hear be your own voice beggin' for mercy."

Reavis was perched on the hood of a LeBaron convertible parked next to the Ford van. He took a long pull on his bottle of Budweiser and nodded several times at Angela and Troy, who were sitting on the couch.

"I'd a' moved all the way to Alaska," Reavis said, "but my wife has to take care of her daddy and he ain't about to go nowhere at his age, so this had to do."

Troy lit a cigar and leaned back on the couch. Angela took a small sip of her beer and set the bottle down on the concrete floor between her legs.

"Tell me something, Oliver," she said. "Are there any tile fields left up north of my place? Along the river?"

"Tile fields?" Reavis said. "What you wanna know about tile fields for? Ain't nothin' but bad memories connected to tile fields, you understand what I'm sayin'?"

"I need to know, Oliver," Angela said. "There could be something hidden in one of them that'll help break this case. Maybe catch the man responsible for killing Smooth Lee."

"Poor Smooth," Reavis said. "Poor fuckin' Smooth. Never hurt nobody his whole life." He took another pull on the bottle and stared out of his garage into the bright sunlight. For a long time he was silent. "They be three, maybe four tile fields that I know of," he finally said. "Small ones. They all got history to 'em though."

"Is one of them near some railroad tracks?" Angela asked.

Oliver Reavis continued to gaze into the distance, out beyond the garage, and at first didn't answer. Angela thought that perhaps he hadn't heard her question and was about to ask it again when suddenly he turned and looked at her and Troy.

"There's an overgrown tile field south and east of Enterprise," he said. "An abandoned narrow-gauge spur of the old Deland and St. Johns River Railway runs right next to it. The field belongs to an old woman named Flybird Mims. She and her husband, Lamont, used to farm it. They grew peppers, corn and celery, but since Lamont died, Flybird's let it go. There's nothing there but weeds now. In the old days I used to hunt with Lamont. We'd walk along those tracks looking for hogs and deer. I still go up there now and again to fix Flybird's car. She must be nearly ninety but she still drives. Her field is just off the little back road that runs all the way up to Velvet."

"Let's you and us go pay Flybird Mims a visit," Troy said to Reavis.

Oliver Reavis stared hard at Troy for a moment. Angela thought maybe he was going to throw his beer bottle at him but instead Reavis nodded again. "Yeah," he said. "We can do that."

As they drove north, Angela told Oliver Reavis the story of Leo Weiser.

"Could be that's the place," Reavis said when she was through. "It's so overgrown now you'd never know the spur was there except for a broken-down loading platform and what's left of an old wooden water tank right next to Flybird's field. You can see the tank from the road. Could be that one day this Leo Weiser took a ride and saw that tank. Could be that tank reminded him of something and he stopped his car to check it out. If that's what happened he must've been a decent dude. Flybird Mims shot a white man who came on her property one time. Got away with it too. Not very many black women can say that."

"Your parents stick you with a name like Flybird, God smiles on you and let's you get away with damn near anything," Troy said.

"Ain't that the truth," Oliver Reavis said.

"Of course I 'member him," Flybird Mims said. "He was a very polite man. He come one day and ask me could he take a picture of that ole' water tank. I tol' him help yourself. Next time he come he brung me a great big jar of honey from a beekeeper he say he knew. He wanted to take my picture but I tol' him uh uh. I say, 'who the hell want a picture of an ole' woman like me?' Then he come with a picture got these wavy shapes and say they be my spirit guides. He say they watchin' over me. I tol' him 'Baby, all the trouble I been through that sure ain't no surprise.' "

Flybird Mims was a tiny, dark-skinned woman, and very thin, with snow-white hair and oversized, gnarled hands. She was wearing jeans and a Florida State sweatshirt. She saw Angela staring at it.

"Yeah, sugar, I'm a Seminole fan through and through. My great grandson's playin' for them right now. On the line. Bustin' holes. Got them a runnin' back fine as they can be. Lil' bitty fella, but slipp'ry as a greased eel. His mama was a cop. She was shot and killed, way on over in Louisiana. You be a cop too, ain't that right? I can tell. I can always tell. Y'all be careful some'n like that don' happen to you."

"Did he come here often?" Angela asked. "The man who took pictures?"

"He come time after time, sugar, drivin' that busted-up ole' car. Ole' Toyota. He took picture after picture of that tank. Sometime he jes come and sit on de platform, and don' do nothin' but look. One time it seem like he was cryin'. When he was fixin' to leave I ask him if he all right. He say he fine, it was jes the sunlight in his eyes, but I knew better. I ain't seen him for a year or two. Sumpn' happen to him, did'n it?"

"Yeah," Troy said.

"That's a shame," Flybird said. "That's truly a shame. He was a nice man."

"You mind if we take a walk down in your field?" Angela asked. "Down there by the siding?"

"Hell no," Flybird said. "Why I mind that? You walk and I'll chat with Oliver. My car ain't holdin' the road like it should, Oliver. You gotta see to it. Make it drive straight."

"It ain't the car," Oliver Reavis said.

They found the inlet pipe twenty feet from the spur at the base of a bottlebrush tree. It was the only inlet with a clear view of both the siding and the broken remnants of the tank. It had to be the one. Troy lifted off the perforated circular tile cover, set it on the ground, and stuck his arm inside the pipe. He reached down almost to his shoulder, to where the vertical and horizontal pipes were joined, and groped around for a few seconds, then pulled out a thick black plastic garbage bag. The bag was empty.

"Seems like someone beat us to it," he said.

"Are you sure it was in that bag?" Angela asked.

"Look," Troy said, turning the bag inside out and shaking it. A few fragments of brownish paper floated to the ground. "That's where it was."

Angela shook her head and sighed. She walked over to the platform, sat down, and held her head in her hands. Troy put the cover back in place and folded up the garbage bag.

"Why do you think they left the bag?" she asked him after a while.

"Maybe they were in a hurry," Troy said. "Maybe they pulled the album out, saw they had what they came for, and didn't want to leave anything above ground to show they'd been here. Maybe something startled them and they stuffed the bag back in the pipe, put the cover on and ran. Who knows, Angela? Who knows why people do the things they do?"

Troy called Jack Ubinas as soon as he and Angela got back to his house and came straight to the point.

"Who took the album, Jack?" he asked.

"I have no idea what you're talking about, Roland," Ubinas said.

"Justine Fallon paid me a visit," Troy said. "You've been jerking me around, partner. You knew the score all the time. Where's DuCharme?"

"You're misinformed," Ubinas said. "You've been talking to the wrong people. Justine Fallon is deranged, or didn't you notice. Justine Fallon converses with the dead."

"I want DuCharme," Troy said. "He's an ex-Nazi who's responsible for killing more fucking people than either you or I have fingers and toes. Novac DuCharme isn't even the motherfucker's name."

"There's no evidence to support that," Ubinas said.

"Not anymore," Troy said. "Now that someone you sent found Justine Fallon. What did they have to do to make her talk, Jack? What did they do to make that poor woman tell 'em about the album?"

"You're imagining things, Roland," Ubinas said. "You need a rest. Go back to Vermont. Take your ex-partner with you. Pay a visit to your daughter. Enjoy life a little and forget about Novac DuCharme before you make a serious mistake. It'll be better for your health. Better for everyone's health."

"It ain't me who's making a mistake, Jack," Troy said. "And if anything should happen to my daughter or to Angela Becker it won't be my health that's in jeopardy, it'll be yours."

"I thought he was on our side," Angela said when Troy hung up the phone. "I thought he was your friend."

She was lying on the couch, wrapped in a blanket. She looked pale and her eyes were glazed. Troy thought she might be running a fever.

"Men like Jack Ubinas don't have friends," he said. "They have contacts and allies. They have all sorts of markers they can call in, but they don't have friends."

During the night Angela's fever spiked at 103 and she began to shake uncontrollably. Troy bundled her into his truck and took her to the emergency room. Her white blood count was extremely high and her blood pressure had jumped to 180 over 110. She was admitted and placed on intravenous antibiotics. Within two days her fever broke and her pressure returned to normal, but the doctors insisted on keeping her in the hospital for a week. The diagnosis was chronic fatigue immune dysfunction; she was so physically and emotionally depleted her immune system had simply shut down.

Troy brought her to his house from the hospital and took care of her for two weeks while she lay in bed and read, or watched TV, or simply looked out the huge windows of the bedroom at the wildlife on the pond. Soon her strength returned and they began canoeing together and jogging on the paths through the woods. One evening, as they sat out on the porch, he told her that he loved her. She said she loved him too, but when he asked her to go north to Vermont with him she said no.

"I'm going back to work," she told him. "I have to, Roland. I can't come out in the open. I don't want to wander the earth like Justine Fallon wondering whether the next time I go to the store for bread I'll wind up in the trunk of a car, so I can't say who I really am. I have to go back to my job. It's the only way I'll keep from going nuts."

He told her in that case he would stay too and keep trying to dig up something on DuCharme, but when a month passed, and then another, and nothing at all turned up, he decided he needed a break. It was March. He'd arranged to have the maples tapped on his land in Vermont and now that the sap was flowing he made plans to travel north and bring it in the old way, with a team of horses and a sleigh. He talked Halpatter into going with him, which was no small task.

"I'll have to wear things on my feet," Halpatter said. "Those big heavy rubber-bottomed things with felt linings."

"They're called boots," Troy said. "We'll get you a pair you can wear without socks. How's that for a compromise?"

"I've never been up there before," Halpatter said. "I understand the country's very beautiful. I guess I'll go."

They were packing for the trip, loading their supplies into the bed of Troy's truck, half an hour from being on the road, when the phone rang.

"Mr. Troy, I'm calling for your old friend," the woman on the line said.

He knew instantly who it was.

"How you doin' Madeleine?" he asked.

"I'm fine, thank you," she replied. "Your friend wonders whether you could join him in an hour for a bite to eat at a little Japanese restaurant not too far from your house. He thinks you'll find the food very . . . satisfying."

"It's eight-thirty," Troy said. "The only Japanese place near here closes at nine."

"I think tonight they plan on staying open later," Madeleine told him.

"I'll be there," Troy said.

XXVII

The restaurant was at the far end of a strip mall dominated by a large electronics store that was closed. When Troy pulled his El Camino into the parking lot the only other cars there were a Lincoln Town Car and a new Corvette. Someone was sitting in the driver's seat of the Town Car. As Troy walked past it he saw there was someone else in back. A wiry, tough-looking Oriental studied Troy for a moment through the restaurant's door, let him in, then locked the door and hung the closed sign in the window. The large, muscular black man Troy knew as Tim was sitting at the sushi bar. Other than the man behind the counter, Chotoku Nakama was the only person in the place. He was seated at a small table, partially shielded from the door by a hand-painted rice-paper screen.

"Roland-san, it is good to see you again," he said, standing up as Troy approached and spreading his arms wide. Nakama looked tanned and fit, though a trifle thin, as though he'd just come back from a long vacation climbing a mountain or sailing on the open sea. Troy thought for an instant he was going to hug him, but instead he vigorously shook Troy's hand.

"Sit down, sit down," he said. "Are you hungry?"

"It's good to see you too, Bassai," Troy said. "No, I ate earlier. I don't eat late anymore. I find I sleep better if I don't."

"You know, I find the same thing," said Nakama. "Less chance of having a bad dream, né? But how about just a bowl of miso soup. It's never too late for something simple and restorative."

"You talked me into it," said Troy, "but only if you join me."

"Join you I will," Nakama exclaimed, signaling to the chef, who immediately hurried to their table, took their order, and hurried away.

"I would have joined you earlier, in fact, or seen to it that you joined me, but there were things that needed to be attended to," Nak-ama said. "I had no choice. But now here we are."

"That's for sure," Troy said. "Not exactly where I might have expected, but here we are."

"I was in the air when I heard you were about to travel north," Nakama said, smiling at Troy. "I wanted to catch you before you left. This seemed as good a place as any."

"Hell, Bassai, you should have just come over to the house," Troy said. He had no idea how Nakama knew he was heading north to Vermont and decided not to ask.

"Indeed I could have," Nakama said. "I am sure you would have been delighted to have me there. But of course there was no way I could know in advance who might be there with you. And then," he said, nodding to the chef who placed their bowls before them and departed, "who would have served us fresh miso soup while we talked? The soup is good, né?"

"The soup is just fine, Bassai," Troy said.

"But of course soup is not the reason I had Madeleine give you a call."

"I didn't think so," Troy said.

"What kept me from contacting you sooner, Roland-san, were matters that were very urgent. However, if I'd known someone else would find that album before you did I assure you I would not have waited."

"You knew about the album?" Troy asked.

"I knew that there was something," Nakama said. "I knew there was evidence proving who Novac DuCharme really is. You're a wonderful detective. I had faith that you would find that evidence. I didn't know it was an album until after it was found."

"You know where DuCharme is?" Troy asked. "Where I can find him?"

"No," Nakama said. "That I do not know. But I know you will find him."

"Thanks for the vote of confidence, Bassai," Troy said. "But I'll be honest with you. In terms of the Novac DuCharme case, as of this moment I'm fucked. Up, down, backwards and forwards. Fucked."

"That is where you are wrong, Roland-san," Nakama said. "Novac DuCharme is the one who is fucked."

Troy finished off the last of his soup, wiped his mouth with his napkin, and nodded at Nakama. "Bassai," he said. "You were right. That was wonderful miso soup. Now tell me how Novac DuCharme is fucked."

"What do you know about leverage?" Nakama asked.

"With a good lever, an old woman can move a ton of bricks," Troy said.

Nakama raised his eyebrows, nodded to Troy and smiled. "You are an honorable and noble Prancing Tiger, Roland-san. But you are not a good businessman. If you were, you would have waited to sell the land you sold until the buyers were crawling on their bellies through the mud of the swamp to reach your front door. True, you made a considerable amount of money, but if you had waited and not sold for emotional reasons you would have made much more. I, on the other hand, am not as noble a Prancing Tiger as you . . ."

Troy began to say something but Nakama stilled him with an upraised palm.

"No, Roland-san. What I say is true. I am honorable, but to my own code. I am not a romantic like you. However, I am a good businessman, probably for that very reason. Business, Roland-san, is nothing but leverage. You know that saying that appears on bumper stickers, 'He Who Dies with the Most Toys Wins'? That is the saying of a fool. When you are dead the game is over, and winning or losing is irrelevant. The truth is that he who lives with the greatest leverage wins. Now let me ask you something. Do you imagine that album still exists?"

"Oh yeah," Troy replied. "It still exists."

"Correct," said Nakama. "And you know why. For leverage. Do you think I look well?"

"I think you look terrific, Bassai," Troy said, wondering what Nakama had up his sleeve, what game he was playing now. "I was remarking on that to myself when I came through that door."

"I think so too," Nakama said. "But in fact, Roland-san, I am dying. There is a tumor inside me that is inoperable and has failed to respond to standard protocol. I am flying from here to Mexico for experimental treatment that will probably not succeed. Don't speak. Listen. I want to give you a lever before I go. A straight flush against whatever hand your old associate Ubinas and his friends are holding."

"What sort of lever is that?" Troy asked.

"Forty pounds of weapons-grade plutonium," Nakama said. "Put that on the table, Roland-san. See who wants to play then."

Jack Ubinas was a creature of habit, a man compelled by his nature to a life of absolute regularity. In the old days, when he traveled the world running covert operations, he fought against this predilection. A spook with a schedule, he had been taught, was a spy who would die. Now, however, he worked at home, in the bright airy room at his farmhouse in Virginia where he kept his computer and was free to indulge his passion for uniformity. With his enormous storehouse of information Ubinas controlled dozens of other people's lives. With rigorous attention to a precise and unvarying daily agenda he attempted to control time. Ubinas would never have admitted to this, since he considered himself above the foibles that plagued lesser mortals. He was disdainful of anything that smacked of human weakness and re- garded his own solitary lifestyle and compulsive behavior as masterful rather than bizarre.

Still the sleuth, he dressed in flannel shirts, rumpled khakis or corduroys, and work boots in order to project the image of a semi- retired college professor to his neighbors, but he dressed in those clothes every morning at precisely ten minutes after six, not a minute earlier or later, and removed them at ten-thirty each night. If he worked past ten-thirty, which sometimes happened, he did so in pa- jamas and a flannel robe. Ubinas smoked a pipe, but never lit the first bowl until exactly 8 A.M. when he returned from his morning walk along the south fork of the Shenandoah River. The walk began at seven on the dot, no matter what the weather. He had snowshoes for bliz- zards and high-tech rainwear for torrential nor'easters and boots that were good for springtime mud. Should someone need to reach him while he walked, he carried a cell phone. Jack Ubinas was never out of touch.

Ubinas's other obsession was the security of his computer. Now that his only exposure was to the elements when he was walking or working in his vegetable garden, his concern was not for his own safety but for a possible raid on his computer when he wasn't home. The security system at the farmhouse was such that any breach would automatically render the computer useless. Furthermore, three of Ubinas's operatives were skilled computer hackers who kept abreast of all the latest piracy techniques. Ubinas knew that no electronic information system was invulnerable, but his came close.

Every Saturday morning Jack Ubinas drove into the town of Front Royal for supplies. After breakfast, his morning walk, and a shower, he climbed into his Grand Cherokee and left for town, precisely at nine o'clock. As time went by, these trips to and from Front Royal assumed for him the characteristics of an automobile rally, a form of competition he devised that pitted him against the clock. There were specific landmarks he noted along the way—a particular maple tree, for example, a certain curve in the road, or the converted barn now used by a river-guiding outfit. To win the game he had to pass these landmarks at precisely the same time each week: the tree at 9:18, the curve at 9:25, the river guide's barn at 9:31, all while driving exactly at the speed limit. For accuracy, he had installed a digital timer with a split-second stopwatch in the Jeep.

It was only a game, Ubinas told himself, something to maintain his edge now that his job was completely sedentary, but on the Saturday morning in late March when the Grand Cherokee wouldn't start, he felt a decided surge of anxiety. Despite the cold early morning air he began to sweat. It wasn't a problem, he told himself. He would simply take the timer and put it in his other vehicle, an old Nissan pickup parked next to the Grand Cherokee in the small wooden barn behind his house. He could drive the truck to town and compute his score based on his new time of departure. He got out of the Grand Cherokee, opened the door of the pickup and realized he didn't have the keys. He would have to go back inside the house.

Ubinas was much calmer now that he had devised a solution to his problem, and as he pressed the buttons on his remote control deactivating the house security system he actually laughed at himself for becoming so upset. He went inside, retrieved the keys for the pickup, and walked back to the barn, reactivating the security system on the way. He climbed into the Nissan, but like the Jeep, although the engine had no problem turning over, the truck wouldn't start. Then his cell phone rang.

"Guess you're going to have to postpone your trip to town," Roland Troy said. "Unless you want to strap that timer on your back and walk. Or swim down the river. You know all these years I never knew the Shenandoah ran south to north. I always thought it was the other way."

"Where are you?" Ubinas asked.

"I'm sitting in your kitchen," Troy said. "Nice place you got here, Jack. I should have paid you a visit sooner. Then again, you never invited me. I think maybe you ought to get out of that rust bucket and come on inside so we can talk. You can say hello in person to my ex-partner on the way. The one you've been wanting to meet so bad. You'll recognize her. She's standing right outside your barn. Five-eleven, skinny, long blond hair, diamond stud in her nose, tattoo of an angel on her ankle, forty-four magnum in her right hand. I know you've seen the kinda hole a forty-four can make, so you better be moving slow when you come. Oh by the way, the twenty-two rifle you keep out there is long gone, so don't bother looking for it."

"You've stepped over the line this time," Ubinas said. "You've stepped way over the line. You've screwed yourself right to the wall, buddy."

They had moved from the kitchen into the room where Ubinas kept his computer. Angela was sitting in the chair in front of it, her .44 still in her right hand pointed straight at Jack Ubinas, who sat on the floor against a windowless wall. Roland Troy, his .45 in a shoulder holster, was in an armchair facing him. Although he'd done numerous undercover jobs for Ubinas, Troy hadn't seen him in fifteen years. In spite of his daily walks, he saw that Ubinas had grown soft during that time. A thick roll of fat hung around his waist, and his thighs and buttocks strained the seams of the corduroy pants he wore. Ubinas's thick lips were white with fury, and his fleshy neck trembled. No one had ever held him at gunpoint before.

"Now Jack, I can understand you being upset at having your schedule disrupted," Troy said. "And I know how much you hate uninvited guests, or any guests for that matter. But see, what you have to do is relax and get your mind straight. Angela and I haven't come here to hurt you. We've come to offer you a deal."

"What the hell kind of deal do you have to offer me?" Ubinas asked angrily. Even greater than his fear of being shot was his rage at having lost control. "What could someone like you possibly have to offer me?"

"Thirty years I've been knowing you and this is a side I've never seen," Troy said. "But then the shoe was always on the other foot, wasn't it, Jack? I was the golf ball and you were the club. Drive me this way. Chip me that way. Hook me into the rough. Just as long as I kept flyin' straight and true I was in the game. Well, I'm fixin' to make you an offer just the same, and it's better than a Ferrari for that piece of shit truck in your barn. Better even than a jet airplane for a Piper Cub. I'm ready to give you forty pounds of weapons-grade plutonium and all you gotta give me in return is a dog-eared old photo album and the whereabouts of Novac DuCharme. Plus one or two little extras that don't amount to a hill of beans."

"You're crazy," Ubinas said. "You've lost your mind. You don't have any plutonium. You're bluffing, and you're not doing a very good job of it."

"You ever hear of a woman named Claudia Muller?" Angela asked. "The late Jergen Muller's wife? The woman Novac DuCharme debased, humiliated and then ripped off? You ever hear of Claudia's partner, Rafiq Said? How about Nick Sharifi? We've got a videotape Claudia Muller made of Said and DuCharme discussing the plutonium deal in great detail. We've got another one of Nick Sharifi singing louder than Luciano Pavarotti. We've got Nigel Fullerton on tape too. You know, the captain of the tanker that hauled the stuff into the offshore oil depot at Lafourche Parish, Louisiana. We've got that and more, Mr. Ubinas. One phone call and it all gets sent to the *New York Times* along with directions to the plutonium's hiding place. You still think we're bluffing? Maybe you'd like to see the plutonium. It's right outside in your barn, where we found it just before we captured you, the government man who's been hiding an ex-Nazi nuclear terrorist."

"The thing is, Jack, you can still be the hero," Troy said. "We don't care. We just want the album and DuCharme. And the little extras I referred to a minute ago. You give us that, we'll let you find the plutonium anywhere you want. Personally, I'd go for a place like DuCharme's electronics company, but you're good at that sort of shit. I'm sure you'll make the right decision."

"Tell me about the extras," Ubinas said.

XXVIII

The woman who ran the call-girl service from an apartment on Sutton Place in Manhattan prided herself on two things: absolute discretion and the ability to cater to the very specific desires of her clients no matter how unusual they might be. For her services she was paid very large sums of money but the wealthy men who paid her never objected.

This madam, who went by the name of Celeste, had a staff whose job it was to find girls particularly suited to each client's needs, but occasionally Celeste conducted the search herself. This was the case with a man named Mr. Sloane who lived on the corner of Seventy-second Street and Central Park West in an apartment building known as the Majestic. The woman stipulated by Mr. Sloane had to be in her thirties, tall and thin, very pretty in an aloof, haughty way, impeccably groomed, and with straight hair that hung just to her shoulders. A further requirement was that she be married to a man of considerable means.

Celeste found this last requirement an interesting challenge and chose to take it on personally. She prided herself on being able to read people by watching them and would frequent certain expensive shops along Fifth Avenue, as well as fashionable coffee shops and the bars of certain very expensive hotels, studying the faces of women who were alone and fit the physical profile Mr. Sloane desired. She searched for a certain look on the faces of these women, a certain expression that almost invariably signaled boredom, sexual neglect, or outright dissatisfaction with a marriage.

Celeste, herself a product of an upper-class environment, knew exactly how to approach one of these women. She knew just how to comment on the inventory of the shop they were in, how to compliment something the woman might be wearing, or, if the two of them were in a bar or coffee shop, exactly what to say in order to join the woman for a drink or a bite to eat. Once the ice was broken it didn't take Celeste long to find out whether the woman she was talking to had fantasized about working, just once, as a highly paid call girl, not for the money, but simply for the thrill of it. Of course the hunt was not always successful and often she was rebuffed, but surprisingly, even to Celeste, she had had no trouble providing Mr. Sloane with five different women in the six months he had been her client.

One morning in early April Celeste struck gold. She met a woman in an antique shop who fit Mr. Sloane's prerequisites to a T. The woman was a redhead with a diamond on her finger. She was just the right age and size, expensively dressed, with a look on her face that could freeze molten lead. Celeste approached her and began chatting. They had coffee together and she found the woman not only interested in her proposition but available at once. She would be willing to spend an entire weekend with the right man. Her husband was in Europe on business and wouldn't be back for two weeks.

At first, after he decided to locate in New York City, Novac DuCharme spent almost all his time in the apartment on the twentieth floor of the Majestic. He conducted business, worked out in a room filled with exercise equipment, or sat sunning on the balcony overlooking the park. Sometimes he went out to one of several carefully selected restaurants, but always late at night and never alone. Then, as time passed and it was apparent he was once again safe, he began leaving the city on weekends, driving either to a secluded country house north of New York City in Dutchess County, or to a boatyard on the north shore of Long Island where a fifty-eight-foot cruiser owned by a Mr. Sloane was moored. His house on Long Island, his old apartment in Manhattan, and his villa in Switzerland had all been sold, but in addition to the country house in Dutchess County, DuCharme had recently purchased a chalet in the Bavarian Alps where he intended to spend his summers. While there, his boat would be taken south to the Bahamas, where he would winter. He had considered moving it to Florida, but decided not to push his luck.

The boat was DuCharme's weekend destination when Klaus, his

muscular bodyguard, ushered the beautiful redhead into his study early on a Friday afternoon. The price DuCharme agreed on with Celeste for the entire weekend was five thousand dollars, payable in advance in hundred-dollar bills, assuming he was satisfied with what he saw.

DuCharme was sitting in an armchair when the woman walked into the room. For several seconds he watched her standing just inside the doorway and was pleased. She seemed to be just what he wanted. She didn't look in the least bit nervous. She looked bored and a trifle disdainful and DuCharme was instantly aroused. The pleasure of humiliating her would be exquisite.

"Walk across the room and stand in front of the window," he told her. Saying nothing, the woman did as he asked. The only sound was the clicking of her high heels.

"Now raise your arms as high as you can and put your hands on the window," he said. "Then turn your head, but not your body, and look at me."

As he had ordered, the woman wore a short skirt, a matching jacket, and no blouse. When she raised her arms he could see her waist which was lean and supple, and the bottom portion of her ribs. Her fingernails were painted crimson and stood out against the glass. As she stood there eyeing him coldly, DuCharme removed an envelope from the drawer of the desk next to his chair and held it out.

"This is for you," he said. "I'm hoping it will be money well spent."

"Oh it will," the woman said.

The phone rang and DuCharme answered it.

"My car is waiting downstairs," he said. "I understand you like boats."

"My husband has one," the woman said. "Celeste told me yours was bigger."

"Indeed," said DuCharme.

They left the study and were walking toward the front door when the phone rang again. Slightly annoyed, DuCharme went back into the study to answer it. Angus Elliott was on the other end of the line. He had been living in DuCharme's country house for six months and was looking forward to the summer in Bavaria. He believed the atmosphere there would give him inspiration for their cause.

"Don't go to the boat," he said to DuCharme. "Come up here instead."

"Why should I do that?" asked DuCharme.

"Something isn't right. I think the weekend weather will be nasty," Elliott replied. "Just a feeling I have. I woke up with it this morning. The boat is not where you want to be."

"A change of plans," DuCharme said, returning to the foyer where the woman waited. "I hope you like the country as much as you like boats."

"Do you always have this much trouble making up your mind?" she asked.

DuCharme smiled contentedly as his cold eyes looked into hers.

"Not about most things," he said.

A black BMW 850Ci was waiting for them at the curb. The doorman opened the back door of the car and held it for the woman and DuCharme. When she got in she saw that the muscular man with short blond hair, the bodyguard, was behind the wheel.

"Don't you like to drive?" she asked DuCharme, as the car swung onto the West Side Highway heading north.

"I drive when it is necessary," he said, smiling at her again. "Does your husband like to drive, or does he prefer being driven?"

"I never asked him," the woman said.

DuCharme unfolded a copy of the *Wall Street Journal,* put on a pair of reading glasses, and ignored the woman until they had traveled a good distance up the Taconic Parkway. They had left the city before the weekend crush and there was little traffic on the road. Abruptly, DuCharme put the paper away and took off the glasses.

"Unbutton your jacket," he said.

The woman, who had been staring out the window, raised her eyebrows and glanced at the back of the bodyguard's head.

"Don't worry about him," he said. "Klaus does not like women. He has other interests."

"I see," the woman said, turning toward DuCharme and undoing the buttons of her jacket as he watched. The lace bra she wore underneath was midnight blue, the color Celeste told her DuCharme preferred.

"Now tell me about your husband," said DuCharme.

"He makes money," the woman said. "Like you."

The BMW swung off the parkway onto a two-lane country road, then after about a mile turned onto an even narrower winding lane that climbed steeply and ended at an open iron gate. The bodyguard turned his head and looked questioningly at DuCharme.

"Angus knew we were coming," DuCharme said. "But call him anyway to make sure."

The bodyguard did as he was told, nodded his head, and drove on. The lane was gravel now and crunched beneath the BMW's tires.

"Tell me about the tattoo on your ankle," DuCharme said to the woman as they pulled to a stop in front of a large stone house, a fortress actually, built into the side of a small mountain.

"It's an angel," she said, as the bodyguard climbed out of the car. "A messenger from God. Do you believe in angels, Mr. DuCharme?"

DuCharme began to say something but then Roland Troy stepped from the bushes and shot the bodyguard three times in the chest.

For a moment nothing moved and there was only sound. Then DuCharme bolted from the car and ran along a path behind the house. Angela kicked off her heels and went after him, oblivious to the flapping of her jacket and the pebbles on the path. She held the pistol she had hidden in her purse. Troy raced by her yelling not to shoot, yelling that they had to have the son of a bitch alive.

The path ended at a low stone wall. On the other side, a craggy cliff with evergreens and brambles clinging to its face dropped sixty feet straight down, where it ended in a rocky, shallow stream. Novac DuCharme was trapped and knew it. He reached the wall and there was nowhere left for him to go. He whirled around and now his ice-cold eyes were truly mad. Angela saw something in his hand, a gun she thought, and when he raised his arm she felt she had no choice. She fired and fired again. DuCharme spun, pitched over the low wall, and disappeared.

He was still alive when they found him, sprawled on his back at an impossible angle across a rotting log. A trickle of blood ran from his mouth. More blood seeped from the bullet wound in his shoulder and from a gash across his scalp. It dripped into a little pool formed where the rotting log had blocked the stream. The blood had turned the water dark.

DuCharme's breath came in short, ratcheting gasps, and his legs twitched slightly. Troy knelt beside him and saw that he was clutching something in his hand. It was a small leather pouch drawn together at the top with rawhide lace.

"Who killed my wife?" Troy shouted. "Who killed the filmmaker, Bruno Schleifer, and my wife?"

DuCharme's wild eyes bore into Troy's and his hand opened, offering the leather pouch. A raspy growl came from somewhere in his throat. Troy knelt closer and placed his ear next to DuCharme's mouth.

"My little Jews," DuCharme whispered. Then his eyes went blank.

EPILOGUE

"Daddy, I can't believe you let Angela go up to that monster's apartment alone and then get in a car with him," Troy's daughter, Katherine, said.

"What do you mean 'let'?" said Troy. "It was her idea. She set it up, not me. She even paid six hundred dollars of her own money for that damned red wig. I was against the whole thing, but she convinced me. We wanted to get him and Angus Elliott at the same time. We did get 'em, except the one who really mattered wasn't any use to us in the end. There would have been no deal for Novac DuCharme. He would have gone to trial. Hold on a sec."

He set the phone down, lit a cigar, then picked it up again. He was sitting on his porch, watching the old mama gator cruise across his pond, checking out the great blue herons on the other side. It was a standoff that had been going on for years and looked like it would never end.

"I'm back," he said.

"So that was one of the extras," Katherine said. "Getting to go after Novac DuCharme."

"Yep," Troy said. "That and having Angela made a special federal agent just like me."

"Just like you," Katherine said. "That's wonderful. Now you never will retire. You know the two of you deserve each other. You're both insane. Putting that plutonium in Ubinas's barn. You had to be out of your minds."

"What the hell you talkin' about," Troy said. "There wasn't nothin' in his barn but vehicles and tools. You think I'm gonna go drivin' up the interstate with weapons-grade plutonium in the bed of my truck? Come on girl. Get a grip."

345

"Angela was bluffing?"

"Well, we had the stuff. It just wasn't in his barn. It was buried in the mountains of North Carolina. Maybe 'embellish' is a better word than 'bluff.' Either way, she hooked Ubinas like he was a starving bass. He'd have signed over the deed to his farm when she was through. It was a performance the likes of which you wouldn't believe. I just sat there listening and watching. When Ubinas took the album out of his safe and handed it to her he was sweatin' like he'd just run a marathon. He could hardly hold onto it, he was shakin' so bad. She cried later, when we were alone, but when she took it from him she stared him down cold as ice and never flinched. I'll tell you this, I'd marry her, but I wouldn't play poker with her."

"Daddy? . . . What don't I know?"

"You know everything, honey."

"I'm not so sure."

"We're gonna take a trip to Israel first. Then we'll see. Angela wants to donate the album to the Holocaust Museum at Yad Vashem. I'm going with her in the fall, for the Jewish New Year."

"How's Nakama?" Katherine asked.

"I don't know how he is," Troy said. "I think he's still in Mexico but I'm not sure. I know he's still alive. I would have heard if he wasn't."

"Daddy?"

"Yeah."

"Did he do it? Did DuCharme kill Clara?"

"Honey, I'm still not sure. Elliott says he was involved, but Elliott's singing for his supper. His contacts in the spirit world told him Leavenworth wasn't where he ought to be. If he gives up enough they'll put him in witness protection, so who knows. He says the guys who did it wound up at the bottom of an Austrian lake. No witnesses. No fingerprints. Nobody left to tell the tale."

"What about that group?" she asked. "The white mushrooms?"

"El Hongo Blanco," Troy said.

"Does it exist?"

"Always," Troy said. "In one form or another. The names change. Their intentions don't."

"The never-ending war, huh, Daddy?"

"So it seems. Although this time the good guys won the battle."

"And Jack Ubinas is the hero."

"Yup. He broke the case. He found the goods at DuCharme's electronics company. He sent me out to get DuCharme. They pin a medal on his chest and he goes back to his computer."

"You don't sound pissed."

"Why should I be? You know what the *Zenrin Kushu* says. 'Entering the forest he moves not the grass; entering the water he makes not a ripple.' You can't do that with a chest full of medals. Anyway, he got a good look at the woman that I'm living with and that sucker sleeps alone."

Roland Troy and Angela Becker traveled to Israel in September. On the way they stopped off at the estate where she was raised. The leaves were changing and the air was cool and the day they went there the water sparkled in the sun. While Troy made small talk with her stepbrother and his wife, Angela excused herself and walked down to the barn. She got a shovel and carried it twenty paces from the barn's back wall where she began to dig. She was expecting to find nothing and was ready to give up when the shovel struck the metal box she'd buried there twenty years earlier, just before she first went off to boarding school.

She got a hack saw from the barn and cut the lock off; she didn't remember where she'd put the key. The old owl's nest was still inside, along with a book of poems she had loved, a bag of marbles, some letters from her childhood friends, a lock of hair tied with a ribbon, and a tiny pair of baby's socks that once were white but now were dirty gray. She put the socks in the pocket of the down vest she was wearing, closed up the box, and buried it again where it had been.

They held a ceremony at Yad Vashem, a very small one at Angela's request. She handed the museum director the album and the leather pouch filled with gold teeth, then hesitated and told him she had something else.

"What's that?" he asked her.

"A pair of baby's socks," she said.

"Did they belong to a victim?" he asked.

"They belonged to the daughter of a survivor," she told him. "She had them on her feet the last time that he saw her. I was hoping you could make an exception and put them with the album."

"I think I understand," he said. "I don't see any problem."